Simon Scarrow work [   ] becoming a full-time writer. In the past he has run a Roman history programme taking parties of students to a number of ruins and museums across Britain. Having enjoyed the novels of Forester, Cornwell and O'Brian, and fired by the knowledge gleaned from the exploration of Roman sites, he decided to write what he wanted to read – military page-turners about the adventures of the Roman army from AD 43 onwards.

Simon Scarrow's earlier novels featuring Macro and Cato are all available from Headline – see page ii for a full list of titles. He is also the author of the REVOLUTION series about the lives of the Duke of Wellington and Napoleon Bonaparte.

Simon Scarrow lives in Norfolk.

For more information on Simon Scarrow and his novels, visit www.scarrow.co.uk

THE
EAGLE
IN THE SAND

SIMON SCARROW

headline

First published in 2006
by HEADLINE PUBLISHING GROUP

First published in paperback in 2007
by HEADLINE PUBLISHING GROUP

3

ISBN 978 0 7553 2775 1

Typeset in Bembo by Avon DataSet Ltd,
Bidford-on-Avon, Warwickshire

Printed and bound in Great Britain by
Mackays of Chatham, plc, Chatham, Kent

Headline's policy is to use papers that are natural, renewable and recyclable
products and made from wood grown in sustainable forests. The logging and
manufacturing processes are expected to conform to the environmental
regulations of the country of origin.

HEADLINE PUBLISHING GROUP
A division of Hachette Livre UK Ltd
338 Euston Road
London NW1 3BH

www.headline.co.uk
www.hodderheadline.com

To Timoor Daghistani
In gratitude and friendship

As the first five books in the Eagle series were set in Britain it was easy enough to walk the ground and get a feel for the landscape that Macro and Cato would be fighting over. Setting the latest book in the desert, on the extreme fringe of the Roman Empire, proved to be more of a problem. Until I received a call from Mr Daghistani at the Jordanian Embassy and was told that His Majesty, King Abdullah, was a keen reader of the series and would like to invite me and my family out to Jordan to see the Roman sites that cover much of the country.

I would like to express my sincere gratitude to His Majesty for being such a kind host. I extend that gratitude to all the Jordanian people who made our visit to the country such a pleasure. Thanks to Rozana Abu Hamdi, of the Royal Protocol Office, for organising a wonderful itinerary of sites; to our driver Moraud, who proved a patient teacher of the Arabic we tried our best to learn; and finally thanks to Samer Mouasher, who knew exactly where to find a certain desert fort that was crucially important to the setting of this novel.

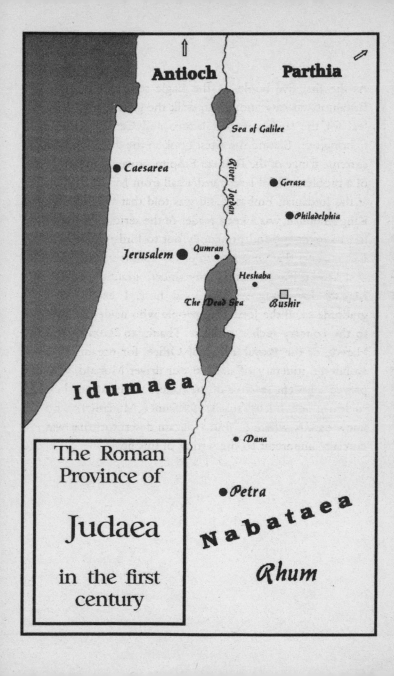

Antioch ↑

Parthia ↗

Sea of Galilee

River Jordan

● Caesarea

● Gerasa

● Philadelphia

Jerusalem ● · Qumran

Heshaba ·

The Dead Sea □ Bushir

Idumaea

· Dana

The Roman
Province of

Judaea

in the first
century

● Petra

Nabataea

Rhum

CHAPTER ONE

Centurion Macro noticed them first: a small band of men with hoods drawn over their heads casually entering the crowded street from a dark alley and merging with the flow of people, animals and carts heading for the great market in the outer court of the temple. Even though it was only mid-morning the sun was already beating down on Jerusalem and ripening the air in the narrow streets with a stifling intensity of smells: the familiar odours of cities throughout the empire, and other scents that were strange and evocative of the east – spice, citron and balsam. In the glaring sunshine and baking air, Macro could feel the sweat pricking out all over his face and body, and he wondered how any man could bear to go hooded in this heat. He stared at the band of men as they made their way along the street, not twenty paces ahead. They did not talk to each other, and barely acknowledged the jostling crowd around them as they moved forward with the flow. Macro switched the reins of his mule to the other hand and nudged his companion, Centurion Cato, riding alongside him at the head of the small column of auxiliary recruits shuffling along behind the two officers.

'They're up to no good.'

'Hm?' Cato glanced round. 'Sorry. What did you say?'

'Up ahead.' Macro quickly gestured towards the men he was watching. 'See that lot with covered heads?'

Cato squinted for a moment before he fixed his eyes on the men Macro had indicated. 'Yes. What about them?'

'Well, don't you think it's odd?' Macro glanced at his companion. Cato was a bright enough lad, Macro thought, but sometimes he would miss a danger or a crucial detail that was right under his nose. Macro, being somewhat older, put it down to lack of experience. He had served in the legions for nearly eighteen years – long enough to develop a profound appreciation of his surroundings. Life depended on it, as he had discovered on rather too many occasions. Indeed, he bore scars on his body for not being aware of a threat until it was too late. That he still lived was proof of his toughness and sheer brutality in a fight. Like every centurion in Emperor Claudius' legions, he was a man to be reckoned with. Well, perhaps not every centurion, Macro reflected as he glanced back at Cato. His friend was something of an exception. Cato had won his promotion at a distastefully early stage of his army career by virtue of his brains, guts, luck and a little bit of favouritism. The last factor might have irked a man like Macro who had clawed his way up from the ranks, but he was honest enough to recognise that Cato had fully justified his promotion. In the four years since Cato had joined the Second Legion, years in which he had served with Macro in Germany, Britain and Illyricum, he had matured from a fresh-faced recruit to a tough, sinewy veteran. But Cato could still lose his head in the clouds.

Macro sighed impatiently. 'Hoods. In this heat. Odd, wouldn't you say?'

Cato looked at the men again and shrugged. 'Now you mention it, I suppose so. Maybe they're part of some religious sect. Jupiter knows how many of them there are in this place.' He scowled. 'Who would have thought one religion could have so many? And from what I've heard, the locals are about as pious as you can get. You don't get much more religious than the Judaeans.'

'Maybe,' Macro said thoughtfully. 'But that lot up there don't look very religious to me.'

'You can tell?'

'I can tell.' Macro tapped his nose. 'Trust me. They're up to something.'

'Like what?'

'I don't know. Not yet. But keep watching them. See what you think.'

'Think?' Cato frowned irritably. 'I was already thinking when you interrupted me.'

'Oh?' Macro replied, keeping his attention on the

men ahead of them. 'I suppose you were contemplating something of earth-shaking importance. Must have been from that vacant look on your face.'

'Nice. As it happens, I was thinking about Narcissus.'

'Narcissus?' Macro's expression darkened at the name of the Imperial Secretary, on whose orders they had been sent to the east. 'That bastard? Why waste any time on him?'

'It's just that he's stitched us up nicely this time. I doubt we're going to see this mission through. It stinks.'

'What's new? Every job that bastard has given us stinks. We're the sponge-sticks of the imperial service. Always in the shit.'

Cato looked at his friend with a disgusted expression and was about to reply when Macro suddenly craned his neck and hissed, 'Look! They're making their move.'

Just ahead was the lofty archway which marked the entrance to the great outer court of the temple. The light was dazzling and for an instant silhouetted the heads and shoulders of those in front of them, and it was a moment before Cato's eyes fixed on the hooded men again. They had thrust their way over to one side of the street as they passed through the arch, and were now walking quickly towards the tables of the moneylenders and tax collectors in the centre of the court.

'Let's go.' Macro kicked his heels into the side of his mule, causing it to bray. The people in front glanced back over their shoulders nervously and shuffled out of the animal's path. 'Come on.'

'Wait!' Cato grabbed his arm. 'You're jumping at shadows. We've hardly reached the city and you're spoiling for a fight.'

'I'm telling you, Cato, they're up to no good.'

'You don't know that. You can't just wade in and trample down anyone who gets in your way.'

'Why not?'

'You'll cause a riot.' Cato slipped out of his saddle and stood beside his mule. 'If you want to follow them, then let's go on foot.'

Macro took a quick glance towards the hooded men. 'Fair enough. Optio!'

A tall, hard-faced Gaul strode up from the head of the column and saluted Macro. 'Sir?'

'Take the reins. Centurion Cato and myself are going to take a little stroll.'

'A stroll, sir?'

'You heard. Wait for us just inside the gate. But keep the men formed up, just in case.'

The optio frowned. 'In case of what, sir?'

'Trouble.' Macro smiled. 'What else? Come on, Cato. Before we lose them.'

With a sigh Cato followed his friend into the flow of bodies entering the great courtyard. The men they were following were already some distance away, still heading towards the stalls of the moneylenders and tax collectors.

The two centurions threaded their way through the crowds, jostling some of the people as they passed and drawing angry glances and muttered curses.

'Roman bastards . . .' someone said in accented Greek.

Macro stopped and whirled round. 'Who said that?'

The crowd shrank from his enraged expression, but stared back with hostile eyes. Macro's gaze fixed on a tall, broad-shouldered youth whose lips had curled into a sneer.

'Oh, so it was you, was it?' Macro smiled, and beckoned to the man. 'Come on then. If you think you're man enough.'

Cato grabbed his arm and pulled Macro back. 'Leave him be.'

'Leave him?' Macro frowned. 'Why? He needs a lesson in hospitality.'

'No he doesn't,' Cato insisted quietly. 'Hearts and minds, remember? That's what the procurator told us. Besides,' Cato nodded towards the stalls, 'your hooded friends are getting away from us.'

'Fair enough.' Macro quickly turned back to the young man. 'Cross my path again, Judaean, and I'll take your bloody head off.'

The man snorted with derision and spat on to the ground, and Cato hauled Macro after him before the latter could respond. They hurried on, quickly closing the distance between them and the small knot of men picking their way through the crowd towards the stalls. Cato, taller than Macro, was easily able to keep them in sight as the two centurions pressed on through the exotic mixture of races that filled the great courtyard. Amongst the locals were darker-featured Idumaeans and Nabataeans, many wearing turbans wound neatly round their heads. Cloth of all colours and patterns swirled amongst the crowds, and snatches of different languages filled the air.

'Look out!' Macro grabbed Cato's arm and pulled him back as a heavily laden camel crossed in front of them. The beast's wooden-framed saddle was weighed down with bales of finely woven material and it let out a deep grunt as it stepped aside to avoid the two Romans. When it had swayed past, Cato pushed on again, and suddenly paused.

'What's the matter?' asked Macro.

'Shit . . . I can't see them.' Cato's eyes hurriedly skimmed over the section of the crowd where he had last seen their prey. But there was no sign of the hooded men. 'They must have lowered their hoods.'

'Oh, great,' Macro muttered. 'What now?'

'Let's make for the tax collectors. That's where they seemed to be heading.'

With Cato leading the way, the two centurions moved over to the end of the line of stalls stretching alongside the steps that led up to the walls of the inner temple. The nearest stalls belonged to the moneylenders and bankers, who sat in comfortable cushioned chairs as they conducted business with their customers. Beyond them was the smaller section where the tax collectors and their hired muscle sat waiting for payment from those who had been assessed for taxation. At their sides were stacked the waxed slates that detailed the names of those to be taxed, and how much they should pay. The tax collectors had bought the right to collect specific taxes at auctions held by the Roman procurator in the province's administrative capital at Caesarea. Having paid a fixed sum into the imperial coffers, they were legally entitled to squeeze the people of Jerusalem for any taxes they might be deemed to be liable for. It was a harsh system, but it was one that was applied right across the Roman Empire, and the tax collectors were a deeply resented and despised social class. That suited Emperor Claudius and the staff of the imperial treasury very well indeed, since the odium of the provincial taxpayers was invariably focused on the local collectors and not the people from whom the latter had bought their tax-collecting rights.

A sudden outburst of shouting and screaming drew Cato and Macro's attention to the far end of the line of stalls. A group of men had charged out of the crowd. Sunlight flashed off the side of a blade and Cato realised the men were all armed as they closed in round one of the tax collectors, like wolves at the kill. His bodyguard took one look at the blades, turned and ran. The tax collector flung up his arms to protect his face and disappeared from sight as his attackers fell on him. Cato's hand automatically snatched at his sword as he ducked round behind the line of stalls.

'Come on, Macro!'

There was a rasp as Macro's blade was drawn behind Cato and then the two of them sprinted towards the killers, thrusting the moneylenders aside and leaping over their stacks of record slates. Ahead of him Cato saw the men draw back from the tax collector, now slumped over the top of his stall, his white tunic torn and bloody. In front of the stall the crowd drew back in a panic, crying out in terror as they turned and ran. The attackers turned on the men behind the next stall. They had frozen for an instant before realising the terrible danger they were in, but now they attempted to scramble away from the men brandishing the short curved blades that gave them their name: the sicarians – assassins of the most extreme fringe of the Judaean zealots resisting Roman rule.

The sicarians were so intent on their killing frenzy that they did not notice Cato and Macro until the last moment, when the nearest killer glanced up as Cato thrust a collector aside and leaped forward, teeth bared and sword thrust out in front of him. The point took the attacker just to one side of the neck, split his collar bone and drove deep into his chest, piercing his heart. With an explosive gasp the man slumped forward, almost wrenching the blade from Cato's grasp. Cato raised his boot and kicked the body back, yanked the blade free and crouched, looking for his next target. To one side there was a blur as Macro ran past and hacked his sword into the arm of the next sicarian, almost severing the limb. The man fell away, howling in agony as his nerveless fingers released his blade. The other men abruptly abandoned their attack on the tax collectors and turned to face the two Romans. Their leader, a short swarthy man with powerful shoulders, snapped out an order and the sicarians swiftly fanned out, some circling round the stalls while others climbed the steps and moved to cut off Macro and Cato from the direction they had come. Cato kept the bloodied point of his sword raised as he glanced round.

'Seven of them.'

'Bad odds.' Macro was breathing heavily as he took up position with his back to Cato's. 'We shouldn't be here, lad.'

The crowd had fled back towards the gate, leaving a clear space round the two Romans and the killers. The paving slabs of the outer court were littered with discarded baskets and half-eaten snacks, hastily flung aside as people fled for their lives.

Cato laughed bitterly. 'Your idea, remember?'

'Next time, don't let me do the thinking.'

Before Cato could respond the leader of the sicarians snapped an order and his men closed in, moving quickly, blades held out ready to strike. There was no way out for the Romans and Cato crouched lower, limbs tensed as his eyes flickered from man to man, none more than a spear's length away from him and Macro.

'What now?' he whispered softly.

'Fuck knows.'

'Great. Just what I needed to hear.'

Cato sensed a movement to one side and turned just as one of the killers lunged forward, stabbing towards Macro's side.

'Watch it!'

But Macro was already moving, his sword a glittering blur as it swept round and knocked the blade from the man's hand. Even as it clattered to the ground another sicarian feinted, causing Cato to turn towards him, ready to parry. As he moved, another of the men jumped forward, knife point flickering out. Cato turned back just in time to meet the threat. He lowered his spare hand and snatched out his dagger, broad-bladed and unwieldy compared to the narrow-bladed weapons of the killers, but it felt good in his hand all the same. The leader shouted another order, and Cato heard the anger in the man's voice. He wanted this finished at once.

'Macro!' Cato shouted out. 'With me! Charge!'

He threw himself at the men backing onto the courtyard and his comrade followed him, bellowing at the top of his voice. The sudden reversal of roles startled the sicarians and they paused for a vital instant. Cato and Macro slashed at the men in front of them, causing them to jump aside, and then the Romans were through, running across the paving, back towards the entrance to the Great Courtyard. There was a cry of rage from behind and then the scuffling pad of sandals as the sicarians chased after them. Cato glanced back and saw Macro close behind, and just a few paces behind him the leader of the killers, lips drawn back in a snarl as he sprinted after the Romans. Cato knew at once they would never outrun them. They were too heavily weighed down and the sicarians wore nothing but their tunics. It would all be over in moments. Just ahead lay an amphora, abandoned in the rush to escape from the courtyard. Cato jumped over it and immediately turned round. Macro, with a puzzled expression, leaped past him just as Cato slashed his sword down, shattering the large jar. With a gurgling rush the contents sloshed across the paving slabs and the air filled with the aroma of olive oil. Cato turned and raced after Macro, and glanced over his shoulder just in time to see the leader of the sicarians slither, lose his footing and tumble back on to the ground with a thud. Two of the men immediately behind him also slipped over, but the rest skirted the spreading slick of oil and chased after the Romans. Cato saw that they were only a short distance from the stragglers of the crowd: the old, the infirm and a handful of small children, crying out in terror.

'Turn round!' he shouted to Macro and scraped to a halt, swivelling to face their pursuers. An instant later

Macro was at his side. The sicarians charged forward for a moment before they suddenly drew up, glaring past Cato and Macro. Then they turned away and ran back towards their leader and the others who were back on their feet, and the sicarians raced towards a small gate on the far side of the Great Courtyard.

'Cowards!' Macro called after them. 'What's the matter? No balls for a real fight?' He laughed and slapped a thick arm round Cato's shoulder. 'Look at 'em go. Bolting like rabbits. If two of us can scare them off then I don't think we've that much to worry about in Judaea.'

'Not just two of us.' Cato nodded towards the crowd and Macro glanced back and saw the optio and his men shouldering their way through the edge of the crowd and hurrying to the aid of the centurions.

'After them!' the optio bellowed, thrusting his arm out towards the fleeing killers.

'No!' Cato commanded. 'There's no point. We won't catch them now.'

Even as he spoke the sicarians reached the gate and ducked out of sight. The optio shrugged, and could not hide a look of resentment. Cato could understand how the man felt and was tempted to explain. Just in time he stopped himself. He had given an order – that was all there was to it. There was no point in letting the auxiliaries go on a wild and dangerous goose chase through the narrow streets of Jerusalem. Instead, Cato gestured towards the overturned stalls and the dead and injured victims of the sicarians.

'Do what you can for them.'

The optio saluted, recalled his men and hurried over to what was left of the tax collectors' area of the market. Cato felt blown from his exertions. He sheathed his sword and dagger and leaned forward, resting his hands just above his knees.

'Nice move, that.' Macro smiled and thrust the point of his sword back towards the shattered jar of oil. 'Saved our skins.'

Cato shook his head and drew a deep breath before replying. 'We've only just arrived in the city . . . haven't even reached the bloody garrison, and already we've nearly had our throats cut.'

'Some welcome.' Macro grimaced. 'You know, I'm beginning to wonder if the procurator was having us on.'

Cato looked round at him with a questioning expression.

'Hearts and minds.' Macro shook his head. 'I get the distinct impression that the locals are not warming to the idea of being part of the Roman Empire.'

CHAPTER TWO

'Hearts and minds?' Centurion Florianus laughed as he poured the new arrivals some lemon-scented water, and slid the cups across the marble top of the desk in his office. His quarters were in one of the towers of the massive fortress of the Antonia, built by Herod the Great and named after his patron Mark Antony. These days it was garrisoned by the Roman troops charged with policing Jerusalem. From the narrow balcony outside his office he had a fine view out over the temple and the old quarter of the city beyond. He had been roused from his seat by the terrified cries of the crowd and had been witness to Macro and Cato's desperate skirmish. 'Hearts and minds,' he repeated. 'Did the procurator really say that?'

'He did.' Macro nodded. 'And more besides. A whole speech on the importance of maintaining good relations with the Judaeans.'

'Good relations?' Florianus shook his head. 'That's a laugh. You can't have good relations with people who

15

hate your guts. This lot would stick a knife in your back the moment you dared turn away from them. Bloody province is a disaster. Always has been. Even when we let Herod and his heirs run things.'

'Really?' Cato cocked his head slightly to the side. 'That's not what you hear back in Rome. As far as I was aware the situation in the province was supposed to be improving. At least, that was the official line.'

'Sure, that's what they tell people.' Florianus laughed bitterly. 'The truth is that the only places we control are the larger towns and cities. All the routes between are plagued by bandits and brigands. And even the towns are riven by political and religious factions jockeying for influence over their people. It's not helped by the fact there are so many dialects that the only common tongue is Greek, and not many of 'em speak that. Hardly a month goes by without some trouble flaring up between Idumaeans or Samaritans or someone. It's getting out of hand. Those people you had a fight with in the Great Courtyard were from one of the gangs hiring themselves out to the political factions. They use the sicarians to kill off rivals, or make a political point – like this morning's demonstration.'

'That was a demonstration?' Macro shook his head in bewilderment. 'Just making a political point? I'd hate to get into a full scale row with those bastards.'

Florianus smiled briefly before he continued. 'Of course, the procurators rarely see that side of things from

Caesarea. They just sit on their arses and send out direc-
tives to the field officers, like me, to make sure the taxes
are paid. And when I send them reports on how shit the
situation is, they bury them and tell Rome that they're
making great progress on settling things down in the
sunny little province of Judaea.' He shook his head.
'Can hardly blame them, I suppose. If they told the
truth it'd look as though they were losing their grip. The
Emperor would have them replaced at once. So you can
forget about what you've been told back in Rome.
Frankly, I doubt we'll ever tame these Judaeans. Any
attempt to Romanise them slips away quicker than crap
through a goose.'

Cato pursed his lips. 'But the new procurator —
Tiberius Julius Alexander — he's a Judaean, and he seemed
more Roman than most Romans I've ever met.'

'Of course he does.' Florianus smiled. 'He's from a
wealthy family. Wealthy enough to be raised and educated
by Greek tutors in expensive Roman academies. After
that someone was kind enough to set him up with a
glittering commercial career in Alexandria. Surprise,
surprise — he ends up rich. Rich enough to be a friend of
the Emperor and his freedmen.' Florianus snorted. 'Do
you know, I've spent more time in this land than he has.
That's how much of a local boy he is. The procurator may
have pulled the wool over the eyes of Claudius, and that
Imperial Secretary of his, Narcissus, but the people here
can smell a rat. That's always been the trouble. Right from

the outset, when we made Herod the Great their king. Typical one pattern fits all approach to diplomacy. Just because we've managed to impose a king and ruling class in other lands we assumed the same thing would work here. Well, it hasn't.'

'Why not?' Macro interrupted. 'What's so special about Judaea?'

'Ask them!' Florianus waved his hand towards the balcony. 'Eight years I've been posted here and there's hardly a man amongst them I can call a friend.' He paused to take a long draught from his cup and set it down with a sharp rap. 'So you can forget any notion of winning their hearts and minds. It's not going to happen. They hate the *Kittim*, as they call us. The best we can do is grab 'em by the balls and hang on until they cough up the taxes they are due to hand over.'

'Colourful image.' Macro shrugged. 'Reminds me of that bastard Gaius Caligula. What was it he used to say, Cato?'

'Let them hate, as long as they fear me . . .'

'That's it!' Macro slapped his hand down. 'Bloody fine piece of advice that, even if Caligula was barking mad. Sounds as if it might be the best approach to these people, if they're as difficult as you say.'

'Take it from me,' Florianus replied seriously. 'They're as difficult as I say. If not, worse. I blame that self-righteous religion of theirs. If there's any slight to their faith they take to the streets and riot. A few years back, during the Passover, one of our men stuck his arse over the battlements and farted at the crowd. Just a crude soldier's joke you might think, but not to that lot. Scores of deaths later we had to hand the soldier over for execution. Same thing with an optio up at some place near Capernaum who thought he would burn a village's holy books to teach them a lesson. Nearly caused a revolt. So we let them have the optio and the crowd tore him to pieces. It was the only way to restore order. I warn you, the Judaeans are not prepared to compromise on the slightest detail of their religion. That's why we have no cohort standards here and no images of the Emperor. They look down their nose at the rest of the world and cling to the idea that they have been singled out for some great purpose.' Florianus laughed. 'I mean, look at this place. It's a dusty little rat-hole. Does it seem to you like the land of a chosen people?'

Macro glanced at Cato and shrugged. 'Perhaps not.'

Florianus poured himself another cup of water, took a sip and considered his guests thoughtfully.

'You're wondering why we're here.' Cato smiled.

Florianus shrugged. 'It had crossed my mind. Since I doubt the Empire can spare the services of two centurions to nursemaid a column of recruits to their new postings. So, if you don't mind my being blunt, why are you here?'

'Not to replace you,' said Macro and smiled. 'Sorry, old son, but that's not in the orders.'

'Damn.'

Cato coughed. 'It seems that the imperial staff is not as ignorant of the situation in Judaea as you think.'

Florianus raised his eyebrows. 'Oh?'

'The Imperial Secretary has heard some worrying reports from his agents in this part of the Empire.'

'Really?' Florianus looked steadily at Cato, his face expressionless.

'More than enough to doubt the reports given out by the procurator. That's why he sent us here. Narcissus wants the situation assessed with fresh eyes. We've already spoken to the procurator, and I think you're right about him. He simply can't afford to see things as they are. His staff are well aware of what is going on, but know that Alexander isn't best pleased by any views that contradict his official line. That's why we needed to see you. As Narcissus' chief intelligence agent in the region, you would seem to be the best person to speak to.'

There was a brief, tense silence before Florianus nodded his head slightly. 'That's right. I assume that you made no mention of this to the procurator.'

'What do you take us for?' Macro said flatly.

'No disrespect, Centurion, but I have to guard my true role here very carefully. If the Judaean resistance movements got wind of it, I'd be food for the vultures before the day was out. Only after they'd tortured me to get hold of the names of my agents, of course. So you can see why I have to be sure that my secret is quite safe.'

'It's safe with us,' Cato reassured him. 'Quite safe. Otherwise Narcissus would never have told us.'

Florianus nodded. 'True . . . Very well then, what can I do for you?'

Now that the air had been cleared Cato could speak freely. 'Since much of the information Narcissus has gathered comes from your network you'll be familiar with his most obvious concerns. The most dangerous threat comes from Parthia.'

'And there's nothing new there,' Macro added. 'As long as Rome has had an interest in the east we've been facing those bastards.'

'Yes,' Cato continued, 'that's right. But the desert forms a natural obstacle between Parthia and Rome. It's allowed us to have some kind of peace along that frontier for nearly a hundred years now. However, the old rivalry remains, and now it seems that the Parthians are playing politics in Palmyra.'

'So I've heard.' Florianus scratched his cheek. 'I have a merchant on the payroll who runs a caravan to the city. He tells me that the Parthians are trying to stir up trouble between members of the royal household at Palmyra. It's rumoured they've promised the crown to Prince Artaxas if he agrees to become an ally of Parthia. He's denying it of course and the King dare not have him removed without hard evidence, in case he panics the other princes.'

'That's what Narcissus told us,' said Cato. 'And if

Parthia should get its hands on Palmyra, then they'll be able to march their army right up to the boundaries of the province of Syria. At the moment there are three legions at Antioch. Arrangements are being made to send a fourth, but therein lies the other problem.'

They had reached the limit of Florianus' knowledge of the situation and now he stared at Cato intently. 'What's that?'

Cato instinctively lowered his voice. 'Cassius Longinus, the Governor of Syria.'

'What about him?'

'Narcissus doesn't trust him.'

Macro laughed. 'Narcissus doesn't trust anybody. Mind you, nobody in their right mind would trust him.'

'Anyway,' Cato continued, 'it seems that Cassius Longinus has some contacts with those elements back in Rome who oppose the Emperor.'

Florianus glanced up. 'You mean those bastards who call themselves the Liberators?'

'Of course.' Cato smiled grimly. 'One of their men fell into the hands of Narcissus earlier this year. He gave up a few names before he died, including that of Longinus.'

Florianus frowned. 'I've heard nothing from my sources in Antioch about Longinus. Nothing to arouse suspicion. And I've met him a few times. Frankly he doesn't seem the type. Too cautious to strike out on his own.'

Macro smiled. 'Having three legions at your back has a wonderful way of stiffening a man's spine. Four legions even more so. To have that much power in your grasp must be quite inspiring to a man's ambition.'

'But not enough to turn him against the rest of the Empire,' Florianus countered.

Cato nodded. 'True, as things stand. But suppose the Emperor was compelled to reinforce the region with yet more legions? Not just to counter the Parthian threat, but to put down a rebellion here in Judaea.'

'But there isn't a rebellion here.'

'Not yet. But there's plenty of ill feeling brewing up, as you yourself have reported. It wouldn't take much to incite an open revolt. Look what happened when Caligula gave orders for a statue of him to be erected in Jerusalem. If he hadn't been murdered before work could begin then every man in the land would have risen up against Rome. How many legions would it have taken to put that down? Another three? Perhaps four? In addition to the Syrian legions, that's at least seven in all. With that kind of force at his disposal a man could easily make himself a contender for the purple. Mark my words.'

There was a long silence as Florianus considered Cato's proposition, and then he suddenly looked back at the young centurion. 'Are you suggesting that Longinus might actually provoke such a revolt? To get his hands on more legions?'

Cato shrugged. 'Maybe. Maybe not. I don't know yet. Let's just say it's a sufficiently worrying prospect for Narcissus to send us here to investigate it.'

'But it's preposterous. A revolt would lead to the deaths of thousands – tens of thousands of people. And if Longinus was intending to use the legions to force his way into the palace in Rome he would leave the eastern provinces defenceless.'

'The Parthians would be in here like a shot,' Macro quipped and then raised his hands apologetically as the other two turned to him with irritated expressions.

Cato cleared his throat. 'That's true. But then Longinus would be playing for the highest stakes of all. He would be prepared to sacrifice the eastern provinces if it meant becoming Emperor.'

'If that is his plan,' Florianus responded. 'Frankly, that's a very big if.'

'Yes,' Cato conceded. 'But still a possibility that has to be taken seriously. Narcissus certainly takes it seriously.'

'Forgive me, young man, but I've worked for Narcissus for many years. He is inclined to jump at shadows.'

Cato shrugged. 'Longinus is still a risk.'

'But how exactly do you think he is going to cause this revolt? That has to be the key to the situation. Unless there's a revolt he'll not have his legions, and without them he can do nothing.'

'So, then, he needs a revolt. And isn't he lucky to have someone here in Judaea who has sworn to provide one.'

'What are you talking about?'

'There's a man named Bannus the Canaanean. I assume you've heard of him.'

'Of course. He's a minor brigand. Lives in the range of hills to the east of the River Jordan. He's been preying on the villages and travellers in the valley, besides raiding a few of the wealthy estates and some of the caravans making for the Decapolis. But he's not a serious threat.'

'No?'

'He has a few hundred followers. Poorly armed hillsmen and those on the run from the authorities here in Jerusalem.'

'Nevertheless, according to your most recent reports, his strength has grown, he's becoming more ambitious in his attacks, and he's even claiming to be some kind of divinely chosen leader.' Cato frowned. 'What was the word?'

'*Mashiah*,' said Florianus. 'That's what the locals call them. Every few years some crazy fool sets himself up as the anointed one, the man to lead the people of Judaea to freedom from Rome, and eventual conquest of the world.'

Macro shook his head. 'An ambitious-sounding lad, this Bannus.'

'Not just him. Almost every one of them,' Florianus responded. 'They last a few months, gather a desperate mob behind them and eventually we have to send the cavalry out from Caesarea to knock a few heads together and crucify the ringleaders. Their followers melt away readily enough and then we just have a handful of anti-Roman fanatics and their terror tactics to worry about.'

'So we saw,' Macro said. 'I can tell you, there was nothing low-level about that.'

'You get used to it.' Florianus waved his hand dismissively. 'It happens all the time. They pick on their own more often than not, those people they accuse of collaborating with Rome. Usually a quick kill in the streets, but when their targets are hard to get at the sicarians are not above using suicide attacks.'

'Shit,' Macro muttered. 'Suicide attacks. What kind of madness is that?'

Florianus shrugged. 'You make a people desperate enough, and there's no telling what horrors they are capable of. Give it a few months here, and you'll see what I mean.'

'I want to leave this province already.'

'All in good time.' Cato gave a thin smile. 'This Bannus. You said he operates on the far side of the Jordan.'

'That's right.'

'Near the fort at Bushir?'

'Yes, so?'

'That's the fort where the Second Illyrian Cohort is stationed, under Prefect Scrofa.'

'Yes. What of it?'

'Our cover story is that we have been sent to relieve Scrofa. Macro is to take command of the cohort and I'll act as his second in command.'

Florianus frowned. 'Why? What possible use will that serve?'

'I believe Prefect Scrofa was appointed directly on the orders of Longinus?'

'That's true. He was sent down from Antioch. But it's not unusual. Sometimes a new commander is needed and there's no time to refer the matter to Rome.'

'What happened to the previous commander?'

'He was killed. In an ambush, while he was leading a patrol in the hills. That's what his adjutant said in the report.'

'Quite.' Cato smiled. 'But the fact that his adjutant was named by the same man who told Narcissus about Longinus is more than a little intriguing, to my mind at least.'

Florianus was still for a moment. 'You're not serious?'

'I've never been more serious.'

'But what is the connection with Longinus?'

Macro smiled. 'That's what we're here to find out.'

Centurion Florianus called his orderly and sent for some wine. 'I think I could use something a little stronger. You two are beginning to frighten me. There's more to this than you've let on.'

Macro and Cato exchanged a brief look and Macro nodded his assent. 'Go on then. You know the background to this better than I do.'

CHAPTER THREE

Cato was still for a moment, focusing his thoughts before he told Florianus about the meeting with Narcissus in the imperial palace nearly three months earlier, at the end of March. Before then Macro and Cato had spent several months training recruits for the urban cohorts – the units assigned to police Rome's streets. The recruits were the type of men who would never be selected for the legions, and the two centurions had done their best to kick them into shape. It had been a thankless task, but even though Cato had been desperate to return to active service, the summons of the Imperial Secretary had filled him with foreboding.

The last mission that the imperial agent had sent them on had been a near suicidal operation to retrieve some scrolls, vital to the security of the Empire, from the clutches of a gang of pirates who had been preying on shipping along the coast of Illyricum. The Sybilline scrolls completed a set of sacred prophecies that were supposed to describe in some detail the future of Rome, and its ultimate fate. Naturally, the Emperor's right hand man had to win possession of such a treasure to safeguard his master and the Empire he served. Cato and Macro had been assigned training duties as a 'reward' for successfully finding the scrolls and delivering them safely into the hands of the Imperial Secretary. Macro was on leave when the messenger from Narcissus arrived at the barracks and so Cato approached the palace alone just as dusk thickened about the grimy walls and sooty tiles of the city.

An early spring storm was raging across the city as Cato entered the palace complex. He was escorted to the suite of the Imperial Secretary and then ushered into Narcissus' office by one of his neatly groomed clerks. Cato handed his drenched cape to the clerk before he crossed the room and sat on the chair that Narcissus waved him towards. Behind the Imperial Secretary was a glazed window through the panes of which the view of the city was distorted. Black clouds billowed across the sky, illuminated every so often by a dazzling flash of lightning that, for an instant, froze the city in brilliant whiteness, before the vision was snatched away and Rome was plunged once more into the shadows.

'Rested, I hope?' Narcissus attempted to look concerned. 'It's been several months since that campaign against the pirates.'

'I've been keeping fit,' Cato replied carefully. 'I'm ready to return to active service. So is Macro.'

'Good. That's good.' Narcissus nodded. 'And where is my friend Centurion Macro?'

Cato stifled a choke. The idea that Macro and this effete bureaucrat might be considered friends was sublimely ridiculous. He cleared his throat. 'On leave. He went to Ravenna to see his mother. She hasn't got over her loss.'

Narcissus frowned. 'Her loss?'

'Her man was killed during the final attack on the pirates.'

'Oh, I'm sorry,' Narcissus replied flatly. 'You must pass on my condolences, when you rejoin him. Before you take on your new task.'

Cato froze for a moment, feeling a sick sense of inevitability rise up as he realised the Imperial Secretary had further plans for him.

'I don't understand,' he said. 'I thought Macro and I were waiting to be reassigned to a legion.'

'Ah, well, the situation has changed. Rather, a new situation has emerged.'

'Really?' Cato smiled mirthlessly. 'And what would that be?'

'Those scrolls you recovered, I've been studying them closely for some time now, and I appear to have stumbled on to something quite interesting.' He paused. 'No. Not interesting. Frightening . . . As you might imagine, I concentrated on the prophecies relating to the immediate future, and I came across something that rather jarred my mind. You see, the seeds of the eventual downfall of Rome are being sown even now.'

'Let me guess – a plague of tax collectors?'

'Don't be glib, Cato. Leave that to Macro – he's better at it.'

'But he's not here.'

'What a pity. Now if I might continue?'

Cato shrugged. 'Go on then.'

Narcissus leaned forwards, clasped his palms together and propped up his chin as he began. 'There was a passage in the scrolls which predicted that in the eighth century after the founding of Rome a great power would stir in the east. A new kingdom would be born that would destroy Rome utterly, and build a new capital on her ruins.'

Cato sniffed with derision. 'Every mad prophet on the streets of Rome is spouting that kind of prediction.'

'Wait. It's more specific than that. It said the new empire would rise out of Judaea.'

'That's nothing I haven't heard scores of times before. Hardly a year goes by without the Judaeans discovering another great man to lead them to freedom from Rome. And if I've heard about these men, then you surely have.'

'Granted. But there is a new sect amongst the Judaeans that has come to my attention. I'm having my agents investigate them even now. Seems they are followers of a man who claimed to be some kind of divinity. Or at least that's what my agents say his followers

31

are claiming now. I'm told that in reality he was the son of some rural craftsman. Jehoshua was the man's name.'

'Was? What happened to him?'

'He was accused of inciting civil disorder by the high priests in Jerusalem. They insisted that he be put to death, but lacked the guts to do it themselves, so the procurator at the time had this Jehoshua executed. Trouble was that, like so many of these prophets, he was quite charismatic. So much so that his coterie have managed to attract a large following in the years since his death. Unlike most other Judaean sects, this one promises them some kind of glorious afterlife when they die and go into the shades.' Narcissus smiled. 'You can see the appeal.'

'Perhaps,' Cato muttered. 'But it sounds like the usual religious quackery to me.'

'I agree with you, young man. But that's not stopping these people from finding new adherents.'

'Why not just stamp them out? Proscribe their leaders?'

'All in good time. If the need arises.'

Cato laughed. 'Are you saying these people are threatening to overthrow Rome?'

'No. At least not yet. But we're keeping an eye on them. If I judge them to be the threat identified by the scrolls then they will be . . . removed.'

Cato reflected that it was typical of the man to talk in such euphemisms. For an instant he felt contempt, then with a sudden flash of insight he wondered if the Imperial Secretary could only carry out his work because of a euphemistic frame of mind. After all, the decisions that Narcissus made frequently resulted in deaths. Necessary deaths perhaps, but deaths all the same. Opponents of the Emperor consigned to oblivion at the stroke of a pen. How that must weigh on a man's conscience. Far better for Narcissus to see them as a problem removed, rather than a string of corpses littering his wake. Of course, Cato thought, that presupposed the man had a conscience to be perturbed by the decisions of life and death that he made every day. What if he didn't? What if the euphemisms were merely a matter of rhetorical style? Cato shuddered. In that case Narcissus was completely without ethics. The ideal of Rome was no more than a hollow edifice whose real centre was the simple, unadorned greed and lust for power of the elite few. Cato tried to shake off such thoughts as he forced his mind to focus on the matter at hand.

'I didn't think you placed much faith in such prophecies?'

'Normally, I don't,' Narcissus admitted. 'But it so happens that the same day I read of this supposed threat to Rome, a rather disturbing intelligence dossier, compiled from reports from my agents in the eastern provices, happened to cross my desk. It seems that there is a confluence of dangers in the region. For one thing, these followers of Jehoshua are divided. One tendency, the version that even has its adherents in Rome, preaches some kind of unworldly pacifism. That we can live with. After all, what possible danger could come from such a philosophy? It is the second tendency that concerns me. The movement is led by Bannus of Canaan. He preaches resistance to Rome, by any and all means available to the people of Judaea. If that kind of philosophy overspilled the borders of the province then we really would be in trouble.'

'Indeed.' Cato nodded. 'But you implied there were more threats. What else is there?'

'Our old adversary, Parthia, on the one hand. Parthia is making a play for Palmyra; territory that directly encroaches on our frontier. Unhappily, this, the worsening situation in Judaea, and the rise of this man Bannus are further complicated by the fact that the Governor of Syria has been linked to the Liberators. Put it all together and even a cynical rationalist like me would consider it more than a little foolhardy to ignore the words of the prophecy.'

'What are you saying exactly?' Cato frowned. 'The prophecy could refer to any of these threats, assuming it has any validity at all.'

Narcissus leaned back in his chair and sighed. For a moment he said nothing, and Cato was conscious for the first time of the rattling of rain against the window. The wind must have changed. A distant flash of sheet lightning momentarily silhouetted the Imperial Secretary and after a pause the sound of thunder grumbled across the city.

Narcissus stirred. 'That's my problem, Cato. The wording is vague enough to embrace all of those threats. I need someone to investigate the matter further, assess the dangers, and if possible resolve them.'

'Resolve?' Cato smiled. 'Now that's a vague term if ever I heard one. Covers a multitude of possibilities.'

'Of course it does.' Narcissus smiled back. 'And it's up to you to discern the best means of resolving any issue you judge to constitute a threat to the Emperor.'

'Me?'

'You and Macro, of course. You can pick him up in Ravenna when you board a ship bound for the east.'

'Now, wait a moment—'

'Unfortunately, we can't wait. There's no time to waste. You must leave Rome immediately.'

Cato stared back at Narcissus with a hostile expression. 'That last mission you sent us on nearly got us killed.'

'You're a soldier. Getting yourself killed is an occupational hazard.'

Cato stared at the Imperial Secretary for a moment, consumed with rage and a sense of injustice. He forced himself to answer as calmly as he could. 'Macro and I don't deserve this. Haven't we done enough for you already?'

'No man can do enough in the service of Rome.'

'Find someone else. Someone better suited to this

kind of work. Let Macro and me get back to soldiering. It's what we do best.'

'You're both fine soldiers,' Narcissus agreed smoothly. 'As good as they come. And being soldiers is a useful cover for your real mission. You and Macro will be assigned to a frontier unit in the province. Since you belong to the select few who know about the prophecies you are the most obvious choice for the job.' He shrugged. 'In a way, you are victims of your own success, as the saying goes. Come now, Cato. It's not as if I'm asking you to risk your lives. I just want you to assess the situation.'

'And resolve it.'

'Yes, and resolve it.'

'By what means?'

'You will be acting with the full authority of the Emperor. I have prepared a document to that effect. It's waiting in another office, together with Centurion Macro's letter of appointment, the report from Caesarea and all the other material I felt it was relevant for you to see. I'd like you to read through it tonight.'

'All of it?'

'Yes, I think that would be wise, since you will be leaving Rome at dawn tomorrow.'

Centurion Florianus shook his head as Cato finished relating the details of the meeting. 'That's tough. The Imperial Secretary seems determined to make you boys earn every sestertian of your pay.'

Macro rolled his eyes. 'You can't imagine.'

'Of course,' Cato said quietly, 'you are never to speak to anyone else about the scrolls. Narcissus instructed me to inform you alone. Only a handful of people are aware of their existence, and we are the only three in all of the eastern provinces in the know. That's how Narcissus wants it to stay. Is that understood?'

Florianus nodded.

'Very well,' Cato continued. 'I won't insult you by asking you to swear to secrecy. Knowing the Imperial Secretary as we all do, it's enough to imagine what he might do to us if we ever revealed the secret.'

'Don't worry,' Florianus replied casually. 'I know what becomes of those who fall foul of Narcissus. Before I came here, I was one of his interrogators.'

'Ah . . .' Macro made to speak, thought better of it, closed his mouth and impulsively thrust his cup towards Florianus. 'I think I need some more of your wine.'

As Macro took a hefty gulp from his replenished cup Florianus continued, 'So what is your plan?'

'We'll start with Prefect Scrofa and Bannus,' said Cato. 'If we can sort them out then we might be able to prevent an uprising. Without that Longinus will have no reason to call for reinforcements. He won't be strong enough to march on Rome. If he's forced to hold his position, then, with luck, the Parthians will not dare to push their ambitions too far.'

'That's two ifs too many for my taste,' Macro muttered.

Cato shrugged. 'There's nothing we can do about it. At least until we reach the fort at Bushir.'

'When will you go?' asked Florianus.

'A fine host you are!' Macro laughed, and Florianus tried to stop himself blushing as he replied.

'I'm not trying to get rid of you. It's just that since you killed some of the sicarians in that skirmish down in the temple, their friends will be looking out for you. I'd advise you to look to your safety until you reach Bushir. Don't go anywhere alone. Always keep armed men close to you and watch your backs.'

'We always do,' Macro told him.

'Glad to hear it. Now, I imagine you'll want a guide. Someone who knows the route, as well as the lie of the land around Bushir.'

'That would be helpful,' said Cato. 'Do you know anyone we can trust?'

'None of the local people, that's for sure. But there's a man who should serve your needs. He usually works as a guide on the caravan routes to Arabia so he knows the land and the people well. Symeon's not exactly a friend of the Empire, but he's smart enough to know that nothing good will come out of any attempt to defy Rome. You can trust him that far at least.'

'Sounds useful.' Macro smiled. 'My enemy's enemy is my friend.'

Florianus nodded. 'Thus it ever was. Don't knock it, Macro. The adage works well enough. Now is there anything else I need to know? Anything I can do for you?'

'I don't think so.' Cato stared out over the ancient city. 'Given what you said about the sicarians, I think we should leave Jerusalem as soon as possible. Tomorrow morning, if possible.'

'Tomorrow?' Macro repeated in surprise.

'We should leave at first light. Try to put as much distance between us and Jerusalem as we can before nightfall.'

'Very well,' Florianus nodded. 'I'll get hold of Symeon and organise a mounted escort for you. A squadron of horse from the garrison should be enough to guarantee you reach Bushir safely.'

'Is that really necessary?' Macro asked. 'We can move faster on our own.'

'Believe me, if you left here without an escort, the bandits would track you down and kill you before the day was out. This is a Roman province in name only. Outside the city walls there is no law, no order, just a wasteland ruled by the local thieves, murderers and the odd religious cult. It's no place for Romans.'

'Don't worry. The lad and I can look after ourselves. We've been in worse places.'

'Really?' Florianus looked doubtful. 'Anyway, keep me informed of the situation at Bushir, and I'll pass the reports on to Narcissus.'

Cato nodded. 'Then it's all settled. We leave in the morning.'

'Yes. One last thing,' Florianus said quietly. 'A word of advice. When you reach Bushir watch your backs. Seriously. The commander before Scrofa was killed by a single sword blow, from behind.'

CHAPTER FOUR

The small column prepared to leave the city just after the sun had risen, bathing the walls of the Antonia fortress in a warm rosy glow. The air was cool and after the heat of the previous night Macro relished its refreshing embrace as he ensured that his bags were securely tied to his saddle horns. Like every man in the legions he had been taught to ride after a fashion, but still distrusted and disliked horses. He had been trained as an infantryman, and from long experience he preferred the company of 'Marius' Mules', as the footsloggers were known the length and breadth of the empire. Still, he was respectful enough of the fierce heat that blasted the rocky landscape of Judaea to know that it would be far more exhausting to reach Bushir on foot. So by horse it would be.

He glanced round at the cavalry squadron detailed to accompany the two centurions to the fort. These men were Greek auxiliaries, recruited from the population in Caesarea. There were no native units in the province now that Rome had taken Judaea under direct control. The army of Herod Agrippa, largely composed of Gentile mercenaries, had been disarmed and dispersed after his death two years ago. With all the inter-faction fighting that had plagued the kingdom of Judaea the authorities in Rome had decided that it would be foolhardy in the extreme to make any attempt to raise local forces and provide them with weapons. Besides, the peculiar requirements of the local religion, with all the fasting and days of abstaining from any labour, did not sit well with the routines of the Roman military system.

Macro cast an experienced eye over the cavalrymen. They seemed competent enough, and their kit was well maintained and their mounts well groomed and healthy-looking. If there was any trouble on the road then he and Cato could count on these men to put up a good enough fight to beat off an ambush. A quick charge and any band of robbers would bolt like rabbits, Macro decided. He turned to look for Cato.

His young friend was talking earnestly to the guide, and Macro's eyes narrowed slightly. Centurion Florianus had brought the man to them as Cato and Macro were packing their saddlebags by the wan light of oil lamps in the last hour before dawn. Symeon was a tall, broad-shouldered man in his forties. He wore a clean but plain tunic, sandals and a simple keffiyeh held in place by an ornate headband that was the only outward sign of opulence. Indeed, he carried little on his horse apart from a small bundle of spare clothes, a thin curved sword, and a compound short bow and a quiver of arrows. He had a pleasant, round face and spoke Greek fluently. More than fluently, Macro realised. Macro's grasp of the language was limited, no more than the basics learned from Cato on the voyage from Ravenna. With the diversity of languages at this end of the Empire, the common second language was Greek and Macro had to be able to make himself understood. The guide's accent was flawless. The effect was so unexpected that Macro was instinctively suspicious of the man. Yet he seemed friendly enough and had clasped forearms in a firm and frank manner when he had been introduced. Cato was smiling at some comment the guide had made, and then he turned away and strolled over to join Macro.

'Symeon has been telling me about the route to the fort.' Cato's eyes glinted with excitement. 'We go east to Qumran, on the shore of the Dead Sea, then cross the River Jordan and climb the hills on the far side up on to the escarpment. That's where the desert begins, and that's where the fort is.'

'Oh joy,' Macro replied tonelessly. 'A desert. Can't wait to discover what they do for entertainment out that way. Finally, after all these years, I make it out to the eastern provinces. Do I get to see the fleshpots of Syria? I do not. Instead I spend the time in some far-flung fort in the middle of a bloody desert where I'll be lucky if the sun doesn't fry my brain to a crisp every day. No. I'm sorry,

Cato, but I just can't seem to share your obvious pleasure at the prospect. Sorry.'

Cato punched him on the shoulder. 'We're going to spend tonight by the Dead Sea, you idiot. Surely you want to see that?'

Macro stared at him. 'Dead Sea? Does that sound like a nice place to you?'

'Oh, come on.' Cato grinned. 'You must have heard of it.'

'Why?'

Cato looked stunned. 'It's a natural wonder. I read about it back in Rome when I was a boy.'

'Ah, well. You see, while you were busy reading about natural wonders, I was busy learning how to be a soldier and sticking it to those barbarians up on the Rhine. So excuse me for not being up to speed on sightseeing attractions at the arse end of the Empire.'

Cato grinned. 'All right then, misery-guts. But just you wait until you see it tonight.'

'Cato,' Macro began wearily. 'Once you've seen one sea, you've seen 'em all. There's nothing special or even nice about the sea. After all, fish fuck in it and shit in it. That's as magic as a sea gets.'

Before Cato could respond the decurion in command of the squadron bellowed the order for his men to mount and the courtyard of the fortress was filled with the sounds of horses stirring and scraping their hooves across the paving stones as their riders swung themselves up on to their saddles. The leather seats gave under the weight of the riders and the saddle horns squeezed slightly inwards, giving the cavalrymen a steady position on top of their mounts. The two centurions abandoned their conversation and climbed on to their horses in a somewhat ungainly manner, and then steered their beasts over to the middle of the column. Florianus had suggested that this would be safest for them until they were outside the walls of Jerusalem, when they could join Symeon and the decurion at the head of the column. Macro was not entirely happy about the precaution.

'I don't like being nursemaided,' he grumbled.

'Better than being assassinated,' Cato replied.

'Let 'em try.'

The decurion glanced round at his squadron, saw that all was ready, and raised his arm.

'Column! Advance.' His arm swept down towards the gate and the sentries stood aside under the great arch as the column clopped forward, out into the street that ran down from the Antonia, alongside the north-facing mass of the temple complex towards the Kidron gate. As they emerged from the shadows of the gateway Cato blinked at the sunlight shining directly into his eyes. This was a mistake, he suddenly realised. The sun would blind them to any ambush the sicarians might attempt along the street and he squinted painfully as he scanned the buildings crowding in on each side. But there was little sign of life. A few early risers were abroad, some beggars were taking up their pitches for the day and a mangy dog trotted from one pile of refuse to the next, sniffing for morsels of food. The handful of people on the street gave way as the column approached and stared expressionlessly at the mounted soldiers as they passed by. Ahead of them, Cato saw the watchmen on the city gate draw back the locking bar and begin to ease back the heavy slabs of timber that protected the city. A short while later, without incident, the squadron rode out of the city and began to descend the steep track leading down into the valley of Kidron. Cato breathed a sigh of relief.

'Glad we're out of there.'

Macro shrugged. 'It'd take more than a few fools who fancy themselves with a blade to worry me.'

'That's a comfort to know.' The dust from the mounts ahead of them was already filling the air and Cato pressed his knees into the flank of his horse and twitched the reins to the side. 'Come on, let's get to the front.'

By the time the column had crossed the valley and climbed the Mount of Olives on the far side, the sun had risen far enough into the sky for its heat to begin to be felt. Macro, far more used to the climate of the northern provinces, started to dread the prospect of spending the rest of the day swaying in the saddle under the direct blaze of the sun. His helmet hung from the saddle frame and like the rest of the soldiers he wore a straw hat over his felt helmet liner. Even so his sweat soon made the liner feel hot and prickly and he silently cursed Narcissus for landing them with this job. As the horses picked their way along the track that led towards the River Jordan where it fed into the Dead Sea, they soon left behind the large estates of the wealthier Judaeans. Most of the great houses were closed up, their owners no longer daring to live under the threat of a brigand's knife. Instead they had retreated to their houses in Jerusalem where they could live more safely. The land steadily became more sparsely populated and the villages they rode through comprised huddles of mudbrick hovels surrounded by small strips of cultivated land.

'This is crazy,' Macro commented. 'No one could live off these scraps of dirt. Hey, guide!'

Symeon turned in his saddle and smiled. 'Yes, my friend?'

Macro stared at him. 'You're not my friend. Not yet. You're just a guide, so watch your lip.'

'As you wish, Roman. What did you want of me?'

Macro indicated the intricate patchwork of fields around the village they were passing. 'What's going on here? Why are their plots so small?'

'It's the Judaean way. When a man dies his land is divided between his sons. When they die in turn it is divided between their sons. So, every generation the farms get smaller and smaller.'

'That can't go on for ever.'

'No, indeed, Centurion. That is one of the problems

that blights this land. When a man can no longer support his family, he is forced to take a loan against his property.' Symeon shrugged. 'If there's a bad harvest, or if the market is glutted, he can't pay the loan off and his land is forfeit. Many drift to Jerusalem looking for work, the rest go into the hills and become brigands, preying on travellers and terrorising some of the smaller villages.'

Macro pursed his lips. 'That's not much of a life.'

'Still less of a life, now that the people have to pay Roman taxes.'

Macro looked at him sharply, but the guide just shrugged. 'I mean no offence, Centurion, but that's how it is. If Rome wants peace here, then she must look to the needs of the poor, before she adds the spoils of Judaea to her coffers.'

'The Empire's not a bloody charity.' Macro sniffed. 'It has an army to run, borders to maintain, roads to build, aqueducts, and . . . well, other things. Doesn't come cheap. Someone has to pay. And without us, who would protect these people, eh? Answer me that.'

'Protect these people?' Symeon smiled thinly. 'Who from? They would scarcely be any worse off under the heel of another empire.'

'I was referring to people like Bannus and his brigands. Rome will protect them from Bannus.'

'The people don't see him that way. Many are inclined to see Bannus as some kind of hero. You won't defeat Bannus unless Rome governs Judaea with a lighter hand, or garrisons these lands from top to bottom. I don't see that happening in my lifetime.'

'So what would you do then, Symeon? How would you improve the lot of these Judaeans?'

'Me?' The guide paused for a moment before he answered. 'I would rid them of their burden of Roman tax for a start.'

'Then there'd be no point in having Judaea as a province. Is that what you want for your people?'

'My people?' Symeon shrugged. 'They're not really my people any more.'

'Aren't you a Judaean?'

'I am. But I am no longer so sure that I share their beliefs. I have not been living in the province for many years.'

'So how did you end up as a guide?'

'I had to leave Judaea in a hurry over ten years ago.' Symeon glanced at Macro. 'Before you ask, I had my reasons, and I won't go into them.'

'Fair enough.'

'Anyway, I went south, to Nabataea, where no one would come looking for me. I joined one of the companies of men who guard the caravans. That's how I learned to use weapons properly. I'll never forget my first caravan. Twenty days across deserts and through mountains. I'd never seen lands like it before. Truly, Centurion, there are certain places in this world where the hand of God can be seen.'

'I think I've seen enough already,' Macro grumbled. 'Give me Campania or Umbria any day. Sod all this desert and rock.'

'It's not always like this, Centurion. In spring, it's cool and there's rain and the hills are covered with flowers. Even the desert across the Jordan blooms. And there's a kind of majesty in the desert. To the south there's a wadi where the sand is bright red and great cliffs of coloured rock rise up to the skies. At night the heavens are filled with stars and travellers gather round fires and tell tales that echo back off the cliffs.' He paused and smiled self-consciously. 'Perhaps one day you'll see for yourself, and understand.'

He clicked his tongue and urged his horse forward, until he was a short distance ahead of the column. Macro stared at him for a moment and spoke quietly to Cato. 'Well, what do you make of him?'

'I'm not sure. If he knows the area as well as he says, then I can see why Florianus uses him. But there's something about him that doesn't seem right.'

'What is it?'

Cato shook his head. 'I'm not quite sure. I just can't believe a man turns his back on his family and friends for such a long time so easily. He's interesting.'

'Interesting?' Macro shook his head. 'Mad more like. Maybe he's just had a little too much of the desert sun.'

* * *

The column of horsemen reached the small Essene community of Qumran as the sun dipped down behind them, casting long distorted shadows before the riders. Qumran was a small settlement made up of simple houses that lined dusty narrow streets. The people warily acknowledged the greetings offered to them by Symeon as he led the column through the village towards the small fort built on a slight rise a mile beyond Qumran. Beyond the fort lay the Dead Sea, stretching out towards the mountains that rose up, fiery coloured and forbidding, in the red glow of the sun settling in the west. The fort was little more than a fortified signal station and a thin trail of smoke wafted from the brazier in the main tower that was kept alight at all times. It was defended by a half-century of Thracian auxiliaries under an ageing optio who greeted them warmly as the column rode in through the gateway.

'Glad to see some new faces, sir.' He smiled as Macro dismounted and returned the optio's salute. 'Haven't seen any Romans for over a month now.'

Macro yawned and stretched his back before giving his buttocks a firm rub to restore some of the circulation lost after a day in the saddle. He ached, stank of sweat and was covered in dust.

'I need a bath. I don't suppose there's a bath-house here.'

'No, sir.'

'What about back there, in Qumran?'

'There is, sir. But we're not allowed to use their baths.'

'Why's that?' Macro said irritably. 'I'll pay 'em good money.'

'They're Essenes, sir. Friendly enough but they won't share any food or facilities with us, in case we contaminate them.'

'What is wrong with this fucking land?' Macro exploded. 'Has the sun boiled everyone's brains? What are Essenes? Not another bloody sect, surely.'

'Sorry, sir.' The optio shrugged. 'That's how it is. My men are under strict orders not to cause the Essenes any offence.'

'Oh, very well then. Just find quarters for our men and then feed 'em. I'm going for a swim.'

'A swim, sir?'

'Yes. In the sea.'

Macro noticed the surprised look on the optio's face and continued irritably, 'Don't tell me our Essene friends are going to take exception to sharing a whole bloody sea with me?'

'No, sir. It's not that, it's just—'

Macro cut him off. 'See to the men and their mounts.' He turned to Cato. 'Coming?'

'Oh yes.' Cato smiled. 'I wouldn't miss this experience.'

From the corner of his eye Macro saw Cato exchange a knowing look with Symeon and turned on them suddenly. 'What?'

Cato feigned innocence. 'It's nothing. Let's go and swim.'

The two officers stripped down to their tunics and boots and descended the stony slope to the shore. They picked their way a short distance along until they found a stretch of pebbled beach and undressed, leaving their clothes, belts and daggers on top of a rock. Macro trod warily down to the edge of the water and began to wade out, under the amused gaze of his young friend. When he was up to his waist Macro raised a hand and rubbed his fingers together.

'Odd . . . Feels kind of oily.' He raised his fingers and sniffed them for a moment before dabbing them with his tongue. At once his face tightened into a grimace. 'Ugh!'

'What is it?'

'The water. It tastes awful. Far too salty.'

'Then don't drink it,' said Cato. 'Just swim in it.'

'For someone who is such a poor swimmer, you're awfully keen to get stuck in.'

Cato laughed. 'You'll understand in a moment.'

Macro was too weary to continue playing Cato's games and turned away. Stretching his arms out he thrust himself forward into the gently lapping sea. Instead of plunging down beneath the surface he bobbed up like a cork. As soon as he tried the first stroke his legs seemed to come up out of the water behind him.

'What the hell is going on?'

Cato laughed as he waded out towards his friend, and

was treading water even before the sea came close to his shoulders. It was a strange sensation and he smiled in delight. Macro was still floundering, trying to swim a few strokes further out from the shore.

'This is ridiculous.' He gave up and turned on to his back. Floating effortlessly, he looked at Cato. 'I suppose this is why it's some kind of natural bloody marvel.'

Cato settled into the water and raised his legs. 'Strange, isn't it?'

Now that he had got over his surprise Macro found that the experience was quite agreeable after all and for a while he experimented with propelling himself around, finding that the best way was to stay on his back and use his arms like oars. Cato followed his example, whooping like a small boy.

They were splashing about so much that they did not hear the warning shouted from the walls of the fort until it was far too late. Cato was aware of the sound of hooves first. He craned his neck round and saw a small party of horsemen, five of them, racing along the track that ran along the shore of the Dead Sea.

'Macro! Get out!'

'Eh?'

Cato pointed to the horsemen, now less than three hundred paces away. At once they stroked back towards the pebbly beach and as soon as their feet gained purchase on the stony bottom they surged ashore. Already the horsemen had closed the distance and Cato could see the glint of the swords they had drawn. There was no time to run back for their daggers.

'Forget the clothes! Make for the fort!'

They ran awkwardly across the rocks, wincing as the rough surface jabbed and cut into the soles of their feet. Then they reached the track and sprinted across it and started up the slope towards the gateway. The sentry on watch was shouting down into the courtyard and moments later two men emerged from the fort, stared at the approaching horsemen and then started down the slope towards the two officers. Cato risked a glance back along the track and was horrified to see the horsemen no more than a hundred paces behind, closing fast as they bent forward along the sides of their horses' necks, urging their mounts on as they prepared to strike with their swords. Cato knew that he and Macro would be run down before they could reach the fort, long before the first of the auxiliaries could reach them.

'Keep going!' Macro shouted, scrambling up the slope beside him. 'The bastards are almost on us.'

Cato ran on, head hunched down into his shoulders as if that would somehow make him a more difficult target for the horsemen's swords. He was barely aware of the pain from his torn feet as he focused on the gateway and ran towards it with all his might. The pounding of hooves from behind was deafening and at the last moment he risked a look back over his shoulder.

'Shit!' he cried out, as the leading man loomed high

above him, sword raised ready to slash down with a killing blow. Cato saw the triumphant glint in the man's dark eyes and the teeth clenched in a feral grin. Then Cato stumbled and sprawled painfully on the ground. Instinctively he rolled over and raised his arm. The man was as before, only now his eyes were wild with surprise. The shaft of an arrow protruded from his chest. His sword slipped from his hand and clattered on to the track beside Cato. Then he slipped from the saddle and fell to the ground with a heavy thud that drove the wind from his lungs in an explosive grunt of agony. Cato snatched up the weapon and rose into a crouch. The other horsemen were only an instant away, already swerving round the riderless horse. Cato glanced at Macro, who had stopped several paces further on and turned towards him.

'Run, Macro! Don't stop!'

'Fuck that.'

Macro took a step towards Cato but the latter shouted, 'There's nothing you can do. Go!'

Momentarily torn, Macro delayed for a fatal instant and the next horseman clattered forward, his mount knocking Macro flat on his back. But before the man could strike an arrow thudded into his stomach, doubling him over in the saddle before he rolled off to one side. The men behind, confused and frightened by the unerring accuracy of the bowman, reined in and looked up towards the fort. A third arrow tore through the throat of the nearest rider and he toppled from his saddle clutching at his neck with a strained gurgling noise as the blood poured from his wound. Then one of his comrades shouted something and the two survivors wheeled their mounts round and galloped back down the track, bent flat over their horses, not daring to look back. Cato watched them for a moment, chest heaving, and then he let his grip on the sword relax. They were saved. He turned to Macro.

'All right?'

'Fine.' Macro gulped down some breaths. He nodded at the three bodies on the ground. 'Bloody good piece of archery that.'

Cato turned to glance up at the parapet above the gatehouse. Brightly lit by the setting sun, Symeon lowered his bow and waved.

Cato bowed his head, and behind him Macro chuckled.

'Remind me never to try to raid one of his caravans.'

CHAPTER FIVE

The next morning, as the column left the fort, the men eyed the landscape around them warily. The previous evening's attack was not the work of simple thieves. It had been a deliberate attempt on the lives of the two centurions and it was clear that they had been followed from Jerusalem. The survivors of the attack would now shadow them, waiting for another opportunity to strike. It was also possible, Cato thought, that the five men were part of a larger group, in which case the column must guard against ambush.

'What is the lie of the land between here and Bushir?' Cato asked their guide as they left Qumran behind and continued along the shore of the Dead Sea.

'We should be safe enough this side of the Jordan, and some way into the east bank. The danger lies there.' Symeon raised his arm and indicated the mountains on the far side of the sea. 'To reach Bushir we're going to have to climb up a steep wadi. We won't reach the plateau before dark. If our friends are going to try another attack that's where it'll happen.'

'Is there no other route?'

'Of course. We could head further north, where there's a more open road to Philadelphia. Then turn south along the caravan route to Petra. That will add two or three days to the journey. Do you wish me to take you that way?'

Cato thought about it a moment and shook his head. 'I don't think it would be wise to give those people any more time to make another attack. What do you say, Macro?'

'If they're going to come for us, let them come tonight. I'm ready.'

'Very well then.' Cato smiled. 'We'll take the direct road.'

They continued in silence for a moment, and Macro's eyes alighted on the horned tip of the bow protruding from Symeon's saddlebags.

'That was fine shooting yesterday.'

'Thank you, Centurion.'

Macro paused for a moment before continuing awkwardly, 'You saved our lives.'

Symeon turned and flashed his white teeth. 'I would hardly be doing my job if the men whose lives I had been charged with guarding had been killed. Why, Florianus would have demanded a refund of my fee.'

'So you're a guard as well as a guide?'

'As I told you yesterday, Centurion, I spent many years in the desert escorting caravans. More than enough time to learn how to use my weapons. And I was taught by the best warriors in Arabia.'

'Why did you give it up? Escorting the caravans?'

'It's a hard life. I was growing weary of it. And now my adopted son has taken over from me. Murad commands a company of escorts and works the route from Petra to Damascus.'

'Is he as good as you with the bow?'

Symeon chuckled. 'As good? No, Murad is far better. Far tougher, and so are most of his men. Murad would have taken down all five of those riders before they had even got close to you.' He spat on to the ground in disgust. 'I only managed three.'

Macro glanced at Cato. 'Only three. The man's slipping.'

'Please don't mention it again,' Symeon said quietly. 'I'm ashamed enough as it is.'

'Fair enough.' Macro smiled. 'Still, your son sounds like the kind of man the Empire could use. He'd make a fine auxiliary soldier. I wonder if he's ever considered it.'

'Why should he?' Symeon seemed surprised by the suggestion. 'Murad lives well enough as he is. Your Empire could not afford to pay him a tenth of what he earns from guarding the caravans.'

'Oh,' Macro responded with embarrassment. 'Just a thought.'

* * *

The day wore on, much like the day before, and soon the heat was stifling. Far up the flat Jordan valley the air shimmered like quicksilver. They crossed the river late in the morning, at a point where it meandered between great clumps of reeds. There was a ford where the river ran across a wide bed of sand and pebbles and the horses kicked up a foam of white spray as they surged across. Glancing upriver Cato saw a large shelter on the far bank, thatched with palm leaves. In the shallows below the shelter stood a small crowd of people, gathered around a man who immersed each in turn.

Cato tugged Symeon's arm and indicated the gathering. 'What's going on over there?'

Symeon glanced up. 'That? A baptism.'

'Baptism?'

'Local tradition. Supposed to wash away the sins of the person being baptised. It's popular with some of the sects. The Essenes, back at Qumran, for one.'

'I meant to ask you about that,' Cato said. 'These sects. How many of them are there? What makes them different?'

Symeon laughed. 'Less than you imagine, yet they seem to hate each other with a passion. Let me see . . . Best to start in Jerusalem. The main sects there are the Sadducees, the Pharisees and the Maccabees. The Sadducees are the hardline traditionalists. They believe that the holy books represent the incontrovertible will of

God. The Pharisees are a little more pragmatic and argue that the will of God can be interpreted through the holy books. The Maccabees, on the other hand, tend towards the hardline position. They hold that Judaeans are the chosen people who are destined to rule the world one day.' He smiled at Cato. 'So you can imagine how they feel about being ruled by Rome. They hate you even more than they hated Herod and his heirs.'

'Why hate them?'

'Because they were Idumaeans, and not descended from one of the original twelve tribes of the Hebrews.'

Macro shook his head. 'These Judaeans sound like a pretty stuffy lot. Fuck knows why, given that they've been rolled over by every empire that's passed through the region.'

Symeon shrugged. 'Perhaps they believe their god is saving them for something special.'

'Their god?' Cato looked at the guide curiously. 'Yours too, surely?'

'I told you. I no longer subscribe to the faith.'

'What do you believe in?'

Symeon did not reply straight away, but glanced briefly at the distant crowd of people being baptised before he spoke. 'I'm not quite sure what I believe in any more . . .'

'What about that lot we passed yesterday?' Macro broke in. 'The Essenes, or whatever you called 'em.'

'Essenes,' Symeon confirmed. 'They're simple enough.

The Essenes believe that the world of men is corrupt, evil and unspiritual. That is why God has not favoured Judaea. They try to live a simple, unadorned life. All possessions belong to the community and they live strictly according to the word of the holy books.'

'Not the best of drinking companions, then?'

The guide glanced at Macro. 'No. I suppose not.'

'Any more sects worth mentioning?'

'Just one. Most of them live in a small settlement near Bushir. They're a lot like the Essenes. At least some of them are. The ones who call themselves the true followers of Jehoshua. The trouble is, they have a rival faction.'

'The one led by Bannus,' said Cato.

'Yes, that's right.' Symeon glanced at him in surprise.

'I must have heard of him in Jerusalem,' Cato explained quickly.

Symeon continued. 'Bannus claims that Jehoshua meant his people to use force to establish the authority of his teachings, and that the Essenes are attempting to take over the movement and corrupt Jehoshua's creed. He says they have watered it down into a powerless set of beliefs. The irony is that although they have a limited number of followers in Judaea, there are cells springing up all over the Empire according to my friend Florianus.'

'Who is the leader of this faction?' asked Cato.

Symeon looked at him closely. 'Do you really need to know? Bannus is the real danger. Remove him, and the province might have a chance to be at peace.'

'You're right, of course,' Cato replied smoothly. 'I just like to know the full details of a situation, that's all.'

The far bank of the Jordan rose slowly and the track passed by groves of trees and scores of small farms, drawing on irrigation water from the river that gave life to the entire valley. In the afternoon they approached the line of mountains that climbed up to the great plateau beyond and the land became far more barren with little sign of life apart from the occasional herd of sheep tended by children. As soon as they saw the horsemen approach they hurriedly drove their beasts in the opposite direction, disappearing into the small gullies that meandered across the plain.

As the sun began to sink towards the horizon Symeon led them into the wadi and the track clung to the steep slope as it wound its way up into the rocks. Very soon the track became so narrow that the column could only continue in single file, the horses carefully picking their way along, keeping away from the crumbling edge of the track. Every so often one of the beasts dislodged a small rock that skittered down the slope, trailed by a shower of shingle. The wadi was quite dry and exposed to the full strength of the sun so there was almost no vegetation and the noises made by the passage of the column echoed off the walls of the rock above them.

Cato glanced back and saw they had little more than an hour of light left.

'Symeon . . . We can't spend the night along this track.'

'A little further. There's a wide ledge. We'll camp there.'

'Is it safe?'

'Yes. The path continues like this at either end of the ledge. There's no other way to reach it. Not even for a goat.'

Cato nodded with relief.

The horsemen emerged onto the ledge just as the last glimmer of the sun disappeared over the horizon and the sky flared up in brilliant hues of orange and purple. The riders dismounted wearily and roped their mounts together away from the edge. Feed was taken out of the coarse bags hanging from the saddle frames and spread around the animals for them to graze on. Once the optio had posted sentries on the track at each end of the ledge the men settled down for the night.

Macro gave the order that no fires were to be lit. In the clear mountain air they would be visible for many miles and alert any bandits, or worse the sicarians, to their precise position. Once the last of the light had faded Macro, Cato and Symeon sat on a flat rock and stared back across the Jordan valley. To their left the Dead Sea stretched out dark and forbidding as its name. A scattering of tiny lights flickered across the wide floor of the valley, and so clear was the air that beyond, far away, Cato could just make out a cluster of sparks.

He raised his hand and pointed it out. 'Is that Jerusalem?'

Beside him Symeon squinted for an instant and then nodded. 'It is. Your sight is good, Roman. Very good indeed.'

'In our line of work, it needs to be.'

Macro shivered. 'It's cold. I'd never have thought it after the heat down there.'

'The nights will get colder still when we reach the plateau,' said Symeon as he rose up. 'I'll get our cloaks.'

'Thanks.'

As the guide strode away towards the scattered dark shapes of the men settling down for the night Cato tipped his head back and stared into the sky. It was, as Symeon had indicated, quite beautiful. Overhead hundreds of stars gleamed with cold ethereal brilliance.

'You know, I think I can begin to see why our friend likes this life.'

'What's to like?' Macro muttered. 'We're cold, surrounded by hostile natives and as far from a decent inn and a warm woman as I ever want to be.'

'True, but look at the stars . . . the view. It's magnificent.'

Macro fixed his gaze on the darkened features of his friend and shook his head pityingly. 'You've been in the army for what, nearly four years?'

'Yes . . . So?'

'So when are you going to stop talking like some poncy poet?'

'I don't know,' Cato said quietly. 'When I've seen enough of this world to grow tired of it, I suppose.'

'I can hardly wait,' Macro said quietly as Symeon trudged back to them with the thick army cloaks bundled under his arm.

In the morning, they continued up the path, still in single file. Most of the men had been too cold to sleep through the night and were stiff and tired. Nevertheless, they kept a wary eye on the cliffs above them for any sign of trouble. Soon the path broadened out into a track and the slope became more gentle. Cato breathed a sigh of relief as he urged his mount alongside Symeon and Macro.

'Looks like we've given them the slip.'

'Bunch of women,' Macro growled. 'That's what they are.'

Symeon did not reply. Instead he was scanning the low ridge ahead of them that marked the beginning of the great plateau. Suddenly he reined his horse in.

'You spoke too soon, Centurion,' he said softly. 'Look up there.'

Cato's eyes flickered along the ridge and stopped as he saw a small group of men rising up from the rocks, so that they were starkly silhouetted against the sky. More men appeared, scores of them, and then a line of horsemen, directly across the breadth of the track where it crossed the ridge. As the optio bellowed orders for his men to dump their kit, put on their helmets and prepare their weapons, Macro's hand instinctively grasped his sword handle.

'Now we're for it,' he said quietly

Symeon glanced round at the centurion with a grim smile. 'Not bad work for a bunch of women.'

As he spoke, one of the horsemen edged his beast forward, down the track towards the Romans.

CHAPTER SIX

'It's Bannus,' Symeon said quietly.

As Cato threw his straw hat aside and jammed his helmet on to his head he looked at their guide in surprise. 'You know him?'

'We've met before.'

'As friends, I hope.'

'We were friends, many years ago.' He glanced quickly at Cato. 'But not now.'

'You might have mentioned this before,' Cato muttered.

'I didn't think it was important, Centurion. Besides, you didn't ask.'

'If we get out of this, I think there might be a few questions I'll want answers to.'

Bannus reined his horse in when he was a short distance away and smiled as he recognised the guide. He addressed him in Greek.

'When my men told me about the archer in the fort, I should have guessed. These Roman soldiers are not welcome here, but peace be with you, Symeon of Bethsaida.'

'And with you, Bannus of Canaan. How may we be of service to you?'

'I want those two Roman officers surrendered to me. You and the others can return to Jerusalem, after we have disarmed you.'

Symeon shook his head. 'You know that is impossible. You would dishonour me, and my family.'

Bannus stared at him a moment before he continued. 'For the sake of the old days, I will ask you again to hand over those two men, and your weapons. I would not have your blood on my hands.'

'Then stand aside and let us pass.'

'No. Those two have slain three of my men in Jerusalem. They must be executed to serve as an example to the people of Judaea.'

'And what of me? I slew three of your men at the fort.'

'My fight is with Rome, Symeon. As yours should be.' He stretched out his hand. 'Join us.'

'No.'

Bannus let his hand drop, and turned his attention to the men of the cavalry squadron. 'Surrender these two officers to me and you will live. Now lay down your arms!'

Macro nudged Cato. 'Who does he think he's fooling? He'd kill the auxiliaries the moment he'd taken their weapons.' Macro took a breath, drew his sword and shouted towards Bannus. 'If you want our weapons, come and get them!'

'Shhh!' Cato hissed. 'Who do you think you are – Leonidas?'

Bannus glared at them a moment, then nodded his head in farewell to Symeon and turned his horse to gallop back up the slope towards his men. Macro called the decurion over to them. 'What are our chances?'

'None, if we stay put and try to defend ourselves. We have to charge, cut our way through and run for it. Just give the order, sir. But do it now, before they attack.'

Macro nodded. 'Let's go.'

The decurion turned back to his men. 'Form tight wedge!'

As the horses shuffled into position, Macro and Cato fastened their helmet straps, untied their baggage and tossed it aside. Symeon reached for his bow and carefully unwrapped it, strung it, then loosened the end of his quiver. By the time the three men joined the formation Bannus had reached his men and was barking out a string of orders. He had positioned slingers and archers on either flank, and in the middle, astride the track, stood a band of swordsmen on foot, mostly poorly armed and carrying wicker shields. Some had helmets and leather cuirasses. A short distance behind them, right on the crest of the ridge, stood Bannus and his horsemen, armed with a mix of spears and bows. As soon as he saw the slingers begin to fit stones to their pouches Cato turned to the decurion.

'Now! Give the order now!'

The decurion nodded, drew a breath and called out. 'Squadron! Advance!'

The rough wedge formation rippled forward, the auxiliaries grasping their reins tightly in the hand behind their shields. In the other hand they held their spears, vertically, so as not to risk injury to their comrades before they made contact with the enemy. Above them, on each flank, the slingers were starting to whirl their weapons up above their heads, as the archers drew their bows. Cato found himself angrily willing the decurion to order his men to charge forward, before it was too late. Then he chastened himself. The decurion was a professional, and knew his business.

'Squadron, at the trot, advance!'

His men kicked in their heels and the formation lurched forward, just as the first ragged volley of slingshot and arrows arced into the air. The abrupt change of pace confounded the brigands' careful aim and most of the missiles clattered on to the ground a short distance behind the wedge. A handful of shots found the shields of the rearmost men. One horse whinnied in terror as an arrow plunged into its rump. It reared up, but the rider managed to keep his seat and urged his mount back into the formation.

'Charge!' the decurion cried out from the front of the

wedge, stabbing his sword into the air. His men roared out their battle cry, kicked in their heels and the wedge surged forward. In the second rank, Cato and Macro gripped their reins and hung on grimly as their mounts flowed onward with the rest, manes and tails streaming. Dust and grit filled the air as the charge burst up the slope towards Bannus and his brigands. From the flanks the attackers aimed more arrows and slingshot at the Romans and this time more missiles found their targets. Ahead to his left Cato saw a stone strike the head of one of the auxiliaries. The blow knocked the man's head to one side and his spear, shield and reins dropped from his nerveless fingers, causing the horse to swerve. Then the rider toppled to one side and the riderless horse galloped on regardless. To his right Cato caught a glimpse of Macro, grim-faced, and bending forward as low as his saddle horns would allow. Beyond him was Symeon, superbly poised as he notched an arrow and raised his bow, ready to shoot.

Ahead of them Bannus raced down to his footmen and urged them to hold their ground. But the sight of the oncoming cavalry proved too much for some, and they melted away, rushing out of the path of the horsemen. Then, before Cato realised it had happened, they crashed into the enemy line. Abruptly the air was filled with the scrape and clatter of weapons, grunts and cries from the men, snorts and whinnying from the horses. There was a blur low and to his right and Cato thrust his sword towards a lithe man in a dirty turban. He ducked aside, the tip of the sword grazing his shoulder. With a snarl he slashed back at Cato with a thin curved blade and Cato wrenched his sword back just in time to block the blow with his guard. Then Cato cut down, striking the turban hard with the edge of his sword. The material absorbed the cutting force of the blade but the weight of Cato's blow knocked the man senseless and he collapsed into the dust swirling about the feet and hooves of those locked in the deadly skirmish. Cato glanced round. Macro was slashing at a pair of swordsmen, shouting insults into their faces as he dared them to fight him. Symeon drew an arrow, swivelling in his saddle as he swiftly notched a bead on his target, and released the string. The arrow flew ten paces through the air, punched into a man's chest and burst out of his spine in a bloody welter of torn flesh.

'Forward!' Cato shouted. 'Don't stop! Go forward!'

The decurion glanced back, nodded, and took up the cry. His men urged their mounts on as they fought free of the brigands, and as soon as they were clear they surged up the last stretch of the slope towards the waiting horsemen. Bannus drew his sword and grasped a round shield tightly across his left side as he shouted an order to his followers. With a cry they launched their mounts forward, down towards the auxiliaries. The wedge formation was long broken and now the Romans charged in a ragged mass. The two sides came together in a swirl of gleaming swords, horseflesh, flowing robes and glinting armour. Without a shield Cato felt horribly vulnerable and he hunched down, sword held low as he urged his horse through the mêlée, trying to break through the brigands. He could hear Macro roaring above the din. 'Cut through them! Cut through!'

Something glinted to Cato's right and then he saw a flash of blinding white as a blade rang off the side of his helmet. He kicked his heels in and the horse jumped forward, just in time to avoid the return cut as it hissed through the air close to his neck. Bright spots flickered before his eyes as his vision cleared and he turned back towards his foe. There was a dark face fringed by a mat of black hair and a beard and the man snarled as he raised his sword to cut again. Cato swept his sword up, blocked the blow, slid his weapon down the curve of the man's blade and chopped into his hairy wrist. He felt a solid connection and the man cried out, snatching his arm back, as blood spurted from the deep gash. Cato leaned nearer and thrust his sword into the brigand's stomach, twisted it and yanked it free. He quickly glanced at the other figures looming in the haze of dust, trying to orient himself. Then he saw a patch of open ground between two riderless horses and turned his mount's head towards it, slapping the flat of his sword on the horse's rump. It burst through, out of the billowing dust, and Cato saw that he had broken through Bannus' men.

'On me! Romans, on me!' he cried.

More figures emerged. There was Symeon, bow and reins in one hand, sword in the other as he slashed at a turbaned man trying to catch up with him. More of the auxiliaries, and then Macro, one arm locked tightly about a man's neck as he dragged him from his horse and dumped him on the ground. Suddenly the world was spinning crazily, and then it went out of focus. Cato blinked his eyes but his vision remained blurred, and an awful nausea made him retch.

'Cato!' a voice called out close by and a dark shape loomed up. His vision cleared a little and he saw that it was Macro. 'Are you all right?'

'Hit on the head,' Cato said thickly as he fought to keep his balance. 'Be fine in a moment.'

'We haven't got a moment. Give me your reins.'

Before he could assent, Cato felt them being pulled from his left hand. He grabbed one of the saddle horns as Macro urged his beast on, drawing Cato's horse abruptly after him. As they fled from the brigands Cato's vision cleared a little more, but he was still terribly dizzy and the urge to throw up was stronger than ever. Around him he saw that most of the auxiliaries had broken from the fight and were galloping away from the brigands, along the ridge. Behind them the struggle continued round the handful who were still trapped. But already some of the footmen were pointing excitedly at the fleeing Romans and shouting to their mounted comrades. Bannus quickly tried to bring his men to order, but his prey had half a mile's start on him by the time his horsemen began their pursuit. However, their beasts were light, and the riders wore little or no armour, so they moved swiftly and soon began to catch up with the Romans. But the auxiliaries were well mounted, having the pick of the horses in the province, and soon the greater stamina of the army mounts began to tell as the brigands became strung out, only a handful of their horses able to keep up with the auxiliaries.

'Stay on the track!' Symeon called out. 'Follow it all the way to the fort!'

Cato's dizziness came and went more and more frequently and he feared that he might lose consciousness. Macro kept glancing back with a concerned expression; it was clear that Cato's head injury was more serious than it had first appeared. Then it happened. Cato blacked out and started to topple from the saddle. Macro saw it just in time and reined his horse in, letting Cato's draw level so that he could catch his friend and hold him up. He looked round desperately, but most of the auxiliaries were already ahead of them.

'Help me here!' he bellowed.

The rearmost man glanced back, met the centurion's eyes for an instant and then turned away and urged his horse on. Symeon too heard the call, and instantly wheeled his mount about and galloped back towards Macro.

'What's happened to him?'

'Took a blow to the head. He just fainted. How far are we from Bushir?'

Symeon glanced round at the track. 'Two, maybe three hours' hard ride.'

'Damn. They'll catch up with us long before then.'

Symeon said nothing. He knew it was true. With Cato needing to be supported Macro would steadily lose ground to their pursuers.

'What will you do, Centurion?'

Macro looked back at the distant figures of the horsemen following them. He frowned for a moment and then nodded to himself. 'All right. You take him on. I'll try to delay those bastards for as long as I can.'

Symeon stared hard at him. 'Leave him.'

'What?'

'I said leave him. You won't delay them long enough for the two of us to get away. Either he dies, or all three of us will.'

'I can't,' Macro said helplessly as he glanced down at Cato's pale face slumped against his shoulder. 'He's my friend. More than a friend: he's like a son. I won't leave him to die.'

Symeon glanced at their pursuers and then turned back to Macro with a grim expression. 'All right, you lead him on. Stay on the track. I'll ride with you and hold them off.'

'What with?'

'This.' Symeon raised his bow. 'A few miles further on

the track branches off towards a village. There's a winding gully beside the road. When we reach it, do exactly as I say. Understand?'

Macro stared a moment, tortured by doubt, then nodded.

'Good! Now let's go!'

They rode on, either side of Cato, bracing his limp body so that he stayed in the saddle. But their speed was greatly reduced and every time Macro looked back he saw that the fastest of the enemy riders was drawing closer. Ahead, the rearmost of the auxiliaries was steadily drawing away, a dim shape amid the dust kicked up by his comrades in front of him. Macro cursed them for a moment, before he realised that, because of the dust, the decurion and his men could not be aware of his situation.

Behind them a group of four brigands was swiftly catching up, some distance ahead of the weaker mounts of their comrades. They knew they would soon have the Romans at their mercy and whipped their horses on in frenzied anticipation of catching their prey.

They had ridden down through some hills and now they were emerging on to the plateau: an undulating expanse of stony ground through which a thin strip had been cleared for the track. Symeon steered his horse away from Cato's and called out to Macro, 'Keep going. I'll be a short distance behind.'

Macro nodded, took a tighter grip of Cato's shoulder

and continued riding on. Behind him Symeon flipped open the lid of his quiver, drew an arrow and fixed the nock precisely to his bowstring while his horse continued down the track at an even canter, directed by pressure from Symeon's knees. He let the pursuers get closer, and still closer, until they were no more than thirty paces behind him. Only then did he swivel round in his saddle, revealing his bow as he took careful aim at the nearest brigand. The man looked startled and crouched low to present a smaller target. But Symeon was not aiming at the man. He released the string and the arrow shot straight into the chest of the oncoming horse. With a shrill whinny of pain and terror the horse stumbled, then cartwheeled over, crushing the rider. Symeon had already notched his second arrow and twisted to draw a bead on the next target. The brigands had lost a little ground as they swerved round the downed horse, which was writhing on its back, kicking the air as it tried to dislodge the barbed shaft lodged in its chest. Then they came on again, close enough for the guide to see their grim, determined expressions. One by one he shot their horses down and left them in the dust. Then with a nod of satisfaction he flipped his quiver shut and hung the bow on the saddle horn and caught up with Macro.

A short distance on, they reached the place that Symeon had spoken of where the track divided, a smaller way dipping off into a shallow valley that meandered down towards a broad wadi. The decurion and his men were waiting at the junction, unsure of which branch to take. Their horses were blown and their sides heaved and shrank like bellows. The decurion looked relieved to see them, and then he saw that Cato was unconscious.

'Is he injured?'

'No,' Macro responded coolly. 'He's having a bloody nap. Of course he's injured.'

The decurion realised the problem at once. 'He'll slow us down.'

Symeon pointed down the main branch of the track. 'Keep going that way. It'll take you to the fort. Centurion, you go with them.'

'What?' Macro started. 'Not likely! I'm staying with him.'

'They will still catch you long before you reach the fort if he stays with you.'

'I told you. I'm not leaving him to Bannus.'

'Bannus will not have him. I'm taking him to a safe place.'

Macro laughed. 'A safe place? Out here?'

Symeon pointed down the side track. 'There's a village a mile down there. People I know and trust. They will shelter us. When you reach the fort, come back with a relief column. I'll watch for you.'

'This is madness,' Macro protested. 'Why should I trust these villagers? Why should I trust you?'

Symeon stared at him intently. 'I swear to you, on the

life of my son, that he will be safe with me. Now, hand me the reins.'

For a second Macro was still, weighing up the situation. He did not want to leave Cato, yet to try to continue with him to the fort would almost certainly mean death for both of them.

'Sir!' One of the auxiliaries pointed down the track. 'I can see 'em!'

Macro let the reins drop from his grip and shaded his eyes. Symeon scooped the reins up before the centurion could change his mind. With one hand steadying Cato he led the horse down the side track.

'Wait here a moment,' he called back. 'Until I'm out of sight. Then go. They'll follow you.'

As soon as Symeon and Cato had dropped below the level of the main track the decurion wheeled his horse round. 'Let's go!'

The auxiliaries followed him, kicking their heels in and yelling at their mounts to urge them on. Macro waited a moment, torn between staying with his friend and getting to the fort as swiftly as possible to give the order to send out a column to rescue him. Then he gripped the reins and thrust the heels of his boots into the side of his horse and set off after the auxiliaries. As he took a last glance towards the gully into which the two figures had disappeared, Macro vowed to himself that if any harm came to Cato he would not rest until Symeon paid for it with his life.

* * *

Symeon steered the two horses into the dried river bed and followed its course for a moment until there was a looping bend. Then he reined the animals in and waited. The horses were exhausted, and snorted and breathed heavily as they scuffed the ground with their hooves.

'Shhh!' Symeon said softly, and gently patted the neck of his horse. 'Let's not give ourselves away, eh?'

In the distance he could hear the faint drumming of a number of horses, getting closer. Symeon offered up a silent prayer that his pursuers would be single-minded enough to chase after Macro and the others and ignore the quiet side track. The sound of their approach swiftly grew louder and Symeon felt his body tense as he waited for them to pass. Beside him, Cato suddenly straightened up in his saddle, his eyes flickering open and then staring about as he gazed at his surroundings in confusion.

'What . . . Where am I?'

'Quiet, boy!' Symeon grabbed his forearm tightly. 'I beg you.'

Cato stared at him, then clenched his eyes shut as another wave of dizziness overcame him. With a convulsive heave he threw up, over his mail vest and down the glistening flank of his horse. He spat weakly to clear his mouth, then slumped forward again, his mind wandering as he muttered, 'Because it's my fucking tent . . . that's why.'

Symeon's shoulders sank in relief as the Roman fell

silent again. He strained his ears and listened as the brigand horsemen galloped closer, shouting wildly with the thrill of the chase with the auxiliaries clearly in view. There was no sound to indicate they had divided or even slowed down at the junction of the two tracks, and they galloped on until the sounds faded in the distance. Symeon waited until it was quiet again, listening for any sounds of stragglers, but there was nothing. With a click of his tongue he turned the horses round and headed back up the gully to the track. Then, supporting Cato as carefully as he could, he steered the horses in the direction of the village.

Cato awoke from a bad dream with a start. Instantly, whatever terror it was that had spurred him into consciousness was gone, even before he could remember it. His head hurt horribly, the pain pounding away at his skull. He opened his eyes and at once the pain was worsened by the searing brightness of the sunshine. Cato blinked and squinted and then his nostrils filled with the acidic odour of his vomit and he retched, clasping a hand to his mouth.

When he opened his eyes again a moment later, the stabbing pain of the light had subsided a little and he saw that he was riding into a small settlement. Small, neatly kept houses of stone, plastered with mud, were on either side. Sun shelters of thatched palm leaves leaned against the sides of buildings and here and there the long slender trunks of palm trees stretched up. Then Cato was aware of the people, Semitic and dressed in light-coloured flowing robes. Children wore simple tunics. Women and men were grinding grain in stone basins, and a small group of people seemed to be engaged in some kind of meeting outside the largest of the buildings. They paused and stared at him as Symeon led the horses past. Symeon bowed his head in greeting to each person in turn and then stopped outside a small house at the centre of the village. Sliding down from his horse, he turned and helped Cato down, straining as he took the centurion's weight. As he pulled Cato's arm across his shoulders and struggled towards the doorway an older woman emerged from the house.

She was grey-haired, with strikingly beautiful features and dark eyes. Although she was small and slender, she carried herself with graceful authority and stared a moment at the two men approaching the threshold of her house.

'Symeon ben Jonas,' she said sternly, in Greek. 'I have not seen you for over a year and you turn up on my doorstep with a drunk Roman soldier. What's the meaning of this?'

'He's not drunk. He's injured and he needs your help. He's also heavy . . . I could use a hand.'

The woman tutted and stepped forward to support Cato on his free side. As she took up some of the weight Cato stirred, rolled his head round and smiled as he introduced himself. 'Centurion Quintus Licinius Cato, at your service.'

'You are welcome to my home, Centurion.'

'And whose home would that be?'

'This is an old friend of mine,' Symeon explained. 'Miriam of Nazareth.'

Cato's mind was still reeling, and he struggled to make sense of his situation. 'Nazareth. This can't be Nazareth.'

'It isn't. This is the village of Heshaba.'

'Heshaba. That's nice. Who lives here?'

'It's a commune,' said Miriam. 'We're followers of Jehoshua.'

Jehoshua . . . Cato struggled for a moment before he recalled that this was the man who had been executed by Rome. He glanced round at the faces of the villagers as a cold trickle of fear traced its way down his spine.

CHAPTER SEVEN

Macro deliberately slowed his pace as the brigands reached the junction, to make sure that they came after him. As soon as he saw them gallop past the side track he stabbed his heels in and his horse burst forward again, pounding over the ground. He glanced back and saw that the brigands were keeping up with him, some two hundred paces behind. If his mount fell, or tired too quickly, they would be on him in a moment. One Roman against thirty or more. Not good odds, he thought grimly. If only he could do that trick of Symeon's with his bow. He had never seen archery like that before. He had heard of it. Only one nation in the east had archers who were reputed to be able to perform such feats. Parthia. In which case . . . he felt his stomach turn to ice. If Symeon was a Parthian spy then he had left Cato in the hands of one of Rome's longest-standing and bitterest enemies. But surely not. Symeon did not look like a Parthian. He certainly did not sound like one, and after all, he had saved their lives only the day before. So who exactly was Symeon of Bethsaida?

If he escaped his pursuers, Macro told himself that he would find out. But for the present only one thing mattered: staying out of the hands of Bannus and his men. He had little doubt that the revenge Bannus would seek for the death of his sicarian gang members would be agonising and drawn out. He glanced back and saw that they were still some way behind him, and did not seem to be closing the distance.

'Go on, my girl!' he called out to the horse. 'Run like we're on the last lap in the Circus Maximus.'

The beast seemed to sense his will to live and stretched out its sleek neck as the hooves pounded across the crude track. Ahead, Macro could see the auxiliaries and was sure that he was gaining on them. That gave him a slender shred of comfort. At least it would improve the odds, if the brigands did catch up with them. Better odds, same result, Macro thought. But at least, with a few men fighting at his side, he should be able to take more of the bastards down with him before his turn came.

He raced on across the desert, and as the distance took its toll on the horse's reserves of energy it began to slow down, and soon was barely able to do more than a canter. A quick glance forward and another over his shoulder revealed that all the mounts were suffering fatigue, and with the sun rising higher into the sky, the heat soon sapped their fast dwindling strength. They had been ridden far longer and harder than they were used to and were blown. One by one, the auxiliaries' horses stopped running and slowed to a weary walk, and Macro had closed up with the stragglers by the time his mount too had had enough.

The decurion dropped back to ride at his side. 'Where's Centurion Cato, and the guide?'

'Couldn't keep up with us,' Macro explained. 'They're hiding back there. We'll go back for them with men from the fort.'

The decurion shrugged. 'If they're still there.'

The auxiliary officer left Macro to continue along the track and rode back to round up his stragglers Half a mile behind the brigands came on in a haze of dust. Twice they forced their horses into a canter and the Romans followed suit, driving their mounts on harshly, until the brigands gave up and continued at a steady walking pace, at which point the Romans reined in as well, and both parties continued along the track in the grilling heat of the midday sun.

Then, ahead, where the heat shimmered off the ground like water, Macro saw a low wavering silhouette. He squinted and it took a moment before he realised what he was seeing, and his heart soared. Turning in his saddle he called out to the auxiliaries.

'It's the fort, lads! Straight ahead.'

The men instantly lifted themselves and stared along the track, some shielding their eyes to cut the glare and see Bushir more clearly, no more than two miles away. As they drew nearer and the heat haze dissipated Macro could make out more detail. The fort was constructed from stone, with four massive towers, one at each corner. In between stretched long curtain walls with a smaller tower either side of the main gate on the wall facing the track. A short distance from the fort was a reservoir, built into a dip in the ground where two shallow gullies converged. Macro could just make out the tiny dark shapes of a group of men watching their approach from one of the towers.

Behind them, a faint cry rose up from the brigands as they too caught sight of the fort, and forced their mounts to make one last effort to catch the Romans before they reached safety.

The decurion responded immediately. 'Squadron . . . forward!'

He kicked his heels in and his tired mount lurched into a canter, and his men followed suit, pounding along the track as their pursuers started to close the distance, desperate to make the kill. Macro did his best to keep up with the auxiliaries, but he was an infantryman and not used to getting the best out of his mount, and so he gradually slipped behind. As the auxiliaries approached the fort the gate opened and fully armed men piled out and quick-marched towards their comrades, ready to provide a defensive screen against the pursuers. Some officer in the fort had acted very quickly and Macro made a mental note to thank the man, if he got away from the brigands pursuing him.

The first of the auxiliaries passed through the gap in the infantry line and then reined in quickly and dismounted from their exhausted horses. Macro glanced back and saw that Bannus' men were much closer now, foam flicking back from the muzzles of their driven mounts.

'Come on, you bastard!' Macro growled at the two ears rising stiffly at the end of his horse's neck. 'Run! Or we're both food for the jackals.'

The horse sensed his urgency and struggled on, as fast as its trembling limbs could carry it, towards the line of infantry striding towards them. Then it seemed to miss a step, and staggered on for an instant before its front legs began to buckle. Macro released the reins and grabbed the saddle horns with all his might to stop himself being thrown forward. The beast slowed and then collapsed, thudding belly first on to the ground. At once Macro heaved himself off, and sprinted towards the oncoming infantry. Behind him he heard the exultant cry of the brigands as they scented his blood. He glanced back and saw them only a short distance behind, blades drawn, the leading man leaning out to one side, sword rising up ready to strike. Just beyond the line of infantrymen the decurion suddenly wheeled his horse round, drew his weapon and spurred his mount back down the track, knocking aside one of the infantry as he charged towards Macro. At the last moment, he cried out, 'Get down!'

Macro's ears were filled with the pounding rhythm of hooves as he threw himself to one side, off the track, and rolled heavily, the impact driving the breath from his lungs. A large shadow danced across the ground beside him and he heard the swish of a blade cutting through the air. Then the legs of horses were all about him and Macro curled into a ball, shielding his head in his burly arms as he was sprayed with gravel. Blades clashed with a shrill ring and the decurion shouted, 'No you don't, you bastard!' Each time Macro tried to glance up, he was blinded by grit and dust, and only heard the fight going on around him. Then something spattered down on him, hot and wet, and a voice grunted in triumph.

'Get 'em!' a voice shouted. 'Stick it to 'em, Second Illyrian!'

Then there were booted feet all round Macro, more shadows, and someone grabbed him under the arms and hauled him up.

'You all right, mate?' A man's face loomed in front of him. Then the soldier saw Macro's mail vest and the medallions on his harness. 'Sorry, sir. You all right?'

Macro was dazed. 'Yes, fine.'

Then he noticed the doubtful look on the man's face and glanced down and saw that a great streak of bood splashed across his shoulders and down his left arm. His fingers fumbled over the blood, but found no injury. 'Not mine.'

The soldier puffed out his cheeks in relief, nodded

and turned away, hurrying after his comrades as they drove the brigands back. Macro closed his eyes and wiped the grit from his face on the back of a hairy forearm, then looked around. The men from the fort were chasing after the surviving brigands, thrusting at them and their mounts with spears. On the ground close to Macro lay the bodies of three of the brigands, and the decurion. The latter lay sprawled on his back, eyes staring up at the sun, mouth hanging open. A sword blade had opened his throat to the spine and the ground about him was drenched with blood.

'Poor bastard . . .' Macro mumbled, before he realised that the decurion had sacrificed himself to save the man he had been charged with escorting safely to Bushir. 'Poor brave bastard,' Macro corrected himself.

'Who are you?' a voice demanded.

Macro turned and saw an officer approaching him. At the sight of the plumed feathers in the man's helmet crest, Macro instinctively stiffened to attention before what he assumed was a superior.

'Centurion Macro!' he snapped, and saluted.

The officer saluted back, then frowned. 'Mind explaining what's going on, sir?'

'Sir?' Then it dawned on Macro that the officer was a centurion like himself, and only a freshly minted one at that. He regarded the man anew. 'Who are you?'

'Centurion Gaius Larius Postumus, adjutant at the fort, sir.'

'Where's Scrofa?'

'Prefect Scrofa? He's in the fort, sir. Sent me out to cover your force.'

'Leads from the front, eh?' Macro couldn't help sneering for a moment. 'Never mind. I've been sent to take command of the Second Illyrian. These men are my escort. We were ambushed several miles back.'

Macro glanced round and saw that the fight was over. Most of the brigands had pulled back and were staring silently at the fort from a small rise some distance away. The officers of the Illyrian troops had recalled their men and were forming them up beside the survivors of the cavalry squadron. Two of their men lifted the decurion off the ground and gently placed his body across the saddle of his horse before leading it towards the gate. Macro shook his head. It had been a close thing. But even though he had escaped this time he didn't suppose that Bannus would abandon his design on Macro's life. And Cato's. At that thought Macro stared back along the track.

'Sir?' Postumus tilted his head and looked questioningly at Macro. 'Anything the matter?'

'Yes. My friend's out there. We need to go and find him as soon as possible. I want you to give orders for the cavalry contingent to mount up.'

'With respect, sir, that is a decision for Prefect Scrofa to make.'

Macro rounded on the man. 'I told you. I'm in command now.'

'Not until the appointment has been properly authenticated, sir.'

'Authenticated?' Macro shook his head. 'We can deal with that later. Right now, what matters is Centurion Cato.'

'I'm sorry, sir. I take my orders from Prefect Scrofa. If you want to help your friend, you'll have to speak to the commanding officer.'

Macro fumed for a moment, balling his hands into fists as he glared at the young centurion. Then, with a sharp intake of breath, he nodded. 'Very well. There's no time to waste. Take me to Scrofa.'

They made their way back into the fort with the last of the troops who had been sent out and Macro was able to take a closer look at the men as he made his way through them. Their kit was only adequately maintained, but they looked tough enough. Certainly, they had moved to engage the enemy horsemen willingly. That was always something of a test of any unit. The men in the legions could be counted on to hold their ground against any kind of attack. It was different with auxiliaries since they were more lightly armoured and not so well trained. But these lads had faced the enemy horsemen without any trouble. Macro nodded approvingly. The men of his new command – the Second Illyrian – seemed to have some potential and Macro was determined to build on that. Then he stepped through the gateway and saw the poorly maintained barrack blocks stretching out in rows on either side of the gate. There would be plenty of work to do before the cohort came up to Macro's standards. Opposite the barracks were the grain stores, infirmary, stables, headquarters building, officers' quarters and the cohort commander's house.

The Second Illyrian was a mixed cohort. Of over nine hundred men who served in the unit, a hundred and forty were mounted. There were cohorts like this on every frontier, where the mixture of cavalry and infantry allowed for greatest flexibility for those officers charged with policing the local tribes and keeping watch for any attempt by barbarians to cross the border. A strong force of cavalry allowed the cohort commander to scout a wide area, chase down any barbarian raiding parties, and when necessary, launch quick punitive raids into enemy territory.

Such cohorts were usually commanded by centurions who had transferred from the legions, a process regarded as a promotion for those who were judged ready to hold independent commands. Despite his earlier reservations, Macro realised that Scrofa had to have shown some promise to be selected for this command. Macro did not fool himself that he too must be a cut above the rest. His own command of the cohort was to be a temporary affair; little more than a cover until the present crisis had been resolved.

Once the last man had passed through the gates,

Centurion Postumus ordered them closed and the locking bar replaced in its sockets. Macro indicated the survivors of the cavalry squadron, leading their exhausted mounts away from the gateway. 'You had better organise some stabling and quarters for the men.'

'Yes, sir. After I've shown you to the prefect.'

'Where is he?'

'In his quarters, sir.'

'Right, I can find him. You see to these men, all right?'

'Very well, sir,' Postumus responded reluctantly. 'I'll join you as soon as they have been taken care of.'

Macro entered the prefect's house, which was guarded by two well-turned-out men in full equipment. Even though they stood under a sun shelter, they were sweating profusely in the heat. They snapped to attention at Macro's approach and as he passed between them he noticed, with wry amusement, a bead of sweat suspended on the tip of one man's nose. Inside he paused momentarily to adjust to the shaded environment. An orderly was sweeping the hall and Macro turned to him.

'You there!'

'Yes, sir?' The man stiffened his back at once and saluted.

'Show me to Prefect Scrofa's office.'

'Certainly, sir,' the orderly responded with a deferential bow of his head, and led Macro through the hall to a staircase at the rear. They climbed to the next floor where the rooms were spacious and designed to allow any available breeze to be channelled through them by well-placed windows.

'This way, sir.' The orderly indicated an open door at the end of the landing. Macro strode past him and entered the commander's office, and paused in surprise at the luxurious appointments. The walls were richly painted with mythic scenes of a heroic nature. The furniture was well crafted and finished with neat decorative flourishes, and there was a couch to one side covered in comfortable cushions. A glass bowl stood on a small side table, filled with dates and figs. Prefect Scrofa, wearing a light tunic, sat behind a large wooden desk. To one side of him stood a huge red-haired slave, steadily directing air at his master with a fan. Scrofa was a wiry man in his early thirties with pale skin and dark hair that had receded on either side of his central fringe. On his left hand he wore the ring signifying that he came from the equestrian social class. He looked up irritably as Macro marched into the room, covered in dust and stained with the decurion's blood.

'Who the hell are you?'

'Centurion Macro. Sent from Rome to assume command of the Second Illyrian. You are hereby relieved, Prefect Scrofa. Please send for your senior officers at once, so they can be told of my appointment.'

Scrofa's mouth sagged open. The slave continued fanning without any change in his expression.

'What did you say?'

'You're relieved.' Macro leaned back and popped his head round the door frame. The clerk was heading back to the top of the stairs. 'Hey!'

The clerk turned round and stared at Macro for a moment, then glanced past him towards Scrofa with a questioning expression. 'Sir?

'Centurion Scrofa is no longer in command.' Macro stepped between them and continued, 'I want to see all the centurions and decurions in here straight away.'

'Even the duty officers, sir?'

Macro paused. With Bannus and his men still in the area, that would not be wise. 'No. Not them. I'll meet them later. Now go!'

When he turned back into the office Scrofa had recovered some composure and was sitting back in his chair. He looked at Macro with an angry frown. 'Explain yourself. What in Hades is going on here?'

Macro, conscious of his pressing need to collect a strong force of men and go in search of Cato and Symeon, strode across the room and stood in front of the table. 'It's simple. Your appointment was temporary. I have been given orders by the imperial staff to take command of the Second Illyrian. There's no time for any change-over ceremony, Scrofa. I need the mounted contingent ready for action immediately.'

Scrofa shook his head. 'Impossible! Cassius Longinus assured me that he would send to Rome to have my appointment made permanent.'

'Look,' Macro said in a gentler tone, desperate to take command as soon as possible, 'I don't know anything about that. All I know is that I was sent to Bushir with orders to take command.'

The sound of footsteps came from the landing and a moment later Centurion Postumus strode into the room. Scrofa raised an arm and pointed at Macro. 'This man says he has been sent from Rome to take command of the cohort.'

Postumus shrugged. 'He was with the auxiliary cavalry being pursued to the fort, sir.'

'There is another officer, and a guide, still out there, hiding,' Macro said urgently. 'I must take some men out to find them.'

'I'll deal with that in a moment,' said Scrofa. 'Once we've sorted the situation out.'

'There's nothing to sort out!' Macro shouted, his temper finally snapping. 'I'm in command! You have been replaced. Now stand aside. I'm meeting the cohort's officers in here. Take your slave and return to your quarters.'

'I'll do no such thing! How dare you come in here and treat me like this? Who sent you from Rome?'

'I told you. I'm acting on the orders of the imperial office.'

Centurion Postumus coughed loudly and stepped up to the table to confront Macro. 'Excuse me, sir. If you're acting on orders, might we see them?'

'What?' Macro stared at him.

'Your orders, sir. The confirmation of your appointment.'

'Bloody hell! All right then. I'll get them. They're in my saddlebag . . .'

Abruptly, Macro's lips froze as his mind flashed back to the morning ride up towards the plateau, the sudden appearance of Bannus and his brigands, and then the dumping of all the baggage as the cavalry squadron desperately prepared to fight its way through to the fort.

Macro's lips moved again. 'Oh, shit.'

CHAPTER EIGHT

Once again Cato faced the druid, but this time his foe was far taller than Cato, dwarfing him so that he felt like a child. The druid's eyes were jet black and his teeth were needle sharp, as if they had been filed. In his hand he held the scythe, and as Cato's eyes fixed on the glinting edge the druid raised it high. For an instant the blade glittered as it caught the moon's silvery rays. Then it slashed down, slicing towards Cato's throat.

He woke with a cry, and jerked up on to his elbows. His eyes were wide open, darting from side to side as he took in his surroundings. A small, darkened room, unfurnished apart from the bedroll he was lying on. He made to move, but there was a sudden pounding in his skull as if a heavy mallet was rhythmically beating the side of his head. Nausea welled up from the pit of his stomach and he quickly turned on one side and retched. The door opened, and light flowed into the small room.

'Lie down, Roman.' A woman spoke softly in Greek. She crouched beside the bedroll and gently pressed Cato back so that his head was resting on the bolster again. 'You're still suffering from the effects of that blow to your head. It will pass, but you must lie still and rest.'

As his eyes grew used to the light Cato glanced up at the woman. Her face and voice were familiar, and memories flashed into his mind of the ambush, the flight from the brigands and his arrival in a village where he had glimpsed this woman between blackouts.

'Where am I?'

'Safe.' She smiled. 'For the moment.'

'This place. What was it called?'

'Heshaba. You are in my house, Roman.'

Cato remembered another detail. 'Symeon . . . where is he?'

'He's taken the horses further into the wadi to hide them. He'll be back soon.'

She shuffled round behind the bolster and Cato heard the swill of water. A moment later she placed a damp cloth over his head and squeezed gently so that a dribble of water trickled down over his temples.

'That feels good. Smells good too. What is that? Lemon?'

'I squeezed some into the water. It'll refresh you and ease the sick feeling.'

Cato made his body relax, working the tension out of his muscles until his limbs felt loose, and the pounding in his head subsided. Then he rolled his head to the side to better see the woman.

'I can't remember your name.'

'Miriam.'

'Yes.' He nodded faintly. 'You and Symeon know each other.'

'He's a friend. Not as good a friend as he used to be.'

'Miriam, why are you helping me? I'm a Roman. I thought everyone in Judaea hated us.'

She smiled. 'Most people do. But this community is different. We try not to let our lives be ruled by hate. Now lie still.'

She reached a hand up to his head and he felt her fingers stroke lightly through his hair, until they grazed the point on his skull that seemed to be the centre of the pain. He winced, gritting his teeth.

'It's a bit swollen there. But you seem coherent enough. I don't think the injury is too serious. You should be back on your feet in a few days, Roman.'

Cato waited until the pain had passed before he unclenched his eyelids and looked at her again. Despite her obvious age, Miriam had striking features. Not conventionally beautiful, but she looked wise and had an air of calm authority. He reached his hand up, took hers and gave it a light squeeze.

'Thank you, Miriam. I owe you my life.'

'You owe me nothing. All are welcome here, Roman.'

'My name is Cato.'

'Cato . . . Well then, Cato, if you want to repay me, please be quiet and rest.'

'Miriam,' a voice called from somewhere else in the house.

She turned to the door and spoke in Aramaic. 'In here.'

A moment later a boy stood on the threshold. He was perhaps thirteen or fourteen, with a shock of dark hair. He wore a tunic of coarse material and was barefoot. He stared at Cato for a moment before he turned his gaze back towards Miriam. 'Is he a soldier? One of the Romans?'

'Yes.'

'Must he stay here?'

'Yes, Yusef. He is injured. He needs our help.'

'But he is an enemy. An enemy of our people.'

'We have no enemies. Remember? That is not our way.'

The boy did not look convinced and Miriam sighed wearily as she stood up and took his hand. 'I know this is not easy for you, Yusef, but we must care for him, until he is well enough to leave. Now be a good boy, and finish the threshing. There's bread to be made for this evening, and I haven't even done the grinding yet.'

'Yes, Miriam.' He nodded, cast a last glance at Cato and turned away. As the bare feet pattered off Cato smiled.

'I take it that's one of the Judaeans who still hates Rome.'

'He has his reasons,' Miriam replied, watching the boy from the doorway. 'His father was crucified by the Romans.'

Cato's smile faded. He felt awkward. 'I'm sorry. It must be terrible for him.'

'He takes it too hard.' Miriam shook her head. 'He never knew his father. He wasn't born until after his death. Still, he feels a sense of loss, or lack, and he has filled the void with anger. For a long time his life centred round hatred of Rome and Romans. Until his mother abandoned him and he came to live with me.' She turned towards Cato and he saw the look of sadness in her eyes. 'I was all that he had left in the world. And he was all that I had left.' Cato did not understand and she smiled at his confused expression. 'Yusef is my grand-son.'

'Oh, I see.' Then Cato felt the sudden chill of realisation as his eyes met Miriam's.

'His father was my son. My son was executed by Rome.' Miriam nodded sadly, then slowly turned away. She left the room and gently closed the door behind her.

For what seemed like a long time Cato lay still in the dark room. When he tried to move the pain in his head returned with a vengeance and pounded away so that he felt sick. With what Miriam had told him he knew he must get away from this house, these people, before they turned on him. Despite Miriam's claims about the forbearance of the villagers, Cato knew human nature well enough to know that old wounds never heal. As long as he stayed in Miriam's house, he was in mortal danger. But he could not move without being racked with agony. As he lay still, straining his ears to pick up the sounds of the people in the house and the village beyond, he cursed Symeon for leaving him here. Leaving him alone. If he was just concealing the horses, then why in Hades had he not returned long ago? Cato had no idea how long he had been lying there in the dark. He knew that it was light outside, but was it the day of the ambush? Or the next day? How long had he been unconscious? He should have asked Miriam whilst she was there. As his anxiety swelled he rolled his head to the side and glanced round the room.

A short distance away, bundled against the wall, lay his armour, his harness, his boots and his sword belt. He gritted his teeth and shifted himself over, reaching out with his fingers. They groped for the sword belt, grasped it; tugged until the pommel came free of the scale armour. His fingers closed round the hilt, and as quietly as he could he drew the sword. It rasped faintly in the scabbard and he winced. Then the blade was free and he lifted the weapon across his body and wedged it between the bedroll and the wall, out of sight, but to hand if he needed it. The effort had made his arm muscles tremble and Cato had just enough energy to reach over and push the empty scabbard back under his mail vest before he collapsed back on to the bolster, fighting the waves of pain that pounded against the inside of his skull. He shut his eyes, breathing deeply, and slowly the pain subsided, his body relaxed and he fell asleep.

* * *

When he woke again the door was open and from the wan glow of the light shining through the opening he could tell that it must be late in the afternoon. He heard voices outside the room. Miriam and Symeon. They spoke in Greek, in low familiar tones, and Cato strained his ears to catch their words.

'Why did you not come back to us?' Miriam was asking. 'We needed you. You're a good man.'

'But not good enough, it seemed. Not for you at least.'

'Symeon, I'm sorry. I loved you – I still do, but . . . I couldn't, and still can't, love you as you want to be loved. I must be strong for these people. They look to me for guidance. They look to me for love. If I took you as my man I would betray them. I will not do it.'

'Fine!' Symeon snorted. 'Then you will die alone, if that's what you want.'

'Perhaps . . . If that is my fate.'

'But you don't have to. You could have me.'

'No,' she said bitterly. 'You think of nobody but yourself. You renounced the rest of us, because we refused to follow your path. You and Bannus were so convinced that your way was the only way. That's your trouble. That's why you could never be a part of what we are trying to create here.'

'What do you think you can achieve? You are taking on an empire, Miriam. Armed with what – faith? I know who I'd place my money on.'

'Now you sound just like Bannus.'

Symeon took a sharp breath, then continued in a cold rage. 'You dare to compare me to him . . .'

Before Miriam could reply there was a shout from the street and footsteps pattered into the house.

'Miriam!' Yusef was excited. 'Horsemen are coming.'

'Whose?' Symeon asked.

'I – I don't know. But they're riding fast. They'll be here any minute.'

'Damn! Miriam, we must hide.'

'I'm not hiding. Not any more.'

'Not you! Me and the Roman.'

'Oh! All right. Quickly, come this way.' She hurried into the room and pointed to Cato. 'Get him up.'

Symeon squeezed past her, and thrusting his arms under Cato's shoulders he hauled him up and supported him on his feet. Miriam rolled the end of the mattress back to reveal a small wooden hatch. She lifted it by a metal ring and slid it to one side.

'In there! Both of you, quickly.'

Symeon dragged Cato over to the opening and dropped him down. Cato fell four or five feet beneath the floor and landed heavily. He had just enough strength to roll to one side as Symeon lowered his feet and followed him in. A moment later Symeon cursed as Cato's kit dropped on his head. Then Miriam replaced the hatch and rolled the bedding back. A thin slit over by the front of the house let in a shaft of light and the two men crawled cautiously towards it. The space was narrow and as Cato's eyes adjusted to the gloom he saw that it stretched from the front to the rear of the house. It was empty, apart from a small, plain casket towards the back. They heard the sound of horses approaching and shuffled the last few feet to the slit. It was no wider than a finger and sparse tufts of grass grew in front of it, and since it was just below the level of the floorboards Cato had to tilt his head to one side to see out of the slit.

He was staring up the street towards the track that led to the junction. A party of horsemen was riding into the village, and Cato's heart sank as he recognised Bannus at the head of his brigands. Bannus slewed his horse to a halt just in front of Miriam's house, kicking up a small cloud of dust that momentarily obscured the view. They heard a crunch as his booted feet landed on the hard earth.

'What do you want?' Miriam stepped out into the street. 'You're not welcome here.'

Bannus laughed. 'I know. That can't be helped. I have wounded men who need treatment.'

'You can't leave them here. The Romans patrol the land round Heshaba. If they find them we'll be punished.'

'Don't worry, Miriam. I just want their wounds cleaned and bound and we'll be on our way. They'll never know we were here.'

'No. You have to leave. Now!'

As Cato and Symeon watched through the slit, they saw the brigand chief draw his sword and raise it towards her. Miriam did not flinch and just stared back defiantly. For a moment there was a silent confrontation, then Bannus laughed and waved the sword at her.

'This is what makes things possible, Miriam. Not prayers and teaching.'

'Really?' She cocked her head to one side. 'And what have you achieved? Did you win the little fight that caused these men to be injured? No? I didn't think so.'

Symeon whispered, 'Careful, Miriam.'

'The situation is changing, Miriam.' Bannus spoke in a soft, menacing tone. 'We have friends who are about to help us. Soon I will have an army at my back. Then we'll see precisely what can be achieved.' Bannus sheathed his sword, turned to his men and called out, 'Bring the wounded into the house.'

Miriam stood her ground. 'You will not bring them into my house.'

Bannus turned back to her. 'Miriam, you are a healer. My men need your skills. You will treat them, or I will start providing you with patients from amongst your own people, starting with . . . young Yusef over there. Boy! Come here. Now!'

The floorboard above Cato squeaked as Yusef stepped outside and hesitantly approached the brigand leader. Bannus took him by the shoulders and looked down at him with a smile. 'Such a fine boy. His father would be proud of him. Prouder still, if he joined with me and fought to liberate our lands from Rome.'

'He will not join you,' said Miriam. 'That is not his path.'

'Not today. One day, when he is old enough to choose for himself, maybe he will join me and make Jehoshua's vision become a reality. One day. But for now, Miriam, you must choose. Treat my men, or I will cut one of the boy's fingers off.'

Miriam glared at him, and then her shoulders sagged and she nodded. 'Bring them to my door. I will treat them there.'

'No, inside. They would welcome the shade.' Without waiting for her to answer Bannus thrust Yusef to one side and shouted orders. As Cato watched, the brigands dismounted and started helping several men into the house. Above him the floorboards creaked under the weight, and dislodged dust and grit fell on top of Cato and Symeon. A door squeaked on its hinges and with a start Cato realised that someone was entering the room where he had lain on the bedroll.

'Oh, shit,' he whispered.

Symeon looked at him in alarm and raised a finger to his lips.

'My sword,' Cato said as softly as he could. 'It's behind the bedroll.'

'What?'

'I took it from the scabbard and hid it there.'

'Why?'

'I wasn't sure about Miriam, and the boy. She told me the Romans killed his father.'

Symeon frowned at him. 'You're in no danger from Miriam and her people.'

'Shit.' Cato stared at him, then his eyes turned to the hatch beneath the mattress and he looked at it in horror. Any moment now one of the brigands might spot the sword, and know that a Roman had been there. Or worse, they would fling back the mattress to reveal the hatch. There was nothing he could do about it, so he and Symeon sat as still as they could and waited. He felt his heart pounding, and the splitting headache and sickness returned so he had to concentrate his will on fighting off the pain and the urge to groan or cry out.

'Put him on the bedroll,' Miriam said. 'Get me some water.'

This was it, Cato thought. Any moment now, the injured man would feel the hardness of the sword handle through the bedding.

Footsteps thudded overhead, and they heard Bannus speak. 'Don't talk in Greek, Miriam. Some of my men are simple peasants. They only know the dialect of the valley.'

They continued speaking a form of Aramaic and Cato glanced at Symeon. 'What?'

Symeon raised his hand to quiet the Roman and cocked an ear towards the ceiling as he strained to hear what was being said. There were many voices talking now, and feet moving overhead as the men's wounds were treated. Time seemed to slow to a crawl, so that Cato was aware of every instant that passed as his ears filled with the sounds from the room above his head. He willed Miriam to treat the men as swiftly as she could, to get them out of her house, and out of the village.

As the light outside began to grow dim there was a shout from the street and immediately a commotion in Miriam's house as the men piled outside and Bannus bellowed a series of orders. Symeon nudged Cato. 'They've spotted a column of Roman cavalry heading for the village.'

'Macro. It has to be.'

Symeon shrugged. 'I sincerely hope so.'

Bannus' men began to carry the wounded out towards the horses. Then, as they helped them into the saddles, there was a cry from the man on the bedroll. His wounds had made him weak and he paused for breath before he gasped a few more words.

'He's found your sword!' Symeon hissed. 'When they come back for him they'll see it.'

Cato thought quickly, and then winced as he knew what had to be done. He crept over to his equipment, fumbled for his dagger handle and drew the blade. The hatch was old and weathered, and brittle, and Cato summoned up all his energy, grasped the dagger with both hands and punched it up through the hatch, tearing through the wool padding of the bedroll and into the back of the injured man. He heard a faint explosive gasp and his blade was tugged as the man twisted for a few moments before slumping back. Cato sensed no further movement through the handle. He twisted it slightly and wrenched the blade free. Then he crouched down and waited. Shortly afterwards someone padded lightly into the room and paused an instant before moving over to the man on the bedroll.

'Saul!' Bannus shouted from outside. 'Get the last man. In the back room.'

'Yes, sir.'

Footsteps thudded overhead and then they heard Miriam say, 'It's too late. He's dead. You'd better take him with you.'

'Bannus! He's dead,' the man shouted. 'Should I bring his body?'

'Leave it. We have to go. Now!'

Out in the street the brigands wheeled their horses about and began to ride past the house on their way out of the village. More dust obscured the view, and Cato and Symeon could feel the vibrations of the pounding hooves through the earth around them. The sounds quickly receded. There was quiet for a moment, and then Miriam grunted with effort as she shifted the body off the mattress. The hatch was slid to one side and she peered into the hole.

'You can come out now. The Romans will be here any moment.'

CHAPTER NINE

Macro was fuming. Centurion Postumus had him over a barrel. Without written authorisation from the imperial palace he had no power to oust the temporary commander of the Second Illyrian. So when the officers began to turn up, as Macro had instructed, he had to sit in embarrassed silence while Scrofa sent them away again. Not for the first time that day, he cursed Bannus and his brigands with the most heinously dire and painful torments imaginable. Because of the ambush, his letter of appointment was lying out there somewhere in the desert. Worse still, it might have fallen into the hands of Bannus' men as they rifled through the baggage that Macro, Cato and the cavalry squadron had been obliged to abandon. Macro cringed with shame at the thought, even though there had been no alternative in the circumstances. They had barely escaped with their lives on unladen mounts as it was. Indeed, Cato was not yet out of danger. Thought of his friend spurred Macro on and he stood up and approached Prefect Scrofa's desk.

'Sir?' he said as respectfully as he could. 'I accept that I cannot produce my orders, and that means you are entitled to hold on to your command. But you must send men out to search for Centurion Cato. Before Bannus finds him.'

'Must I?' Scrofa smiled coolly. 'As you so rightly pointed out, I am still in command. I don't have to do a thing that you say.'

Macro clasped his hands behind his back and forced himself to nod gently as he fought back his anger and frustration. Anger would only make this man obdurate. 'I know that, sir. But I'm thinking about how this will look back in Rome when word gets out that the commander of the Second Illyrian sat and did nothing while a comrade was hunted down and put to death by a bunch of brigands. It would tarnish the cohort's image for ever, and perhaps the reputation of the commander as well.'

Prefect Scrofa stared up at him in silence for a moment and then nodded. 'You're right . . . That would be most unfair to my men.' Then Scrofa's eyes narrowed a fraction as he sat back and stared blankly at the opposite wall. 'It's bloody unfair. I served my time as a tribune on the Rhine. I've worked my way up through the junior civil appointments, and spent good time and money cultivating the right contacts at the palace.' He looked at Macro suddenly, his eyes flashing with bitterness. 'Do you know how much I paid to have sturgeon's eggs served at a dinner I gave for Narcissus? Well do you?'

Macro shrugged.

'A bloody fortune, that's how much. And that bastard Narcissus pushes them aside and complains that they're too salty.' Scrofa was silent for a moment, wrapped up in the past, before he continued in a resigned tone. 'So I decide to try my hand at winning a little glory on the field of battle. That should add lustre to the name of Scrofa, I thought. You know, my great grandfather fought with Mark Antony at Actium? Martial blood runs in my family's veins. So my father pulled a few strings to get me appointed as a centurion of auxiliaries. I thought I'd carve out a reputation on the battlefields of Britannia. That was my request. And what happens? They send me to Syria. Garrison duty. Can you imagine? A complete waste of my potential. A whole year stuck in a wretched hole on the border with Palmyra. Then I get this appointment. Another bloody frontier fort. But the only enemy I have to deal with is Bannus and his little gang of thieves. Where's the glory in that?' Scrofa sniffed. 'Police work. Might as well have got a posting to the urban cohorts in Rome. At least I'd be out of this damned oven!' He gestured irritably towards the slave holding the fan. 'Faster, damn you . . .' He slumped back in his chair.

Macro's shoulders heaved with relief that the tirade was over, and he tried to steer the cohort commander back on to the subject of sending out a force to find Cato and Symeon. 'You're right. No one should be out in this heat. Especially not an injured Roman officer.'

Scrofa looked at Macro sharply and frowned for an instant. Then he flapped his hand towards the door. 'Very well, Macro! We'll take all four cavalry squadrons. We'll find your friend and bring him back here as quickly as possible.'

'Yes, sir.' Macro turned to the door, but he had not reached it before Scrofa spoke again.

'But we're not taking any risks with my men, you understand?'

Macro paused and looked back over his shoulder and stifled the urge to sneer. Risk was what soldiers got paid for. He had the measure of Scrofa now. The man was simply playing at soldiers. The last thing he wanted was any more injured men cluttering up his fort on the farthest-flung fringe of the Empire.

'I understand, sir.'

'Good. You can organise the men. I've some records that need seeing to. I'll join you when the column's ready to leave.'

'Very well, sir.'

For a man who prided himself on the military blood that coursed through his veins, Prefect Scrofa was a very poor horseman, Macro reflected, as he watched the cohort commander being hoisted up into the saddle by his Celtic slave. Scrofa flung a leg across the animal's back and wriggled into position, then adjusted his helmet, which had slid forward since it had not been tied securely enough. He was little better than the raw recruits Macro had broken in back in the legions. If the man had been a common soldier Macro would have been all over him, bellowing into his face and applying his vine cane in retribution for such slovenliness. As it was, thanks to the imperial policy of directly appointing minor aristocrats to the office of centurion, alongside those who had won the rank on merit, Scrofa was in command of the Second Illyrian. Macro shook his head gently. What was Cassius Longinus thinking of when he picked Scrofa for this post? Surely he had better men backing his cause? Or was he so short of men of quality amongst his plotters that he had been forced to call on the services of Scrofa?

Prefect Scrofa took up his reins and flicked them casually as he tapped his heels into the flanks of his horse. 'Let's be off.'

Behind him the decurions commanding the four mounted squadrons chosen for the task relayed the order in more formal tones and the column clopped out of the fort and on to the track that stretched across the stone-strewn desert to the west. Scrofa led the way at a steady walk and once again Macro found himself simmering with frustration and rage as the column ambled along. A light wind blew in from the deep desert, and the dust kicked up from the track swirled round the men in a choking, blinding cloud. The officers at the head of the column were spared the worst of the dust and occasionally

Macro could see the distant shapes of horsemen along the track ahead. Bannus was keeping them under observation, Macro realised. Even though the brigand scouts kept far beyond the reach of the Roman column, Macro had no doubt that the lightly armoured men on their small, swift horses would easily evade any sudden rush by Scrofa and his men. Not that Scrofa showed any signs of being interested in chasing the enemy down.

At length, as the sun began to sink towards the western horizon, Macro could no longer tolerate the pace and urged his horse forward until he was alongside the cohort commander.

'Sir, at this rate we'll not be able to return to the fort before nightfall. Let me take half the men and go on ahead.'

'Divide my command?' Scrofa frowned and glanced at Macro with a disappointed expression. 'Really, I'm surprised at you. I'd have thought you would be conversant with the basic principles of military campaigning.'

'This isn't a campaign, sir. It's a simple rescue mission. I can ride ahead, scout the lie of the land and search for signs of Centurion Cato and the guide. If I see any sizeable enemy forces I'll fall back and join you.'

Scrofa considered this for a moment and then nodded reluctantly. 'Very well. You're right. It would not be prudent to push on into what could easily be an ambush. Take two of the squadrons up ahead. Make sure you keep me informed of developments, understand?'

Macro nodded.

'And take Centurion Postumus with you.'

'Postumus? Why?'

'I trust him. He's reliable. He'll make sure the men are looked after.'

Macro stared at the cohort commander. Clearly Scrofa did not trust him with his auxiliaries and Macro seethed as he forced himself to nod his acquiescence. He turned and looked round for Postumus and beckoned to him. The younger officer, his helmet still bedecked with a flowing crest, trotted up and Macro quickly briefed him. Shortly afterwards Scrofa stood aside as the two leading squadrons cantered ahead down the track. When they had drawn some distance away Scrofa waved the rest of the column forward and they continued at the same steady pace as before.

Macro did not look back as he rode along the track. Ahead of him he could see Bannus' scouts wheel their mounts about and gallop away, keeping a safe margin between themselves and the Romans. Macro drove his men on, mile after mile, until they reached the junction where he had parted with Symeon and Cato. He plunged off the main route and followed the track until it descended into a long narrow wadi. There, a short distance ahead, lay the village that Symeon had mentioned, and Macro felt his heart quicken at the sight of scores of horses and men filling the open space in the heart of the settlement.

Macro reined his horse in and thrust his arm up to halt the two squadrons of mounted auxiliaries behind him.

'Decurions! On me!'

The squadron commanders trotted up as Macro pointed towards the village. 'That's where we're headed. The guide said he'd shelter there with Centurion Cato. Those brigand bastards are already on the scene. So we go in fast and drive 'em out before we start searching for our men. You — Quintatus, wasn't it?'

The decurion nodded.

'Right. I'll wager they'll run for it the moment they see us. Take your squadron right through the village and keep chasing them until they're well clear of the place. Then fall back and rejoin us. Who knows? By then, the prefect might even have caught up with us.'

The decurions grinned, and Macro kicked his heels in, urging his mount on towards the village. 'Let's go!'

As soon as the two squadrons launched themselves down the slope the brigands burst into desperate activity. Men spilled out of the houses where they had been sheltering from the sun and scrambled on to their horses. Others limped out, supported by their comrades, and were helped into the saddle, to hang on as best they could as Bannus and his men fled from the village.

A few figures stood still, watching the men leave the village, some turning to stare at the approaching Romans. Macro guessed they must be the inhabitants, bewildered and afraid of the violent pursuit their small settlement had been abruptly caught up in. And somewhere, in among the humble dwellings, Cato and Symeon were hopefully still alive and in hiding. The thought spurred Macro on and he crouched over his horse and urged it forward with harsh cries of encouragement as the hooves pounded over the hard ground that sloped down towards the nearest houses. To one side he saw a woman scream and rush to scoop up a small child before she hurried into her house and slammed the door. Then Macro was in amongst the buildings, and there was only a narrow open street before him. He could no longer see the brigands, but the anxious cries of the last of their stragglers carried across the dun-coloured roofs.

The street turned a corner and directly ahead lay the heart of the village. Macro snatched out his sword, his senses tingling now that he was almost on his enemies. Just as he emerged from the end of the street, a horse suddenly bolted across in front of him. There was an instant as Macro's eyes met the terrified ink-dark stare of the other rider, then the centurion's horse slammed into the flank of the other beast. Macro was hurled forward, out of the saddle, straight into the brigand, and both tumbled into the open space in the centre of the village. Macro slammed into the ground, driving the breath from his body, but he rolled over into a crouch and, gasping for air, looked round at his enemy. The other man was still lying on the ground, dazed by the impact and shaking his head. He turned his head and saw Macro, before his gaze dropped to the centurion's sword on the ground in front of him. Macro saw it too, and lurched forward. Too late. The brigand snatched up the blade and quickly clambered into a low crouch, eyes fixed on Macro as he held the sword out and grinned.

'Easy there, sunshine.' Macro backed away. The rest of the auxiliaries were only a short distance behind – the sound of their hooves echoed up the street. The brigand glanced over his shoulder and then turned back to Macro. His grin had vanished and now he scrambled forward with a cold glint in his eyes. Macro felt his back thud up against a wall and turned his head and saw that he would be trapped in a corner if he went to his left. Tensing his legs, he sprang to the right and ran for the edge of the building, just as the brigand thrust the sword. It struck the wall in an explosion of loose plaster, then with a cry of frustration the man ran after Macro. Macro sprinted past a door, which swung open an instant later, straight into the face of the brigand. Cato emerged into the street blinking and jumped as the door rebounded towards him. Then he turned and saw Macro, and smiled.

'I wondered when—' Cato's smile froze as his friend slithered to a stop, reversed direction with a menacing grimace and dived back past the door. The brigand was flat on his back, winded. Macro stamped down on the wrist of his sword arm and the fingers instinctively flinched, releasing the blade.

'I'll have that back, thank you.' Macro dipped down to retrieve his sword, then delivered a savage kick to the side of the man's head, knocking him senseless. There was a confused din of shouts and whinnying and Macro turned to where the street fed into the centre of the village. The horses that had collided were still thrashing around and the cavalry had been forced to stop, piling up into a dense mass just beyond the flailing hooves. Then Macro's horse rolled over, clambered up and lurched nervously to one side. The auxiliaries squeezed past and Macro waved them on.

'Don't stop! Get after the bastards! Go! Go!'

They stumbled by in a rush of horseflesh, kicking boots, and shields as Macro turned back to Cato. Behind them Symeon emerged from the house and watched the riders go past with a relieved grin. He nodded a greeting at Macro.

'Nice timing, Cato.' Macro nodded to the unconscious brigand, then focused on the pallor of his friend's face, which was streaked with blood. 'How's the head?'

'Sore. I feel a bit sick. But I'll live. You got here just in time. They'd have surely found us if you'd been a moment longer.'

'I nearly didn't get here at all. Had a hard time persuading that bloody prefect at the fort to send these auxiliary boys out.'

'Why persuade him?' Cato frowned. 'You've replaced him. You're the new prefect.'

Macro laughed bitterly. 'Not until I present him with the right document. You know how the Roman army loves its procedures. Unfortunately, my letter of appointment was lost with the rest of the baggage.'

Cato shook his head. 'Damn. That's messed things up for us.'

A thought struck Macro. 'What about that warrant from Narcissus?'

Cato instinctively clutched a hand to his chest, and felt the slim leather case that hung from a strap round his neck. 'It's still safe.'

'Good. Then we can use that. Show it Scrofa and take command of the cohort.'

'No.'

'What do you mean, no?'

'Think about it. If we use the warrant now, then our cover is blown. It won't take long for word to get back to Longinus that two of Narcissus' spies are in the region. He'd immediately be on his guard, and you can bet that the first thing he'd do is see to it that we were disposed of.' Cato paused for a moment, then shook his head. 'We daren't use the Emperor's authority unless we really need to.'

Macro laughed bitterly. 'Shit! So what the hell do we do now?'

'We have to send a message back to the procurator in Caesarea, asking for confirmation of your appointment. He'll have it on record.'

'And until then Scrofa will continue to be the prefect of the Second Illyrian.'

'So it seems.'

'That's great, just great.' Macro turned away, trying to contain his frustration, and saw Symeon sitting on a bench in the sun shelter, talking intently to one of the local women. He leaned closer to Cato and spoke softly. 'Who's that?'

'Miriam. She's the one who hid us from Bannus and his men.'

'Really?' Macro looked at her more closely. 'Must be a brave old stick.'

'Brave?' Cato recalled the manner in which she had confronted Bannus. 'That she is. But there's more to her than meets the eye.'

'Oh?'

'She seems to be the leader of this settlement. Or at least one of the leaders.' Cato chewed his lip for a moment. 'She also seemed to know Bannus quite well.'

'Not to mention our guide there.'

Cato looked at Symeon, and saw that he was holding one of Miriam's hands as he spoke earnestly to her. 'Yes. We need to find out more about her. More about what precisely is going on around here.'

'Think we should take her to the fort for questioning?'

Cato shook his head. 'I'm not sure that would be helpful. She could be of some use to us, if we can win her trust. Though, in the circumstances, that might be difficult.'

'What circumstances?'

'It seems that her son was crucified.'

'Ah, that is a little unfortunate,' Macro conceded. 'Still, if we can work on her, maybe we can win her round.'

'It's not a question of winning her round. I'd think she'd see through that in an instant. We're going to have to play this one very carefully, Macro, if we want her on our side. Anyway, quiet! Symeon is coming.'

Symeon had risen from the bench and was making his way to the two Romans. He tipped his head on one side with an apologetic expression. 'Miriam has a favour to ask, Centurion Cato.'

'Oh, yes?'

'She would like us to remove that brigand you skewered. She needs to patch her mattress and wash the bloodstains out before she prepares his body for burial.'

By the time Cato and Macro had heaved the dead brigand out of the house and found a cool spot in the shade for the body, the prefect and the other two squadrons were approaching the settlement. Scrofa rode into the village and halted his column outside Miriam's house, before dismounting in the same ungainly manner in which he had been hoisted into the saddle. He looked at Cato and Symeon.

'The missing centurion and his guide, I presume?'

'Centurion Quintus Licinius Cato, sir.' Cato bowed his head.

'I'm glad that our little expedition managed to find you before Bannus and his scum did.'

Cato smiled faintly. 'They were here not long ago, sir. Macro's men drove them out.'

Scrofa stared back frostily. 'They are not Centurion Macro's men. They are my men until he can provide proper proof that he has been sent to replace me. *My* men, do you understand?'

'Yes, sir.'

'Good.' Scrofa nodded. Then his eyes swept round the village, before fixing on Miriam who was watching them from the bench under her sun shelter. 'You say that the enemy was in the village when Centurion Macro arrived?'

'That's right, sir.'

'So what were they doing here, exactly?'

'Having their wounded seen to,' Cato replied uneasily.

'So the villagers were helping them?'

'No. They forced the villagers to help. They threatened them.'

'We'll see about that.' Scrofa gestured towards Miriam. 'Bring that one over here.'

Miriam had overheard the exchange. She rose to her feet and strode towards the two Roman officers, staring defiantly at the prefect. 'What do you want of me, Roman?'

Scrofa was momentarily taken aback by her forceful manner, but quickly recovered his composure and cleared his throat. 'It seems you gave shelter to the brigands.'

'Yes, but as your centurion said, I had no choice.'

'There is always a choice,' Scrofa replied haughtily. 'Whatever the consequences. You could have resisted them. Indeed, it was your duty to resist them.'

'Resist them with what?' Miriam swept her arm out, indicating the surrounding houses. 'We have no weapons – they are not permitted here. My people believe only in peace. We will not take sides in your conflict with Bannus.'

Scrofa gave a derisive snort. 'Won't take sides! How dare you, woman? Bannus is a common criminal. A bandit. He is outside the law. If you are not against him, then, by default, you are for him.'

Now Miriam laughed and shook her head. 'No. We are not for him. Just as we are not for Rome.'

'Then what are you for?' Scrofa sneered.

'One faith, for all the people, under one true God.'

As Cato watched the confrontation he saw the contempt in Scrofa's expression, and could understand it. Like most Romans Scrofa believed in many gods, and accepted that the peoples of the world were entitled to worship their own. The Judaean insistence that there was only one god, their god, and that all others were merely worthless idols, seemed like simple arrogance to Scrofa. Besides, if the god of these people reigned supreme, then how was it that they were a province of Rome, and not the other way round?

A deep groan broke the tension and they all turned towards the brigand who was stirring on the ground beside the entrance to Miriam's house. His eyes flickered open and he started at the sight of the Roman officers and auxiliaries standing about him. He sat up quickly and shuffled back against the wall as Macro took a pace towards him and gestured at him with his sword. 'What do you want done with this one?'

Scrofa regarded the man for a moment, then folded his arms. 'Crucify him. Here in the centre of the village.'

'What?' Cato could not believe his ears. 'He's a prisoner. He must be interrogated – he might have useful knowledge.'

'Crucify him,' Scrofa repeated. 'And then burn this woman's house.'

'No!' Cato stepped up to the prefect. 'She saved our lives. And risked her own to do it. You can't destroy her home.'

Scrofa's brow furrowed and he took a sharp intake of breath before he continued in a low, furious voice. 'The woman admits to helping the enemy, and she denies the authority of the Emperor. That I will not tolerate. These people must be taught a lesson. Either they are with us, or they are against us.' Scrofa turned back towards Miriam. 'She just might consider that while she watches her house burn.'

Miriam returned his stare with a thin-lipped look of contempt.

Cato's heart was pounding. He was horrified by the rank injustice of the prefect's decision. It was pointless. Worse than pointless – it was wilfully wrong. If this was how Rome rewarded those who risked all to help her soldiers, then the people of Judaea would never be at peace with the Empire. But there was more to it than that, Cato thought. Such punishment was morally wrong and he could not tolerate it. He shook his head and stood stiffly in front of the prefect while he forced himself to speak as calmly as possible.

'You can't burn her house, sir.'

'Can't I?' Scrofa looked amused. 'We'll soon see about that.'

'You can't do it!' Cato blurted out. 'I won't let you.'

The amused expression faded from Scrofa's eyes. 'How dare you challenge my authority, Centurion? I could have you broken to the ranks for that. I could have you condemned. In fact—'

Before he could continue, Macro moved in, took Cato's arm and drew his friend away, towards the sun shelter. 'The lad's had a bad knock on the head, sir. He doesn't know what he's saying. Come on, Cato, sit down in the shade. You need rest.'

'Rest?' Cato glared at him. 'No. I have to stop this folly.'

Macro shook his head. He thrust Cato away from the

prefect, whispering, 'Shut your mouth, you fool. Before I have to shut it for you.'

'What?' Cato looked at him in shock as he was propelled towards the shaded bench.

'Just sit still and say nothing.' Cato shook his head, but Macro clamped his hand on his arm and hissed, 'Sit down!'

Cato's head was reeling with confusion. Scrofa was about to perpetrate a monstrous injustice, one that Cato knew he must resist. And yet Macro was siding with Scrofa. He was clearly determined to prevent Cato's making any further protest, and Cato slumped helplessly as he glanced back towards Miriam. She was grim-faced, but there was no hiding the tears that gleamed in the corner of her eyes. After a moment's hesitation, Symeon put his arm round her and led her back inside the house.

'Miriam, let's save what we can. While there's still time.'

She nodded as they disappeared into the shadows.

Dusk was closing in as the column rode out of the village. Riding between Macro and Symeon, Cato took a last glance back over his shoulder. Flames roared and crackled as the fire consumed Miriam's house. She stood some distance away, embracing her grandson. A handful of the villagers stood still and gazed at the inferno. To one side, silhouetted by the flames, the brigand hung from the makeshift frame that the auxiliaries had erected after ripping the timbers out of Miriam's house. A hastily scribbled message on a wooden plaque had been nailed beneath the brigand's feet, warning the villagers not to render the man any comfort, and not to remove his body once he had died. Otherwise, his corpse would be replaced by one of their own.

As he turned away, Cato felt sick with despair and self-loathing. Rome had taken away her son, and now it had destroyed her home. If this was how they treated those who bore so little malice towards them, then there would never be peace in this land.

CHAPTER TEN

'What the hell were you doing back there?' Cato snapped. 'Why didn't you back me up?'

They were sitting in the room allocated to Macro. Cato had been given a room nearby. Scrofa had explained that until the issue of Macro's appointment had been sorted out there was no question of providing them with quarters appropriate to their alleged status. So the cohort's quartermaster and his assistant had been required to temporarily give up their offices and the clerks had laboured into the evening to clear the rooms and introduce the bare minimum of furniture needed by the newly arrived centurions. The column had returned to the fort some time after dusk, in the silvery light of a crescent moon, and it was not until the fourth hour of the night that the preparation of their hastily arranged quarters was complete. Symeon had been allocated a bunk in the cavalry barracks and had immediately gone off to sleep, leaving the two officers to sit in an atmosphere of muted tension until at last their rooms were ready.

'What was I doing?' Macro looked astonished. 'I was behaving like a bloody officer, that's what I was doing. Not buggering about like some indignant bloody child.'

'Excuse me?'

'Cato, when a senior officer gives an order, you obey it without hesitation.'

'Macro, I know that. But he's not the senior officer. You are.'

'Not until I can prove it. Until then Scrofa is in command, and what he says goes.'

'No matter how wrong-headed the order?'

'That's right.'

Cato shook his head. 'That is ridiculous, Macro. The woman did nothing wrong. Nothing to deserve having her house burned down.'

'I agree with you,' Macro responded with forced calmness. 'It's a bloody great shame. An injustice. Call it what you will.'

Cato was exasperated. 'So why didn't you say anything at the time?'

'You know the score. When an order is given there is no discussion, whatever I might think.'

'But that's madness.'

'No – it's discipline. It's what makes the army work. There's no room for debate. No place for weighing up the pros and cons. The order is given and you obey.' Macro paused and continued in a harsh tone. 'What you don't do – in any circumstances – is question the order of a senior officer, and never in front of the bloody men. Do I make myself clear?'

Cato, surprised at Macro's hostility, nodded.

Macro went on. 'You start down that road, my friend, and discipline crumbles. If men start thinking about orders and not acting on them, then the army falls apart and we become easy pickings for our enemies. There's no shortage of them. Then who's going to protect the Empire, eh? So go ahead and weigh that up against some woman's house going up in smoke. Next time, you think about that before you go and question the orders of a superior.'

Cato was silent as he considered Macro's argument, then he looked up and shrugged. 'I suppose you may be right.'

'Of course I'm bloody right.' Macro sighed with exasperation. 'Look here, Cato. The army's your life now. It's a hard life sometimes I grant you, but I love it. And I will not let anybody fuck it up, however well meaning they be, even if they are my best friend. Make sure you understand that.'

Cato pursed his lips. 'All right. But it was still wrong to punish that woman.'

Macro groaned and cuffed his young friend on the shoulder. 'That's enough. We've got bigger problems to think about. We're not here for the good of our health, Cato.'

'Hardly.'

Macro smiled for a moment, and then looked thoughtful. 'You know, there might be more to this than meets the eye.'

'What do you mean?'

'Burning that house. Crucifying that brigand.' Macro raised his eyebrows. 'It's just that, now I think about it, there's little more he could have done to deliberately provoke the people of that village, and at the same time lose the chance to get some good intelligence from the prisoner.'

'I see.' Cato nodded. 'In that light it certainly seems to back up Narcissus' suspicions about what's going on here.'

'And if he's right about Scrofa, and that adjutant of his, Postumus, then we're going to have to tread carefully, and watch our backs all the time. I don't fancy going the way of Scrofa's predecessor.'

The next morning, at first light, the survivors of the cavalry escort set off on the return journey to Jerusalem. Scrofa had appointed one of his junior officers to temporary command of the squadron and ordered Symeon to guide them safely to Jerusalem by a different route from the one they had taken to reach the fort. The veteran carried a message from Macro for delivery to the procurator at Caesarea requesting urgent confirmation of his appointment as commander of the Second Illyrian. Given the distances involved it would take at least several days for a reply to reach them. Until then, the two centurions would be regarded as supernumeraries – free of duties and free to come and go around the fort. Macro and Cato, mindful of the true purpose behind their presence there, joined the other officers for the prefect's morning briefing immediately after breakfast in the mess.

The centurions and the junior officers of the cohort crowded the benches in the hall of the headquarters building, and as they talked idly while waiting for Scrofa and his adjutant to appear Cato scrutinised them surreptitiously. The officers seemed somehow distracted and edgy and spoke in subdued tones. Occasionally one of them would glance in the direction of the new arrivals, but no one came over to introduce himself. It was as if they were suspicious, Cato decided. But suspicious of what? They could not know that Macro and Cato were working for Narcissus. The appointment of Scrofa had been temporary so they would be expecting a permanent commander to replace him. There should be nothing untoward about the arrival of Macro and Cato and yet Cato sensed that something was amiss.

His speculations were interrupted as Centurion Postumus marched through the door and barked out, 'Commanding officer present!'

With a scraping of benches the assembled officers rose to their feet and stood stiffly at attention while Scrofa entered the hall and made his way to the desk at the end and sat down.

'Be seated, gentlemen.'

The officers relaxed and sat back down on their benches. When all was still, Scrofa cleared his throat and began the briefing.

'First, let me formally introduce you to Centurions Macro and Cato.' He gestured to them and the new arrivals briefly rose to their feet in acknowledgement as Scrofa continued. 'Now, I'm aware that there have been a few rumours doing the rounds about the reason for their presence at Bushir. For the record, Centurions Macro and Cato claim to have been sent out from Rome to replace myself and Centurion Postumus. Unfortunately, in the rush to escape his pursuers yesterday, Centurion Macro was obliged to drop his baggage, which contained his orders from the palace.'

There was a ripple of light laughter and amused expressions amongst the officers and Macro flushed with embarrassment and anger. Scrofa smiled as he continued.

'So, until his appointment is confirmed we welcome them as honoured guests to Fort Bushir. You gentlemen might want to take the chance to make yourself known to the commander designate in the coming days, if you wish to thrive under his command, as you have under mine. Centurion Macro will need to learn how we do things here, if he is to enjoy your confidence in the months ahead . . .'

The prefect glanced through the notes on the waxed slate in front of him and went on. 'We've had word that two caravans bound for the Decapolis are due to pass through our area in the next few days. The first belongs to Silas of Antioch. We'll be sending out our usual welcoming committee and should have no trouble getting their agreement to escort the caravan as far as Gerasa. The second belongs to one of the Arab cartels that's just started up in Aelana. Since they're new to the game, Centurion Postumus will lead a strong force out to greet them and explain the procedure. Then escort them safely up the trail as far as Philadelphia before returning to the fort . . . On to more onerous tasks. There's been a band raiding the borders of the Decapolis from somewhere out in the desert. Decurion Proximus will take a patrol to Azrakh, and offer their headman a bounty for tracking down and eliminating these raiders.' Scrofa paused and glanced round the room before he spotted Proximus. 'Make sure you agree a good deal. No point in cutting too deeply into our profit margins.'

The decurion grinned and nodded.

'Good man. That's the last of our commerce excursions. Any questions?'

One of the older centurions raised his arm and Scrofa regarded the man with a weary expression as he responded. 'Yes, Parmenion?'

'What about that business yesterday, sir? Are we going after Bannus and his gang? It's time we settled the score with them.'

Scrofa glanced at his adjutant and Postumus leaned closer. The two men conferred quietly for a moment before Scrofa turned back to the questioner. 'You are right, of course. We cannot tolerate such attacks on Roman forces. The Judaeans need to be taught a lesson. To that end I'm sending you out with a squadron of horse and an infantry century to make a circuit of the local settlements. If you find any evidence that their people have been offering any assistance to the brigands then you are to burn a few houses to the ground. If there's no evidence then I want you to flog a few of the locals to give them a taste of what's to come if they ever feel tempted to aid men like Bannus. Make sure they get the message.'

'Yes, sir,' Parmenion replied. 'But wouldn't it make more sense to try to track down the brigands themselves? Rather than mount another punitive expedition?'

'There's no point in exposing our men to the danger of an armed clash with these brigands,' Scrofa responded uneasily. His adjutant stepped forward and interceded.

'The brigands can only survive by drawing on support from the villagers. If we can persuade the locals to stop supporting Bannus, then his men will starve and disband and the problem is over.' Postumus smiled. 'Satisfied?'

Centurion Parmenion gave the adjutant a withering stare for a moment before he tilted his head and glanced past Postumus towards the prefect. 'Begging your pardon, sir, but we've been going in hard on the locals for months now. And we're no closer to finishing Bannus off. In fact, I think our actions have only strengthened the man.

Every time we punish the villagers, we drive some of them into joining Bannus. Every time he ambushes one of our patrols and kills a few of our men, the villagers celebrate.' Parmenion paused, and shook his head. 'I'm sorry, sir. But I just don't believe your policy is having the right effect. We should be trying to win these people over, not punishing them for the actions carried out by brigands.'

Centurion Postumus stabbed his finger at Parmenion. 'Thank you, Centurion Parmenion. I am aware of your long experience in this province, but that will be all for now. You have your orders. All you have to do is carry them out. Trust me, when the locals understand that Rome will brook absolutely no hint of defiance, then we will have order in this area. Besides, according to my sources, the number of Bannus' men has been exaggerated. They're poorly armed, and equipped with little more than the rags they stand up in. They're nothing more than a handful of wretched robbers.'

'Sir, I'm not sure how far we can rely on those sources of yours. They've not been much help so far, and anyway, men who are paid to inform tend to say what they think their paymaster wants to hear.'

'I trust them,' Scrofa said firmly. 'The threat from Bannus is minimal.'

Parmenion shrugged and nodded towards Macro. 'They seemed to give the centurion's escort a pretty good hiding.'

Postumus smiled. 'Let's just say, the centurion's escort must have had an inflated sense of any danger they might have been in.'

Parmenion turned to Macro. 'What do you think, sir? You were ambushed by them. How much danger do you think Bannus poses to us?'

Macro pursed his lips a moment before he replied. 'It was a well-worked trap. He caught us on a narrow track, and must have had three, maybe four hundred men with him. Yes, they were poorly armed, and only a small proportion had mounts. But if that's how many men he can call on for a simple ambush, then I should imagine his entire force is something to be reckoned with. Or will be, if he can ever train and equip them adequately. As it was, we only managed to break through because they weren't expecting us to charge them.'

As his friend spoke, Cato felt a chill run down his spine. What was it that Bannus had said as he stood outside Miriam's house? Something about friends who were about to help them. And that soon he would have an army behind him. But was it mere bluster? The vain boasts of a desperate man condemned to spending the rest of his days as an outlaw and fugitive? Yet Prefect Scrofa seemed content to let the brigand remain at large while he attacked what he perceived to be his supporters. And with Scrofa's current approach to the problem, if they weren't already supporters of Bannus they soon would be.

Centurion Postumus again responded on behalf of his commander. He nodded his head, as if in agreement with Macro, and then smiled faintly. 'Of course, in your haste to escape it is possible that you might have overestimated the danger.'

Macro stared hard at the adjutant. 'Are you calling me a liar?'

'Of course not, sir. I'm just saying that in the heat of, er, shall we say battle, it must be hard to know exactly how many men you were facing.'

'I see.' Macro's expression darkened. 'If you don't believe me, then ask Centurion Cato here how many men he thought we were facing.'

'What would be the point, sir? He was in the same predicament as yourself. Why should his judgement be any less clouded? Besides, he had a head injury. He could easily have been mistaken about the size of the force you encountered. I assure you, we have perfectly good intelligence that the threat from Bannus is minimal.'

Cato leaned forward. 'Then why go to the trouble of all these punitive raids on local villages?'

'Because we need to dissuade them from any further support for Bannus. If we go easy on them it can only make us look weak. Bannus will be able to claim that, given enough men, he can guarantee to deliver the people of Judaea from Roman rule.'

'Surely, if you treat the Judaeans harshly, you'll only drive them into his arms, as Centurion Parmenion pointed out. Perhaps we should be trying to win these people over.'

'No point,' Scrofa interrupted. 'It's clear that they hate our guts. We'll never win them over as long as they cling to their faith. In which case we can only hold them in line through fear.'

Macro leaned back and crossed his arms. 'Let them hate, as long as they fear, eh?'

The prefect shrugged. 'The dictum seems to work well enough.'

Cato felt his heart sink. Scrofa's was a short-sighted and dangerous approach, particularly in the present situation where Bannus offered its victims a chance to fight back. Every village that the Romans made an example of would become a recruiting ground for Bannus and swell his ranks with men who had a fanatical hatred of Rome and all those they perceived as serving Roman interests.

'Anyway,' the prefect concluded, 'I've made my decision. The orders stand and will be carried out. The briefing is over. Centurion Postumus will have written orders prepared for the relevant officers. Good day, gentlemen.'

The benches scraped over the flagstones as the officers rose and stood to attention. Scrofa collected up his slates and left the room. Once he was gone Postumus called out, 'At ease!' and the officers relaxed again.

Cato nudged his friend. 'I think we should have a word with Centurion Parmenion.'

Macro nodded, then glanced round at the other officers, slowly dispersing to carry out the day's duties. 'Yes, but not in front of the rest. Perhaps we should ask him to show us round the fort. No harm in that. Only natural that new arrivals should want to look over the place.'

CHAPTER ELEVEN

Fort Bushir, like nearly all Roman forts, followed a roughly standard design. The commander's house, the headquarters, hospital and stores all occupied a central position and lined the two main thoroughfares that ran through the fort at right angles to each other. On either side stretched the long, low roofs of the barrack blocks where the cohort's men were accommodated eight to a room in the buildings allocated to each century or cavalry squadron. The stables took up one corner of the fort and the smell of the animals permeated the hot air that hung over everything like a stifling blanket. As Centurion Parmenion gave them a detailed tour Cato noted examples of a slackness that would not be tolerated in most other auxiliary cohorts, let alone the huge fortresses of the legions he was more familiar with. There were broken doors and shutters, food slops left in the street and several items of poorly maintained equipment, most notably the dried-out wood on the bolt-throwers mounted in each of the towers. They were quite useless;

sure to split the moment the arms were placed under any strain if the weapons should ever be made ready to shoot. There was also a discernible listlessness amongst the rankers of the cohort and Cato wondered if it might be more than just the natural reaction to years spent in such a desolate posting.

As the three centurions climbed the ladder to the watchtower built over the main gates Macro decided it was time to speak directly.

'Have you always served with the auxiliaries, Centurion Parmenion?'

'No chance. I'm a proper soldier. Spent seventeen years with the Third Gallica up near Damascus, the last as an optio. Then I took a transfer into the Second Illyrian with promotion to centurion. Been here ever since. Should be demobbed within the next year or two.'

'I see.'

'Why do you ask?'

'With someone of your background here, I was just wondering how the place came to be in such a state.'

Parmenion did not respond until all three of them were standing on the small platform of the watchtower, in the shade of the palm thatch roof. Around them the desert unravelled to the horizon, shimmering in the glare of the sun. But Parmenion's gaze was fixed on Macro. 'There's nothing wrong with the cohort, Centurion Macro. Not the rankers at least,' he said guardedly.

'And the officers?'

Parmenion stared back at Macro, and glanced at Cato. 'Why are you asking me that? What are you after?'

'Nothing,' Macro replied easily. 'It's just that I should be assuming command of the cohort soon, and I'll want to make a few changes . . . a few improvements. I was just curious about how the cohort came to be in the state that it is. In my experience, a unit is only as good as its officers.'

Parmenion seemed satisfied by the explanation and he tilted his head slightly. 'Most of 'em are sound enough. Or were, until Centurion Postumus turned up. That was under the previous commander.'

'What difference did Postumus make?' asked Cato.

'None, at first. The previous adjutant had died after a long illness. Postumus was sent down to us from Damascus as a replacement. Like Scrofa after him. He did his duties conscientiously enough. Then he started volunteering for command of the patrols into the desert. You can imagine that made him very popular amongst those of us who had no great desire to spend days riding around in the sun and the dust. Anyway, that was the situation until the previous commander received a visit from the representative of one of the caravan cartels. Seems that he accused Postumus of operating some kind of protection scam on his caravans. The prefect wanted some hard evidence and went on the next patrol with Postumus. And didn't come back.'

Cato raised his eyebrows. 'That might be seen as quite convenient for Centurion Postumus, from a cynical point of view.'

'Quite.' Parmenion smiled. 'Anyway, Scrofa turned up and nothing has been done about the accusations since then.'

There was a pause before Cato asked, 'Are you saying that the prefect has been cut in on the deal? What about the other officers?'

Parmenion shook his head. 'I don't want to talk about it.'

'About what?' Cato persisted.

Macro interrupted impatiently. 'Something is going on here. The officers appear divided and the men don't seem to care about their duties. Any fool can see it.'

'If any fool can see it then you don't need me to inform on my fellow officers.'

'No one is asking you to be an informer,' Cato replied gently. 'But a veteran like you must know what is going on. Why didn't you complain to the prefect, or someone higher up the chain of command?'

'I did. I had a word with Scrofa. Told him standards were slipping amongst the men. He seemed a little bemused by my complaint. Anyway, I haven't been assigned any desert patrols since then. He's kept me well away from the caravan routes. And now he wants me to go in heavy on the local villages.' Parmenion sniffed derisively. 'What good's it going to do sticking it to a bunch of farmers scraping a living in this wasteland? We should be going after Bannus.'

'Yes,' Macro replied thoughtfully. 'We should.'

Parmenion turned to face him. 'Is that what you plan to do, sir? When word comes of your appointment?'

'Seems the logical way to proceed.'

Parmenion nodded with satisfaction. 'Be good to get the officers back to proper soldiering. Do the men good as well.'

'True. But there's nothing I can do about it right now.' Macro scratched his chin and turned to stare out into the desert. 'I think it's time I had a look at some of the territory the Second Illyrian is supposed to be covering.'

Cato looked at him with narrowed eyes. 'What's on your mind?'

'I think I'll join one of those patrols Scrofa is sending out.' Macro smiled. 'You might want to join Parmenion here, see what the situation is in the local villages.'

Cato shrugged. 'Fair enough. There's nothing else we can do until we hear back from the procurator.'

Prefect Scrofa stared at Macro and Cato. 'Why would you want to do that? You've only just arrived here and you want to leave the fort already?'

Cato answered for them. 'As you yourself pointed out, sir, we are surplus to requirements, as things stand. So we might as well get some experience of the area. See how the men perform. That sort of thing.'

Scrofa exchanged a look with his adjutant before he responded. 'I'm not so sure about that. I mean, we have our own way of doing things here. Perhaps it's best if you spend some time observing how we run the cohort before you throw yourselves into action.'

Macro smiled back. 'No point in wasting any time. There's an expression we had in the Second Augusta, back on the Rhine. Best thing a soldier can do is get his arse in the grass.'

Scrofa frowned. 'I don't understand.'

'Field experience,' Macro explained. 'There's no substitute for it. Though, I admit, the saying doesn't seem to have much currency out here. What with grass being in such short supply.'

'Get your bust in the dust?' Cato suggested.

Macro looked at him irritably. 'Helpful, as always, Centurion Cato.'

'Yes, sir. Sorry, sir.'

'Anyway, that's why I think I should accompany Centurion Postumus on his patrol, while Cato heads out with Parmenion. We'll just be along for the ride, and won't get in the way.'

'Hm.' Scrofa folded his hands together and rested his chin on the fingertips. 'I'm still not sure it's a good idea.'

'Why not?' Postumus interrupted. 'I'd be honoured if Centurion Macro joined me. And I'm sure that once he sees how we operate he will be only too happy to continue our methods. That'll ensure a smooth transition, if confirmation of his appointment turns up.'

'When it turns up,' Macro corrected him with an icy glint in his eye.

'Yes, sir. Of course. When it turns up. Meanwhile, I think you'll quickly come to appreciate how well we deal with the people passing through our territory.'

'I'm sure.'

'Just as Centurion Cato will come to understand that the only authority the Judaeans will respect is one backed up by the harsh application of force.' Postumus bowed his head towards Macro. 'An excellent suggestion, if I may say so, sir.'

Macro nodded. 'Then we'll draw some kit from the quartermaster and prepare for the patrols.'

'Where you're going, you'll find this far more suitable than a helmet,' Centurion Parmenion explained as he picked up a folded cloth from one of the shelves in the quartermaster's stores. 'Here, let me show you.'

He flicked the cloth out and then folded one corner diagonally across so that the light material formed a triangle. He raised it over his head so that the long side faced forward, and then he secured the material over the crown of his head with a double loop of braid. 'There, you see?'

'I can see you look like a native,' Macro grunted. 'Is that really necessary?'

Parmenion shrugged. 'Only if you don't want the sun to boil your brains. You can cross the ends in front and throw them over your shoulders to keep the dust from your face as well, if needed. Useful piece of gear all round. And in this place, yes, necessary.'

Parmenion removed the keffiyeh and handed it to Macro who regarded it with little enthusiasm. Cato took his more willingly and tried it on.

'Like this?'

'Not bad,' Parmenion conceded. 'And you'll need a linen cuirass. There's a few sets we keep for officers. That scale armour of yours might be fine for Germania or Britannia, but it'll kill you out here if you have to wear it for too long.'

He searched along the shelves until he found what he was looking for and returned with a set of the light-weight armour. It was made from sheets of linen, glued together to make stiff, hard breast and back plates that were joined by a tie at each side.

'Here, Cato. Try it on.'

Once Parmenion had fastened the ties Macro could not help laughing.

'What's so funny?'

'Those bits that stick up at the back look like wings.'

Parmenion pulled each of the plates over Cato's shoulders and fastened them to the front of the breast-plate. 'There you are. You'll find that it lacks the flexibility of scale or mail armour, but it's much lighter and almost as tough.'

Cato flexed to each side and performed a slow twist from his midriff. 'See what you mean.' Then he rapped the breastplate and was pleased that it seemed resilient enough. Fine for most sword cuts, although a determined thrust with a spear, or an arrow strike, would be a different matter. He looked up at Parmenion and nodded. 'It'll do.'

Parmenion turned to Macro. 'Now you, sir.'

While Parmenion went to fetch some more armour Macro muttered to Cato, 'All this cloak and dagger stuff is bad enough already, without having to muck about with all this fancy dress crap.'

The patrols left the fort the following morning, just after sunrise. The air was cool and Cato relished it, knowing full well how hot the day would become. A squadron of horse and a century of infantry had been allocated to Centurion Parmenion, since he would be marching from village to village and would not need to move swiftly. The infantry were equipped with the light headgear and armour, but retained their heavy oval shields and sturdy spears, together with their marching yokes from which hung their bedding, rations and mess kits. The column tramped out through the gate, horsemen at the front in a cavalcade of clattering accoutrements. From the gatehouse Macro watched them march off down the track for a while, and then turned away to join the two mounted squadrons that Centurion Postumus was about to lead in the opposite direction, out into the desert.

CHAPTER TWELVE

The patrol had stopped for a rest at an abandoned Nabataean way station, and while the men tended to their horses in the shaded courtyard Macro and Postumus climbed into the small signal tower and gazed down the trade route leading into the heart of Nabataean territory. To their left stretched a vast flat plain, covered in small black rocks, that wavered in the heat of the midday sun. Despite his earlier reservations about the headpiece Macro had come to realise its practicality in this searing, dusty climate. He had never experienced temperatures like this before. Heat, like the blast from a suddenly opened oven, during the day, and cold nights that reminded him of the winter in Britannia. The previous night the patrol had camped out in the open, sheltering in a gully as they huddled inside their cloaks, shivering. Now, Macro wiped the sweat from his forehead as he stood alongside Centurion Postumus and gazed down the trade route.

'What are we looking for? I can hardly make anything

out in all the shimmering. Looks like water.' Macro sighed. 'I'd kill for a swim right now.'

Postumus smiled. 'Me too. Anywhere far from this place.'

Macro grunted his agreement, and then glanced at the young officer. Postumus was a few years older than Cato, in his mid-twenties, slim, darkly featured, with the kind of looks that Macro guessed would make him popular with the ladies. 'So, then, what's your story?'

Postumus turned towards him and cocked an eyebrow. 'My story?'

'Where are you from, Postumus?'

'Brindisium. My father owns a few ships. He carries cargoes to and from Piraeus.'

'Rich?'

'He has done well enough to have bought himself into the equestrian class. So yes, he's rich, I suppose.'

'So why are you here?'

'Couldn't stand the sea. I thought I had a taste for adventure, so I joined up as a legionary.'

'Which legion?'

'I chose the Tenth.' He gave a self-deprecating smile. 'I wanted to come east and fight the Parthian hordes.'

'And did you?'

Postumus laughed. 'No chance! The imperial palace has been stitching up one deal after another with Parthia in recent years. And with Palmyra sitting pretty between the two empires that's how it will remain.'

Macro shrugged and made no comment. According to the intelligence that he and Cato had been made aware of, Parthia had designs on Rome's eastern provinces. If there was any truth in the rumours about Cassius Longinus then there was every prospect that the Parthians would storm across the eastern frontier the moment the legions garrisoned there pulled out to support Longinus' bid for the imperial throne.

Postumus went on. 'So with Parthia out of the picture I had to find something else to do. I applied to train as a scout.'

Macro looked hard at him. On campaign scouts acted in a traditional role. But in garrison postings their skills were directed more towards the black arts of espionage and torture. Macro had never liked the scouts in the legions he had served with. Soldiering was supposed to be a straightforward business as far as he was concerned, and he regarded with distaste the kinds of duties that the scouts were required to undertake.

'I had some fun,' Postumus continued, 'before I came to the attention of Cassius Longinus. He took me under his wing, gave me a promotion into the auxiliaries and sent me to Bushir. That was over a year ago. Can't tell you how much I've missed Antioch.'

'I can imagine,' Macro responded with feeling. 'I've heard a lot about it. Is it all true?'

Postumus nodded. 'Every word. There's not a vice you can't buy. The place is an Epicurean's heaven.'

Macro licked his lips. 'When I've finished my duty here, Antioch is going to be my first stop on the way back to Rome.'

The other man looked at him closely. 'How long are you expecting to stay here then?'

Macro cursed himself for the slip. He forced himself to grin. 'As little time as possible. Knowing the army, that probably means I'll end up dying of old age at Bushir. Long after the army bureau has forgotten that they sent me here in the first place. If I'm really lucky they might remember me, and even cough up a small pension.'

'Small is the word,' Postumus said with feeling, and then stared into the distance as he continued, 'That's why a man should build up a little contingency fund, if circumstances permit.'

Macro looked at him. 'What do you mean?'

Postumus' lips flickered into a quick smile. 'You'll see. All in good time. No . . . Wait.' He suddenly thrust his arm out and pointed towards the horizon. 'There! Look.'

Macro followed the direction of his finger and squinted at the shimmering haze. 'What? I don't see anything.'

'Look again. Closely.'

At first Macro could see nothing, but when he strained his eyes a small black dot blinked into sight, and then another to one side. In the next few moments several more appeared and the first slowly resolved itself into the distant silhouette of a man riding a strange-looking mount. It took a while before Macro realised that it must be a camel.

'Who are they?'

'Traders,' Postumus replied. 'They come from Aelana. It's an Arab colony on the coast. They land goods from the far east and load them into caravans bound for Palestine, Syria, Cilicia and Cappadocia. It's quite a haul from Aelana, and parts of the route pass through some pretty wild territory. That's where the Nabataeans come in, and more recently us.'

Macro frowned. 'I don't get it.'

'How do you think the Nabataeans became so wealthy?'

Macro shrugged.

'It's a protection racket. Their kingdom sits astride some of the most profitable trade routes in the known world. So they sit pretty in Petra and demand a toll on any caravans passing through their lands. At the same time they offer their services to protect the caravans from those tribes deep in the desert that occasionally raid the trade routes.'

'I see,' Macro replied. 'So what's our part in this?'

'It's our duty to police the trade route passing to the east of the fort. That's where Roman territory begins and Nabataea ends. That's why we're here, to protect caravans, like that one. It's a mutually beneficial arrangement.'

'I see.' Macro stared at him. 'You mean, you protect them at a price?'

'Of course.' Postumus laughed. 'All part of the service that the Second Illyrian provides to its regular customers.'

'I see,' Macro said again. He stared at the caravan, his mind racing. It was as he suspected. The question was what should he do about it, if anything. 'How does it work?'

Postumus had been watching him closely, and appeared relieved that Macro did not seem to be one of the sticklers for the strict letter of the law. 'It's simple enough. We have a regular deal with most of the caravan cartels. Just as the Nabataeans do. They get an escort from Aelana to Petra and from there to Machaeros, where there's another way station like this. That's the limit of Nabataean authority. They used to escort them as far as Damascus, but we handle the last stage of the job these days. They tried to undercut us, but we made it clear that this is now our turf and the Nabataeans keep clear of us. We pocket the fee and see them safely as far as the Decapolis.'

'Not exactly by the book, is it?'

'No. But not exactly illegal, either.' Postumus replied. 'We carry out our duties patrolling the frontier, and the caravan cartels get their escort. Everyone's happy. The thing is to make sure that word of this doesn't spread too far, or pretty soon we'll have Cassius Longinus clamouring for a cut, and the procurator in Caesarea. So we keep it quiet.'

'I can imagine.'

'Of course, the only really tricky issue is when we have to deal with fresh customers. Those caravan cartels that are new to the area. Like that one.'

'Oh? What happens then?'

'You'll see.' Postumus turned towards him. 'When they reach us, let me do the talking, sir. Chances are they'll know some Greek but they prefer to negotiate in their lingo and I know enough to get by.'

'All right then.' Macro nodded. 'I'll follow your lead.'

The caravan emerged from the heat haze and slowly drew closer to the way station. Macro watched them from the tower, and saw that there must be at least a hundred camels, weighed down by great baskets stuffed with bales of material, jars tightly packed into straw and other less discernible goods. Towards the front of the caravan were two large ox-carts laden with stout lengths of timber. The camels came at a steady swaying pace, goaded on by the herders walking at their side, who occasionally flicked the beasts with the ends of the slender canes they carried. On either flank of the caravan rode a handful of guards: warriors swathed in dark robes, with swords and bows slung from the wooden frames of their camel saddles. They looked fierce enough, Macro decided, but there were only twelve of them, hardly sufficient to beat off a spirited attack.

Down below in the courtyard of the station Postumus was ordering his men to mount up, and with a last look at the approaching caravan Macro descended from the tower to join them. As soon as he was in the saddle Postumus gave the signal to move and the horses clopped out of the way station and into the harsh light outside. They quickly fanned out and formed a line two deep across the track, the standards of both squadrons prominently on display a short distance in front of the main body.

'Just to make sure they know we're Roman,' Postumus explained to Macro. 'No sense in panicking them.'

Even so, the caravan halted. The escorts formed a small party with the merchants in charge of the caravan and warily approached the Romans. They stopped the moment they were within speaking distance and one of the merchants waved a hand in greeting.

'Remember, sir,' Postumus muttered, 'let me do the talking.'

'Be my guest.'

Postumus clicked his tongue and walked his horse forward. Macro followed him, keeping a short distance behind. They reined in a few paces from the other men.

Postumus flashed a smile and addressed them in Greek. 'I bid you welcome to the Roman province of Judaea. Do any of you speak Greek?'

'I speak it, a little.' One of the men lowered the veil covering his mouth so that Postumus would know who was speaking for the caravan. 'What can I do for you, Roman?'

'It's more a question of what I can do for you.'

Postumus bowed his head. 'The route ahead is plagued by raiders from the desert. You will need a stronger escort than that afforded by your twelve companions, no matter how formidable they might be. My men and I can ensure your safe passage through this area as far as Gerasa, should you wish it.'

'Most kind of you, Roman. I imagine you will require us to pay a fee for this service?'

Postumus shrugged. 'A small consideration is all that is required.'

'How much?'

'A thousand drachma.'

There was a stony silence from the leader of the caravan, until one of his fellow merchants broke the silence and spoke harshly in their tongue. A conversation ensued and Macro caught the angry tone in their voices. At length the leader hushed his friends and addressed the centurion again. 'It is too much.'

'It is what all caravans who pass this way pay us, should they require our protection.'

'And if we don't pay?'

'You may freely pass. But you continue your journey at your own risk. It is not advisable. You are new to this route, are you not?'

'Perhaps.'

'Then you might not be fully aware of the dangers.'

'We can look after ourselves.'

'As you wish.' Postumus twisted round in his saddle

and bellowed an order for his men to move off the track. Then he turned back to the leader of the caravan, bowed his head politely and turned his horse about to trot off and join his men. Macro caught up with him and edged his beast alongside.

'That didn't seem to go very well.'

'Oh, it's not over yet. We sometimes get this reaction from merchants new to this route. But he'll change his mind soon enough.'

'You seem very sure of yourself.'

'I have every reason to be.'

Postumus did not elaborate and Macro sat irritably in his saddle as the long procession of laden camels and their herders swayed by. The escorts stood between the caravans and the Roman cavalry, and eyed Postumus and his men warily until the end of the caravan had passed. Then they turned their camels and trotted them back on to the flanks of the caravan. Once they had gone Macro turned to Postumus.

'What now?'

'We wait a little while, and then follow them.'

Macro had had enough. 'Look, you'd better just tell me what's going on here. No more of your games, Postumus. Just tell me.'

'Maybe nothing will happen, sir. Maybe they will complete their journey in safety, but I wouldn't bet on it. The route between here and Gerasa is the haunt of a number of raiding parties.'

As soon as the rear of the caravan was a mile or so distant Postumus gave the order for his men to advance slowly along the track behind it, making sure that they kept their distance as they followed. The hours passed slowly and Macro began to feel the effects of the previous night's sleeplessness. His eyes felt heavy and sore and he had to blink frequently to try to refresh them. Ahead, the distant figures of the caravan loomed hypnotically, only increasing his sense of weariness. It was late in the afternoon when Postumus halted the column so abruptly that Macro almost slipped from his saddle. He shook his head to clear the heaviness that shrouded his mind.

'What? What's happening?'

'It's just as I anticipated, sir.' Postumus smiled. 'Raiders, coming out of the desert. Over there.'

He pointed to the right and Macro saw a line of camels emerge from beyond a low dune and swoop in towards the straggling length of the caravan. At once Macro's hand reached for his sword as his mind cleared at the prospect of action.

'Let's get moving.'

'No.'

'What do you mean no?' Macro growled. 'Those men are attacking the caravan.'

'Precisely.' Postumus nodded. 'And don't those merchants wish that they had taken us up on our offer to protect them? Now they'll learn just how expensive it can be to travel without a proper escort.'

'They'll be massacred!' Macro said angrily. 'We have to do something.'

'No,' Postumus replied firmly. As the raiders charged in towards the caravan, the Roman cavalry column stood still. 'For the moment, we're going to do precisely nothing.'

CHAPTER THIRTEEN

The settlement of Heshaba was the first village on Centurion Parmenion's patrol route, and the column of Roman cavalry and infantry descended the slope from the main track late in the morning. The blackened remains of Miriam's house were clearly visible and once again Cato felt consumed with guilt that this woman had been so cruelly rewarded for saving his life. As the column approached the village, Parmenion led them in a wide circuit round its periphery. He did not halt the column but kept them marching down the wadi, away from Heshaba.

'I thought we were supposed to stop there.' Cato spoke quietly to the veteran as they rode side by side at the head of the cavalry squadron.

'They've had enough of us for the moment,' Parmenion replied. 'We're coming back the same way, so we can let them know the score then.'

Cato looked at him shrewdly. 'Still out to win their friendship?'

Parmenion glanced back at him. 'Perhaps I'm just trying not to lose whatever good will remains between us. If we go in hard today, it might just be the final straw for those people. Then they'll go over to Bannus. And if the people of Heshaba turn against us, then what hope have we with the rest of the province? Strictly between us, Cato, there are times when I doubt that there's anything more the prefect could do to stir up bad will amongst the people in this area. It's almost as if he wants to goad them into open rebellion.'

'And why would he want that?' Cato responded evenly.

Parmenion thought it over for a moment and shook his head. 'I don't know. I really don't. Doesn't make sense at all. The man must be mad. Quite mad.'

'Does he strike you as mad?'

'No. I suppose not.' Parmenion sounded confused, and glanced round at Cato again. 'What do you think? There has to be more to it. Any fool could see where these orders will lead. They are going to provoke a rebellion, or at least drive far more men into Bannus' clutches. I just don't get it.'

Cato shrugged, then stared back towards the village. He reined his horse in, steering it out of the path of the following column as his mind turned over the wanton injustice that Miriam had suffered. He made a decision, and spurred his mount back alongside Parmenion.

'Where are we camping tonight?'

'There's a spring and some trees halfway along the wadi. About another four miles from here. Why?'

'I'll join you there at dusk,' Cato replied, before he urged his horse back along the column and headed for the village.

'Where are you going?' Parmenion called after him.

'I have to speak to someone!' Cato shouted back, and then muttered, 'I have to apologise.'

As his horse climbed back up the slope towards the cluster of houses that made up the small community of Heshaba, Cato mentally composed the words he wished to say to Miriam. He had to make it quite clear that the prefect was not representative of other Romans. That his actions must not be understood to be typical of Roman policy. It might yet be possible to mend some of the damage that Scrofa had caused.

He entered the village and was immediately aware of the hostile expressions in the faces of the few people who met his gaze through open doors and windows as his horse picked its way down the street and into the open space at the heart of the community. The air still carried the sharp tang from the burned-out shell of Miriam's house. The brigand hung from his cross and Cato hoped that the man was dead, spared from any further suffering. A short distance away from the smouldering ruin Cato saw her grandson, Yusef, squatting on a small chest on the ground next to the meagre pile of goods that she had been able to rescue from the house before the auxiliaries had set fire to it. Yusef looked up at the sound of hooves and stared at Cato with wide terrified eyes. Cato dismounted, and led the horse over to one of the blackened uprights that had supported Miriam's sun shelter. He tethered the animal to it and slowly approached the young boy.

'Yusef, do you know where your grandmother is?' he asked in Greek.

The boy did not respond for a moment, and then shook his head quickly. 'She's not here. She's gone. So you can't hurt her any more, Roman!' He almost spat out the last word, and Cato paused a short distance away, not wanting to alarm the boy any further.

'I mean her no harm. You have my word on that, Yusef. But I must speak to her. Please tell me where she is.'

Yusef stared at him for a moment, then slowly rose to his feet. He pointed at the ground. 'Wait here. Don't move. Don't try to follow me.'

Cato nodded. With a last careful look at the Roman, Yusef turned and ran off, disappearing round the corner of the nearest building. Cato glanced round and saw that there was no one else in sight. The village was as quiet and as still as the vast necropolis that spread out to either side of the Appian way outside the gates of Rome. Not the happiest of comparisons, Cato thought wryly, and turned his attention to the pile of belongings in the street. Aside from the bundles of clothing and cooking pots there were several baskets of scrolls, and the small casket that Yusef had been sitting on. Something about the casket struck Cato, and then he remembered that he had seen it in the hiding place beneath Miriam's house. What could be so precious about it that it had to be hidden from sight? His curiosity aroused, Cato glanced round to make sure that he was unobserved. After a moment's hesitation he approached and squatted down to examine it more closely. The casket was quite plain, with no ornamentation and a simple catch fastening.

He was interrupted by the sound of footsteps and hurriedly stood as Miriam and Yusef turned the corner and saw him squatting down by their belongings. Miriam's eyes went immediately to the casket as she strode across towards the centurion.

'I'll thank you to leave my property – what remains of it – alone. My son made that for me. That, and the contents, are all I have to remember him by.'

'I'm sorry. I . . . ' Cato stared at her helplessly, then hung his head in shame. 'I'm sorry.'

'My grandson says you wish to speak to me?'

'Yes. If you will permit me.'

'I'm not sure that I want to speak to you. Not after . . . ' Miriam swallowed as she gestured towards the scorched remains of her house.

'I can understand that,' Cato replied gently. 'The prefect was wrong to do it. I tried to stop him.'

Miriam nodded. 'I know, but it made no difference.'

'What happens to you now? Where will you go?'

Miriam blinked back the tears that glistened at the corners of her dark eyes and nodded vaguely towards the street she had emerged from. 'One of my people has provided a room for me and the boy. The villagers will build us a new home.'

'That's good.' Cato tilted his head slightly to one side. 'You said your people. Are you their leader?'

Miriam pursed her lips. 'In a manner of speaking. They hold me in some regard as followers of my son. It's almost as if I was their mother as well.' She smiled weakly. 'I suppose they're just sentimental.'

Cato smiled back at her. 'Whatever the reason, you clearly hold some power over them, as well as Symeon and Bannus, it appears.'

Miriam's smile froze, and she looked at Cato suspiciously. 'What do you want of me, Centurion?'

'To talk. To understand what is going on. I need to know more about your people, and about Bannus, if we are to bring his ambition to provoke an uprising to an end, and save lives. Many lives, Roman and Judaean alike.'

'You want to understand my people?' Miriam replied bitterly. 'Then you'd be one of the few Romans who ever did try to understand us.'

'I know that. I cannot apologise for what has been done in the name of Rome. I am only a junior officer. I cannot change imperial policy. But I can try to make a difference. That's all.'

'Very honest of you, Centurion.'

'We could start improving relations if you would call me Cato.'

She stared at him for a moment and then smiled. 'Very well, then, Cato. We'll talk.' She bent down to pick up the casket and tucked it securely under her arm before she rose up and nodded to him. 'Come with me. You too, Yusef.'

She led Cato through the quiet streets and a short distance out of the village to a small reservoir that collected the rain that ran off the slopes of the wadi during the winter and spring. Now it was nearly dry and a few goats chewed at the tufts of grass growing in the cracked earth at the water's edge. Miriam and Cato sat in the shade of a handful of palm trees while Yusef ambled off to find some pebbles for his sling and began to practise against a distant rock.

'He's got a good eye for that,' Cato commented. 'He'd make a fine auxiliary when he grows up.'

'Yusef will not be a soldier,' Miriam replied firmly. 'He's one of us.'

Cato glanced at her. 'One of what, exactly? I am told that you, and these people, are Essenes. Yet you don't seem to wholly embrace their way of life.'

'Essenes!' Mirian laughed. 'No, we are not like them. The pleasures of life are to be enjoyed, not denied. Some of my people were once Essenes, but they didn't want to spend the rest of their days dead to the joys of the world.'

'Pardon me, but Heshaba is hardly my idea of paradise.'

'Perhaps not,' Miriam conceded. 'But it is our home, and we are free to make it as we will. That was always my dream. After my son was executed I turned away from Judaea. I'd had enough of their petty factions, playing one sect off against another. The high priests in Jerusalem were the worst of the lot. Endlessly splitting hairs over interpretations of the scriptures, while their families grew wealthier and wealthier. That's why my boy, Jehoshua, became involved in the political struggle. Not just against Rome, but against those who exploited the poor. He was quite a speaker, and at the end huge crowds used to come and listen to him. That was when the priests decided that Jehoshua had to be silenced. Before he persuaded the people to turn on them. So they had him arrested and saw that he was executed.'

'I thought you said he was crucified?'

'He was.'

'But only the procurator could authorise that.'

'The procurator at the time was a weak man. The priests threatened to stir up trouble against the authority of Rome unless my son was executed. They made a deal and my boy was killed. His closest followers were hunted down and the movement was broken up. Some of the leaders wanted to avenge Jehoshua. They took to the hills and have been raiding the estates of the rich and attacking Roman patrols ever since. In Jehoshua's name.

Bannus became their leader. He had been a follower of my son, and claimed to be carrying out his will.'

'That's how you know him, then.'

Miriam nodded. 'He was a fiery young man, even in those days. Very idealistic. Jehoshua used to joke that Bannus was the living spirit of the movement. I often thought they were like brothers. Bannus looked up to him all the time, so he took his death very badly. He became very bitter towards those of us who still believed in peaceful resistance and reform. Eventually he killed a tax collector and went on the run. There were plenty of others like him in the hills, and he gradually won them round. He must have picked up some of my son's speaking skills, I suppose. He visited me regularly for a while, trying to win me over to his point of view. If the mother of the movement's figurehead was on his side then he knew he could draw on far more support. I refused, and he no longer regards me with the affection he used to show me. Anyway he has acquired a large enough following of his own now, as you Romans have discovered.'

'True enough.' Cato nodded. 'But as long as they hide out in the hills we can contain the problem. The thing is, I overheard that comment he made about having some outside help.'

'What comment? When was this?'

'That day when Symeon and I hid beneath your house. I overheard you speaking with Bannus outside. He said he was expecting aid from some friends.'

'I remember now. He seemed quite excited by the idea. I wondered who he was talking about.'

Cato stared at the ground between his boots for a moment before he responded. 'The people who would have most to gain by arming Bannus are the Parthians. That's my fear.'

'Parthians?' Miriam stared at him. 'Why would Bannus go to them for aid? They're more of a danger to us than Rome will ever be.'

'I think you're right,' Cato replied. 'But it seems that Bannus must hate us more than anything else in this world. I guess he subscribes to the "my enemy's enemy is my friend" school of thought. He wouldn't be the first man in history to fall for that. And if it's true, then there's every danger that he can stir up a rebellion large enough to draw down the full might of Rome in this region.' Even as he said the words Cato felt a twinge of guilt over his duplicity. They were true only if Cassius Longinus proved not to be a traitor. Otherwise there would be no army to counter Bannus, only the scattered garrisons of auxiliary forces, like the cohort at Bushir. If there were no legions in Syria, and Bannus struck quickly, the Roman presence in Judaea could be swept away very easily. He could not trust Miriam with that knowledge. She must be made to believe that Bannus could not succeed, and would only bring fire and the sword to her fellow Judaeans. Only then would she be sure to do everything she could to dissuade Bannus and those who might support him. Cato decided to change the subject.

'So if Bannus is a warmonger, what exactly do you and your people here stand for?'

'Bannus is not a warmonger,' Miriam said quietly. 'He is a tormented soul whose grief has been twisted into a weapon. He has lost the person closest to him in life, and does not know how to forgive. That's how we differ, Cato. At least that is our most important difference . . . My people are almost all that's left of the true movement. Once we saw what a nest of vipers Jerusalem had become we decided to find somewhere to live alone and apart from other people. That's why we came here. I did not want to be reminded of those who took away my son's life . . .' Her lip quivered for an instant, then she swallowed and continued. 'We are outside their law, and we welcome all others who wish to join us.'

'All others?' Cato smiled. 'Even Gentiles?'

'Not yet,' Miriam admitted. 'But there are those amongst us who wish to broaden our movement, spread our beliefs amongst other peoples. It is the only way to guarantee that my son's legacy does not eventually follow him into the grave.' She paused, and gently stroked her hand along the casket. 'But for now, this village is virtually all we have. As you said, it is no earthly paradise, but at least we are free of the ideas that turn people against each other. That is a paradise of sorts, Cato. Or at least it was, until you turned up with Symeon.'

Cato looked away, back towards the village where he could just make out the blackened corner posts of Miriam's house.

'Tell me about Symeon. How is it that you know him as well?'

'Symeon?' Miriam smiled. 'He was another of my son's friends. A very close friend. I suppose that's why there's no love lost between Bannus and Symeon. They were good friends before they became rivals for Jehoshua's affection. Towards the end I think it was clear that he preferred Symeon. He had a nickname for Symeon. What was it? Ah yes, *Kipha*.' She smiled fondly. 'It means "rock" in our tongue.'

'Did Bannus know that Symeon was your son's favourite?'

'I fear so. I'm sure that's part of the reason for his bitterness.'

'What happened to Symeon after your son's death?'

'He tried to keep the movement going in Jerusalem for a while. But the priests hired men to hunt him down. They killed his wife and sons and Symeon fled the city and disappeared. For a long time. Then he appeared here a few years ago. Since then he has spent his time travelling across the region. He keeps in touch with my son's followers whenever he can, though I don't see much of him out here. Not as much as I'd like. He's a good man. Heart's in the right place, and one day he'll settle down and commit himself to something.' Miriam smiled. 'At least I hope he will.'

'I can trust him, then.' It was meant as a question, and Cato was relieved when Miriam nodded.

'You can trust him.'

'Good. That's what I need to know. That, and the location of Bannus and his men.'

Miriam looked sharply at him. 'I don't know where his lair is, Centurion. And even if I did, I wouldn't tell you. Just because I saved you doesn't mean that I am on your side. I would no sooner betray Bannus to you than you to him. If the opportunity arises, I will do all that I can to persuade Bannus and his followers to end their struggle and return to their families. Meanwhile I will have no part in your conflict. Nor will my people. I would ask you to just leave us alone.'

'I'd like to,' Cato said quietly. 'You've endured more than enough hardship already. The thing is, I'm not sure whether you can stay out of it. At some point you may have to choose a side, if only to save yourselves. And that time may come sooner than you think. If I were you, I would reflect on that.'

'Don't you think I haven't already?' Miriam said wearily. 'I think about it every day, and always I ask myself what Jehoshua would have done . . .'

'And?'

'I'm not sure. He would say we should not take part in this fight. That we should argue for peace. But what if no one listens? At times I think that Symeon is right.'

'And what does he say?'

'That sometimes people cannot just argue for peace, they have to fight for it.'

'Fight for peace?' Cato smiled. 'I'm not quite sure I understand how that works.'

'Nor do I.' Miriam laughed. 'You men aren't exactly the most coherent thinkers when you start spouting your philosophies. Anyway, Symeon told me that it would make sense when the time came.'

Cato shrugged. It all sounded like the usual mystical nonsense that arose whenever politics and religion intermixed. One thing was certain. Bannus did not sound like the kind of man who could be reasoned with. His confrontation with Rome was inevitable. All that mattered now was to see to it that his rebellion was crushed and that Bannus did not survive to breed more trouble in the future.

Cato stood up. 'I have to go. I have to catch up with the patrol before dark. I just wanted to apologise for what happened. Centurion Macro will be taking over command of the Second Illyrian very shortly. He will make sure that your people are treated fairly from now on. You have my word on it.'

'Thank you, Cato. But what happens until then?'

'Prefect Scrofa is still in charge.'

'So the violence will continue against the villages in the area?'

Cato shrugged helplessly. 'As long as he is in command he can do as he wishes. All I can do is try to soften the blow.'

'Why can't your centurion take over from Scrofa right now?'

'He can't.' Cato's hand went to the bulge of the thin scroll case beneath his tunic. 'Not without the proper authorisation. We're waiting for it to arrive.'

'Then you had better pray that it arrives quickly, Centurion Cato. Before Bannus and his Parthian friends start a general revolt. If that happens, then God help us all.'

CHAPTER FOURTEEN

'We can't just stand here and watch,' Macro said angrily.

'Why not?' Centurion Postumus replied. 'We offered them our protection and they turned us down. Perhaps next time they'll think twice before they spurn my offer.'

'Next time?' Macro's eyes widened in surprise. 'There isn't going to be a next time. They're being slaughtered over there.' He gestured down the track to where the raiders from the desert had charged in amongst the caravan's small force of armed escorts. The latter were hopelessly outnumbered and it was clear that they were being cut to pieces. Beyond them the camel herders were streaming away from their charges, abandoning them, and their precious cargo, to the raiders. The merchants in charge of the caravan had wheeled their camels round and were now riding them back up the track towards the Roman cavalry patrol as fast as they could go. Postumus watched them with an amused expression.

'I can't wait to see their faces when I tell them the price has doubled.'

Macro turned to him. 'What did you say?'

'It's at this stage that we double the price for escorting them the rest of the way. Oh, don't worry, they'll agree to pay it without any argument.'

'Then what?'

'Then we charge in. The raiders take what they have and run for it, and it's all over and another contract is in the bag. A few months of this, sir, and you'll be sitting on a small fortune.'

'And if the raiders decide to fight it out?'

'They won't. We have an unspoken understanding with them.'

'What?'

'Think about it, sir. It's important that the threat is real. So if they see us riding behind a caravan, they have come to know we'll let them carry out a quick attack. For our part, when we ride to the rescue, they know that we won't pursue them into the desert. Neither side loses any men and both sides get to profit. The only losers are the caravan cartels, and the next time they come this way, they'll pay up without any fuss.'

Macro shook his head in disbelief. He stared towards the caravan where the raiders had dealt with the escort and were now busy looting the leading camels.

'How long has this been going on?'

'Since I arrived here, sir.'

'Was Scrofa's predecessor in on it?'

'No,' Postumus admitted guardedly. 'He didn't approve, but then again, he just turned a blind eye to those of us who had joined the scheme. I think I would have talked him round, if he hadn't died in that ambush.'

'I bet.' Macro had heard enough. He drew his sword and tightened his hands on the reins.

'What are you doing, sir?' Postumus asked in alarm.

'I'm doing my duty,' Macro growled, before he took a sharp breath and bellowed his orders. 'Deploy into line!'

'No!' Postumus cried out. 'No! Stay as you are!'

Macro whipped round towards him. 'Shut your mouth! Not one more word from you.' He turned back to the auxiliaries. 'Deploy into line!'

'I'm in command here!' Postumus called out.

Macro let go of the reins and slammed his fist into Postumus's face. The centurion's head snapped back and he dropped from the saddle and hit the ground with a jarring crash. Macro shook his head. 'Not any more you're not, sunshine.' He turned to the auxiliaries and shouted, 'Well? What are you bloody waiting for? Deploy into line!'

Behind him, obedient to his order, the decurions were marshalling the two squadrons into line. As soon as they were ready, Macro raised his sword to get their attention and swept it down towards the caravan.

'Charge!'

The horses broke into a trot, quickly accelerating into

a canter, straight at the oncoming owners of the caravan. They just had time to register a look of surprise and fright before they wheeled their beasts aside, out of the path of the charging Roman cavalry. Then they flashed out of Macro's field of vision, and he concentrated on the situation ahead as the auxiliaries whooped their war cries and brandished their spears as they closed on the raiders. Already, the first of them was breaking away from the caravan, hurriedly herding a cluster of laden camels ahead of him, back into the desert. As the auxiliaries neared the tail end of the caravan the rest realised the danger and mounted their camels and turned them away. They were in for a nasty shock, Macro thought, when the cavalry didn't give up the chase and charged right after them. He turned his head to call back to the men behind him. 'Keep going! Go for them! Don't stop!'

He wanted them to be quite sure of the order, given that Postumus must have got them used to drawing up as soon as they had chased the raiders away from previous caravans. The auxiliaries pounded round the end of the caravan and headed diagonally across the level ground towards the fleeing raiders. Greed had got the better of the bandits and they did not abandon their loot and the camels they had driven off. Macro smiled. Perhaps they still thought that the Roman cavalry, true to form, was merely making a show of chasing them off. They'd soon discover the folly of that notion.

Macro, at the head of the auxiliaries, was within

bowshot of the nearest raiders when they began to understand their peril. One of the camel riders, leading a string of laden beasts, abruptly threw down the lead rope and whipped his camel into a loping run towards the distant dunes. At once his companions did the same, releasing the animals they had seized and desperately racing to escape the horsemen charging towards them. Macro ignored the discarded baggage and waved his sword towards the black-robed figures making for the open desert.

'Stay on them! Don't let them get away!'

The nearest of the raiders was just a short distance ahead now, and Macro drew his shield against his left side and held his cavalry sword out to the right in readiness. The raider, his head swathed in black turban and veil, glanced back and his eyes widened at the sight of the Roman officer bearing down on him. At once he reached forward and snatched out one of the short javelins from the sheath hanging from his saddle frame. As his camel loped on towards the desert the raider twisted round, took aim and hurled the javelin at Macro only a short distance behind. The shaft flew flat and true towards him. He jerked the reins to the left and leaned as far as he dared to the side and ducked his head. The javelin flicked past his right shoulder and the raider uttered an angry curse and snatched at another. For an instant Macro's horse staggered as it struggled to fight the inertia opposing the rapid change in direction and Macro hung on tightly, clamping his legs against the horse's side as he tried to shift his weight to the right. Then, with a power-ful thrust from its front legs, the horse regained control and galloped after the raider once more.

The second javelin was thrown as Macro closed in, and it was deflected off his shield with a sharp clatter. There was no time for another javelin and the raider drew a curved blade and swung it at Macro's head. With a metallic ring, Macro parried the blow and then swept the point of his sword towards the man's side and thrust home, through the dark robes and into his chest. The raider gasped as the impact drove the air from his lungs; then, as the blade ripped free, he galloped on several more paces before the reins slipped from his fingers and he toppled from the saddle, hit the stony ground, rolled over a few times and was still. His camel lumbered on, riderless, into the desert.

Macro reined in and glanced round. Scattered ahead of him the rest of the raiders were drawing away. He turned as the first of the auxiliaries streamed past him on either side. None of the men were riding their mounts at full stretch and Macro felt his guts churn with anger and contempt. The bandits were going to escape. True, they would have little to show for their attack on the caravan, but they would survive to strike another day, thanks to Postumus and his ongoing scam.

'Don't just ponce around!' Macro bellowed after them. 'Get after them. Get stuck in, before I have your bollocks for breakfast!'

The nearest men made a show of bending low and urging their horses on, but there was little chance of catching up with the raiders now and Macro sheathed his sword and sat erect as he surveyed the scene. Beyond the auxiliaries, the raiders were rapidly disappearing over the nearest dunes. Elsewhere, the herders were returning to the caravan and restoring order to the nervous animals, who were milling about where they had been left. Some of the merchants were retrieving the loot that been spilled on the sand and repacking it into the baskets hanging over the backs of the pack camels.

A pounding of hooves drew Macro's attention and he saw Centurion Postumus approaching him across the desert. At the last moment, Postumus reined in, his horse kicking up a cloud of dust and loose stones, so that Macro's horse recoiled with a nervous whinny.

'What the hell d'you think you're doing?' Postumus screamed at him, thrusting an arm towards the dead raider.

Macro glanced at the body and shrugged. 'I'm doing your job, Postumus. At least, I'm doing the job you *should* be doing.'

Postumus clenched his teeth and stabbed a finger at Macro. 'You've fucked it up, Macro! It's taken months to set this up. It was going like a dream . . . Now?' Postumus looked at the body again and shook his head. 'I don't know what's going to happen. There'll be reprisals.' He turned back to Macro with a bitter grin. 'You're going to pay for this.'

'I don't think so. Not when word gets back to Rome about the little deal you had with that lot.' He gestured towards the last of the raiders, already far off, half hidden by the dust kicked up by their flight.

'What makes you think you'll live to expose us?'

Macro laughed. 'Are you threatening me?' His hand dropped to the hilt of his sword as he watched Postumus closely. 'Go on then, if you've got the balls to do it. Draw your sword.'

Postumus stared at him, then shook his head and sneered. 'I don't have to fight you, Macro. I have powerful friends who could swat you like a gnat.'

'Really? Then let them try.'

'In any case, aren't you forgetting something?'

'What?'

'You struck me. In full view of the men. As soon as we get back to Bushir, I'll bring charges against you. Make no mistake, you'll pay for this.'

'So you say. We'll see. But for now, I'm relieving you of command for the rest of this patrol.'

'On whose authority?' Postumus smirked. 'Aren't you forgetting something? Until your appointment is confirmed you have no—'

'I know all that,' Macro cut in. 'But in this situation it doesn't matter. First, you have failed to carry out your duty. I could have you charged with cowardice when we return to Bushir. Second, I am the senior officer present. Unless you have written authority that supersedes my seniority there's nothing you can do about it. I don't suppose you have such a document on you, Centurion Postumus? No? How unfortunate.' Macro smiled. 'I can only imagine how frustrated you must feel.'

Postumus glared at him, opened his mouth to protest, and then shut it again. Macro had him. The same rigorous adherence to rules that had cost Macro his appointment had now robbed Postumus of command over the two cavalry squadrons. It took all of Macro's self-control not to laugh now that the tables had been turned on the smug younger officer. He let Postumus stew for a moment before he continued.

'I will remain in command until we return to Bushir. Until then, you are to assume the duties of an orderly. Is that clear?'

'You can't do this,' Postumus said quietly. The decurions of the two cavalry squadrons had called off the pursuit and were rallying to Macro and Postumus.

'I already have. You can sort it out with the prefect when we return to Bushir.'

'Trust me, I will.'

As the decurions trotted up Macro turned to them and announced the change of command. They turned questioningly to Postumus, but before the latter could speak Macro snapped at them, 'Ignore him! I am the ranking officer here! You will obey my orders from now on. Centurion Postumus will be facing a charge of gross neglect of duty when we return to Bushir. If you don't want to join him then I suggest you accept the change of command right away. Do either of you question my authority? Well?'

The decurions shook their heads.

'That's better! Now get your men to help the merchants restore some order to the caravan. Once that's done, we'll escort them to the Decapolis. If there's another attack I don't expect to see your men responding like a bunch of virgins at the Lupercal. I'd better see them go in hard and fast, or I'll personally make sure that both of you are broken back to the ranks.' Macro subjected them to a withering glare, and then concluded, 'Do I make myself clear?'

'Yes, sir!' the decurions chorused.

'Fine, then carry out your orders.' Macro returned their salute and they wheeled their mounts round and trotted back to their units. Macro turned to Postumus and gestured after them. 'What are you waiting for? I want you out there helping to clear up this mess as well.'

'Me?'

'Yes you. And you will call me sir from now on. Get moving before I add insubordination to the charges I aim to bring against you.'

Postumus stabbed his heels in, wheeled his horse and galloped past Macro, back towards the caravan.

Macro watched him go, and breathed a sigh of relief. Corruption had made the officers go soft. If they had had the guts to stand up to him a moment earlier then Macro feared he might have gone the way of Scrofa's pre-decessor. As it was, Macro had the whip hand and they had cringed like curs in front of him. In some small way that saddened him. If they buckled before the wrath of a superior officer so easily they would be little good against Bannus and his men when the time came to fight the brigands on the battlefield. As soon as his appointment as prefect of the Second Illyrian was confirmed he was going to have to crack down on the officers even more harshly than on the men. They had to be hardened up, and quickly, if they were to be a match for the Judaean rebels, and any Parthian allies.

For the next four days the caravan ambled along the track towards Gerasa. With a squadron of auxiliary cavalry on each flank there were no more attacks, and when the walls of the hill town that overlooked the sea of Galilee came into sight the merchants approached Macro to make their farewells.

'We'll leave you here,' Macro announced. 'You're safe now.'

'Only thanks to you, Centurion.' The merchant bowed his head, and then looked up awkwardly. 'The other merchants and I wish to offer you a gift, in thanks for saving our property and, perhaps, our lives.'

'No,' Macro replied firmly. He was not going down that route. He'd not end up like Postumus and most of the officers of the Second Illyrian. 'We were just doing our duty. No gift is necessary. There'll be no more bribes paid to the Roman soldiers protecting travellers along this route. That's finished with. I give you my word on that.'

The merchant looked pained. 'You do not understand, Centurion. It is our custom to offer a gift. If you do not accept, we are shamed.'

Macro looked at them and scratched the stubble on his chin. 'Shamed, eh?'

The merchant nodded his head vigorously.

Macro felt irritated by the situation. He was not one to tolerate the customs of other cultures easily and did not know how to get out of this predicament. Then an idea that he had been brooding over for the past few days came back to him and provided a very neat and useful solution.

'I will not accept a gift,' he repeated. 'But I will require a favour of you in the near future. When the time comes, where may I find you gentlemen?'

'When we have concluded our business here we will be returning to Petra, to make arrangements for the next caravan. We should be there for a month, maybe two.'

'I'll send word to you in Petra, then.'

Macro watched as the merchants returned to the long stream of camels swaying up the slope towards the gate of Gerasa. He smiled. If his plan was workable at all, then the merchants were going to prove vital to its success.

CHAPTER FIFTEEN

The day after Centurion Parmenion's force left Bushir they marched through the hilly landscape around Herodion, keeping close watch on the terraced olive groves that climbed the slopes on either side. This was the kind of country that favoured the light troops that Bannus had at his disposal, and Cato could well imagine the damage that a small force armed with slings and javelins might inflict on the Roman column. Fortunately there was no sign of the brigands and at midday they reached the large village of Beth Mashon, surrounded by dusty clumps of palm trees. Their approach was spotted by a handful of children tending their goats, and as they drove their bleating charges out of the path of the soldiers one of them raced ahead to warn the villagers.

Cato glanced at Parmenion. 'Do you think we should deploy the men?'

'For what?'

'In case they're preparing a surprise.'

'Who do you think we're up against, Cato?'

Parmenion asked wearily. 'Some crack Parthian cavalry, or something?'

'Who knows?'

Parmenion laughed bitterly. 'There's nothing in there apart from the usual peasants. Believe me. And right now they'll be scared as hell and hoping that we don't add to their difficulties. Fat chance of that, of course. About the only time outsiders ever visit places like this is when they've come to collect the taxes or make some other trouble.'

Cato looked closely at the veteran. 'Sounds to me like you're on their side.'

'Their side?' Parmenion raised his eyebrows. 'They don't have a side. They're too bloody poor to have a side. They have nothing. Look around you, Cato. This is about as close to desolation as you can get. These people are scraping a living off the dust. For what? So that they can pay their taxes, their tithes, their debts. And in the end when the tax-farmers, temple priests and bankers have had their cut, and there's nothing left, they have to sell their children. They're desperate, and desperate people having nothing left to lose but their hope. When that's gone, who do they go for?' He smacked himself on the chest. 'Us. Then we have to go round butchering the poor bastards until they're sufficiently cowed again to let the same old parasites resume squeezing the survivors for every last shekel they can get.'

He took a deep breath and made to continue, but

shook his head in frustration and clamped his mouth shut.

'Got that off your chest, then?' Cato said quietly.

Parmenion glared back at him and then smiled. 'Sorry. It's just that I've served here too long. And it's always been the same.' He gestured towards the village. 'It's a wonder they stick it. Anywhere else the people would be in open rebellion by now.'

'They are,' Cato replied. 'I thought that was why we're out here. To deal with Bannus.'

Parmenion pursed his lips. 'Bannus? He's just the latest in a long line of bandits. Soon as they get a large enough following they claim to be the *mashiah*, here to deliver the people of Judaea from our clutches.' He laughed. 'I've yet to see one who wasn't the *mashiah*. And still they come . . . I tell you, I'm sick of it all. I hate this place. I hate these people and their poverty and I hate what it does to them. I'm counting the days to my discharge. Then I can leave this hole for good.'

'Where will you go?'

'As far from here as I can. Somewhere with good soil, and water, where a man can grow crops without breaking his back. I hear Britain's the place to take up a land grant these days.'

Cato laughed. 'I'm not so sure about that.'

'You've been there?'

'Yes. Two years in the Second Legion, with Macro.'

'What's it like?'

Cato thought for a moment. 'In most ways it's as different from Judaea as you can get. A good spot for that farm of yours, Parmenion, but the people are just as unwelcoming. They'll not bend to our ways very soon, I imagine. It's funny, here I am at the other end of the empire and it seems we're making the same old mistakes.'

'What do you mean?'

'These Judaeans. They have a religion that will not bend, will not compromise. And one Roman procurator after another is doomed to resort to force to make sure the Judaeans accept Roman rule on our terms. It's the same story in Britain, with the druids. As long as they hold to the old ways and we insist on the new, then there's little chance of long-term peace in either province. Not a rosy outlook on both fronts, I'm afraid.'

'You may be right.' Parmenion shrugged his shoulders wearily. 'Seems that the people who run the Empire are never going to learn. Anyway,' he glanced up at the nearest houses, 'here we are. Better get on with it.'

The column entered the edge of the village and Cato felt the familiar chill of tension tighten round his spine as he glanced down each side of the narrow street that wound through the blocks of sun-bleached houses. It followed the same pattern as all the other villages he had seen since arriving in Judaea. It was comprised of several households clustered around courtyards, where the inhabitants shared a cistern, an oven, a grain mill, an olive press and the other facilities which made them self-sufficient. Most of the houses were single-storey, but some had internal stairs that led up to the roofs where sun shelters were erected. Where the plaster was cracked and chunks had fallen away Cato could see the basalt blocks beneath, with mud and pebble mortar to make them weatherproof. From its size Cato guessed that as many as a thousand people lived in the village, but when he mentioned this to Parmenion the veteran scoffed.

'More than that. Much more. The families at the bottom of the pile live pretty much cheek by jowl. Land is in short supply. When a father passes it on, it is divided equally amongst his sons, so each generation had less and less land to work, and cannot afford to build their own homes.'

The column emerged from the winding street into a broad paved square in front of a large building with a domed roof. Parmenion summoned one of his men and handed over the reins.

'That's the synagogue,' Parmenion muttered as he dismounted. 'That's where I'll find the priest. He'll be the headman, or at least someone who knows him. Optio!' he bellowed back towards his men and a junior officer came trotting over and saluted.

'Yes, sir.'

'You can pass the word for the men to stand down. But have detachments posted on each street leading out of the square. A section on each should do. Got that?'

The optio nodded and turned away to carry out his orders. Cato slid off the back of his horse and handed his reins to Parmenion's groom.

'Mind if I come with you?'

Parmenion stared at him. 'If you really want.' Then he took a deep breath and strolled over to the door of the synagogue, with Cato following at his shoulder. The door opened inwards as he approached and a tall man in a long black tunic cautiously emerged. He wore a red skullcap and long, dark locks hung down over his shoulders.

'Who are you?' Parmenion asked, in Greek.

'Sir, I am the priest.' The man stiffened and tried not to show any fear of the soldier. 'What do you want of us, Roman?'

'Water for my men and horses. Then I need to speak to the village elders. Have them summoned immediately.'

The priest's expression darkened as he endured the centurion's peremptory tone. 'The water is there in our public cistern.' He pointed across the square to a low stone trough that rose knee high from the ground. 'Your men and beasts can help themselves. As for the village elders – that will not be easy. Some of them are still at the festival in Jerusalem. Others are out tending to their land.'

Parmenion raised his hand to cut the priest off. 'Just find as many as possible. We'll wait in the square. But be quick about it.'

'I'll do what I can.' The man's eyes narrowed

202

suspiciously. 'But tell me, for what purpose do you want them?'

'You'll see,' Parmenion replied curtly. 'Now fetch them.'

The priest stared at him for a moment before he nodded, closed the door of the synagogue behind him, and made his way into one of the alleys leading off the square. Once he was out of sight Parmenion relaxed. He sat down on the edge of a stone trough and took a drink from his canteen. After a moment Cato followed suit and they sat and watched as the soldiers slumped down in whatever shade they could find and talked quietly. A few of the more curious were having a look round the square but when one of them reached for the synagogue door Parmenion snapped at him, 'Not in there, Canthus! Keep away from the building.'

The man saluted and backed off at once.

'What's so special about their place of worship?' Cato asked.

'Nothing, to our eyes. Just a square meeting room. A few old scrolls in a box and that's it. But to them?' Parmenion shook his head. 'You have no idea how touchy they can be. I've seen more than one riot kick off when one of our lads has overstepped the mark.' He suddenly looked hard at Cato. 'No offence meant, but you've not been here long enough to know the ropes. So watch what you say and do around the locals.'

'I will.'

A short while later the priest returned with a small crowd of villagers, mostly older men, almost all of them wearing long smocks and skullcaps. They glanced round nervously at the soldiers filling the square in front of the synagogue as they followed their priest towards the two Roman officers. Parmenion eyed them coldly, and muttered to Cato, 'I'll talk. You watch, listen and learn.'

The village elders and Parmenion exchanged a brief bow of the head and then Parmenion addressed the priest. 'I need to talk to them somewhere cooler. Where can we go?'

'Not in our synagogue.'

'I assumed that,' Parmenion said shortly. 'So?'

The priest gestured towards one of the alleys. 'Our threshing room will do. Come with me.'

'All right.' Parmenion turned to Cato and spoke softly. 'Get two sections and follow me.'

The younger officer nodded, and as Parmenion went off, surrounded by the local people, Cato felt a twinge of anxiety for the man. Even though he had implied that the villagers were quite submissive, it still seemed risky to go with them alone. He shrugged the feeling off. Parmenion knew these people well enough to know how far he could trust them. Calling on the nearest men, Cato formed them up, and marched quickly to catch up with Parmenion and the village elders who were just disappearing into one of the alleys. Cato found the threshing room a short distance down the alley, where a long sheltered space lined the thoroughfare. Inside, the village elders were sitting on the ground facing Centurion Parmenion, who glanced round as Cato and the soldiers arrived on the scene.

'Form them up along the side there.'

Once the men were in place Parmenion began to address the locals in Greek. Without any kind of preamble he gave notice of Prefect Scrofa's threat to punish any person who offered any aid or shelter to Bannus and his brigands. The locals listened with sullen expressions as some whispered a translation in Aramaic to those that had little or no Greek. They listened calmly, having often heard such threats from Roman officials, and before them the representatives of Herod Agrippa. As ever, they were caught between the rapacious forces of authority on the one hand, and on the other their instinctive loyalty to the outlaws who tended to be from the same peasant stock as themselves.

Parmenion concluded by reminding them that Rome expected them not only to withhold aid from the brigands, but also to actively help in locating and destroying Bannus and his men. Anything less would be considered proof of abetting the criminals and the punishment would be swift and severe. Parmenion paused, and drew a breath before he continued with the most contentious aspect of his orders.

'In order to ensure your co-operation in these matters Centurion Scrofa has instructed me to take five hostages from your village.' He quickly indicated some men sitting nearest to Cato and the soldiers. 'They'll do. We'll take them. Put them under guard.'

As soon as Parmenion's words had been spoken a chorus of angry voices filled the threshing room and several of the locals jumped to their feet and approached him, shouting into his face. Cato's hand slipped down to the handle of his sword, but the veteran officer stood his ground, and suddenly swept his arms open, causing the nearest villagers to cringe back.

'That will do!' he bellowed. 'I will have quiet in here!'

The villagers subsided, grudgingly, and the priest spoke up for them. He indicated the five hostages. 'You cannot take these men.'

'I can, and I will. I have my orders. They will be well treated, and returned safely the moment Bannus is destroyed.'

'But that could take many days, months!'

'Perhaps. But if you co-operate we can finish Bannus off sooner rather than later.'

'But we know nothing of Bannus!' the priest protested, struggling to contain his rage. 'You cannot hold our people in this manner. We'll protest to the procurator.'

'You can do what you like, but those men are coming with me.'

'Who will run their businesses and tend their crops while they are gone?'

206

'That's your problem, priest, not mine.' Parmenion turned to Cato. 'Get 'em on their feet. We're heading back to the column.'

The five men were pinioned between two lines of soldiers as they headed back to the square. The priest and the other village elders bustled after the Roman troops, shouting and gesticulating angrily. Parmenion ignored them, and Cato tried to follow his lead, facing straight ahead as the other soldiers tramped along at his back. When they emerged into the square the soldiers were already looking their way, to see what the shouting was about. Parmenion directed his men to take the prisoners over to where the groom was holding his horse and Cato's. The priest hurried alongside, still protesting that the men's families would be ruined in their absence. His words had no effect and Parmenion ignored him as he bellowed orders for his officers to get the column ready to move.

The priest suddenly stopped shouting and stared past Parmenion, towards the synagogue, and let out a shrill cry of outrage as he started to run across the square. Cato, startled, turned to look and saw that the door to the synagogue was open, and that men were moving in the gloomy interior.

'Shit.' Parmenion slammed his fist against his thigh. 'The fools!'

He ran after the priest, and Cato followed. Inside was a square space with sloped stone seating and a large pillar in each corner to support the dome above. At the far end was a wooden cupboard, round which several soldiers had clustered. The doors of the cupboard were open and the men were rifling through the scrolls stacked inside, pulling them out and dropping them on the flagstones as they searched for anything of value.

'Get away from there!' Parmenion shouted. But it was too late. The priest flew across the floor, and snatched a scroll from the hand of the man closest to the cupboard. Then he screamed in rage and slapped the soldier, who Cato realised was the same man who had approached the synagogue earlier. Before Parmenion or Cato could react, Canthus slammed his fist into the priest's face, knocking him down, and then scooped up the scroll, and let it spool out over the floor. Looking down at the priest, he spat and tore the scroll in half.

'That's enough!' Parmenion ran over to the group and thrust the soldier aside. 'You bloody fool! You don't know what you've done!'

The soldier stared back at his superior and then indicated the priest. 'Sir, you saw him! The bastard slapped me.'

'Nothing compared to what I'll do to you. Get out of here and form up. All of you!'

The men scrambled away. On the ground the priest sat up, rubbing his jaw, then froze as his eyes beheld the torn scroll. He uttered a terrible shriek and clawed his way across to the scroll and picked it up with a look of horror. Then he raced for the door and cried out to the rest of the village.

'We've got problems,' Parmenion said quietly. 'We have to get away from here, as soon as possible. Come on!'

The two officers hurried to the door. Outside the auxiliaries had paused to look round at the priest who was shrieking hysterically. Parmenion glowered at them. 'What the hell are you waiting for? I gave orders to form up!'

The men started guiltily and moved back towards their standards, hurriedly picking up their packs and equipment, while the priest continued to cry out. The village elders looked inside the synagogue and then turned back, aghast, and joined in the wailing. Cato turned to Parmenion. 'Should I shut them up?'

'No. We've already done enough damage. Let's just get out of here.'

Already more villagers were entering the square, hurrying towards the synagogue with anguished expressions that quickly turned to anger as they started shouting at the Roman soldiers.

'Get the men moving!' Parmenion roared out.

But it was already too late. The routes into the square began to fill with villagers, men, women and children, rushing in from the alleys. The soldiers closed ranks, and raised their shields as they eyed the growing crowd anxiously. Then the first of them lowered his pack and drew his sword. More followed suit and stood ready to move into action the moment the order was given, or the crowd began to edge too close. There was a blur and Cato turned to see a rock arc over the front of the crowd towards the Roman line. At the last moment one of the auxiliaries ducked and threw his shield up and the rock clattered harmlessly to one side.

Centurion Parmenion stepped back towards his men and drew his sword. Cato felt a sick feeling turn his guts to ice. The situation was rushing out of control. Unless some kind of order was quickly restored the square would be awash with blood in moments. He saw the priest close by and strode over to him.

'Tell them to disperse!' He gestured frantically towards the crowd. 'You have to get them out of the square, or the soldiers will charge.'

The priest stared at him defiantly, and for an instant Cato feared that he too was caught up in the wild rage of the moment. Then the man looked round at his people and seemed to realise the danger. He advanced to stand beside Cato, then flung his arms up and waved wildly as he shouted at the villagers. The grim-faced soldiers looked on while the crowd slowly quietened, until there was a tense hush hanging over both sides. Cato spoke quietly to the priest.

'Tell them to leave the square. Tell them to go home, or the soldiers will charge.'

The priest nodded and called out to the people. At

once they stirred angrily and several voices shouted back, and the crowd roared in support. Again the priest quietened them, and then one of the men ran forward, snatched up the torn scroll and waved the pieces in the face of the priest. Then he turned to glare at Cato and spat on the ground, just in front of the centurion's boots. Cato forced himself to stand still and show no reaction. He stared back at the man for a moment and then looked at the priest.

'What does he want?'

'What they all want. The man who did this,' the priest replied. 'The man who profaned the scriptures.'

'Impossible.' Cato had no doubt what the mob would do to him.

'What's going on?' Parmenion growled, approaching to stand beside Cato.

'They want the soldier who tore up their sacred book.'

Parmenion smiled grimly. 'Is that all?'

'No,' the priest cut in. 'Some of them are calling for the hostages to be released.' He glanced back at the crowd before he addressed the two officers again. 'They will accept nothing less.'

'We're keeping the hostages,' Parmenion said firmly. 'And our man. He will be disciplined for his actions when we return to the fort. You have my word on it.'

The priest shook his head and gestured to the mob. 'I don't think they'd accept the word of a Roman.'

'I don't care. We're not giving anyone up. Now, you'd better persuade them to move, before my men do.'

The priest eyed the Roman officer shrewdly before he replied. 'They will not let you leave, unless you hand your soldier over.'

'We'll see about that,' Parmenion growled.

Cato coughed and gestured casually over the crowd. 'Look up there.'

Parmenion's gaze flickered to the roofs of the buildings surrounding the square, where more of the villagers were gazing down at the Romans. Several, he noted, were carrying slings – the hunting weapon of the Judaean peasant.

'Looks like we're going to have to fight our way out,' Cato said quietly.

'Not if you hand the man over.' The priest spoke urgently, with a discreet nod towards his people. 'That's what they want. Then you can go. With the hostages.'

'And let our man be torn to pieces?' Cato shook his head.

'It's his life, Roman, or the lives of hundreds of my people and your men.'

Cato could see no way out of the impasse. So there would be a fight. He swallowed nervously and felt his heart beat quicken.

'Shit,' Parmenion hissed through clenched teeth. 'We have to give the man up.'

Cato turned to him in astonishment. 'You're not serious. You can't be.'

'We're caught in the heart of the village, Cato. I've seen it before when I was in Jerusalem. There was a riot. We chased them into the old city and they hit us from all sides and above. We lost scores of men.'

'You can't do it,' Cato said desperately.

'I have to. As the priest says, it's one life weighed against many.'

'No! All he did was tear up a scroll. That's all.'

'Not to him, and the rest of them.' Parmenion jerked his thumb at the mob. 'If we don't hand the man over, we're going to have to fight our way out of here, and all the way back to the fort. And once word of this gets out you can count on every village in the area rising up. Bannus will have an army in a few days. It's that, or hand the man over.'

The priest nodded and Cato opened his mouth to protest. But the veteran was right and there was nothing more he could do to save Canthus without provoking a bloodbath. He nodded his assent. 'Very well, then.'

Parmenion turned towards his men. 'Canthus! Step forward!'

There was a short pause, then a man shuffled through the line of oval shields. He stepped hesitantly towards the two centurions and the priest, who eyed him with bitter hostility, and stood to attention.

'Sir!'

'You're being relieved of duties, soldier. Disarm.'

'Sir?' Canthus looked confused.

'Lower your shield and hand me your sword. Now,' Parmenion added harshly.

After a instant's hesitation, Canthus leaned over and placed his shield on the ground. Then he drew his sword and handed it, pommel first, to his superior. Parmenion tucked the blade under his arm and tapped his vine cane on the ground. 'Now stand to attention! Don't move until I give the order.'

Canthus drew himself up and stared straight ahead, still unsure of what was happening to him, and Cato felt sick with pity over the man's fate. Then Parmenion turned to Cato.

'Get the column moving. Out of the village as quick as you can. I'll follow on.'

Cato nodded, keen to be as far from this place as he could be. He paced over to his horse, slid awkwardly on to its back and gave the order for the column to move out of the square. At first the crowd stood firm, blocking the route by which the Romans had come. The horsemen at the head of the column walked their beasts steadily towards the silent villagers, and then the priest shouted out to them and with dark expressions they shuffled aside and let the head of the column through. Cato waited for the last of the mounted men to pass and then eased his horse into position ahead of the standard carried at the head of the infantry.

'What's going on with Canthus?' a voice cried out.

Cato swung round and shouted, 'Silence! Optio, take the name of the next man to utter a word. He'll be flogged the moment we return to the fort!'

The men trudged on, casting wary glances at the villagers massing on either side of them. But the crowd just stared back, glowering with hatred, and made no threatening moves as the Romans passed. Once he was out of the square Cato tried not to look up at the figures looming above him on either side of the narrow street. Parmenion had been right. If there had been a confrontation then the Romans would have been caught like rats in a trap, showered with missiles and unable to strike back. Cato shuddered at the thought and then stiffened his back and stared straight ahead, refusing to appear intimidated.

When the column had cleared the village Cato eased his mount to the side of the track and called over the centurion in command of the infantry. 'Get 'em up that track there. I'll wait for Parmenion.'

'Yes, sir.'

As the men marched away Cato sat in the saddle and gazed back at the village. The crowd was no longer silent; an angry chorus of shouts sounded from its heart and Cato willed the veteran to hurry up and quit the place. Just when Cato had gripped his reins and was about to ride back to find him there was the dull thrumming of hooves and Parmenion came trotting out of the alley. A vest of mail armour hung over his saddle horn and a shield hung from straps tied to his belt. His face was set in a grim expression and he barely acknowledged Cato as he rode by and continued towards the column, a short distance off. Cato turned his horse and followed. When they reached the brow of the small hill that Cato had indicated to the centurion the two officers halted and turned to stare down into the centre of the village.

At first all that Cato could see was a dense mass of dark heads and skullcaps, all facing the synagogue expectantly. 'What did they do to Canthus?' he asked quietly.

'I didn't wait to find out. The priest and some of his men took him as I rode off.' Parmenion glanced down. 'He begged me not to leave him.'

Cato did not know what to say.

A fresh roar rose from the village. A small group of men had emerged on the roof of the synagogue, all but one of them clad in the flowing shirts of the local people. Writhing in their midst was a man in the red tunic of a Roman soldier.

'That's Canthus!' someone called out, and the nearest soldiers glanced back over their shoulders.

'Silence there!' Parmenion bellowed. 'Mouths shut, eyes front and keep marching!'

There was a thin scream in the distance and a fresh roar from the crowd. Cato looked back and saw that Canthus had his arms pinioned tightly behind him.

Someone had wrenched the tunic over his head and he stood naked above the crowd. Another man bent down to pick something up, and as he rose to his feet the sun glinted brilliantly off a curved blade. A reaping tool, Cato realised. As he and Parmenion watched, the man swung the blade into the Roman soldier's side, and then wrenched it across his stomach in a sweeping movement. Blood and intestines burst out from Canthus's body and spilled down the front of the synagogue, leaving a bright red smear on the white plaster wall. The crowd let out a shrill cry of delight that echoed up the slope and Cato felt the bile rise in the back of his throat.

'Come on,' Parmenion said huskily. 'We've seen enough. Let's go. We need to reach the next village before nightfall.'

'The next village?' Cato shook his head. 'After that? Surely we'd better get back to the fort and report to Scrofa.'

'Why? Because of Canthus? The fool should have known better. We still have our orders to carry out, Cato.' Parmenion pulled his reins harshly, turning his horse away from the scene below. 'Maybe next time, our men will have learned a lesson.'

CHAPTER SIXTEEN

'We've got ourselves into a right nasty situation here,' Macro mused, when Cato had finished telling him about the patrol through the local villages. Parmenion had taken hostages from every one of them, including Heshaba, and now forty men were languishing in a store shed, fed and watered, but forced to stay inside. In the days that followed the incident at Beth Mashon Parmenion had made no mention of the fate of Canthus and curtly rebuffed any attempt by Cato to raise the matter. The death of their comrade had soured the rest of the men and their grim mood was reflected in their treatment of the other villagers they encountered, with the result that, far from subduing the locals, Scrofa's measures had made them hate Rome even more. Cato had little doubt that the ranks of Bannus' band of brigands would be swelled in coming days by young men from the villages visited by Parmenion.

Cato had stripped down to his loincloth and was busy washing the dust and grime from his skin. He was as sombre as Macro had ever seen him. Macro leaned back on his bed and gazed at the ceiling. 'I don't see how we can do any good here, Cato. Scrofa's got most of the officers involved in his protection scam; the rest of 'em are trying not to notice and losing heart. The men are pissed off that they aren't getting a share of the spoils, and now it seems that Scrofa is pushing the locals towards open revolt. If that happens then the Second Illyrian is going to land right in the shit, at least while Scrofa is in command, which won't be for much longer, I hope. We should hear from the procurator any day now, confirming my appointment.'

'Assuming the message got through to Caesarea,' Cato said quietly.

'What do you mean?'

'If the officer tasked with carrying the message was one of those on the take, I suspect he would be in no hurry to see Scrofa replaced. It would be an easy thing to do to lose the message.'

'He wouldn't dare.'

'We'll see. And what if the message was lost in an ambush? Or what if the message got through to the pro-curator, but the orders were lost on the return journey?'

Macro propped himself up on one elbow and stared at Cato. 'Cheery little devil, aren't you?'

'Just pointing out the possibilities.' Cato shrugged, and dabbed at his skin with a woollen cloth. 'Besides, you've hardly mentioned half our problems.'

'Do, please, enlighten me. I could do with some light relief.'

'All right.' Cato sat down on the couch opposite Macro's and sat forward, leaning his elbows on his knees. 'As you say – the cohort's in poor shape. The locals are after our blood. If Longinus really is trying to provoke a revolt then he's almost got what he's after. And if it happens then we'll be facing Bannus with an enlarged force, armed to the teeth, with little prospect of receiving any reinforcements, or even the despatch of a relief column to help us reach safety. My main worry is Bannus. At the moment he is a brigand chief, but if he manages to raise a force large enough to take us on, then there's every chance that he will try to present himself to the Judaeans as the *mashiah*. Only the latest in a long line of claimants to the title, of course. But if he has an army of thousands, equipped with Parthian armour and weapons, then he's going to look very credible to his people. If the rising spreads beyond this area, the whole of Judaea could join in the revolt.'

'Oh, sure!' Macro laughed. 'Come now, Cato, that's just not going to happen.'

'Why not?'

'They wouldn't stand a chance. A bunch of farmers and sheep herders up against professional soldiers? Auxiliary troops admittedly, but still good enough to scare a bunch of peasants back into line. Even if they were thinking of rebelling, they'd know that the Syrian legions were on their doorstep. No amount of rebels would be a match for the legions. As far as the local people are concerned, the moment they get stroppy the legions are going to jump on them and kick them into the dust.'

'Yes,' Cato conceded. 'I'm sure they believe that . . .'

'But?'

'I'm not sure.' Cato frowned. 'Ever since we arrived in the province, I've had the feeling that this place is like a tinderbox. One spark could set it off, and Judaea will go up in flames. If Narcissus' suspicions about Longinus turn out to be well founded, then there won't be any help coming from Syria.'

'Yes. But Bannus and his boys don't know that.'

'Don't they?' Cato looked up. 'I wonder.'

Macro snorted. 'What are you suggesting now? That Longinus has cut a deal with some hairy-arsed barbarian bandit hiding out in the hills? Don't you think that's a bit far-fetched?'

'Not really.' Cato stared back wearily. 'If Bannus knows that Longinus will refuse to march, then he can launch his revolt in the knowledge that he will only be opposed by auxiliary troops. That's quite an incentive to action. And Longinus gets his revolt, and justifies his request for reinforcements. Both men get what they want. Coincidence? I think not.'

Macro was silent for a moment. 'A Roman general bargaining with a common bandit . . . that's quite a nasty thought.'

'No. Just straightforward politics.'

'But how would Longinus have got in touch with Bannus?'

'He must have some kind of intermediary. A dangerous job to be sure, but at the right price I'm sure Longinus could have found someone to approach Bannus and make him aware of the Governor's offer not to intervene. All that would remain to be done would be to provoke the locals into rebellion, and Scrofa and Postumus have been doing their best to fan the flames of discontent.'

'Fan the flames of discontent?' Macro smiled. 'You've not been writing poetry on the sly, have you?'

'Just a figure of speech. Be serious, Macro.' Cato concentrated again before continuing. 'The thing is, I'm not sure that Longinus is fully aware of what he is unleashing. It seems that Bannus has also been in contact with the Parthians. So far I imagine they've promised him some weapons for his men. Of course, they'd never own up to it. Anything they can do to undermine Roman power in the east is all part of the great game as far as they are concerned. However, if they got wind of an arrangement between Bannus and Longinus then they'd instantly see the chance to settle the score with Rome once and for all. The moment Longinus leaves Syria with the eastern legions at his back, Parthia would have a free hand in the region. If they moved quickly enough they could overrun Syria, Armenia, Judaea, Nabataea, and maybe even Egypt.' Cato's eyes widened as the implications of what he had said hit home. 'Egypt! If they took that then they'd have a stranglehold on the grain that feeds Rome. They could force peace on Rome on almost any terms they wanted.'

'Hold on there!' Macro raised his hand. 'You're jumping at shadows. Remember, Cato, you're just outlining possibilities.' He smiled. 'There's still a long way to go before the situation represents any serious threat to Rome.'

Cato couldn't help smiling at the way his thoughts had run away with him. Nevertheless, there was a great deal at stake, and not much time to try to do something about it. Until confirmation of Macro's command of the Second Illyrian came through there was little action that the two officers could take except observing events as they unfolded. 'All right then, I'll keep my mind focused on the here and now.'

'For the moment, that would be best.'

Cato nodded, and then reached for a spare linen tunic and pulled it over his head. 'What about you? How did your patrol go with Postumus?'

'Aside from a bit of a punch-up with some desert raiders, I was let in on the little arrangement that Scrofa and most of his officers are operating with the caravans from Nabataea. It's a protection racket, pure and simple. They blackmail the caravan owners into making a payment or let the desert raiders carve them up and make off with their goods. Seems that almost everyone out here is doing business with the enemy. Postumus was kind enough to offer to cut me into the deal. Needless to say I politely declined, tempting as it was.'

'I bet.'

'Anyway, I've had an idea about how we can put an end to their arrangement. But I have to take command here first, and I'll need to get in touch with some people in Petra.'

Cato looked at him curiously. 'Hardly been here a few days and you're already in with the locals. I'm impressed.'

'So you should be.' Macro looked pleased with himself. 'Best idea I've had in ages, and I can't wait to see the raiders' faces when they try it on with the next caravan to pass through our turf.'

Macro carried on smiling and Cato finally gave in. 'All right. I'm intrigued. Now would you care to explain your brilliant plan?'

There was a loud knock at the door, and Cato shook his head in frustration as he called out, 'Come in!'

The door swung open and one of Scrofa's clerks stepped inside, stiffened his back and saluted. 'The prefect sends his compliments, and requires you at headquarters immediately.'

Cato and Macro exchanged a look before the latter responded. 'All right. We're coming. Soon as Centurion Cato has finished dressing.'

'Sir?' The clerk frowned. 'I was only instructed to summon you.'

'Well now you have. And I'll deal with it from here. Now go.'

'Yes, sir.' The clerk saluted and turned to leave.

Cato turned to Macro. 'What's up?'

'I imagine Scrofa wants to resolve a confrontation I had with Centurion Postumus while we were out on patrol.'

Cato did not hide his exasperation. 'Oh, fine. Another fight?'

'Kind of. Postumus was pretty keen to even the score once we got back to the fort. Looks like he's trying to do it through official channels. Anyway, I want you there as a witness.'

Prefect Scrofa was not alone when Macro and Cato were shown into his office in the headquarters building. Postumus was standing behind and to one side of his commanding officer. They turned to look at the new arrivals.

'Not before time,' Scrofa said harshly. 'And what is Centurion Cato doing here? I didn't send for him.'

'He's here on my say-so,' Macro responded. 'And we came as soon as we got your message.'

Scrofa stared at him for a moment. 'While I am prefect of the Second Illyrian, I am the senior officer in this fort. Therefore you will defer to me, Centurion Macro.'

'Fair enough, *sir*.' Macro bowed his head. 'While you are the prefect, that is.'

Scrofa clamped his lips together for a moment to bite

back on the flash of rage Macro's reply had prompted. Then he drew a deep breath and continued. 'Very well. I think we understand each other well enough. But I wouldn't feel too smug about replacing me if I were you. Not for a while yet.'

Centurion Postumus coughed. 'Sir, I am sure Centurion Macro is perfectly aware of the correct protocol in this situation. If we might move on to more important issues?'

'What?' Scrofa turned irritably to look up at his sub-ordinate. 'Oh, very well then.' He turned back to Macro and composed himself before continuing in a more formal tone. 'Centurion Postumus has filed an official complaint about your conduct in relation to an event which occurred while you were on patrol.'

Macro could not help smiling briefly at the prefect's pompous manner and ponderous choice of words.

'What's so amusing, Centurion?'

'Nothing, sir.'

'Well, then, it seems that you struck Centurion Postumus in front of his men, and then seized control of his auxiliaries and ordered them to attack some Arabs who were obstructing the progress of a caravan.'

'Obstructing the progress . . .' Macro had to laugh. 'That's a fine use of words, Centurion Postumus. If you mean that I took command of your men to rescue the caravan from desert raiders, because you refused to, then yes I agree with your allegation.'

Postumus tilted his chin up as he replied. 'Whatever the words, the fact of the matter is that I was the lawful commander of those men, and therefore you illegally usurped my authority.'

'Because you were failing in your lawful duty.' Macro stabbed a finger at him. 'You would have sat on your arse and let those raiders completely destroy the caravan.'

'That is immaterial to the charge I'm bringing against you.'

'Immaterial?' Macro scoffed. 'It is the reason why I was forced to take command.'

'What about striking a fellow officer?' Scrofa interrupted, leaning forward across his desk. 'What about that, eh? Do you deny it?'

'No. And I'd do the same again,' Macro snapped back. 'And with good cause. Now, if you really want to try to make something of this, I will be happy to submit to a proper military tribunal, back in Rome. It's my right to insist on that, as you well know. So then, Prefect, do you wish to continue with this foolishness?'

Scrofa glared back at him for a moment and then eased himself back into his chair and forced a smile. 'I don't think it is really necessary, Centurion Macro. I merely wanted you to be aware of the disciplinary charges that could be brought against you. Rightly or wrongly, you have committed a serious breach of the military code and it is within my powers to bring you before a military tribunal. I could, if I wanted, carry that out in a summary manner, here in this fort.'

'You could,' Macro conceded. 'But I could equally insist on my right to appeal to the Emperor for a hearing back in Rome. And I think we both know how that might turn out, given the way you are running things here.'

It was an impasse, and all the men in the office knew it. For a while no one spoke, until Scrofa continued in the same placating manner.

'There is no need for that, Centurion. Let's just agree that you have acted unacceptably, and that you will give me your word not to commit any further such breaches of the military code. After all, we would not wish you to assume command of this cohort with such an unpleasant disagreement hanging in the air, would we?' He smiled. 'Now then, I can understand that you might see things a little differently from us. You and Centurion Cato have only just arrived in the province and haven't yet acclimatised to the way things are done here. I think Centurion Postumus might accept that he was a trifle brusque in the manner in which he introduced you to the little arrangement we have concerning the caravans that pass through the territory policed by the Second Illyrian.'

'That's putting it mildly, sir.'

Scrofa laughed lightly, and then licked his lips. 'I can assure you that there is nothing unusual about the situation. It's common practice amongst units stationed on this frontier.'

'That's not my understanding, sir,' Cato intervened. 'We were told that this, er, arrangement of yours has only been running since Centurion Postumus arrived at the fort.'

'It must have lapsed,' Postumus explained. 'I merely resurrected it, for the benefit of the officers of the cohort.'

'Naturally.' Macro smiled. 'Very altruistic of you, Centurion Postumus.'

'If I can serve our interests as well as the Emperor's, then I can see no harm in the situation.'

'I doubt the Nabataean caravan cartels see it like that.'

Postumus shrugged. 'They go along with it.'

'They have no choice in the matter,' Macro pointed out. 'They pay up, or you leave them to the mercy of the desert raiders. Somehow, I doubt that is helping cement good relations between the Nabataean kingdom and Rome. If I were a suspicious man I might well think that you were deliberately undermining our relationship with Nabataea, as you are undermining the stability of the territory around this fort.'

A look of alarm flitted across the prefect's face and he glanced quickly to his subordinate for reassurance before he responded. 'What are you implying, Centurion Macro?'

'I'm simply saying that an outsider might think that

you are deliberately trying to undermine the security of this region.'

Cato, standing at Macro's shoulder, winced. His friend was in danger of exposing the true nature of their mission to the area. He shuffled on his feet, and gently tapped Macro's heel with the toe of his boot. Macro shot a withering glance at him, and then turned back to the prefect as Scrofa gave a false laugh.

'And what possible reason could I have for doing that?'

'We'll see. Soon enough,' Macro responded quietly. 'Once I assume command here, I'll make damn sure that I expose your games, and then maybe I'll dispense a little summary justice of my own.'

'Ah, that reminds me.' Scrofa leaned back in his chair and folded his hands together and interlaced his fingers. 'Perhaps I should have mentioned it earlier. A message from Caesarea arrived at the fort shortly before this meeting. That guide of yours, Symeon, brought it. Apparently the procurator decided that your request for confirmation of the appointment is outside his jurisdiction. So he's referred the matter to the Governor of Syria. I'm afraid that means it'll be a while yet before we receive any news. In the meantime, I'm obliged to remain in command of the cohort.' He feigned an apologetic expression. 'I assure you that I regret the delay as much as you do. But I am confident that Cassius Longinus will give the matter his immediate attention.'

'I'm sure he will,' Macro murmured. 'Where is Symeon? I want to speak to him.'

'I'm keeping him on the strength – we can use a good guide. But there's no need for you to see him. Not for a while at least. Meanwhile, I'm confining you two to your quarters.'

'Confining us to quarters? You mean you're placing us under arrest?'

'Not yet. But I will do if you give me any further trouble. Centurion Postumus will arrange for a guard to be set up outside your quarters.'

Macro turned to Cato and smiled grimly. 'I came here to become prefect of the cohort. Now it seems I'm to be a prisoner of the cohort instead.'

'You're dismissed,' Scrofa concluded curtly. 'Postumus, see to it that they are escorted to their quarters and kept there.'

Postumus smirked. 'With pleasure, sir.'

CHAPTER SEVENTEEN

Postumus had them moved into one room to make guarding the two centurions easier. Macro endured the first few days of confinement well enough, while Cato sat at the window and gazed out over the fort towards the battlements, fretting at their inactivity. Around them the men went about their duties in a routine and unhurried manner. The watches changed at regular intervals. The men rose at first light, drilled for an hour and then took their morning meal. Afterwards there was more training until the sun had risen high enough to beat down on the fort and the surrounding desert in a searing glare. Then the soldiers retreated to the shade and only the sentries remained, patrolling the walls in the sweltering heat that even the lizards avoided as they clung to the rough plaster in patches of shadow and waited for the stifling midday hours to pass.

Their guards brought them food twice a day, and readily responded to any further requests for food and drink since the two centurions were technically not under arrest. Yet. The window of their shared room overlooked a narrow alley between the headquarters and the single storey hospital building. Cato had considered dropping down into the alley as a means of escaping their confinement, but then reflected that there was no point. What could it achieve? They couldn't leave the fort, and any attempt at escaping from their room would simply give Scrofa the excuse to have them placed in a cell. So Cato sat at his window and reflected on the wider situation with a growing sense of frustration, and anxiety.

The days passed, and every so often a patrol left the fort and marched off in a faint haze of dust that was visible for a while over the squat towers of the main gate.

Then, after several days, as the men of the cohort took shelter from the midday sun, Cato was sitting at the window, hands propping up his chin as he stared towards the distant foothills that marked the entrance to the wadi leading down to Heshaba.

'Centurion . . .' A voice called out softly.

Cato started, turned back to Macro. 'Did you hear that?' But his friend was sound asleep on his bed.

'Centurion, down here.'

Cato cautiously leaned out of the window, and saw Symeon pressed against the wall directly beneath him. The guide waved a hand and smiled a greeting.

'Symeon! What are you doing here?'

'Sh! Not so loud. I need to speak to you. Here, take this.' The guide took aim and tossed a loop of rope up to

Cato, who caught it awkwardly and then glanced inside the room to find something secure to tie the end to. He turned back to Symeon.

'Wait.' Cato crossed the room to Macro and shook his friend's shoulder. Macro stirred, then sat up with a jerk, eyes blinking.

'What? What's going on?'

'Quiet,' Cato said softly and pressed the end of the rope into Macro's hand. 'Take that.'

Macro frowned as he looked down at the rope. 'What's this for?'

'Just take the strain and help me.' Cato crossed back to the window and nodded down into the alley, before grasping the rope and bracing one foot against the window sill. Macro felt the line tighten and grasped it in his powerful hands as someone scrambled up the wall outside, grunting with the effort. A moment later fingers groped over the sill and Symeon heaved himself up and over, and rolled on to the floor.

'What the hell are you doing here?' Macro asked in surprise.

Symeon looked past Macro towards the door with an alarmed expression, and pressed a finger to his lips. 'Speak softly, Centurion.'

'Sorry,' Macro whispered. He clasped the guide's arm. 'Good to see you! A welcome change from the ugly mugs who bring our food. What's going on?'

'I tried to speak to you when I brought the

procurator's message back to the fort, but the prefect sent me out the next day to visit the local villages, to try to get news of Bannus. I only returned this morning.'

'Well?' Cato raised his eyebrows. 'What's the mood in the villages?'

'Not good. I travelled on foot, claiming I was on my way back from the festival in Jerusalem, but they were still suspicious of me. The ones who did talk were reluctant to tell me too much, but it seems that Bannus is growing in strength every day. They say he has promised to prove to them that the Romans can be beaten. There are even rumours that he is a prophet. Or maybe the *mashiah*. And that he has powerful allies who will help sweep the Romans from our lands and cast them into the sea.'

Cato nodded bleakly. Then it was as he had feared and time was running out. The area around Bushir might break out in open revolt at any moment. He looked closely at the guide. 'Why did you return to the fort?'

'Centurion Florianus sent me. He told me to watch out for you. Make sure you were safe.'

'Safe?' Macro chuckled and gestured round the room. 'We're as safe as it gets cooped up in here. No chance of us coming to any grief. Unless this revolt actually happens. Then we're all for the chop, of course. Symeon, excuse us a moment.' He turned to Cato and continued in Latin. 'It's time we brought that scroll into play.'

Cato's hand instinctively went to the leather thong round his neck, as Symeon watched them curiously. 'I'm not sure. Once we use it then our true role out here is exposed. Longinus will know the score, and rush to hide his tracks.'

'If he is plotting something,' Macro reminded him. 'Look here, Cato. If he is plotting against the Emperor, then what's the worst that can happen? He plays clean and drops any plots he might be hatching against Claudius. He spends the rest of his days looking over his shoulder and acting the model citizen. The longer we wait to use that document, the less chance we have of keeping a lid on all the trouble that is brewing around here. We need to take command of the Second Illyrian now. We have to find Bannus and crush him before he has sufficient strength to destroy us and spread his rebellion. So what if we lose the chance to prove Longinus is a traitor, if indeed he really is? What's that against the prospect of letting Judaea flare up into open rebellion if we do nothing?'

Cato looked at his friend for a moment while he weighed up Macro's argument. It made sense, even if they failed to carry out Narcissus' original design to expose a conspiracy at the heart of the eastern empire. He nodded. 'All right then. How should we proceed? We can't just show Scrofa the scroll and tell him to move over.'

'Why not?'

'Supposing he decides to ignore it. Hush it up by having us thrown into a cell, and destroying the document?'

'Then we have to make sure there are witnesses at the time.'

'How? If we're in here, or in his office, he will have us on our own.'

'True.' Macro frowned, then clicked his fingers. 'All right, so we tell the other officers to join us for the meeting.'

'How?' Cato waved towards the door. 'We're being guarded.'

Macro nodded towards Symeon. 'He can do it. He can get a message to the others. The ones that Scrofa hasn't bought out. Starting with Parmenion.'

'It might work,' Cato conceded. 'But how would Parmenion know when to act?'

'Symeon can keep watch. We tell the guards that we want to speak with Scrofa. The moment we are escorted from here, or Scrofa leaves his quarters and heads this way, Symeon fetches Parmenion and the others to join us. As soon as the witnesses turn up we produce the imperial authority and kick Scrofa out on his arse.'

'Very well.' Cato stroked his chin. 'But once you have control of the cohort, what happens next?'

'We have to deal with Bannus.'

'Then we're going to need more men.'

'Maybe. We can ask Longinus for reinforcements.'

'Why should he give us any help?'

Macro smiled. 'Trust me. He'll be more than willing. If Longinus knows that Narcissus is watching him closely he'll need to prove his loyalty to the Emperor any way he can.'

'True. But what we need are light troops, cavalry, that sort of thing. Not heavy infantry. Longinus should be able to spare some auxiliary forces. In any case, I think we might be able to call on help from other quarters.' Cato turned back to Symeon, who had been sitting impatiently, watching the two centurions talking in their tongue. Cato switched back to Greek. 'Symeon, you told us you that you have family in Nabataea? At Petra?'

'That's right.'

'And they run mercenary caravan escorts down into Arabia?'

Symeon nodded.

'Is there any chance that we might persuade them to help us against Bannus? After all, his men have been raiding the caravans between here and the Decapolis.'

Symeon sucked at his teeth. 'Difficult to say. Thanks to Prefect Scrofa the Second Illyrian has earned itself quite a lot of bad feeling down in Petra. I'd imagine there're plenty of merchants down there who'd be quite happy to see the garrison at Bushir destroyed.'

'Then we have to win back their friendship.'

'Easier said than done.' Symeon smiled. 'Words will not be enough, Centurion. They will need to be persuaded by deeds.'

'Ah!' Macro rubbed his hands together. 'Then they can have their deeds. I've had an idea about those caravans, and how we can persuade the desert raiders to give them a wide berth from now on.'

Cato and Symeon turned to him expectantly.

'Not so fast.' Macro grinned. 'Before that we have to deal with Prefect Scrofa. It's time we had a word with him. I'll have one of the guards send our message. But first, I need you to do something for us, Symeon. Listen here.' Macro lowered his voice and began to outline his plan.

Postumus rapped on the door and from inside the prefect called out, 'Enter!'

The latch lifted and the door swung open to admit Postumus, and behind him Centurions Macro and Cato. The three men approached the prefect's desk and Postumus halted some distance before it, the others following his lead. Postumus patted his sword meaningfully as he met his superior's gaze.

'Macro and Cato, as requested, sir.'

'Thank you, Postumus.'

'There are four men just outside the door, sir.'

'I'm confident they will not be needed, but, er, there's no need to send them away now they're here. Very well then, gentlemen.' Scrofa drew himself up in his chair. 'What is the meaning of this? What is this information that is so important for me to hear?'

Macro glanced at Cato and the latter gave the slightest nod towards the window that overlooked the courtyard.

But outside the fort continued to bask quietly in the heat. Macro coughed to clear his throat. 'We need to talk about the situation.'

'What situation?'

'The, uh, situation pertaining to the command of this cohort.' Macro spoke with slow deliberation, as if weighing each word that he uttered as he played for time. 'That is to say, the correct protocol for the, uh, transmission of authority from the present command to the assumption of command by, er, me. As it were . . . sir.'

'Get to the point, Centurion,' Scrofa snapped irritably, and jabbed his finger towards Macro. 'You'd better not be wasting my time. So spit it out. Tell me what's so bloody important that I must interrupt my afternoon rest to hear it, or I'll send you back to your quarters at once.'

'Very well.' Macro nodded. 'I'll tell you. Your command of this cohort is forfeit. Your confinement of me and my fellow officer is illegal. The protection racket you operate on the caravan route passing through your territory is a corruption of your duty, responsibility and rank, for which I will bring charges against you and Centurion Postumus in due course, once I have assumed command of the Second Illyrian.' Macro paused to draw breath and glanced out of the window and down into the courtyard. His heart sank a little as he saw that it was still empty. He took a breath and continued. 'Moreover, I will add to the charges against you that through deliberate provocation you endangered the security of the Roman province of Judaea and—'

'Be quiet!' Scrofa interrupted. 'This is pointless!'

'I haven't finished saying my piece.'

'Oh yes you have. Centurion Postumus!'

'Sir?'

'Take these two back to their quarters. And don't let them waste my time again.'

'Yes sir.'

Cato had been listening to the exchange with growing concern. He felt his pulse quicken as he knew it was time to act. His hand was being forced, but there was no alternative.

'Wait a moment!'

He reached for the leather thong round his neck and pulled the scroll case from under his tunic.

'What's that?' asked Scrofa.

Cato pulled the cap off the case and pulled out the roll of parchment inside. He approached the desk, unrolling the document, and spread it out across the flat surface, the right way up for the prefect to read it. Scrofa's gaze went straight to the imperial seal and he glanced up at Cato with a surprised expression. Cato tapped the document.

'Read it, sir.'

As the prefect glanced over the authority that Narcissus had penned for Macro and Cato, Centurion Postumus edged closer and moved round to read over his superior's shoulder.

Cato waited until Scrofa had finished examining the document before he broke the silence.

'As you can see, we have been empowered to act in the Emperor's name in all areas of Roman jurisdiction within the provinces of Judaea and Syria. We now invoke our powers under the terms of this authority.' Cato took a breath and continued. 'You are hereby stripped of your command of the Second Illyrian cohort.'

Scrofa looked up from the document with a shocked expression. 'You can't speak to me like that!'

Macro grinned as he leaned forward over the table and tapped the parchment. 'Read it again, sunshine. We can do what we like. Anything we like. Now, citizen, I'd be grateful if you got out of my chair. I've got work to do. A lot of work, thanks to you.'

Scrofa wasn't listening. His eyes scanned the document again, as if he could somehow change its meaning. Centurion Postumus straightened up and laughed. 'This document is obviously a forgery. Something you two have cooked up while you've been stewing in your quarters.'

'Forgery?' Macro shook his head and smiled. 'Look at the seal, Postumus. You should recognise it well enough.'

'I still say it's a fake. If you two think this is going to change things here, then you are bigger fools than I thought.'

The sound of voices drifted up from the courtyard.

Cato hurried over to the window and glanced down. Behind Symeon, Centurion Parmenion and a handful of other officers were walking through the archway. Symeon looked up and waved. More men were emerging from the alley between the barracks opposite, heading towards the prefect's quarters. Cato felt the knotted tension in the pit of his stomach begin to ease. He turned back, crossed to the desk and picked up the document. Before Scrofa or Postumus could react he returned to the window and held it out so all below could see it.

'Gentlemen! By order of Emperor Claudius and the Senate of Rome, Prefect Scrofa has been removed from command of the Second Illyrian Cohort. As of this instant he has been replaced by Centurion Macro. Now, I'd be greatly obliged if you joined us in Prefect Macro's quarters immediately.'

After the briefest of hesitation, and to Cato's great relief, the officers shuffled towards the main entrance to the building, just below the window. As he turned back into the room Scrofa stared at him, thunderstruck. Postumus instantly grasped the implications of what was happening and a look of fear flitted across his handsome features, making Macro laugh. He could not contain the light-hearted thrill at having turned the tables on Scrofa and his subordinate. He leaned towards Postumus and tapped him on the chest. 'Now who's the bigger fool, eh?'

CHAPTER EIGHTEEN

The main hall in the headquarters building was filled with all the officers who could be spared from their duties. Every other centurion, decurion, optio and standard bearer of the Second Illyrian cohort was present. The senior officers occupied the chairs and benches in the centre of the floor, while the rest crowded along the sides of the room. The men spoke in muted tones and from the doorway Cato noted their anxious expressions. Barely an hour had passed since he and Macro had presented the imperial authority to Scrofa and removed him from command. Since then all sorts of rumours had swept round the fort as the officers were summoned to headquarters. Cato smiled. They would find out exactly what had happened soon enough. The question was, would they accept it? Scrofa and Postumus had been conducted to a cell in the basement of the building and placed under a reliable section of men selected by Centurion Parmenion. They were not going to be allowed to make any case against the new commander, and they were not going to be given access to any of the officers or men of the cohort. Macro had been quite firm about that when he had given Parmenion his orders.

'What's the mood like?' Macro asked quietly from behind him. Cato turned and saw his friend a few paces down the corridor, out of sight of any of the men in the hall. Macro held the imperial authority in his hand, rolled up, and was tapping it against his thigh.

Cato raised his hand to cover his mouth and muttered back, 'Curious rather than disgruntled. I doubt there will be any effective opposition to the takeover.'

'Right.' Macro shrugged his shoulders and drew a deep breath. 'Better get it over with. You can announce me.'

Cato stepped inside the room and stood to attention as he called out, 'Commanding officer present!'

At once every tongue was stilled and nail-soled boots scraped over the flagstones as the officers rose to their feet and stood with their backs as straight as javelin shafts. When all was still and silent Macro strode into the hall and marched to the raised dais at the end of the hall from where the cohort's commander habitually addressed his men. He noted the surprised expressions in some of the faces looking towards him and fought the urge to smile, and thus betray the nervousness which had seized him. The dryness in his mouth and the sick feeling in the pit of his stomach were new sensations to him, and Macro was shocked to realise that he was afraid. This was worse than facing a horde of barbarians armed to the teeth and screaming for his blood. He had grown used to commanding a century of legionaries, or a scratch force of native levies, but these men, these officers, were hardened professionals like himself and Cato, and they would know the standard to judge him by.

He swallowed, cleared his throat and began. 'At ease!'

The sound echoed through the hall, as loud as if it had been bellowed across a parade-ground. But the men instantly relaxed their posture and the senior officers resumed their seats. Then all of them looked to him expectantly.

'Right then, I know there's been some wild speculation so I'll make the situation clear at the outset. Gaius Scrofa has been removed from command of the cohort. Lucius Postumus is no longer centurion and adjutant. That post has been filled by Centurion Cato, while I am now the prefect. This action has been taken according to the power conferred on me by Emperor Claudius.' Macro raised the document, and unrolled it, holding it up so that all the men gathered in the hall could clearly see the imperial seal fixed to the bottom of the parchment. 'This authority is without limit. Any doubters are welcome to have a look at it once the briefing is over.'

Macro lowered the scroll to the table and stared at his officers for a moment before continuing. 'As your new commander, I'd like to begin by saying that this cohort is one of the most piss-poor excuses for a unit that I have ever come across.'

Cato winced. Macro had only just taken command of the Second Illyrian and already he was going all out to offend the very men he needed to win over.

'That's right.' Macro glared at them. 'Piss-poor is what I said. And the reason for it has very little to do with all the men out there. They're as good as I could expect a cohort to be, posted out here at the arse-end of the Empire. But you lot?' Macro shook his head. 'You're supposed to lead by example. And what a fine bloody example you've been setting. Half of you have been busy toadying up to Scrofa, so you could take your cut of the racket he was running. The rest of you are little better. Take Centurion Parmenion there. He knew what was going on. What did he do about it? Nothing. Just sat on his arse and pretended to ignore it.'

Cato's gaze flickered towards the old officer and he saw Parmenion lower his head and stare at the ground between his boots.

'Well then, gentlemen,' Macro continued, crossing his arms as he glared at them like a disappointed school-teacher. 'Things are going to change here at Bushir. I'll tell you why. It has nothing to do with the corrupt little scams you were so happy to take part in, though we'll be dealing with that soon enough, as you'll see. No, the reason why things must change is that we are on the verge of witnessing our very own native uprising. All thanks to the former prefect's winning ways with the local villagers, and your willingness to go along with him. As we sit here, Bannus is busy building up a formidable band of followers. What you may not know is that, in all likelihood, he has cut a deal with our Parthian friends who have promised to arm his men.'

This information caused a ripple of anxious murmurs to flow through the officers.

'Quiet!' Macro shouted. 'I did not give you permission to talk.'

The men instantly stilled their tongues and Macro nodded with satisfaction. He was beginning to enjoy this feeling of command. 'That's more like it. So, now I think you can see the scale of the challenge that faces us. It's up to the Second Illyrian to find and destroy Bannus and his brigands, before they grow strong enough to come and destroy us. At the same time, I'll brook no more harsh treatment of the local people. We've already done enough to drive them into Bannus' arms. It's probably too late to win them back on to our side, so we're not going to try. What we will not do is provoke them any further. From now on any man, or officer, who wades into the locals will share the fate of trooper Canthus. You all know what happened to him. Now you know what will happen to any others who follow his example. Make sure your men are aware of that. I'll accept no excuses. We cannot afford to act as recruiting officers for Bannus.'

There were some brief disapproving murmurs and

some officers exchanged disgruntled looks, until they realised that the new prefect was glaring at them and fell silent again.

'I am aware that none of what I have said so far is likely to have gone down well with you, gentlemen. That's just tough on all of us. The question is, what are we going to do about it? For my part, I'm going to let you start with a clean slate. There will be no further mention of your corruption or dereliction of duty. So you all have a chance to prove yourselves worthy. You didn't win promotion to the rank you hold today by taking bribes, so all of you must have been good soldiers at one time. That time has come again. In the next few days you're all going to do some hard soldiering. Your men will need the best from you and I will not hesitate to break any slackers back to the ranks. You will all lead by example. You will all lead from the front.' He paused to make sure that they had got the point. 'Right, well, that's it. You know what I require from you. There's plenty of work to do, and you'll receive your orders as soon as possible. One last thing. I noticed that the standard of the Second Illyrian carries no awards. That's going to change. I have never left a unit without adding at least one medallion to its standard. The same applies to this cohort. So let's all do something we can be proud of, eh? Dismiss!'

The officers rose smartly to their feet and stiffened to attention, saluted, and then began to shuffle towards the doors leading from the hall. Macro watched them carefully as they dispersed, pleased with his performance and feeling that he had put some iron back into his new subordinates. As the last of them left the hall Cato came over.

'How did you think that went?' Macro asked.

'Blunt, but to the point.'

Macro frowned. 'I'm trying to kick them into shape, Cato, not win first fucking prize in a rhetoric competition.'

'Oh, in that case, it went rather well.' Cato smiled. 'No, seriously, I think that was just what they needed to hear. I like the touch about the standard. Is that true?'

'No. Load of bollocks. But it's the kind of thing that goes down well with the glory-hunters. And that's just what we'll need if Bannus decides to take the cohort on.'

'I suppose so.' Cato conceded. 'And what exactly are your first orders, sir?'

Macro was a little taken aback by Cato's last word, but realised immediately that it was right that his friend should defer to his new rank of prefect. It reminded him of the days when they had served in the Second Legion in Germany and Britain, when Cato had been his optio, and then a junior centurion in the same cohort. Much had happened since then, and Macro had grown used to treating the younger officer as an equal in most respects, but now the situation had changed and the professional in him accepted it as a necessity.

'Has Symeon left for Petra yet?'

'Just before the briefing.'

'Did you make quite sure he understood exactly what I wanted him to do?'

'Yes, sir.'

'Good.' Macro nodded. 'Right then, it's time we made preparations for dealing with Bannus, and those desert raiders.'

The new prefect of the Second Illyrian made his presence felt at once. Barracks inspections were made at dawn and dusk and every infringement of rules punished. The men were drilled for twice as long as they had been before, and after each century had completed the regulation manoeuvres it was quick-marched round the fort until noon, when at last the men were permitted to fall out, panting and thirsty in the merciless glare of the sun. The officers quickly recovered their professional edge and worked themselves as hard as their men. There were no further patrols into the surrounding villages. Instead the mounted scouts observed the locals from a discreet distance and concentrated their efforts on searching for signs of Bannus and his men. The geography of the region was such that a large force could hide in the caves of the numerous wadis that cut through the landscape. Their only weakness was a dependence on food and water which they needed to draw from the settlements. Whenever the scouts saw a suspicious-looking party of men arrive at a village they attempted to follow them as they left, but always their prey managed to vanish into the clefts of the mountains that rose up on the east shore of the Dead Sea.

Prefect Macro concentrated his efforts on selecting a detachment for a special task. He needed the pick of the cohort's mounted men, and he needed their riding ability to be matched by their skill with a bow. As in many of the cohorts in the region, there was already a small number of men able to use the powerful compound bow favoured by eastern warriors. These Macro kept practising at the hastily erected target range outside the fort, until they were proficient at a variety of distances.

At the same time the cohort's carpenter had been tasked with designing a saddle frame equipped to carry lightweight burdens which could be jettisoned in an instant. Other men worked hard to create dummy bundles of fabrics to be loaded on to the saddle frames. All was ready by the end of the tenth day after Macro had taken control of the cohort. The same evening a message arrived from Petra. Symeon had done as he had been asked and contacted the merchants whose caravan Macro had saved. They had agreed to meet Macro and his men at the same place as before – the Nabataean way station – at dusk in three days' time.

On the night before Macro and his small force of men left Fort Bushir, he had a final meal with Cato in the dining room of the prefect's quarters. Scrofa, no doubt flush with the money he had extorted from the caravan cartels, had decorated his accommodation lavishly and the walls of the dining room were alive with hunting scenes set in lush green landscapes so utterly different from the barren wilderness stretching out around the fort that it made both men long for the kinder, temperate landscapes of Italy or even Britain.

'Say what you like about Scrofa,' Macro said, as he chewed on a chunk of roast kid, 'at least he knew how to live.'

'So I can see.' Cato was still billeted in the same room at headquarters where he and Macro had been confined. Given the mood of some of the officers it had been felt necessary for Cato to remain at the administrative heart of the cohort and keep watch on their activities. At the same time, he made sure that the two prisoners in the cell did not speak to anyone. Scrofa and Postumus were sent their food, and had their slops bucket emptied, rinsed and returned, and that was all the contact with others that Cato allowed them.

'How is Scrofa coping?' Macro asked.

'Well enough. He's stopped playing the outraged innocent and given up demanding to be set free. What worries me is that the other officers keep asking what is going to happen to the pair of them.'

'Just tell them that those two will be treated fairly and given a proper hearing once we've settled things with Bannus. If that doesn't work then tell them to keep their mouths shut and their noses out of things that don't concern them, unless they want to share the same cell.'

'Do you think they will be given a hearing?'

'Not if Narcissus has anything to do with it. They'll be interrogated to reveal anything they know about Longinus, and then disposed of. You know what Narcissus is like, Cato.'

'I know. But there's no concrete proof that Longinus is plotting anything at the moment. All the evidence we have is pretty weak. In which case Scrofa and Postumus might not be guilty of plotting against the Emperor.'

'Maybe not,' Macro agreed, helping himself to another mouthful of goat. 'But they're certainly guilty of screwing up the situation here on the frontier. Even if we get through this business with Bannus, it's going to take years to mend our relations with the locals. If we ever do.'

Cato nodded thoughtfully, and then replied, 'Perhaps the Emperor should consider abandoning Judaea.'

Macro nearly choked. 'Abandon the province! Why on earth do that?'

'I've seen nothing here that makes me think the Judaeans will ever accept their place in the Empire. They're just too different.'

'Bollocks!' Macro spluttered, and a gobbet of gristle narrowly missed Cato's ear as it sailed over the dining couch. 'Judaea is like any other province. A bit wild and untamed at first, but give it enough time and we'll make them see things our way. They'll embrace the Roman way of life whether they like it or not.'

'You think so? When was Judaea annexed? In the age of Pompey. That's over a hundred years ago. And the Judaeans are still as intractable as ever. They cling to their religious practices as if they were the only things that mattered.'

'The situation could be improved if we could only persuade them to worship our gods, or at least get them to worship our gods alongside theirs,' Macro concluded impatiently.

'Well we won't manage it. So perhaps we should give up the idea of including Judaea in the empire, or we should crush them, destroy their religion and everyone who holds to it.'

'That might do it,' Macro agreed.

Cato stared at him. 'I was being ironic.'

'Ironic? Really?' Macro shook his head and tore off another strip of meat. 'Well I bloody well wasn't. If we're going to make the Empire safe, then we have to make sure that we control this region. Not Parthia. These people will have to accept Roman rule, and like it, or else.'

Cato did not respond. He could see the limitations of Macro's approach all too clearly. As in most provinces the Romans had tried to establish a ruling class to collect tax and administer the law in Judaea. Only this time the common people had seen through those who claimed to be their natural leaders. That's why Judaea had become such a sore in the flesh of the empire. The Judaeans could not be left to run their own affairs on Roman lines because their religion would not permit it. So Rome would have to intervene in order to enforce Roman rule. Unfortunately, she would have to intervene on such a scale that the cost of maintaining Judaea was far in excess of the tax revenue that could be generated, unless the people were squeezed for every coin available, and that in turn would only lead to revolt sooner or later. More troops would be required to restore and then maintain order. More taxes would be required to pay for the enlarged garrisons needed to keep the Judaeans in line, and so the vicious cycle of rebellion and repression would continue on and on. No wonder Centurion Parmenion was so weary and worn out after his years of service in the province.

With a sudden flash of insight Cato realised that this was why Parmenion had been prepared to surrender Canthus to the mob. The soldier had outraged the villagers, and Parmenion had faced a stark choice. If he had tried to defend his man and ignore the offence, or protect him, he would have provoked a riot and simply added to the friction that was remorselessly tearing Judaea to pieces. Canthus' death had served notice on Roman and Judaean alike that no one was above the law. If only such a principle became general policy then some accommodation between Rome and Judaea was possible.

Macro was watching him closely. 'Don't go soft on me now, lad. Whatever you may think are the rights and wrongs of the situation, we have a mission to carry through. About the hardest job that's ever landed on our plate. I can't afford to have you thinking about where all this goes. Keep your mind on what we must do. Worry about the other stuff later on, when it's safe to do it.' He chuckled. 'And if you're still alive to do it.'

Cato smiled back. 'I'll try.'

'Good. I'll feel a lot better knowing that you are keeping an eye on things in the fort while I'm gone.'

'Is it really necessary to do this?'

'We need all the friends we can get in this region. If my plan works out, then it should go a long way towards restoring relations with the Nabataeans. That bastard Scrofa has a lot to answer for.'

'Yes,' Cato replied quietly. 'Are you sure you want me to stay here?'

'Absolutely. Most of the officers are good men, but we've seen how easily they can be led from the straight and narrow. There's a few of them I still don't trust. They'll need watching. The last thing we need right now is some kind of counter-coup to restore Scrofa to command. That would be a bloody disaster. So you have to stay here, Cato. Anyway, I'd thought you'd be glad to have a cohort of your own to command.'

'It's a big responsibility, and given the doubtful loyalty of some of the men I'd rather be out in the field.'

'I'm sure you would.' Macro's expression grew serious. 'But not this time, Cato. You'll be in charge here. You know who you can rely on. Parmenion may be getting on, but he's a tough old bird, and straight as they come. If anything happens to me, then you must take care of Bannus. Don't go tear-arsing around the desert looking for revenge, understand?'

'It's all right, sir. I know what needs to be done. Just make sure you don't take any unnecessary risks.'

'Me?' Macro touched his chest with a hurt expression. 'Take risks? I wouldn't know where to begin.'

Dawn was breaking across the desert as the gates of the fort creaked open and Macro led two squadrons of mounted men through the gatehouse. Despite the heat of the day, the nights were cold, and Cato was wrapped in a thick cloak as he stood in the tower above the gate and watched his friend ride out on to the stony track that led away from Fort Bushir, south and east towards the great trade route along which the caravans brought precious goods into the Empire from lands no Roman had ever seen. The first rays of the sun burnished the sand a fiery red and the dust kicked up by the horses' hooves rose up in swirling puffs of orange. Long shadows flickered across the plateau like ripples of dark water and Cato could not help feeling a sense of foreboding as he watched the small column head out to do battle with the desert raiders. When he could no longer distinguish Macro from the rest of the men, Cato turned away and gazed down at the long barrack blocks stretching away from the wall. The fort was his to command, and to his surprise he found that beneath all his concern about his aptitude for his new role, he was secretly delighted to be the acting commander of the Second Illyrian cohort.

CHAPTER NINETEEN

'They're here, sir,' the decurion said softly.

Macro blinked his eyes open. It was already daylight and the man was silhouetted against a pale blue sky. They had ridden hard for two days after leaving the fort and last night they had eaten and slept well. Macro had insisted on it, firmly believing the old military adage that men fight well on a full stomach. Around him there were the faint sounds of the first of his men waking. Macro threw back his cover and rose stiffly, stretching his shoulders until he felt the joints crack.

'Ahhh! That's better!' He rolled his head and turned to the decurion. 'Right then, show me.'

The two officers strode across the courtyard of the Nabataean way station and climbed the ladder to the lookout tower built over the gateway. As Macro stood beside the decurion, the latter scanned the dimly lit land to the south of the fort and then pointed. 'Over there, sir.'

Macro squinted, and saw a faint flicker of movement, no more than a thin scattering of dots on the desert horizon; the head of the caravan he was waiting for, emerging from a depression in the plateau. 'I see them.'

As the two officers watched, the first riders led out a long train of pack animals as the caravan crawled along the trade route towards the way station. When it drew closer Macro saw a small party of horsemen detach from the vanguard and start trotting towards them. He turned to the decurion.

'Get our men on their feet. I want them ready the moment the caravan reaches us.'

'Yes, sir.' The decurion saluted, climbed down into the courtyard and began shouting out his orders, rousing the last of the grumbling sleepers from their blankets. Macro stared down into the gloomy courtyard and nodded his approval as the decurion kicked some of the slower men into life. No laggard was going to show up the Roman army when those horsemen arrived. The auxiliaries hurriedly pulled on their boots and took up their weapons as the horsemen drew near. Due to the nature of the task ahead they had left their helmets, shields and spears at the fort, but they still wore chain mail over their padded linen tunics and had cavalry swords strapped to their sides. Finally, from each man's shoulders hung a bow case, from which protruded the curved end of an unstrung compound bow and the feathered flights of the arrows. When Macro climbed down from the tower to inspect them he saw that they had all brushed off the fog of sleep and were alert and ready for action.

The sound of hooves drumming across the parched ground drew their gaze towards the arched entrance and a moment later the dark silhouettes of mounted men filled the gate as they swiftly reined in and walked their horses inside. There were four of them, swathed in dark robes and turbans with veils that covered all but their dark eyes. For an instant all was still, and just the heavy bellows breath of the horses and the stamping of their hooves echoed round the station. Then, as his eyes adjusted to the gloom, the leader of the horsemen plucked his veil aside and smiled at Macro.

'Symeon!' Macro grinned back. 'Good to see you. Is everything ready?'

'Yes, Prefect.' Symeon slid down from his saddle and gestured to his followers to do the same. 'All is ready. The caravan is just behind us. It did not take me very long to find a cartel willing to have their revenge on these desert raiders.'

'Good.' Macro was relieved. His plan had hinged on Symeon's persuading some Nabataeans to turn on their tormentors of the last few months. Now all the elements had fallen into place and the trap was ready to be sprung.

Symeon stood aside and gestured to the men with him. They had also lifted their veils and Macro saw two older men, perhaps the same age as Symeon, but darker-skinned. Symeon gestured to them. 'Tabor and Adul, my former business partners. Tabor also represents the cartel that owns this caravan. He and Adul still provide escorts for caravans from Arabia up to Petra. They're travelling with the caravan because they want to extend their escort business towards Syria. Frankly, I suspect they've just come for the fight.' Symeon grinned, and then placed his hand on the shoulder of the last man, who was younger. He was shorter than Symeon, though powerfully built with fierce black eyes and a neatly trimmed moustache. Symeon gazed at him proudly. 'This is Murad, my adopted son. He took over my share of the business when I returned to Judaea. Tough as they come.'

He spoke to the young man in Aramaic and Murad grinned, revealing fine white teeth. He drew his finger across his throat and made a guttural hiss to emphasise the gesture.

'I think I might just get on well with you, young Murad.' Macro smiled back, then bowed his head in greeting to Symeon's companions. 'Did you bring spare robes?'

'Of course, Centurion. They're on the lead camels.'

Macro clapped him on the shoulder. 'Fine work! Now, all that remains is to give those raiders the surprise of their lives.'

The sun was directly overhead and the glare shimmered off the sand and rock of the landscape so that Macro had to squint to avoid hurting his eyes. He rode at the head of the caravan with Symeon and his companions. Behind them came the long column of camels and horses, laden with goods. Macro's men, dressed in the robes of caravan herders, walked along the route, leading small strings of their charges. Their weapons were concealed under the fake baggage on their animals' saddles, the bows strung and ready to use. The real herders had remained in the way station, resting in the shadows of the walls as they waited for word from Symeon. It would have looked suspicious if the caravan had been attended by more men than usual. Macro stared back over his shoulder for a moment. To his eyes the caravan looked just as it did when it approached the way station at first light. With luck, then, it might fool the desert raiders as well. Only a handful of escorts rode out on the flanks and Macro hoped that such easy-looking prey would prove too tempting for the raiders to resist.

After a brief halt, while the auxiliaries had dressed in the robes that Symeon and his men had provided, the caravan had continued past the way station, heading towards Philadelphia. The hours had passed slowly as the laden pack animals and camels trudged on with their endless hypnotic sway. Fearing that an enemy scout might overhear Roman voices, Macro had forbidden any conversation, and the caravan edged forward with only the soft shuffling of camels' feet and the crunch of hooves and boots on the ancient trade route to break the silence of the desert.

Then Murad muttered something and there was a brief exchange of muted conversation between him and Symeon before the latter turned to Macro.

'Centurion, we are being watched, but don't look round. Murad saw a man in the dunes a moment ago. Just for an instant, then he disappeared.'

'One of our raider friends?' Macro responded softly.

'Almost certainly. They will attack us soon, I think.'

Macro glanced ahead and saw that the route would shortly take them through a shallow depression, with a stony rise of ground on each side. A good place for an ambush, he realised. Symeon was right.

'I'll pass the word to my men to make ready.'

Symeon nodded gently as Macro reined in his horse and dismounted unhurriedly. He bent over and made to examine the front leg of his mount. The first of his men came alongside.

'Prepare yourself,' Macro said in a low voice. 'They're close by.'

He repeated the warning as more men passed, then straightened up, as if satisfied by his inspection of the horse's leg, and walked the beast back down the line of the caravan, alerting the rest of his men, until he reached the last string of animals. Then he remounted and trotted back to the front of the caravan, just as it began to enter the depression. The sun's glare reflected off the slopes and made the air even more hot and oppressive as the loose column of men and beasts passed between the two low ridges. Macro kept glancing from side to side as discreetly as he could, the anticipation creating the familiar dryness in his mouth as he waited for the raiders to launch their attack. But nothing broke the quiet as the caravan slowly made its way along the depression. As the sun crept down from its zenith the ground began to rise up gently to rejoin the plateau beyond. Macro felt the tension in his muscles ease and he turned to Symeon, intending to comment sourly on the failure of the desert raiders to snap up this easy prize. Instead he froze, staring over Symeon's head towards the ridge on their right. All along it, figures of men, swathed in black, leaped into view as they urged their camels down on the caravan. At first there was no sound, but as soon as they started down the slope, in a scattered wave, they broke the silence with a shrill ululating cry. Macro's men responded in the manner he had told them to. They took to their heels, drawing their disguised mounts after them. Those at the front and rear of the column seemed to react more slowly, apparently struggling with their beasts as they tried to lead them away from the raiders.

Symeon shouted an order and the thin screen of escorts galloped towards him as Macro drew his sword and held it low, so that the raiders would not see that it was not the curved blade favoured by the other riders. Around him Tabor, Adul and Murad cast aside their outer robes and snatched out their swords, polished blades glittering in the bright sunlight. They raised them overhead and shook them in a brazen challenge at the raiders charging down the slope towards the caravan. As the other escorts reined in and formed up in a mass behind their leaders Symeon turned to Macro with a wild grin of excitement.

'Now we shall see the character of these raiders! Hah!' He snatched out his sword and, like the others, shouted his war cry and challenge to the enemy.

True to their orders, the auxiliaries at the centre of the caravan melted away, leading their horses up the opposite slope as they scrambled over the loose sand and stones. At the sight of the men fleeing from the scene without a fight the raiders urged their mounts on and their shrill cries intensified. The men at each end of the caravan held firm, still jerking the reins of their mounts as if they were having great trouble controlling them. The desert raiders ignored them, as Macro had hoped, concentrating their attentions on the easy pickings at the centre of the caravan. As soon as they reached the first camels they leaped from their saddles and ran to the sides of the loaded animals to search for the richest pickings. Macro waited until most of the raiders had dismounted to seize their spoils and only a handful remained on the backs of their camels, swords drawn as they kept watch on the mounted escort around him. This was the moment that he had been waiting for and he filled his lungs and bellowed the order out to his men.

'Second Illyrian! To arms!'

The shout echoed down the depression, and all the men who had been fleeing up the slope suddenly stopped, casting aside their loose robes. They hurriedly discarded the fake bales of goods from their saddle horns and scrambled on to the backs of their mounts, wheeling them round as they snatched out their swords and charged for the confused tangle of men and animals at the centre of the caravan, letting out loud cries of their own. These were taken up by the men at each end of the caravan, suddenly in full command of their horses as they prepared them to attack the desert raiders.

'Come on!' Macro shouted to Symeon, jabbing his sword at the raiders. 'Get 'em!'

With a savage cry Symeon gave the command to his men and the trap was closed. Over the head of his horse Macro could see the dark-robed figures of the raiders freeze for a moment as they perceived the danger hurtling towards them from three sides. The quickest to react threw themselves back into their saddles and yanked the reins round towards the ridge they had descended from only moments before. Others, more foolhardy, still frantically struggled with the abandoned pack animals in the caravan, desperate to snatch some prizes away before they escaped. As Macro and the escorts raced down the side of the caravan they began to fan out into a line that angled away from the caravan so that they might catch the raiders in the flank before they escaped. They were close now and Macro saw the nearest raider turn towards him for an instant before whipping the rump of his mount with frantic desperation. Macro raised the tip of his sword and angled his horse towards the man, but before he could strike there was a blur of flying robes at his side and Murad surged past, teeth clenched in a triumphant grimace as he swept in between Macro and his man. There was a dazzling flash as Murad's blade scythed through the air and cut deeply into the angle between the man's head and shoulder. With a shrill cry, the raider spasmed and seemed to leap off his saddle, blood spurting from his terrible wound as he tumbled to the ground.

Murad cried out in triumph, laughed madly in Macro's direction, then turned away and spurred his horse towards the next raider. The centurion felt a flicker of anger at the way the man had interposed himself between Macro and his intended target, but then he smiled grimly. It did not matter. Let Murad have his moment of victory. The important thing was to make sure that the trap succeeded as completely as possible. Macro straightened up in his saddle, craning his neck as he tried to get an overview of the fight. There was a dense haze of dust at the centre of the caravan as dark figures hacked away at each other. Raiders were still abandoning the caravan and fleeing back up the slope, chased by Symeon's escorts and the Roman cavalry. Macro spurred his horse on, jerking the reins so that he was galloping straight for the swirling mêlée at the heart of the fighting. A riderless camel galloped out in front of him, and Macro swerved round it just in time as his horse let out a panicked neigh. Then he was in a swirl of dust, blinking as he felt the grit on his face and in his eyes.

Another camel loomed up, this time with a rider on it, and the man's eyes widened as he saw Macro hurtling towards him. His curved blade swept out and up, and then the flank of Macro's horse crashed into the side of his camel and he slashed down at Macro's head. Macro, with the sour scent of the raider's mount filling his nostrils, only just had time to throw out his blade to deflect the blow that would have cleaved his skull to the jaw. The parry jarred his arm; then, as the man was recovering his sword for another slashing attack, Macro leaned in and thrust the point into the man's side, under his raised sword arm. The blow was truly aimed, and crunched through cloth, flesh and ribs before it tore through the man's lungs and pierced his heart. He folded slightly towards Macro before the blade dropped from his limp fingers. He grunted a curse, then flopped forward over his saddle horns.

Macro had no time to react as another shape emerged from the dust and charged at him, the straight-edged blade sweeping round in an arc towards him. He ducked it easily, shouting, 'Bloody fool! I'm Roman.'

The man's eyes opened wide, in panic, and he snatched his sword arm back and wheeled his mount away before the prefect could recognise him.

'Bastard!' Macro grunted, then glanced round and made for another likely-looking target as a raider flitted past, heading for the safety of the slope. Another raider rode by and then another as the sounds of fighting abruptly faded. Macro drew a breath and cried out, 'They're running! Sheathe swords! Draw bows!'

He turned his horse and trotted out of the cloud of dust. Ahead of him the slope was covered with raiders fleeing for their lives, hotly pursued by Symeon and his men. Then, as more mounted auxiliaries emerged from the dust, he waved his sword at the fleeing enemy.

'Finish them! Finish 'em off!'

The men exchanged their swords, drew their bows and spurred their mounts in pursuit of the loping camels of the desert raiders. The horses were faster and quickly made ground on the raiders as Macro's men fitted arrows to their bowstrings. At the last moment, they reined in, took aim and let fly. The range was short and the men had all been selected for their skill with the weapon. Across the slope the raiders tumbled from their saddles; some, wounded, clutched grimly to their reins and rode on until a second or third arrow thudded into them. Only a scant handful reached the crest of the hill and vanished from sight, Symeon's men and the auxiliaries still in pursuit.

Macro sheathed his sword and slumped forward in his saddle, suddenly aware how quiet and still the world around him seemed. His heartbeat was racing and the blood pounded through his head. His throat felt dry and gritty and once again he was aware how hot this cursed land was in daylight hours. The dust was settling across the floor of the depression and the caravans pack animals stood patiently, waiting to be herded into line once more to continue the journey. At their feet were the bodies of those who had fallen in the brief fight. The sand about them was patched with slick dark stains of blood. A few of Macro's men moved from body to body, finishing off the enemy wounded with a swift strike to their throats so that they flailed desperately for an instant before they lost consciousness and died. Only a handful of Romans had been injured, and none killed, and Macro gave orders for a shelter to be erected to save them from the discomfort of the blazing sunshine. A rider was sent back to the way station to bring a cart for the wounded, and summon the herders. Most would live. One man's knee had been shattered by a sword blow and it was clear that his soldiering days were over, even if the surgeon back at the fort managed to save the leg.

As the auxiliaries re-formed the caravan, Macro waited for the rest of his men and the escorts to return. Over the next hour they came back singly or in small groups, tired but jubilant at their swift and thorough defeat of the desert raiders. The men returned to the caravan and rested their horses before feeding and watering them. Symeon and his friends were the last to appear, riding down from the ridge in a compact group, talking and laughing as they came. Adul's arm had been slashed and roughly bound up, but such was his good humour that he seemed oblivious of the pain. Symeon grinned as he rode up to Macro.

'Took your time,' Macro said evenly.

Symeon ignored the brusque tone and spoke excitedly. 'We got them all, save one, as you ordered. We cut off his nose and set him back on a horse. I told him to warn the other desert people of the fate that awaits those who dare to raid the caravan route passing through the Roman province.'

'Good. Let's hope they heed the warning.'

Tabor edged his horse towards Macro and, with a bow of his head, began speaking in a formal tone.

'Wait! Wait!' Macro raised his hands, and turned to Symeon. 'What's he going on about?'

Symeon translated. 'Tabor wants to thank you for this victory over the vermin that have been preying on the route to Decapolis. He says that he, and every caravan cartel in Petra, are in your debt, Centurion.'

'Oh, right.' Macro shrugged wearily. 'Tell him . . .' He frowned, not sure how to respond in the right manner. 'Tell him that from now on the Roman garrison at Bushir will guarantee the safety of this route. There'll be no more corruption. I hope that goes some way to restoring good relations between Rome and Nabataea.'

Tabor nodded graciously as Symeon relayed Macro's words, then spoke again.

'Remember, Centurion, if ever you need his help, you have but to send a message to the house of Tabor in Petra.'

'Yes. Good. Very kind of him.' Macro gestured to the caravan. 'Meanwhile, we'll see this lot as far as

Philadelphia. After that I'm heading back to the fort. Now we've got this flank covered it's time to concentrate on Bannus.' He looked at Symeon. 'I won't pretend that it's going to be easy. There'll be more fighting ahead. I could use a good man like you. Interested?'

'Centurion, it would be an honour.'

Once the wounded had been loaded into a covered cart which set off for Bushir under the protection of one of Macro's squadrons, the rest of the caravan continued along the route to Philadelphia. The journey took a further two days, in which time there was no further sign of any raiders. The desert stretched out in desolate serenity and the men and beasts of the caravan seemed to be the only living things that moved across that wasteland. Towards dusk on the second day they reached a village by a small oasis. Children raced out from amongst the houses at the caravan's approach and ran alongside the leading horse-men. Macro and his men had shed their disguise and the Roman soldiers caused some curiosity amongst the child-ren as they pointed at the men and chattered excitedly. The caravan camped beside the oasis for the night and Symeon's companions bought some sheep from a villager, slaughtered them and roasted the carcasses so that they might share a farewell feast with their Roman friends. As the flames died and the men, well fed and tired, rolled up in their blankets to sleep, Macro lay on his back, arms tucked behind his head, gazing up into the star-sprinkled heavens. A sliver of moon hung in the sky away to the west, in the direction of Bushir, and it reminded him of the glitter of the curved blade Murad had drawn on the day of the ambush. The juxtaposition of the image and the way it hovered over the distant fort of the Second Illyrian brought back all the difficulties that he and Cato faced in the coming days, and suddenly he wanted to quit this peaceful oasis, and be back at the fort, where his men needed him.

Next morning the Roman horsemen mounted up just as dawn glimmered along the horizon. The air was chilly and the breath of men and beasts puffed into the half-light. Macro clasped arms with Symeon.

'I'll see you back at the fort.' He spoke in a questioning tone and Symeon nodded.

'I will be there, Centurion. You have my word.'

'Good. We need men like you by our side.'

There was no more to be said. Macro waved his men forward and the column of horsemen moved out of the oasis, back down the route towards Fort Bushir. Three days later they approached the long lines of the fort's ramparts and Macro noticed that there were more men on the walls than the usual number of sentries on duty. As the column rode up to the gates they swung inwards and there was Cato, standing to one side, waiting for them. The lift in Macro's spirits was abruptly quelled as he saw the strained and weary expression on his friend's face. He knew at once that something had happened.

CHAPTER TWENTY

'Postumus has escaped.'

Cato and Macro were standing to one side of the gateway as the exhausted horsemen rode into the fort, covered in dust. A few of them still wore bloodstained strips of linen from the superficial wounds they had suffered in the fight with the desert raiders.

'What happened?' Macro asked.

'Postumus fell ill. Or at least he seemed to. He collapsed and started vomiting and foaming at the mouth. The duty officer had him moved to the hospital block. By the time I was informed the next morning Postumus had gone. So had one of the horses. He must have got out using one of the sally ports. But they were all locked from the inside when I checked them.'

'Well he didn't ride a horse over the wall, so someone had to open a gate for him.'

'I'd guess that some of our officers are still loyal to Scrofa,' Cato said quietly.

'Scrofa? Is he still here?'

'Yes. Under extra guard now.'

'How long ago was this?'

'The day after you left.'

Macro stared at Cato and they shared an instant understanding of the situation. 'Shit,' Macro said softly. 'You know where he's gone, don't you?'

'I'd guess north to Syria. To find Longinus.'

'Where else?' Macro thumped his fist against his thigh. 'If he rode hard he could reach the Governor in four, maybe five, days. So we can assume that Longinus knows that I've taken command here. That means he knows about the imperial authority and what that implies.'

Cato nodded. 'What do you think he'll do?'

'How the fuck should I know?' Macro suddenly felt more tired than ever with news of this latest setback. He needed a rest. A bath and a rest, he decided. Then he shook off the feeling. He was the prefect in charge of this cohort and could not afford to let his guard down while he was in command. Too much rested on it. Macro rubbed his cheek and looked at Cato. 'What do you think?'

'Once Longinus knows the score he's going to want to see us. To find how much we know, and how much we suspect. My guess is that he's already sent a messenger to summon us to report to him in Antioch.'

'The messenger could arrive at any moment.'

'Yes.'

'Shit.' Macro shook his head. 'One bloody thing after another. We can't spare the time to see Longinus. Not with Bannus on the loose.'

'But we can't ignore the summons. Not without throwing into question the Governor's authority.'

'Our authority overrides his, surely?'

'Of course it does. But I doubt that Narcissus would look favourably on us if we openly confronted the most powerful man outside Rome. What if we precipitated the plot that we were sent out here to investigate and prevent? If Longinus does demand that we report to him, I think we'd better go.'

'Maybe,' Macro responded, before he snatched at one hopeful possibility. 'Of course, Postumus might have fallen foul of some of Bannus' men. After all, he'd have been riding alone. I doubt that any of the villages round here would offer him a safe shelter for the night.'

'If Bannus had taken him I think we'd already know about it. We'd have had a ransom demand, or Bannus would have made some kind of example of him, so that we'd know the fate of any Romans who fall into his hands. Anyway, this is wishful thinking. We should assume that he got through to Longinus. And we should assume that we'll know his response to the news any time.'

'Unless the messenger is taken by Bannus.'

'Now you're clutching at straws.' A smile flickered on Cato's lips before the serious expression returned. 'Let's assume that the summons gets through. In that case we'd better make sure that the cohort will be safe in our absence.'

'Safe?'

'As in making sure that Scrofa doesn't resume control. I think we'd better take him with us. Leave Parmenion as acting prefect.'

'Can we trust him?'

'I think so. One other thing. If we are ordered to report to Longinus I think we should have a little talk with Scrofa as soon as possible and find out how far he is implicated in any plot, and see what he can tell us about Longinus.'

'All right then, we'll speak to Scrofa,' Macro agreed. 'But after I've bathed and rested. I'm too tired to think straight at the moment.'

Cato frowned for a moment in disappointment, before he realised that his friend was truly exhausted. 'Very well, sir. I'll see to it that you're not disturbed.'

Macro smiled and patted Cato on the arm. 'Thanks.'

He turned away and started walking stiffly towards his quarters, then paused and looked back at Cato. 'Any developments on the Bannus front?'

'Nothing, whilst you've been gone, sir. In fact there's been no sighting of the brigands at all. I've got mounted patrols out looking for them. They're due back tomorrow. If there's any news of Bannus, we'll find out then.'

Macro nodded wearily, and headed off towards the comforts of the prefect's quarters.

* * *

That night, Macro and Cato descended the narrow stairs to the cells that lay under one corner of the headquarters building. Cato carried a torch to light their path and it glimmered on the rough stonework as the two officers made their way along the line of cells. Only one was occupied, at the far end, guarded by two auxiliaries. They were sitting on stools, playing dice, and looking up as Macro and Cato approached they jumped up and stood to attention.

'At ease,' Cato said and nodded to the door. 'How's the prisoner?'

'Quiet enough, sir. He's given up demanding better food and quarters.'

'Good.' Cato nodded. 'Because he's not getting them. Open the door. We need to speak to him.'

'Yes, sir.' The guard eased the heavy iron bolt back, lifted the latch and pulled the door open. Cato ducked his head under the lintel and entered the cell, with Macro close behind him. Inside was a small but neat chamber with a bed on either side, and a slop bucket by the door. High up was a grated window which let in light during the day. Now that it was dark a single oil lamp gleamed from a bracket above the bed on which Scrofa lay, reading a scroll by the meagre illumination of the wavering flame. He sat up as they entered, eyeing them warily.

'What do you want?'

Macro smiled. 'Just a little chat, Scrofa. That's all.' He

sat down on the bed opposite Scrofa. Cato placed his torch in a wall bracket and sat down next to Macro. Scrofa's gaze flickered nervously from one to the other.

'No need for alarm, Scrofa,' said Macro. 'We just need to talk.'

'For now,' Cato added darkly.

'That'll do,' Macro said with a look of irritation. 'There's no need to frighten the man.'

'I'm not frightened.' Scrofa tried to sound brave as he glared at Cato. 'I'm not scared of you, boy.'

Cato leaned forward and grasped the handle of his dagger, causing Scrofa to flinch back with a gasp of panic.

Macro clamped a hand on his friend's arm. 'Easy there!'

For a moment the three men were still: Cato leaning forward with a look of intense, cruel anger, Scrofa staring back anxiously and Macro struggling to keep a straight face at the act his friend was putting on. Or at least, he assumed that Cato was putting it on. He cleared his throat.

'It's time you were honest with us, Scrofa.'

'Honest?'

'Yes. I'm sure that it doesn't come easily to you, but you will need to tell us the truth. Now then, in view of the rather unusual manner in which I replaced you as prefect of the Second Illyrian, and given that the Emperor's personal authority was attached to the document you saw, I assume that you have realised who Cato and I are working for.'

'Narcissus.'

'The very man. As you know full well, it is his job to look after the security of the Emperor. So you'll understand why he is a little perturbed by the turn of events out here in the east. Particularly concerning the unwholesome ambitions of your friend, Cassius Longinus – the Governor of Syria.'

Scrofa's brow furrowed in confusion. 'What do you mean?'

'Come now, don't play us for fools, Scrofa. Longinus is deliberately stirring things up here in the east so that he can call on the reinforcements to strengthen his army. That's why he chose you to command the Second Illyrian. It was your job to stir up the local villagers, turn them into rebels. I have to admit, you've done a fine job. Not only that, but you've managed to earn yourself a tidy fortune in the process, thanks to that protection racket you and Postumus set up. Of course, pissing the Nabataeans off must have been something of a bonus for Longinus.' Macro hardened his tone. 'The way things are looking, there's going to be quite a bit of blood spilt over the next few days, months even. Thanks to you and Postumus. You might think about that.'

Scrofa shook his head. 'I've no idea what you are talking about.'

'Liar!' Cato spat at him. 'You're in on the conspiracy! Right up to your stinking neck.'

'No! I have nothing to do with any plot.'

'Bollocks!' said Macro. 'You were appointed to command the Second Illyrian by Longinus. He instructed you to provoke a revolt, and you've done all that he asked, and more. Don't even try to deny it.'

'But it's not true!' Scrofa whined. 'He never gave me such orders. I swear it. It was just supposed to be a temporary appointment. He said it would look good on my record. He said it would help me to find a command of a good cohort in a better posting.'

'I don't believe you,' Macro responded. 'You told me you were waiting for the appointment to be made permanent.'

'I lied! I was only supposed to be the prefect until the man he really wanted for the job could be approved.'

'And who was that?' Cato interrupted. 'Who did he really want for the post?'

Scrofa looked surprised. 'Postumus. Who else?'

Macro and Cato looked at each other, and Macro frowned. 'Postumus? That doesn't make sense. The Governor could have appointed an acting prefect on his own initiative. If he wanted Postumus why didn't he just appoint him from the outset? You're lying, Scrofa.'

'No. Why should I?'

'To protect your scrawny neck. Postumus was just a junior centurion. He'd never have made the cut for promotion to take command of an auxiliary cohort. Why are you lying to us?'

'I'm not,' Scrofa said deliberately.

'Yes. You. Are. And it's time you realised that we're no longer playing games here. The stakes are too high for that. Now, you will tell us everything we want to know and you will tell us the truth. I need to make sure you understand how serious we are. Cato, pass me your dagger.'

Cato pulled the blade from its scabbard with a tinny rasp and offered it to his friend.

'Thanks.' Macro smiled, then launched himself across the gap between the beds and with his spare hand grabbed Scrofa by the neck and slammed his head against the rough stone wall of the cell. 'Take his hand, Cato!'

Cato took an instant to recover from his friend's sudden assault on the prisoner. Then he leaned across, grabbed Scrofa's left hand in both of his and held it tightly as Scrofa tried to wrench it back. Macro punched the pommel of the dagger into Scrofa's kidneys and the man gasped in agony.

'No more struggling, understand?' Macro snarled, and waited until the other nodded quickly. Then Macro turned back to Cato. 'Hold his hand flat on the wall there, where he can see it. Good. Now then, Scrofa. This is your last chance. You'll give me the answers I'm looking for, or I'll cut your thumbs off. To start with . . .'

Macro held the man's neck in a tight grip with one hand while he took a firm hold of the dagger handle with the other, and lowered the edge of the broad blade towards the joint between Scrofa's thumb and the rest of his hand. Scrofa's eyes widened in terror and there was a thin keening noise in his throat before he managed to speak.

'I swear to you – on my life – I know nothing! Nothing! I swear it!'

Macro lifted the blade away from the thumb and stared at Scrofa for a moment, scrutinising his expression. Then he clicked his tongue. 'Sorry, I'm not convinced. Let's see if the loss of one thumb can provide a little incentive. Cato, hold him still.'

Macro lowered the blade so that the edge pressed into Scrofa's flesh. The skin split and there was a small trickle of blood as Scrofa cried out. Macro tensed his arm, ready to begin sawing through the muscle and bone.

'Wait,' said Cato. 'I think he's telling the truth.'

'He's lying.'

'I'm not!' Scrofa whimpered.

'Quiet, you!' Macro shook him by the neck and turned back to Cato. 'What makes you think this worm's telling the truth?'

'He's been set up by Longinus. Think about it. Longinus is shrewd enough to cover his tracks when he can. So he sends Postumus down here to stir things up. Only the previous prefect proved to be something of an obstacle to Longinus' plans. So Postumus removed him. Scrofa is appointed to fill the gap.'

'Why him?'

'Because Longinus knows that he's vain and greedy.

I'll bet you that Longinus told Scrofa that he had been picked for the post because he showed promise. I'd guess that he also encouraged him to go in hard on the locals to prove his mettle. Is that right?'

Scrofa nodded.

'So Scrofa turns up here and Postumus plays him like a lyre. He encourages him to lay into the locals, involves him in the caravan protection racket and is the real commander of the cohort. And if Longinus' plans don't work out in the end then the blame can be laid at Scrofa's door. Longinus blames any rebellion on Scrofa and has him done away with before he can be returned to Rome to be investigated. Longinus is seen to act decisively, the Judaeans get to see us punish the man held responsible for causing the trouble, and Postumus is still in position. Longinus wins every way.' Cato shook his head. 'We've got the wrong man. Postumus is the one. He's Longinus' agent.'

Macro considered this for a moment, then he released Scrofa and backed away, sitting down on the opposite bed again. He handed the dagger back to Cato and nodded towards Scrofa. 'So what do we do with him?'

'Keep him safe. In case he's needed as a witness against Longinus.' Cato glanced at Scrofa. 'You understand what's going on? You've been used all along.'

'No.' Scrofa frowned. 'Longinus is my patron. My friend.'

'Some friend!' Macro snorted and looked at Cato

with a wry expression. 'Oh, you can see why he chose this beauty for the job.'

'Quite.' Cato kept his eyes on Scrofa. 'Listen, you know what I said makes sense. You don't owe Longinus any loyalty. The man has betrayed you. As he'll betray the Emperor and Rome if he gets the chance. You have to help us.'

'Help you?' Scrofa smiled. 'Why should I help you? Until you two turned up I was raking it in. Now, you've taken my command from me, thrown me in this cell and assaulted me. Why should I help you?'

'He's got a point,' said Macro.

'He's got no choice,' Cato replied. 'Longinus can't afford to let him live. He already knows too much, even if he can't quite believe it yet. He helps us or he's dead. Simple as that.'

Scrofa looked at Cato and chewed his lip. 'You're serious about Longinus?'

'Very.'

Scrofa shook his head. 'I don't believe it.'

No one spoke for a moment and Macro could not help feeling sorry for the wretched man on the other bed. Scrofa had no place in the army. He was lazy, corrupt, incompetent and too stupid to see beyond his dreams of glory. But he might yet be of some use. He might yet redeem himself. Macro stood up.

'Come on, Cato. Let's go. There's nothing more we can learn here.'

Just before the door was closed on him Scrofa called out, 'Please, let me out of this cell. I swear I'll cause no trouble.'

Macro considered the request for a moment, then shook his head. 'Sorry. I need every measure of the men's loyalty and obedience. If they see you walking around the fort it'll only confuse the issue. You have to stay here, out of sight and out of mind. For a while at least. It's for the best.'

He closed the door behind him and slipped the bolt back into place as Scrofa started screaming abuse after him. Macro turned to the guards. 'If he keeps that up for long, you have my permission to go in there and belt him.'

'Yes, sir. Thank you, sir.'

'Cato, let's go.'

As they climbed the steps back up to the ground floor of the headquarters building Cato spoke. 'What now? Longinus has been alerted that Narcissus is on to him. He'll be on his guard, and even now I'd bet he's already covering his tracks. We won't have much evidence to offer against him. Only what little Scrofa can offer, that he was ordered to go in hard. The worst that Narcissus can accuse Longinus of will be wilful incompetence.'

'That's enough to justify removing him from office.'

'Maybe.'

'So what do we do now?'

'I'd suggest we concentrate our efforts on Bannus. If

we can destroy him, we can restore peace to the area. If we do that, then we can scupper any attempt by Longinus to request reinforcements.'

Macro nodded. 'Bannus it is, then. We'll talk about it in the morning. I'm so bloody tired I can hardly think straight. You'd better get a good night's sleep too, Cato. Somehow I think there's going to be no chance of a decent rest for some time. Better make the most of it now.'

'Yes, sir.'

Macro smiled faintly. 'It's all right. You can drop the formalities when there's no one else around.'

Cato nodded over Macro's shoulder, and the latter turned and saw the dim shape of one of the standard bearers guarding the entrance to the headquarters shrine where the cohort's standards were kept. Macro cleared his throat and spoke formally. 'Very well, Centurion. I'm turning in. See you in the morning.'

'Yes, sir.' Cato saluted and Macro turned away and walked wearily out of the building, and headed back to his quarters. When he reached the prefect's house he slumped on his bed and closed his eyes for a moment. Then he was asleep. So deeply asleep that he did not notice Scrofa's manservant remove his boots, lift his legs on to the bed and cover him over with a thick blanket. As the manservant closed the door behind him, the first deep rumbling notes of Macro's snoring echoed round the room.

* * *

It was late in the morning when Macro woke up and he cursed himself for not having left orders to be roused at dawn. He was not going to let himself be tarred with the same brush as the previous prefect. Macro prided himself on living as hard as the men he commanded and so he emerged from his quarters in a dark mood and ignored the meal that the manservant had set out in the dining room. Cato was waiting for him in the prefect's office at headquarters, leaning over a map spread out across the desk as Macro strode in.

'Why the hell didn't somebody wake me?'

'You're the prefect. It's not our place to disturb you without orders, unless there's an emergency. Besides, you needed the rest.'

'I'll decide what I need, all right?'

'Yes, sir.'

'Right.' Macro glanced at the map. 'Already planning the next move against Bannus?'

'Just thinking, sir.'

'Oh? That sounds dangerous.' He smiled at Cato's hurt expression. 'When you start thinking, then I know we're in for trouble, Cato. Go on then.'

Cato refocused his mind and stared down at the map. He gestured towards the string of villages that lay between Bushir and the River Jordan. 'Given the size of the force we believe Bannus has at his back, he is going to need access to food and water. He doesn't have anything to fear from our patrols now. The only danger is that we might corner him with the whole cohort and bring him to battle. My guess is that he's come out of the hills and he's camped somewhere close to one of these villages.'

'How can you be sure?'

'I can't. Not until the mounted patrols return. I ordered them to scout the area. They should be back today. Then we'll find out if they've located Bannus. If they have, then you'll need to find some way of forcing him into battle, sir.'

'That won't be easy,' mused Macro. 'You know how these brigands fight. Hit and run. That's their style. So? Any bright ideas?'

Cato tilted his head to one side and considered. Before he could respond there was a clatter of boots outside the room and then a sharp knock on the door.

'Come!'

An orderly stepped through the door and saluted. 'Report from the duty centurion, sir.'

'Well?'

'There's a column of horsemen approaching the fort, sir.'

'That'll be one of your patrols then, Cato. Good. With a bit of luck they'll have some news of Bannus.'

The orderly interrupted. 'Begging your pardon, sir, but the horsemen are approaching from the north. The patrols went to the west.'

'From the north, eh?' Macro began to get a sinking feeling in his stomach. He turned to Cato. 'We'd better have a look.'

By the time they reached the fortified tower above the northern gate, the small column of horsemen was less than a mile from the fort and flashes of light glittered off polished armour and helmets. Cato shaded his eyes and squinted and made out the flicker of a scarlet standard above the head of the column. 'They're ours. Roman, at least.'

'Then what the hell are they doing returning from that direction?' Macro asked.

'I don't know.'

They watched in silence as the horsemen drew closer, and then at last the identity of the party became clear and Cato felt a chill in his guts as they reined in and walked their horses the short distance to the gates. At the head of the column rode a man in a burnished breastplate. He wore a red cloak and an ornate silvered helmet with a red plume.

'It's the Governor,' Macro muttered. 'Bloody Longinus in the flesh.'

'Yes, and look who's riding beside him.'

Macro's eyes flickered to an officer on a horse a short distance to one side and slightly behind the Governor and he took a sharp intake of breath. 'It's that bastard Postumus.'

CHAPTER TWENTY-ONE

Cassius Longinus was shrewd enough to wait until they had reached the privacy of the prefect's quarters before he turned on Macro. As the orderly closed the door, the Governor of the province of Syria crossed over to the desk and eased himself down into the chair. He looked up at Macro and Cato standing to one side of the room. Postumus had sidled across to the opposite side and perched on the window frame so that his shadow was thrown across the floor. Longinus regarded Macro for a moment before he spoke.

'Centurion Postumus has told me that you have unlawfully taken control of this cohort. And that you threw him and Prefect Scrofa into a cell. Is this true?'

'If that's what he told you then Postumus is a damned liar, sir.' Macro smiled. 'Of course, now I wish I had actually thrown him bodily into the cell. Then he might not have been able to sneak off at the first opportunity.'

A smile flickered across Longinus' face. 'That's not a very constructive attitude. If we're going to get to the bottom of this then you're going to need to be a bit more cooperative, Centurion Macro. I've been in the saddle for the last two days, and since I have a province to run, I'd like to sort out this situation and get back to my duties.'

'I'm sure you would, sir.'

'I hope I don't detect a note of insolence in your voice.'

'No, sir. It's just my way. I've been a common soldier for too long.'

Longinus stared at him closely. 'Don't try to mock me. I will not tolerate it . . . I understand that you have a certain document. One that you claim entitles you to dismiss the prefect I appointed, and to assume his office instead.'

'That's right, sir.'

'In which case, I'd like to see it.'

'Very well, sir.' Macro indicated a small chest next to the desk. 'If I may?'

'Be my guest.' Longinus leaned back in the chair as Macro strode over, lifted the lid of the chest and took out the leather case in which the scroll had been replaced to protect it. He flipped the lid back and extracted the document and then placed it on the desk in front of Longinus. The Governor casually picked up the parchment, unrolled it and scanned the contents. Then he placed it back on the table.

'Well, Centurion Macro, and Centurion Cato, your credentials are impeccable. The document appears to be authentic, in which case you are fully within your rights to act as you did.'

Postumus, who had been watching with a faintly smug expression, started at this, and pushed himself away from the window frame.

'Sir, I protest! You are the Governor of Syria, appointed by the Emperor himself. They have flagrantly defied the authority of your office!'

Longinus tapped his finger on the scroll. 'By the terms of this document their authority supersedes mine. Therefore they have acted lawfully, and I'd be obliged if you'd shut up and wait until you are addressed from now on, Centurion Postumus.'

Postumus opened his mouth to protest, thought better of it and closed it. He nodded and stepped back awkwardly towards the window frame.

'That's better.' Longinus smiled. 'Now then, Centurions Macro and Cato, this is something of an unusual situation. It is not customary for officers of your rank to pop up in a far-flung province with the Emperor's permission to act as you please tucked up your sleeve. So, I'd be grateful if you could explain what is going on here.'

Macro turned to Cato and cocked an eyebrow. It was an awkward situation. They had been sent from Rome to quietly investigate the Governor of Syria and their mission had been dogged by bad luck from the moment they had entered Jerusalem. If only Macro had not lost his original letter of appointment then this present situation could have been avoided. Instead, they had been forced to use the Imperial Secretary's document and thereby reveal that they were acting directly on Emperor Claudius' authority. Cato realised that there was nothing to be gained by denying the truth.

'Sir,' he said softly to Macro, 'I think we'd better come clean.'

'What?' Macro shrank from the suggestion. How the hell could he just come straight out and tell one of Rome's most senior officials that the Emperor suspected him of treason? 'Are you mad?'

'Centurion Macro,' Longinus interrupted, then feigned a look of embarrassment. 'I do beg your pardon. Prefect. I think it would be best if we spoke openly. There's nothing to hide any more. I think you should begin by explaining exactly what you are doing here in Judaea.'

Macro swallowed. 'All right then, sir. Since you want it straight. Narcissus had obtained information that you were planning to provoke a revolt in the east in order to gain reinforcements for your army. The same source then said you were intending to use your enlarged army to depose the Emperor and claim the purple for yourself.'

There was a long silence before Longinus produced an amused expression. 'What an astonishing notion. I rather think someone must have been playing a joke on our friend Narcissus.'

'Then he's not seeing the funny side of it, sir. That's

why we were sent out here. To see if that's what you are planning to do.'

'And what is your conclusion?'

Macro cleared his throat. He had not felt so nervous in a long time. 'From what we've seen so far, I'd say that your conduct would seem to support the accusations being made against you.'

'Would you now?' Longinus responded tonelessly. 'If that's what you think, then you'd better be able to justify your conclusions. Because if you can't then you're going to make Narcissus look a fool. In that case I would not like to be in your boots. So what evidence have you got against me, Macro?' Before Macro could respond Longinus held up his hand to silence him, and continued. 'Let me tell you what you have got. Nothing. Nothing more than suspicion and coincidence. There are no documents to back up your version of events. And no witnesses.'

'No?' Macro smiled. 'What about Postumus there? I'm sure that Narcissus has men who are more than capable of getting information out of him.'

'Assuming he was still around to be interrogated.' Longinus smiled back, and then glanced towards Postumus. 'I mean, of course, that he might flee, or go into hiding before he could be questioned.'

'I'm sure that's what you meant,' said Macro. 'After all, you wouldn't want to dispose of such a loyal servant.'

'Quite. So where does that leave us?'

There was another silence as Macro pondered the question. There was no firm evidence against the Governor and everyone in the room knew it. Just as they knew it was clear that he had been plotting against the Emperor. It was Cato who spoke first.

'What if we accept for the moment that Narcissus cannot move against you?'

Longinus raised his eyebrows. 'What if we do?'

'The very fact that we were sent out to investigate the situation means that he must have some grounds for suspecting you, and he will be taking every precaution to ensure that he undermines any plan you might make to turn against the Emperor.'

'So?'

'So there's no chance that you will be given any reinforcements. No matter how much you present the situation as dangerous to Roman interests, Narcissus will not send you extra forces. In which case, any plot there might have been would be doomed to failure. Wouldn't you agree, sir?'

'Maybe. Assuming such a plot existed.'

'On that basis, there is still some advantage to be wrung out of the situation.'

Longinus stared at Cato, and then made an open gesture with his hands. 'Please explain yourself.'

'Yes, sir.' Cato concentrated for a moment and then spoke again. 'You already know the danger we face from Bannus. If his uprising spreads beyond this immediate area, then the whole province of Judaea could turn on Rome. What you may not know is that we have heard rumours that Parthia has offered to assist Bannus. With weapons, maybe even with men as well. If that is the case, then the stakes are even higher. Apart from having to crush the revolt in Judaea you would need to confront the Parthians and persuade them to withdraw their aid. If they had any doubts about your loyalty to the Emperor, the presence of a maverick Roman general on their borders might cause a diplomatic confrontation that Parthia might use to trigger a new war with Rome, sir.' Cato paused for an instant, worried that he had given his imagination too free a rein. 'At least it's a possibility, sir.'

'It's more than a possibility.' Longinus frowned. 'My spies have been reporting that Parthian troops have been spotted moving up the bank of the Euphrates towards Palymra. Their ambassador says they are carrying out exercises. It could be an unfortunate coincidence.'

'It could be, sir. But it would be rash not to make preparations to counter the threat.'

'If there is a threat. How could they know about Bannus' planned uprising?'

'I'm sure they have spies just as we do, sir.'

'You said there was some advantage to be gained,' Longinus reminded him.

'Yes, sir. If you send us reinforcements to help find and destroy Bannus, then the danger in Judaea can be averted. That leaves you free to confront Parthia. A strong show of force should discourage them from breaking the peace. When everything has settled back down, you can report your achievements to the Emperor and the Senate. I'd say they will regard you as something of a hero. Certainly enough to remove any doubts over your loyalty, sir.'

Longinus considered the prospect Cato had envisaged for him, and then looked at the young officer with a cool smile. 'You have a devious mind, Centurion Cato. I would hate to have you as a political opponent. Worse still, as one of Narcissus' lieutenants. Then you would truly be a man to be wary of.'

'I'm a soldier, sir,' Cato replied stiffly. 'That's all.'

'That's what you say, but this document gives the lie to that. There's far more to you and Macro than meets the eye. But no matter.' Longinus tapped his fingers on the desk for a moment and then nodded. 'Very well, let's do as you suggest. But there's one thing that still puzzles me.'

'Sir?'

'I'll accept that the Parthians could have got some intelligence about Bannus, but how could they come to know of Narcissus' suspicions about me? They would have to have spies right in the heart of the imperial service. That, or spies on my staff . . .' A brief startled look flashed across the Governor's face, but before he could continue there was a strident blaring from a trumpet, the notes blasting out across the fort from the direction of the west-facing gatehouse.

Longinus looked at Macro. 'What's that?'

'The alarm signal, sir.' Macro turned to Cato. 'We have to go.'

'Wait!' Longinus rose from behind the desk. 'I'm coming too. And you, Postumus.'

Outside, men were still tumbling from the barracks, clutching equipment as they hurried to take up their positions along the walls of the fort. They stood aside to let the officers trot past and Macro and the others reached the watchtower sweating and breathing heavily. On both sides the auxiliary troops were forming up in sections, sun glinting off their polished helmets as they fastened or adjusted the last items of equipment and then raised their shields and waited for orders. Several sections had been armed with compound bows and they were hurriedly stringing them, one end braced against a boot as the men strained to bend back the other end and attach the loop of the bowstring. The officers in the tower lined the parapet and stared out along the track to where, some distance off, a handful of mounted men were galloping towards the fort. Behind them raced a much larger force.

'Who the hell are they?' asked Longinus.

The two parties of horsemen were still too far away to be certain but as they approached the fort Cato strained his eyes and made out enough details to recognise them for what they were.

'It's one of our patrols.' He turned away, hurried across the tower and called down to the section of soldiers at the gate. 'Open up! Those are our men in front.'

Macro had also summed up the situation, and was issuing orders to the officers on the wall. 'Get some archers ready to cover the patrol! Shoot the moment those bastards behind our men are in range!'

As Macro and Cato returned to the Governor's side, Longinus turned to them and asked, 'So who are those men pursuing your patrol?'

Cato felt a chill feeling in the nape of his neck as he replied. 'I think they're Parthians, sir.'

CHAPTER TWENTY-TWO

'Parthians?' Longinus stared back at him. 'Nonsense! How could they be Parthians? Have you ever seen one?'

'No, sir,' Cato admitted. 'I've read about them. Heard them described.'

Longinus sniffed with contempt and the officers turned back to watch the desperate chase across the desert towards the fort. As the horsemen drew nearer Centurion Postumus glanced at Cato before saying quietly, 'I'm afraid they are Parthians, sir.'

They were clearly visible now and all those in the gatehouse could plainly see the conical helmets and the saddle tassels flapping in the wind. Every so often one of the riders would take careful aim with a bow and loose an arrow after the fleeing survivors of the Roman patrol. But the range was long and the horses galloping at full stretch and only one of the arrows found its mark as the officers in the tower looked on. One of the horses suddenly reared, nearly throwing its rider, and Cato saw the dark shaft of the arrow protruding from a hind leg. As the horse stamped, the shaft caught on the other leg and was ripped out in a bright gush of blood. A major blood vessel must have been severed for the blood continued to spurt from the wound as the rider tried in vain to spur his mount on towards the fort. After several increasingly faltering steps the horse's legs buckled and it sank on to its chest. The rider quickly dismounted and turned to face his pursuers, crouching behind his shield as he drew his sword. They came on, and at the last moment flowed round the man and his dying horse. There was a brief flurry of arrow shafts and the auxiliary spun round under the impacts, and crumpled to the ground.

A deep groan rose up in the throats of the men on the wall and Macro cupped a hand to his mouth and called down to them. 'Archers! Don't just stand there! Hit 'em – soon as they're in bowshot!'

Those men who had already notched their first arrow braced their legs apart, leaned back and drew their bows, adjusting the angle to get the maximum range. Then they waited a moment, until the Roman patrol was close enough to the fort to ensure that the arrows would pass over them. The first man released his bowstring and the shaft shot high into the air, arcing up into the clear blue sky before it seemed to hang a moment and began to fall to earth. From where Cato stood it seemed that it would surely fall amongst the men of the patrol pounding towards the fort. He gritted his teeth as the arrow plummeted down. Only at the last moment was it clear that it had overshot the patrol, and it struck the ground just ahead of their pursuers with a small explosion of sand and dust.

'The range is good!' Macro shouted. 'Let 'em have it!'

More shafts flitted up into the sky and when they fell they were right on target. Cato saw one of the pursuers struck in the face and the man threw his hands up and tumbled off the back of his horse, disappearing under the hooves of the beasts galloping behind. A thin cry cut through the air and the Parthians instantly dispersed, swerving out to both sides to present a more difficult target to the Roman archers. But they had lost their prey. The gate was open and the surviving men from the patrol charged towards it, careering through the arch into the safety of the fort beyond.

'Close the gate!' Macro bellowed an instant later and the hinges grated and then the gate slammed into place with a thud that could be clearly felt in the tower above. At once the Parthians wheeled their mounts round, and then tore off back into the desert and out of range of the archers on the walls. Cato watched them go for a moment and then turned to the other officers.

'I think the situation's just become a lot more serious.'

'Parthians,' Longinus muttered. 'Bloody Parthians. Always the bloody Parthians.'

Macro gestured to Cato. 'Come on. We have to speak to the men from that patrol.'

They climbed down from the tower and joined the cluster of men surrounding the survivors of the patrol and their mounts. The horses' coats were stained with sweat and streaks of foam and their flanks heaved as they snorted. Macro thrust one of the men aside.

'Make way! Make way there!'

The soldiers quickly parted for the officers and a moment later they were standing in front of the decurion who had been leading the patrol. The decurion's arm was slashed and a medical orderly was holding the sides of the cut together while another tied a length of bandage round the injury. They paused at the sight of Macro, unable to stand to attention without interrupting their task. He nodded at them to continue before he turned to the decurion.

'Make your report.'

'Yes, sir.' He glanced at Cato. 'We watched those villages we were assigned to cover. I had five men on each. We saw nothing untoward the whole time. Then, when I gathered my men up yesterday afternoon to return to the fort, we saw a dust cloud, away to the north, coming out of the hills. Heading this way.'

'Hills?' Cato cut in. 'Which hills?'

'Near Heshbon, sir. I decided to investigate. It would take quite a lot of men or animals to make that much dust. So we rode closer until I could make out the details. It was an army, sir. Thousands of men, hundreds mounted and what looked like a baggage train at the rear, although

I couldn't see it clearly. That was when their scouts spotted us. Next thing I knew they were coming at us from all directions, shooting arrows. That's when I realised the mounted fellows were Parthians. They cut most of my men down, but me and these others managed to find a gully and rode through them in the dusk. We carried on through the night, and headed back to the fort. They caught up with us a few miles back.' He shrugged.

Macro stared at him for a moment and then clapped him on the uninjured arm. 'Carry on, decurion. See to your men as soon as that wound's dressed. Get 'em fed and get 'em rested.'

'Yes, sir. Thank you, sir.'

Macro drew Cato away from the men, under the gatehouse, and lowered his voice. 'Coming for us do, you think?'

'I'm sure of it. Bannus needs a victory, to prove that he can beat Roman soldiers. The villages round here only need the slightest excuse to go over to him. He destroys us and they'll swarm to his side.'

'But why us? Why not start with a smaller outpost?'

'We're as far from any large force of Roman troops as you can get in this region. He can easily cut us off from supplies and reinforcements. At the same time, we can only escape by cutting our way through him. There's nothing but desert in the other direction.'

'Shit. We're stuck here.' Macro pressed his lips together

for a moment. 'The Governor can help. If he leaves now, he'll be able to make it back to the legions, and send a column down here.'

'He might. If he can spare the men. Don't forget, there's that force of Parthians moving up on Palmyra.'

'I'm sure he can spare us some men. Enough to deal with Bannus before his army grows much more. We'll stay here until the relief arrives.'

'Stay here?' Cato looked uncertain. 'Is that wise?'

'What else can we do? We'll be safe enough in here.'

'You think so?'

'Why not? He's got a force of brigands, and now, it seems, a few Parthians. They're not going to get over the walls in a hurry. Not without siege weapons.'

'What makes you think they lack those?'

Macro smiled. 'And where would they have spirited them up from?'

'Parthia, that's where.'

'Cato, have you any idea how difficult it would be to move a siege train over the desert?'

'No. How difficult?'

Macro was taken aback, and struggled for an answer. 'I don't really know, but I should imagine it would be bloody difficult to haul anything across the terrain out there. All right?' He gestured vaguely in the direction of the caravan trade route and the desert beyond. 'I'm telling you, he has no siege weapons. We're safe.'

'I hope you're right.'

'I'm right. But we're going to make some preparations all the same.' Macro made a few mental calculations. 'Heshbon, that's what, thirty miles away. They should be here tomorrow then, from noon.'

Cato nodded. 'Sounds right.'

'Then there's not much time. We need to speak to the Governor. Come on.'

They climbed back into the tower. Longinus and Postumus were watching the rapidly diminishing cloud of dust kicked up by the Parthian horses and discussing something in muted tones. They stopped as soon as Macro and Cato emerged from the trapdoor. Macro quickly described what the patrol had seen. There was a momentary look of alarm on the Governor's face before he controlled his feelings again and stood, stroking his chin thoughtfully.

'I'll have to re-join my command before the fort's cut off.'

'Yes, sir,' agreed Macro. 'The sooner you leave, the better. We'll wait here for the relief column.'

'Relief column?' Longinus repeated. 'Yes. Yes, of course. I'll have to send you some more men. Enough to beat Bannus. I'll see to it the moment I return to my command.'

'Very good, sir.' Macro nodded.

'I'd best leave at once then.' Longinus turned towards the trapdoor. Then he paused and turned back, staring hard at Postumus. 'You can stay here.'

'What?' Postumus looked horrified. 'Stay? Sorry, sir, but my place is at your side. It's going to be a dangerous journey back to the legions. You'll need every man you can get to ensure your safety.'

'On the contrary, more men will only slow me down. The prefect has more need of you than I do right now. You will stay here, and help defend the fort.'

'But, sir!' There was a pleading tone to his voice and Macro felt sick with disgust.

'Enough!' Longinus snapped. 'You will stay here! Understand?'

Postumus stared back, and there was a bitter twist to his lips as he replied. 'Oh, I understand, sir. Perfectly.'

'I shall not forget you, Postumus. I never forget those who have served me well.'

'That's a great comfort, sir.'

'Farewell, then.' Longinus nodded, made to hold out his hand, and then let it drop back to his side as he turned away and climbed down from the tower.

A little later Macro, Cato and Postumus looked on as the Governor and his escort galloped out of the fort and immediately swung north to give the approaching rebels as wide a berth as possible before they made for the security of the legions under Longinus' command in Syria. Macro noticed the look of acute bitterness in Postumus' face as he watched them ride off across the desert.

'That's what you get when you play politics, friend.'

Postumus turned to the prefect and laughed. 'You don't get it, sir. He's not going to send us any reinforcements.'

'Why?' asked Cato. 'What do you mean?'

'If you two are the best that Narcissus can come up with, then may the gods help the Emperor. Outside Rome, I imagine that it's only the three of us who know the scale of Longinus' treachery. If he leaves us here to die, then he's in the clear. Of course, the moment Bushir falls, and we're all slaughtered, he'll mount a punitive expedition and grieve over our bodies, and claim that he was just too late to save us.'

Macro and Cato stared at him a moment, then Macro shrugged. 'Fine. Then the only way we get back at that patrician bastard is by making sure we come through this alive.'

'Oh?' Postumus smiled weakly. 'And how do you propose that we do that, sir?'

'The same way we always do. By beating the living shit out of our enemy and dancing on his grave. Cato?'

'Sir?'

'I want every officer at headquarters at once. We've got work to do, and it looks like there's not much time left before Bannus will be breathing down our necks.'

'Including Scrofa? Shall I have him released?'

Macro shrugged. 'Why not? He might as well do something useful before he dies.'

CHAPTER TWENTY-THREE

Macro looked over the faces of his officers, waiting for their complete attention before he began.

'In two days' time Bannus and his forces will be camping outside Fort Bushir. Although we don't know their precise strength yet our scouts report that we are badly outnumbered. Worse still, Bannus and his men have been armed by the Parthians who have also sent him a contingent of their horse-archers. I've sent messengers to the garrison in Jerusalem and the procurator in Caesarea. I doubt whether there will be enough troops to spare to send any to reinforce us. Worse still, it is not likely that any relief column will be sent from Syria.'

This remark brought on looks of surprise, and a tone of muted anger rippled across the hall. Macro raised a hand to attract their attention.

'Gentlemen! Quiet . . . The Governor of Syria is facing a substantial threat from Parthia across the frontier. He cannot spare us any men. We are on our own. I will not pretend that the odds look favourable, but we do have some advantages. The enemy must come to us, therefore we can lay a few traps to greet him. Bannus is at the head of a force comprising untrained villagers for the most part. They'll be brave enough when the time comes but bravery is no match for good training and experience. We also have the benefit of good defences. The walls of Bushir are as strong as they come for a fort this size. Without siege equipment they'll have to come at us over the walls, and if you've ever seen such an assault then you'll know how costly it can be.' Macro paused to let his words sink in, then continued. 'That's the good news. The bad news is that Bannus cannot afford to fail in his attempt on Bushir. He will throw everything he can at us. We cannot be confident of beating him. But even if we do go down to his army of brigands, we must ensure that the cost of his victory is so high that his men will not be prepared to follow him against any other Roman unit. If we can end this rebellion now, before it can spread, then his defeat is certain, even if we don't live to see it.

'Centurion Cato and I have made plans for the coming fight. There's plenty of work to be done before Bannus arrives. My clerks will bring your orders to you. Dismissed!'

The officers filed out of the hall. Postumus looked at the prefect sourly. 'What do you want me to do, sir?'

'I haven't decided yet.' Macro smiled. 'Since you are so keen to get stuck into the enemy I want you right at the thick of things when it comes to the fight. Now wait for me outside.'

'Yes, sir.' Postumus saluted and left the hall.

'You really want him at your side in a fight?' muttered Cato. 'That's asking for trouble.'

'I can handle him. There's no way I'm going to let that scum run out on us. He's the one who turned the villagers against us. Now he can take his full share of the consequences.'

Cato nodded approvingly. 'Still, I'd watch him closely.'

'I will, believe me.' Macro said firmly. 'Do you think he was right about the Governor?'

'Yes. It makes sense. We can't expect any help from that quarter.'

'If only we had more men. I checked the morning strength returns before the meeting. The cohort's down to fewer than seven hundred effectives. It's not looking good.'

'No, sir. It's not. What are my orders?'

'I need a good pair of eyes out there. I want you to command the scouts. Take ten men and ride out towards Bannus. Send back regular reports on his progress. You are not to engage with any of their scouts. No heroics, Cato. Do you understand?'

'Yes, sir. There'll be time enough for that later on.'

Macro laughed. 'That's the spirit! Now, I'd better get on with the preparations. You'll need to leave as soon as you can.'

THE EAGLE IN THE SAND

'Yes, sir.' Cato replied, but did not move towards the door.

'What is it?'

'Those people at Heshaba. I think I owe it to them to offer shelter in the fort. They saved my life.'

'No. They'll be safer in their village, especially if Bannus does take the fort.'

'I'm not sure about that. The Parthians aren't exactly famous for their kind treatment of non-combatants. Besides, I got the feeling that there's not much love lost between Bannus and those people. If we leave them out there, then they'll be at the mercy of the brigands and those Parthians.'

Macro stared at him for a moment before he made a decision. 'Very well. Offer them shelter. But if they accept it, they must come to the fort by nightfall. I don't want them getting caught up between the two sides when the fighting starts.'

'Thank you, sir.'

'Cato, you can ask them, but I doubt whether that woman, Miriam, or her followers, will take up the offer. Those are their people marching on us. It's more likely they'll join them in the attack on the fort.'

Cato shook his head. 'I don't think so. There's something different about Miriam and her followers. I don't think they want to fight us. Or anyone for that matter.'

'Fine.' Macro waved his hand towards the door. 'Then

315

make your offer and be done with it. But get moving. There's not much time.'

As Cato's column of scouts trotted out of the fort there were already many parties of men hard at work, swinging their picks into the ground as they excavated small pits all round the fort. Under the glare of the sun it was exhausting work, but there was no question of rest breaks. These men were digging for their lives. Anything that would stem the tide of the approaching enemy might help to save them. So, with the single concession to comfort of their straw hats, the men swung their picks in the sweltering heat in a desperate effort to prepare for the attack in the short time still left to them.

The villagers of Heshaba were resting inside their houses when Cato and his men rode into the small square at the centre of the village. The man that Scrofa had ordered crucified still hung from his cross. Or at least, what now passed for the man. The sun had baked and desiccated his body so that it had visibly shrunk beneath the dried skin. Crows and other carrion had plucked at the most tender parts of his flesh and lidless, empty eye sockets stared out over the village. Cato ordered the column to dismount. He handed his reins to one of the scouts and ordered the men to water the horses and wait for him in the square. Then he walked into the nearest alley, approached a door and rapped on the frame. A moment later the door creaked open and an anxious male face peered out into the sun-washed street.

'Find Miriam,' Cato said in Greek. 'Tell her Centurion Cato must speak to her on a matter of great urgency. I'll be at the reservoir. Do you understand?'

The man nodded, and Cato turned away and strode up the hill, past the last few houses of the village, until he reached the shade of one of the dusty palms that grew beside the reservoir. There was less water in it than ever, a mere pool surrounded by cracked earth, and he wondered how any people could survive in this arid land. The god of the Judaeans, Yahweh, must be cruel indeed to subject his believers to such a harsh existence, thought Cato. There had to be a better life than this. Perhaps that was why these people were so intensely religious – out of the necessity of finding some kind of spiritual compensation for such a hard and unrewarding physical existence.

The soft crunch of gravel alerted him to Miriam's approach and Cato quickly rose to his feet and bowed his head respectfully.

'I was told that you wished to speak to me.' Miriam smiled. 'You don't need to stand on my account, young man. Sit.'

Cato did as he was told and Miriam knelt down opposite him and made herself comfortable.

'We've been told that Bannus is heading this way with an army. I came to warn you.'

'We already know. A rider came to the village this

morning. We are to offer his men every assistance they require, or we will be deemed to be collaborators and treated accordingly.'

Cato stared at her. 'What will you do?'

'I don't know.' She shook her head sadly. 'If we resist Bannus he will destroy us. If we go along with him, then you Romans will treat us as his accomplices. Where is the middle path, Cato?'

'I don't know. I don't even know if there is one. I came here to offer you and your people shelter in our fort.'

Miriam smiled. 'A kind offer, I'm sure. Tell me, what are your chances of surviving this attack by Bannus?'

'I won't lie to you, Miriam. We're outnumbered, and there will be no outside help. We may well be overrun.'

'In which case it would be as well for my people not to be discovered sheltering in your fort.'

'I agree. If we are overrun. But if you stay here, you will surely fall foul of one side or another.'

Miriam looked down at her hands. 'We came here to escape such conflicts. All we wanted was peace and a chance to live our lives as we wish. Yet it seems that there is no escape from the conflicts that afflict men. They will carry them even here, into the wilderness. Look about you, Centurion. What is there here that is worth having? What is there here to excite a man's avarice? Nothing. That is why my people settled in this forsaken place. We removed ourselves from any land a man could covet. We disowned any possessions that might inspire envy or desire in others. We are all that we are, and nothing more. Yet still we are blighted by the attentions of others. Even though we mean them no harm, they would destroy us.' She reached a hand up and clutched it to her chest. 'That was the fate of my son. I will not let that be the fate of my grandson. Yusef is all that I have left now. That, and the fading memories of an old woman.'

Her head dipped forward and Miriam was silent. Cato could not offer any honest words of comfort and sat and waited. Her shoulders heaved once and a tear dropped on to the sand between her knees and left a dark stain. Cato cleared his throat. 'Will you accept our protection, such as it is?'

Miriam wiped her eyes on the sleeve of her cloak and looked up. 'With all my heart, no. This is our home. There is nowhere else for us to go. We will stay, and either we will be spared, or we will be obliterated. But I thank you for the offer.'

Cato nodded. 'I have to leave.' He eased himself to his feet and looked down into her eyes. 'Good luck, Miriam. May your god protect you and your people.'

She looked up into the sky and shut her eyes. 'Thy will be done . . .'

'Pardon?'

She smiled. 'Just something my son used to say.'

'Oh.'

'Farewell, Centurion. I hope I see you again.'

319

Cato turned away and strode back into the village to rejoin his men, and once he had disappeared between the buildings Miriam gave full vent to her tears with a low shuddering moan.

Bannus and his Parthian allies had not deployed any scouts to mask their movements. Instead they marched directly towards the fort, in full view of Cato and his men. Cato smiled grimly to himself. If Bannus was trying to cow them with the size of his force, then he was succeeding admirably. By Cato's estimate, they were confronted by over three thousand men, perhaps five hundred of them mounted, and most of those would be Parthians, deadly with bow and arrow and skilled swordsmen if it came to a hand-to-hand fight. The enemy column had been easy to locate under the dense cloud of dust that rose up in its wake. At the rear of the column was a small baggage train, with a handful of carts just visible in the dusty haze, although it was impossible to determine what they were carrying. The column advanced at a measured pace, not hurrying to battle, but confident that it could traverse the land with impunity.

As soon as he had estimated their number, and noted the extent of their equipment and weapons, Cato quickly etched the information into the wax on a tablet he took from his saddle bag and called one of his men over.

'Take this back to the prefect. Let him know that at the time of this report the enemy were about twenty miles from the fort. At their current pace they should not arrive before tomorrow evening. Got that?'

'Yes, sir.'

'Then go.'

As the man galloped away, kicking up a thin trail of dust behind him, Cato saw some of the outriders of the enemy column turn and gesture towards the small party of Romans, but no one rode out to chase them away and for the rest of the day they rode ahead of Bannus and his men, being sure to give themselves plenty of room to escape any sudden forays by the Parthian cavalry. As night fell, the enemy column halted. They managed to find enough fuel for only a small number of fires, since firewood was scarce in the barren landscape. Cato did not permit his men to light a fire. It would be dangerous to advertise their presence so openly. Instead, he waited until it was dark, and then moved position across the front of the enemy's line of advance, to the other flank, in case Bannus decided to try to surprise the Roman scouts who had been scrutinising his movements. Then, after his men had dismounted, and a watch had been set, Cato rolled into his blanket and tried to find a comfortable patch of ground to sleep on as the temperature dropped to a freezing chill.

At first light the next day, Macro rode out of the fort to inspect the work his men had carried out. The holes that they had been digging the previous afternoon had been completed and presented a dangerous obstacle to charging cavalry. Behind the pits was the second line of defence. The men had sown a broad perimeter with the four-pointed iron caltrops that had been brought out from the cohort's stores. The spikes would pierce the hooves of any horse, or the boots or bare feet of any attacker who plunged heedlessly towards the Roman line, crippling them instantly. Once past the second line of defence only the ramparts of the fort would stand in their way. Macro offered a quick prayer to Fortuna and Mars asking that the enemy would not have brought many assault ladders or battering rams with them. If they had then it was a only a matter of time before the superiority of their numbers decided the result of the coming battle.

The air was still chilly and Macro shivered as he completed his inspection and headed back towards the fort. As he neared the gate he noticed a rider approaching from the north and reined in, straining his eyes to try to identify the man. No Roman, to be sure, with the swath of cloth covering his body and head. Macro's spare hand shifted to the handle of his sword as he twitched the reins and turned his mount towards the approaching rider. Evidently the sentries had at last seen the man as well, and boots thudded along the rampart as the duty century turned out. Macro frowned at the sloppy watch-keeping. The sentries should have spotted the rider long before Macro. Someone was going to be on a charge for that, Macro decided.

Suddenly the rider was waving his hand at Macro as if in greeting, and a moment later he pulled aside his veil and shouted. 'Centurion! It's me! Symeon!'

Macro relaxed his sword arm and let out his breath in a sigh of relief. He raised his hand and returned Symeon's greeting, and urged his horse forward towards the approaching guide, as Symeon carefully picked his way through the defences.

'You've chosen a poor time to visit us,' Macro said ruefully.

'Is there ever a good time?' Symeon laughed then gestured towards the men busy setting up the caltrops. 'Come, Centurion, tell me: why have you laid out all these trinkets around your fort?'

'Bannus is coming. We expect him to arrive before the walls by nightfall.'

Symeon sucked in his breath. 'How could he have grown so strong, so quickly?'

'He's found some new friends. The Parthians have sent him help.'

'Parthians?' Symeon's expression darkened. 'Bannus is a fool. What does he imagine Parthia will do if Rome is ever forced from this region? He is blinded by his hatred of the *Kittim*. Judaea, Syria and Nabataea would all fall to Parthia.' He grasped Macro's shoulder. 'We must stop Bannus! Right here!'

'Easier said than done,' Macro said wearily. 'He's got us outnumbered. The Governor of Syria has abandoned us.

I'm not sure we can hold Bannus off.' Macro paused as a thought occurred to him. A desperate thought, to be sure. 'Not unless we get help. How soon could you ride to Petra?'

'I could leave at once, Centurion. It's two days' hard ride. Why?'

Macro smiled. 'I need to call in a debt.'

CHAPTER TWENTY-FOUR

'Well, there they are.' Macro scratched his chin as he squinted into the distance. The sun was low in the sky and his eyes watered as he made out the enemy. Two miles away a large party of horsemen were riding over a fold in the land. They reined in and seemed to be observing the fort in turn. 'They won't be able to do anything tonight. They'll make camp, post pickets and get a good night's rest.'

'That sounds like wishful thinking, sir,' Cato responded quietly. 'If I'm any judge of the situation I'd say that Bannus will want to crush us as swiftly as possible.'

'And why's that?'

'As far as he's aware, we would have sent for help the moment we knew that he was making for the fort. If he's going to rouse the rest of the province then he'll need to offer them proof that Rome can be beaten. If he has to give up the attempt on Bushir, then I think his support will melt away quickly enough.'

'But the chances are that there won't be any help coming. Not from Longinus at least.'

'Yes, but Bannus doesn't know that, sir. As far as he's concerned, he's got six or seven days before a relief column turns up. That means he's going to have to move fast to take the fort.' Cato thought for a moment and continued. 'He'll be counting on the threat from Parthia to stop Longinus sending any overwhelming force in response to the situation here. Bannus will hope that with Bushir in his hands he can attract enough recruits to counter any troops that Longinus eventually sends his way.'

Macro looked at Cato. 'How can you know all that?'

'Just thinking it through from the enemy's point of view, sir.' Cato nodded to himself. 'Seems to make sense. In which case I think we shouldn't take any chances. Bannus may even make an attempt on the fort tonight.'

'Let him try.' Macro smiled as he thought of the ground that had been prepared around the fort. Any attempt by the enemy to reach the walls under cover of darkness was going to bring them right on to the obstacles that the cohort had prepared. He indulged himself for a moment, imagining the frustrating delays and injuries Bannus would have to endure. Then his expression hardened. 'All the same, you may be right. I'll have two centuries on the wall at a time.'

'I think that would be prudent, sir,' replied Cato. 'There's one other thing.'

'Yes?'

'That business about letting Postumus and Scrofa return to duty.'

'We need every man who can hold a sword.'

'Maybe, but I still don't trust either of them. Those bastards are bound to betray us the moment our backs are turned.'

'How can they betray us? They're in the same situation as the rest of us. They fight for their lives, or they get massacred by Bannus. They'll fight.'

Cato was silent for a while, then sighed. 'I only hope you're right, sir.'

Macro bit back on his frustration. Cato should not be worrying about Scrofa and Postumus at a time when his mind needed to be concentrating on more important issues. He cleared his throat and turned towards his friend. 'Would you like me to have them arrested again?'

'What?' Cato frowned. 'No, I think not, sir. How do you imagine that would look to the men? The prefect doesn't know whether he's coming or going. That's what they'd say. So we're stuck with Scrofa and Postumus on the strength. I don't suppose they can cause too much trouble in the reserve.'

The two officers had been posted to command a cavalry squadron each. These were being held back from the walls, ready to reinforce any weak points in the defences. That had been Macro's decision.

Macro rubbed his hands contentedly. 'Even if Bannus

tries a direct assault on the walls, he shouldn't get very far without siege equipment. I think we'll get through this without too much trouble, Cato. It's not as if they're going to starve us out. We've provisions for two months for the men and a month for the horses. And if we eat the horses, then we can last for a while yet. The cisterns are full to the brim so we won't be short of water. It's those bastards out there I almost feel sorry for. I doubt Bannus will be able to keep 'em fed for long. And they'll be short of a drink.' Macro nodded towards the reservoir, some way off from the fort. The surface of the water was broken by the carcasses of dead sheep and goats that Macro had ordered to be dumped into the reservoir once the fort's cisterns had been filled.

'We just have to hold them off long enough to make his peasants feel hungry and homesick,' Macro concluded. 'Then, once his support has melted away, we'll get out there and hunt him down. Once Bannus is nailed up, these Judaeans will get the message that there's no point in defying Rome.'

'I hope you're right,' Cato replied. He gazed back towards the distant horsemen. Behind them the head of the enemy column crawled into view over the low ridge and slowly spread on to the barren plain in front of the fort. Thousands of men, and in amongst them, horses and pack animals. The dust that hung over the growing horde filtered the fading sunlight into a glowing red hue that pooled like blood against the paling sky, and Cato felt a cold thrill of fear grip his spine and make him shiver. Macro noticed the sudden tremor in his friend.

'You must be tired. Once the first watch is over, make sure you get some rest. That's an order. I'll need you in good shape over the coming days.'

'Yes, sir.'

Cato was grateful that his friend had misread the gesture, and bitterly reproached himself for letting his fear show in such an obvious manner. If Macro could see it, then so could the men of the cohort, and Cato mentally winced at the impression of weakness he imagined some of the men would see in the officer who had only recently joined the Second Illyrian. Cato glanced at the men spread out along the wall on either side of the gatehouse. A few of them were talking quietly as they watched the enemy approach, but most just stared across the sand and in most cases their expressions were unreadable. Some looked quite calm as they appraised the strength of the enemy they would be fighting. A few of the others fretted, giving away their inner anxiety through a variety of tics as their thoughts were wholly absorbed by the approach of danger: fingers rhythmically rapping the bronze trim of a shield, or the handle of a sword; the tapping of a booted foot, repetitive licking of lips and other gestures that Cato had seen before previous actions.

He forced himself to look upon the approaching enemy again. He tried to imagine how those men would be feeling. Most of them were simple peasants, provoked into this fight by the ceaseless hardship and injustice of their lives. That would embolden them for a while yet, but they lacked training, experience and the confidence of professional soldiers, like the auxiliaries of the Second Illyrian cohort. What were they thinking as they tramped across the dusty plain, and saw the thick walls of Fort Bushir, with its squat towers at each corner and over the gates? Wouldn't they feel a twinge of fear, for all their superiority in numbers? Cato certainly hoped so, for their sake as well as his own. There was no satisfaction, let alone any glory, to be had from killing peasants. It was a dirty, thankless and profitless task that would only add to the misery of the people of Judaea. If they were defeated, yet more fuel would be added to the simmering anger and hatred towards Rome that dwelt in their hearts. That was all that Rome would win if Cato, Macro and the other men managed to hold the enemy at bay. But if Bannus won, Cato reflected, the example of Bushir would sweep through the province. A multitude would swell his ranks and no Roman garrison would be safe between Egypt and Syria. And what then? From what Cato understood of these people, there would be no peace. No unified independent nation of Judaea. The inhabitants were simply too divided by class and religious faction to work as one. In that case, it would be only a matter of time before Judaea was broken apart by civil war and then consumed by another empire whether that be Rome, again, or Parthia. As Judaea had always been consumed by empires throughout history.

Cato smiled as he discovered that he felt sorry for the downtrodden peasants marching towards him.

Bannus marched his army up to within half a mile of the fort before he halted and set up camp as darkness closed in. The sky was clear, and as the orange hue of the setting sun's afterglow faded the stars pricked out brilliantly in the heavens above. The sounds of the enemy carried across the sand to the fort and if he strained his ears Cato could hear snatches of laughter and singing between the shouted orders. One by one, fires were kindled and lit and bright pools of light sprang up across the desert, each illuminating a dense ring of humanity clustering about it as night gripped them in its cold embrace.

Macro waited a while, to make quite sure that the enemy was settling for the night, before he ordered the units that were not on watch-keeping duty to stand down. The men tramped down from the wall and sombrely made their way back to their barracks. Some would find sleep easy enough. Others would continue in the agitated state of anticipation that Cato had observed as they stood and watched the approach of the enemy. At length Macro beckoned to Cato and they returned to the prefect's quarters for a meal with the other officers. Scrofa and Postumus sat as far from the cohort's commander as rank permitted and kept their eyes lowered, refusing to meet the gaze of either Macro or

Cato. The mood was subdued, even though Macro had ordered his housekeeper to bring out the best jars of Scrofa's remaining stock of wine. Conscious that his men were looking to him, Macro made himself appear calm and unflustered by the presence of the enemy. He even attempted a few ribald jokes with some of the officers, and ended the evening with a toast to their inevitable victory. The officers responded with forced enthusiasm and then the dinner party broke up as they returned to their rooms at the end of each barrack block.

'Well, that was a storming success,' Macro muttered as the last of them left and only Cato remained, picking at the dates in the bowl in front of him. 'Might as well surrender the fort to Bannus right now and be done with it.'

'They'll fight hard enough when the time comes, sir.'

'Oh? What makes you think that, my esteemed veteran friend?'

Cato looked up. 'They haven't got any choice. It's fight or die.'

'So what's new?' Macro grumbled. 'I tell you, Cato, if that lot were legionaries instead of auxiliaries the spirit would be different. They'd be thirsting to get stuck into Bannus and his mob.'

'Maybe they would feel the same, if Scrofa and Postumus hadn't got to them. It's a question of leadership. They'd been badly commanded for months before you took over. You've had too little time to return them to battle-readiness.'

'Maybe.' Macro reflected. 'Perhaps the first attack might put a little bit of iron back into them.'

Cato smiled. 'I hope not. A wound is the last thing they need.'

Macro winced at his friend's attempt at humour. 'It's not a laughing matter, Cato. Our lives depend on it.' He snorted. 'The fate of the bloody province depends on it. So no stupid quips please. Not unless we've had a skinful of wine first, eh? Even then . . .'

'All right then, sir. No more jokes.'

'Good.' Macro was silent for a while, deep in thought. Then he suddenly turned to Cato. 'How do you suppose Vespasian did it?'

'Did what, sir?'

'Prepared his officers for battle. You remember, back in the Second Augusta, whenever we were about to go into a fight, the legate would find a few words for us, make a toast, and we'd all head back to our men raring to go? How did he do that?'

Cato recalled their former commander, the stocky frame, the thinning hair crowning the strong-featured face. The steady, deep voice with which Vespasian could equally charm and lambast his men. It was hard to define what made the legate the kind of man you'd fight to the death for. Maybe it was the fact that you believed that he, in turn, would fight to the death for you. Whatever the quality of leadership was, Cato concluded, it was clear that some men possessed it and many more did not.

Macro was one of the former; he just had a different style from Vespasian's.

Cato smiled. 'I can't answer that.'

'Great. Thanks,' Macro responded sourly.

'Don't fret, sir. You'll do well enough. I'd follow you to the ends of the earth.'

Macro looked at him with a surprised expression. 'You mean that, don't you?'

'Of course, sir. And when these men get to know you better, they'd do just the same. Now that we've a battle on our hands they'll see the quality of their new prefect soon enough. Maybe that's what Vespasian had.'

'What?'

'The benefit of an example. We followed him because we'd seen him in battle. He'd proved himself to us. Once a commander's done that, I'd say that was the point where he won his men over. This is your chance to do the same with the Second Illyrian.'

Macro stroked his chin thoughtfully, then refilled Cato's cup and his own before raising the latter in a toast. 'To those who lead from the front.'

Cato nodded. 'I'll drink to that.'

Cato was roused from his sleep in the last hour before dawn. An auxiliary was gently shaking his shoulder. 'Sir, the prefect wants you.'

Cato blinked, yawned and rubbed his eyes. 'Right, where is he?'

'On the main gatehouse, sir.'

'Very well, my compliments to the prefect. Tell him I'm coming.'

'Yes, sir.' The soldier saluted and turned to leave the room. At once Cato threw back his covers and swung his legs over the side of his bed. By the light of a single lamp the soldier had left on his table he pulled on his boots, tied them up and stretched his shoulders before standing up. Then he lifted his chain mail over his head, collected his helmet and sword belt and went to join Macro. Outside headquarters the air was cold and the pale light of the stars provided just enough illumination for Cato to see the barracks on either side of the street as he made for the main gate. Faint glimmers of light showed round the door and window frames of some of the barracks as those auxiliaries who could not find sleep passed the time at dice, or carving, or the myriad ways that soldiers occupy themselves while waiting for action.

As Cato climbed up through the hatch of the gatehouse tower he saw Macro's broad silhouette over by the breastworks.

'You sent for me.'

'Yes, I thought you should see this. Look out there.' Macro extended his arm towards the enemy camp and pointed to an area, perhaps three hundred paces away, where several torches burned, casting a wavering patch of light. In front of the torches was a wicker barricade that concealed the activity beyond. But the sounds of hammering and the shouts of men carried clearly to the two centurions on the gatehouse.

'Any idea what's going on?' asked Cato.

'Could be knocking up some assault ladders, or a battering ram. Not that that worries me, unduly. They still have to cross the dead ground before they can get close enough to use that sort of equipment.'

'Of course, they might be constructing something else,' Cato mused.

'That's what I thought. Perhaps the Parthians have provided Bannus with a company of engineers.'

'As well as arms and those horse-archers? That's uncommonly generous of them. But then again, we're all playing for high stakes.'

'True. Well, there's nothing we can do about it now.' Macro turned away from the enemy camp and glanced at the opposite horizon. 'It'll be light soon. Then we'll see what they're up to.'

It was not long before the darkness began to dissipate and detail by detail the landscape around the fort became visible. Soon the enemy extinguished the torches and Cato, whose young eyes were better than Macro's, strained to make out the details of two thick wooden frames beyond the wicker screen. Then, he felt a sick feeling in his guts as he realised what he was seeing. He waited a moment longer to be sure before he turned to Macro.

'Onagers. Two of them.'

'Onagers?' Macro looked astonished. 'Where the hell

would Bannus have got onagers?' Even as he spoke, a memory flashed through his mind. Weeks earlier, when the caravan had rejected Postumus's offer of protection. In amongst the camels had been two covered ox-carts, carrying heavy timbers. No doubt the iron ratchets and other mechanisms had been hidden beneath the load. Very clever of the Parthians, Macro conceded. Rather than send the siege weapons across the desert, they had shipped them round Arabia and then smuggled them to Bannus under the guise of caravan goods. Macro bunched his hands into fists and thumped them down on the rampart. 'I saw those a while back, broken down for transport. On that first patrol with Postumus. Of course, I was too foolish to recognise the components for what they were. Shit.'

Cato shook his head. 'Well, it's too late to do anything about it now.'

Macro was about to reply when they both heard a sharp shout from the enemy camp. They turned just in time to see the throwing arms of the onagers slash up and forwards until they struck the padded cross pieces. The dull thud of that impact sounded an instant later. Cato saw the first two boulders hurled up through the cold morning air. They rose to the top of the arc that defined their trajectory, seemed to hang there for a moment, and then came down at an alarming speed, rapidly gaining in size as they plunged towards the gatehouse.

Cato grabbed Macro and hauled him away from the rampart. 'Get down!'

CHAPTER TWENTY-FIVE

They hunched down and waited for the impact with gritted teeth. The first rock overshot the gatehouse and smashed through the roof of the barracks block beyond with a shattering crash. Fragments of tiles exploded from the impact and pattered down on to the street around the building. The second missile struck the ground a short distance before the fort sending a shower of stones and grit against the wall, and raising a small cloud of dust above the spot where it had landed. Cato and Macro felt the impact and Macro looked at his friend with a nervous grin.

'That's quite some piece of kit they have there. Good range, and it can throw a decent weight. That's going to be a nuisance.'

Cato stood up and stared towards the onagers. Already the crews were working at preparing them for the next blow. He heard a thin series of clanks as the throwing arm was ratcheted back. Macro had hurried to the other side of the gatehouse and was staring down at the barracks block that had taken the first strike. There was a gaping hole in the roof and a haze of dust hanging over the building.

'Hey, you!' Macro yelled down to one of the soldiers in the street. The man looked round and up and stood to attention.

'Yes, sir!'

'Check inside that building. Make sure everyone's all right. Get any casualties seen to by the medical orderlies. Move!'

As soon as he had given the order, Macro re-joined Cato. The first of the onagers was almost ready to load and in the growing light they could see two men struggling to lift a rock into the cup at the end of the throwing arm. An order was shouted and an instant later the beam of wood shot up again, cracked against the cross bar and another missile arced towards the fort. As before, it seemed to be coming straight for them and Cato glanced at Macro. Macro was tracking the rapid progress of the rock, so Cato forced himself to remain composed and resist the impulse to dive to one side. The rock struck the base of the gatehouse and Cato felt the shock of the impact right through his body. A chunk of masonry fell off the rampart close by and dust and grit tumbled down from the dry thatch roof overhead.

Macro looked at him. 'You all right?'

Cato nodded.

'Better check the damage.'

They leaned over the rampart and gazed down. The rock was still in one piece where it had bounced back from the wall and there was a small crater on the face of the masonry, near the arch, and a skein of small cracks radiating from it.

Macro winced. 'I really hope that was a lucky shot.'

The second onager swung into action and another stone flew through the air towards the fort. Again it fell short and bounced off the stony ground before harmlessly hitting the base of the wall beside the gatehouse. As dawn broke over the desert the bombardment continued in a steady rhythm of the clanking ratchet, the crack of the throwing arm striking the cross beam and the crash of the impact. But nearly half the shots fell short, or went wide and hit the walls, or overshot the defences and smashed into the buildings beyond. Every hit on the gatehouse dislodged more masonry and the fine cracks gradually widened. One lucky shot landed right on the bottom of the gate itself, making the hinges rattle. Macro gave the order for most of the men to shelter behind the wall, leaving those manning the corner towers to keep an eye on the enemy. After a little while Macro and Cato climbed down from the gatehouse and sat down in the watchroom beside the timbers of the gate.

'Have you ever been on the receiving end before?' Cato asked.

'No. Can't say I'm enjoying the experience.' Macro smiled faintly. 'Have to hand it to Bannus and his Parthian friends – they've managed to spring a very nasty surprise on us. And I let those bloody onagers slip by, right under my nose.'

'Don't be hard on yourself, sir. No one could have seen that one coming.'

'Maybe, but that's not going to be much of a consolation if they manage to batter the gatehouse down and swarm all over us.'

'Couldn't we try to destroy the onagers?'

'How do you propose we do that?'

'Send out our cavalry, charge over there before they can react and try to fire the onagers, or at least cut the torsion mechanism.'

Macro shook his head. 'It wouldn't work. There's only one route for horses through the ground we've prepared with caltrops and pits, and that's to the east. We'd have to take that until we were clear of the traps before we could turn towards the onagers. They'd have enough time to get plenty of men between us and their precious siege weapons. It'd just be a waste of men.'

'What if we tried it tonight on foot?'

'Much the same problem. There is a narrow passage through the obstacles to the west, and another to the north. If we lost touch with the paths we'd be caught between the enemy and our own defences. It's almost impossible to find your way in the dark.'

However badly Cato wanted to destroy the onagers he knew that his friend was right. It would be a dangerous operation, by day or night. He ran a hand through his hair. 'If we can't stop these onagers then I suppose we'd better get the counter-measures in place.'

Macro nodded. 'Let's go.'

They strode away from the wall and Macro took a javelin from one of the auxiliaries. He stood to one side of the gatehouse, adjusted his position, and then began to mark out a line in the sand and gravel with the point of the javelin. He continued until he had described an arc round the rear of the gatehouse, and then he returned the javelin to the auxiliary.

'That should do, Cato. I want a breastwork along that line. Build it up as high as you can. Rig a few sheltered platforms on either side. If the enemy comes through the breach then we'll meet them with arrows and javelins from three sides. Got all that?'

'Yes, sir.'

'Then let's get to it.'

Cato assembled a work party and gave orders for the destruction of the barracks blocks closest to the gatehouse. That would provide a ready supply of materials for the second line of defence as well as clearing a space behind the breastwork to mass a force of defenders to meet any attack through the breach. The auxiliaries used iron hooks and lengths of rope to pull down the rafters and then the walls of each block. Other men took up picks and began to dig post holes for the roof beams.

Timbers were nailed across the beams before the largest pieces of rubble were used to build up the foundations of the makeshift wall. The work continued through the morning and into the afternoon, under the glare of the sun, and all the time the onagers continued their assault on the gatehouse. Some rocks still overshot the wall and smashed into a building with a loud crash that made the defenders start and duck for cover, until the officers bawled at them to continue working. They were fortunate enough to escape any serious casualties until noon when one of the rocks pitched down into the middle of a work party, pulverising one man into a barely recognisable tangle of bloody limbs and wounding most of his comrades as splinters of stone exploded from where the rock hit the ground. Cato immediately shouted a string of orders to have the body taken away and the injured removed to the hospital, and sent the other men back to constructing the inner wall.

Then, in the late afternoon, as yet another shot smashed into the gatehouse, there was an ominous rumble of masonry as a crack opened up diagonally from the rampart almost down to the ground. The men paused for a moment to look and then returned to their labours with renewed determination. Cato quietly made his way over to Macro.

'Won't be long now, sir.'

'Maybe,' Macro responded. 'But it's still holding up for the moment. I just hope it lasts until nightfall. I doubt they'll make any direct assaults until they can clearly see what they're doing. Meanwhile, we'll just have to make the best job we can of the inner wall.'

A few shots later, the corner of the gatehouse collapsed on to the ground outside the fort and once the sound of crumbling masonry had died away the defenders could hear the triumphant cries of the enemy. Cato glanced up at the gatehouse and saw the wide gap in the top of the wall next to the collapsed section, as if some great Titan had torn a chunk of the defences away with his teeth. And still the bombardment continued without let-up. Indeed, once the corner had given way, Cato steadily counted between impacts, and calculated that the enemy had increased the frequency of the rocks they were lobbing at the fort. Each blow on the loosened stonework caused more of the structure to collapse on to the existing rubble with a rumble of heavy masonry and the slither and rattle of smaller stones. As the sun sank towards the horizon behind the enemy camp the ruin of the gatehouse became a jagged silhouette, until at last the arch above the gate fell in and all that remained was a tangled heap of rubble and shattered beams of wood.

As dusk fell across the surrounding desert Macro and Cato climbed into one of the corner towers to survey the situation. Some of the enemy, emboldened by the destruction of the gatehouse, had ventured close enough to the fort to attract the attention of the archers stationed at intervals along the wall and every so often an arrow whirred out from the fort towards the nearest men, causing them to scatter and dive for cover. Macro was cheered by the sight of one man, slower to react than his companions, who happened to look up just as the heavy barbed tip of a shaft smashed into his face and burst out the back of his skull.

'Fine shot!' Macro bellowed along the wall and one of the archers quickly turned to bow his head in acknow-ledgement before quickly notching another arrow and looking for his next target.

As the last of the light began to fade the enemy pounded what was left of the gatehouse and then ceased the bombardment. They would resume in the morning and after a few more hours the breach would be practic-able for Bannus and his army to assault. Fires appeared in the enemy encampment and the sounds of singing and laughter could be clearly heard by the defenders as they continued to build up the inner wall. Macro and Cato inspected the work of their men by torchlight. The new wall rose to a height of nearly eight feet and was thick enough to withstand the pressure of a wave of men pressing up against it. On the inside stood a narrow fighting platform from which the defenders could strike down on the enemy as they clambered over the rubble strewn across the ground in front of the wall.

Macro patted the rough surface. 'It'll do.'

'It will have to,' Cato replied softly. 'When they finish

off what's left of the gatehouse, that's all there is to keep them out.'

By the wavering glow of the torch he held in his hand Macro turned to stare at his friend. 'You're right, of course. They will finish the job in the morning.'

'Unless something is done about those onagers tonight.'

'I told you,' Macro responded wearily. 'It's too dangerous.'

'We're in danger either way,' said Cato. 'At least if we try something we might be able to set them back a day or so and buy ourselves some time. It has to be worth trying, sir.'

Macro wasn't convinced. 'I told you, whoever goes out there under cover of darkness is bound to lose their way through the defences.'

Cato was looking at Macro's torch and Macro noticed the excited glint in his friend's eyes that always accompanied the sudden rush of thought when Cato came up with one of his hare-brained schemes. He felt his heart sink.

'Let me lead a raid, sir.'

'Are you so tired of living already, Cato?'

'No, I'm just not terribly keen on sitting here, waiting to be killed. Besides, I think there's a way of safely passing through our defence lines . . .'

'Are you sure about this?' Macro said softly as he looked at Cato. The young centurion had blackened his face and the rest of the flesh that was not covered by the dark brown tunic that he wore. His sword belt was buckled round his waist and a haversack hung from his shoulder containing a tinderbox and several small pots of oil. Behind him stood a party of twenty men, similarly equipped for the night's work.

'I'll be fine, sir. Just make sure those lamps are kept alight.' Cato nodded up to the rampart where the wan glow of an oil lamp flickered in the darkness. Back at headquarters a second lamp had been lit and placed in the highest window in line with the lamp on the wall and the narrow path through the screen of traps and obstacles that stretched out beyond the north wall of the fort.

Macro clasped his friend's arm. 'Do what you have to do and come straight back. Don't get carried away. I know what you're like.'

Cato grinned. 'Trust me, sir. I don't want to be out there any longer than I have to.'

Macro gave Cato's arm a brief squeeze. 'Good luck then.'

He stepped back and nodded to the sentry. As quietly as he could, the sentry slid back the bolts of the sally port and eased the door open. There was a faint grating squeal from the hinges and Macro sucked in his breath at the sound that seemed so loud in the stillness behind the wall. The sentry paused for a moment and then opened the door more slowly, until there was a sufficient gap for Cato and his men to file through.

'Come on,' Cato whispered, and with a last reassuring glance towards the dark shape of Macro he crept out of the fort. The sky was moonless and dim grey strands of cloud covered most of the stars so the landscape was wrapped in darkness – perfect cover for Cato and his party. Of course, the same lack of illumination was the main danger facing the Romans. It would be easy enough to stumble into an enemy sentry or a patrol in such conditions. That was why Cato was determined to proceed as cautiously as possible. As the last man exited the fort the sally port was gently closed behind them. Cato waited a moment for any sign or sound that their presence had been detected, and then he beckoned to the man behind him and began to creep along the foot of the wall. In the distance they could hear the sounds of the men at the main gate, hurriedly trying to repair some of the damage done to the gatehouse during the day. The night's labour would be undone in the first few hours if the bombardment continued in the morning, but it would gain the garrison a little more time. Cato headed towards the narrow path that led from the north face of the fort.

As they reached the point where the lamp glowed faintly on the wall Cato halted, and let his men catch up. Already he was shivering, partly from the penetrating cold of the air and partly from the state of nervous excitement as he led his men on this dangerous raid into the enemy camp. He took a deep breath to try to calm his anxiety, and then headed down into the ditch that surrounded the fort, and climbed up the far side. Picking the black mass of a distant rocky outcrop as a landmark he began to feel his way towards it on hands and knees. His left hand recoiled from contact with the sharp point of a caltrop and he felt ahead and soon found another to give him some sense of that side of the passage. They had crept over a hundred paces from the wall, by Cato's reckoning, before he glanced back and saw the lamp at headquarters as well, almost perfectly aligned with the other one on the wall. He adjusted his position until the two lamps were in line, and then continued forward slowly.

It took a long time to reach the limit of the defences that Macro had prepared and Cato felt a hand on his shoulder as the man behind grasped him suddenly. Cato turned and saw his arm pointing away to the right. Less than a hundred yards away Cato could just make out the silhouettes of two Judaeans against the marginally lighter night sky. There was a snatch of conversation and laughter and the two figures moved slowly away, continuing their patrol around the fort's perimeter. The small party of Romans continued forward until they were well clear of the defences and then Cato turned parallel to the fort's wall and led them towards the red gloom of the fires in the enemy camp.

All his senses strained to detect any presence around him, any sign of danger. The cold had crept into his body and now his chest felt tight and he could do nothing to contain his shivering as they approached the enemy, crouching down as they moved slowly through the darkness. At length he saw the perpendicular frames of the onagers some distance away, picked out by the glow from a nearby fire. He halted his men and indicated to them to form up round him in a loose circle.

'Sycorax?' he whispered.

'Here, sir.'

Cato turned towards the dark figure kneeling a short distance away. 'The carts and their animals are over that way.' He indicated the mass of a rise in the ground a quarter of a mile from the onagers. 'Get rid of the sentries and start a blaze. Make it as large as you can and once you have their attention make as much noise as you can. Then get back to the fort.'

'Don't worry, sir. We know what to do.'

'Good luck then. Off you go.'

Cato watched as Sycorax and his men shuffled off and were swallowed up by the night. Then he waved his men on and they crept closer to the onagers. As they slowly got nearer, the sounds of the enemy camp grew louder and Cato feared that the noise would mask the position of the men guarding the onagers, even as it might help to conceal the approach of Cato and his party. As soon as he saw the first man standing by the onagers, Cato halted his men.

'Wait here.'

Lowering himself on to his stomach Cato slithered

forward, head raised slightly as he scanned the ground ahead. He worked his way to one side of the onagers and saw that there were at least ten men beside the siege engines, an even match for Cato and his auxiliaries should the guards not be tempted to abandon their post when Sycorax started his diversion. Cato crawled back to his men and they lay in the dark and waited.

It was not long before there was a shout in the distance and a moment later the flicker of flames as a heavy cart was consumed by wild tongues of orange and yellow. In the glow cast round the cart Cato could see horses and mules straining at their tethers as they desperately tried to escape the heat. The shrill braying and whinnying rose to a terrified pitch. He turned back to the onagers. The guards had all moved to one side to watch the fire. Beyond them a horn blasted out in the enemy camp and suddenly the dark floor of the desert teemed with figures flowing towards the blaze. One of the guards shouted, and ran a few paces towards the flames, then paused and gestured angrily for the others to follow. One shook his head and shouted back, stabbing his finger to the ground at his feet, refusing to move. But a handful of others rushed to join the first man and they ran off into the night.

Cato turned to his men. 'Follow me. No man strikes until I say.'

Rising to a crouch, Cato ran towards the onager furthest from the remaining guards and with a soft padding of footsteps his men followed. When they reached the onager Cato took off his haversack and opened it.

'As soon as I've got this one alight take down those guards. Draw your swords.'

The was a quiet chorus of rasps as the men slowly took their swords from their scabbards and held them ready. While two of them started dousing the onager's frame and torsion ropes with oil, others found some spare rope and combustibles to place under the frame. Cato prepared some carbonised linen in his tinderbox together with some shreds of dried bark. Then he struck his flints. After the first few frustrating attempts a small shower of sparks caught on the linen and he blew softly over them until, with a tiny pop, a small lick of flame appeared. Carefully he drew some of the bark over to feed the flame and then when there was a healthy crackle he lowered it to the kindling materials. There was a maddening delay before the flames spread from the tinderbox, but at last the flames were licking up from the base of the onager and spread rapidly as the oil caught fire and bathed the surrounding area in a lurid glow.

There was a shout of alarm from the remaining guards as they turned towards the blaze.

'Get 'em!' Cato shouted to his men and they rose up and charged the guards. Cato snatched up a burning length of wood from the fire licking up round the onager and raced after the rest of the incendiary group making for the other siege engine. There was no need to use the tinderbox this time and Cato thrust the burning piece of wood into the kindling his men had swiftly packed under the torsion ropes. The fire caught quickly and Cato watched it long enough to make sure that it was well ablaze before he drew his sword and looked round.

The guards had been quickly cut down by his men, but in the light cast by the flames Cato could see more of the enemy streaming out of the darkness towards the burning onagers. It was vital that he held them off long enough for the eager flames to consume as much of the siege weapons as possible.

'On me!' he called out. 'On me, Second Illyrian!'

As his men came running up Cato formed them into a loose cordon in front of the burning onagers and they stood ready, swords out and slightly crouched as they prepared to take on the enemy rushing into the rippling glow of the flames. With the fire at their backs the Romans were dense black silhouettes casting long dark shadows before them and the first of the Judaeans wavered at the sight. Then, with a snarled shout of anger and contempt, a Parthian thrust his way through them and charged directly at the Roman line. The auxiliary facing him braced for the impact, then at the last moment suddenly kicked sand and gravel into the Parthian's face. Instinctively the Parthian hesitated and raised his arm to protect his eyes. The instinct killed him, as the Roman pounced forward and thrust his sword into the man's guts, then ripped the blade free with a ferocious roar. The Parthian slumped to his knees, glancing down in shock at the blood and intestines bulging from the terrible wound.

Behind him the enemy stopped dead in their tracks, not willing to take on the Romans, and Cato saw his chance. He drew a deep breath and roared, 'Charge!'

He ran straight forward, his men following him an instant later, adding their cries to his. Just before he reached the enemy Cato's mind was blazing with crazy rage and he sensed a current of energy, like fire, coursing through his veins. As he swung his sword in a quick cut at the nearest man, small, dark-featured and terrified, Cato heard himself cry out in meaningless rage. The man threw an arm up, fingers snatching towards the hilt of Cato's sword as it swept towards him. The edge of the blade crushed the man's hand and swept on and down, shattering his collar bone as it cut deep into his shoulder. He cried out in fear and pain, and Cato wrenched his blade free and thrust the man aside as he looked for his next foe. On either side his small force had ploughed into the enemy and were cutting and hacking at them in wild abandon, screaming and shouting all the time as they were caught in the bright red glow of the flames and the leaping shadows of other men.

Cato fixed his glare on a broad man with a long dark beard. He carried a heavy curved sword in both hands, and as soon as he saw that the Roman had singled him out he swung it over his head and rushed towards Cato. The side of the blade gleamed a fiery orange as it caught the light of the flames, then it was a blur as it arced down towards Cato's head. He knew he could not parry the blow. It would mean certain death to even attempt it. Instead he sprang to one side, colliding with another man, and both fell, sprawling on the ground. The curved sword thudded into the ground at Cato's side, striking sparks off the edge of a small rock. Cato lashed out with his boot, feeling the nailed sole strike the man's wrist hard. With a cry of pain the Judaean loosened his grip and the heavy sword dropped to the ground. But before Cato could strike a killing blow, the man he had collided with threw himself on top of Cato, desperate fingers tearing at his throat and face. Cato's sword hand was pinned to his side; he clenched his left hand into a fist and smashed it against the side of the man's head. The blow made him gasp, but he clung on to Cato with gritted teeth and his thumbs clamped down on Cato's windpipe with agonising pressure.

'No!' Cato growled. 'No you fucking don't!'

He brought his knee up hard between the man's legs and felt the kneecap thud into his genitals. The man gasped and rolled his eyes and for an instant his hands loosened their grip. With a convulsive heave of his whole body Cato thrust him off, and then stabbed his sword into the man's side as soon as his right arm was free. The blade slid out of the wound with a wet sucking noise and

Cato scrambled back on to his feet. On either side his men had cut down several more of the enemy, but already many more were appearing in the glow of the flames. Far too many to take on, and with the confidence of numbers the enemy surged towards the Romans. Cato realised that he and his men had done all that they could. To remain here for another instant was to invite death.

'Fall back!' he cried out. 'Go!'

He turned and raced away from the enemy, between the burning onagers, and back towards the safety of the darkness. His men hurried after him, breathing heavily from their exertions and excitement. The enemy came on, rushing after the Romans in a wave. Some realised what their true priority was and leaped towards the blazing onagers, heedless of the scorching heat as they desperately struggled to pull away the blazing wood piled round the thick timbers of the frames. A few scooped up sand and tried to smother the flames, while others pulled off their cloaks and tried to beat the flames out. But more, many more, were filled with a desire for revenge on those Romans who had dared to venture from the fort to attack their camp. They charged past the burning onagers and rushed after Cato and his men, pursuing them into the darkness beyond the orange loom of the flames.

'On me!' Cato called out. He wanted his men close, to make sure that they passed through the defences together. To his right was the dark bulk of the fort, with torches flaring in each of the corner towers. And there, halfway along the wall, the spark of light from the oil lamp, and behind, at an angle, the dimmer flame of the lamp in the window of the headquarters building.

'Keep going,' Cato muttered to the dim shadows beside and behind him. Further off he heard the shouts of the men pursuing them. 'Stay with me.'

They ran on, instinctively edging towards the fort as the two small lights closed on one another. Then the inevitable happened. Just as Cato reached the point where the flames overlapped there was a cry of pain just behind him. He spun round and saw a dark shape rolling on the ground, groaning through gritted teeth.

'What's happened?'

'It's Petronius, sir. He's stepped on a caltrop.'

Cato dropped to the man's side and felt his way down the calf, over the boot, until his fingers brushed the iron prongs. There was no time to spare, and Cato grasped the spikes and wrenched the caltrop from the man's boot. Petronius cried out in surprise and pain and at once there was a shout from the men chasing them as they made for the sound.

'Shit,' Cato muttered. 'Get him up. We're in line with the passage. Head for the wall, and keep those lights in line.'

Cato counted seven men passing him and waited a moment for the rest, but then he heard the enemy shouting close by and he turned to follow his men. Their pursuers were closer than he thought and several figures appeared from the gloom, and shouted to the others the moment they caught sight of Cato making off from them, as fast as he dared, through the fort's outer defences. With their prey in view the enemy ran heedlessly towards Cato, straight across the defences at an angle to the passage the Romans were doing their best to follow. Cato continued for a few more steps before he turned and crouched low, ready to defend himself. There was a shrill cry as the nearest man tumbled over, and clutched at his foot. Then another man went down, and a third stumbled into one of the shallow pits. Only one of them made it as far as Cato and launched himself at the Roman, thrusting a long-bladed sword at the centre of the centurion's body. Cato just had time to sweep his sword over and counter the blow, then the man slashed horizontally, forcing him to drop on one knee and duck his head. As the blade swished overhead Cato slashed out with his own sword at knee height and felt it cut into the joint with a wet, jarring thud that severed tendons and smashed bones so that the enemy fell sprawling on his back, crying out. Cato left him, and shuffled to his side until the lights were aligned. Then he set off again.

Behind him the Judaeans had realised the danger and stopped short of the outer defences. Cato smiled to himself. His plan had worked as he had hoped. All that remained was to gain the wall and move along it to the sally port and then the night's raid was over. Something thudded into the sand beside him. Then again, just behind his boot so that he felt the spray of grit against his calf. Frustrated by the defences, the enemy were throwing stones after the Romans.

Cato hunched his head down and quickened his pace to a slow trot, fearing that at any moment he would feel the stab of iron bursting through the soles of his boots, leaving him crippled and helpless. Suddenly he was upon his own men, and he drew up sharply, almost stumbling over them.

'What the fuck are you doing? Get moving.'

'Can't, sir.' It was one of the men who was helping Petronius. 'Glabarus was hit by a stone. Knocked him cold.'

Cato felt an instant of panic as he stared down at the three men, one lying still on the ground, Petronius slumped to one knee and the third man still holding him under the shoulder and trying to keep him up. Glancing back Cato saw that the Judaeans were moving along the limit of the defences behind them. Any moment they would reach the opening of the passage and it was possible that one of them would be observant enough to work out the significance of the aligned lamps. A moment later his fears were confirmed as the nearest of the men edged cautiously in amongst the narrow path between the traps. Cato swallowed nervously and realised his mouth felt as dry as the sand stretching out around them. He made the only decision that he could and bent down to Petronius' free side and raised the man up.

'Let's get going.'

'What about Glabarus, sir?'

'We have to leave him.'

'No!'

'Shut up and move.'

'But he's my mate.'

Cato fought down the rage that threatened to erupt and spoke as calmly as he could. 'We can't carry both of them. We have to leave him. Or we all die. Now let's go.'

He started forward and as the other man felt the tug of Petronius' weight he was forced to move forward, and only had time to spare his friend a brief last glance. Cato kept glancing up at the lights to make sure they stayed on course and did not dare to look back over his shoulder as the enemy came on behind them. They reached the ditch and half scrambled, half slithered down the slope, across the bottom and up the far slope, under the burden of the injured man. Then they were moving along the narrow strip of flat earth at the base of the wall, making for the sally port. Cato could just make out the shapes of the rest of his party ahead of him and willed himself on. The safety of the fort's walls was mere moments away.

There was a flare overhead and the crackle of burning sticks, and a ball of flame arced down from the wall and bounced into the ditch, lighting up the area around it. Looking back Cato could see the first of the Judaeans to clear the outer defences scrambling down into the ditch, caught in the light of the burning faggot. He heard Macro's voice bellow out.

'Archers! Shoot 'em down!'

Feathered shafts whipped through the air and thudded into the men pursuing Cato and the others, sending several sprawling, and causing the others to halt and stare up at the new danger. More arrows found their target and stopped them dead in their tracks. Cato looked away, back towards the sally port, and hurried on. The thick wooden door was already open and they thrust Petronius inside and then squeezed through after him and slumped to the ground gasping for breath.

'Shut the port,' Cato ordered.

The optio of the section tasked with guarding the sally port glanced out through the wall. 'Where's the rest of your men, sir?'

'They should be here. Sycorax and the others.'

'There's been no sign of them, sir.'

'Shut the gate,' Cato repeated. 'If they're not back yet, then they never will be.'

The optio hesitated for a moment before he nodded and heaved the door back into position and drew the locking bars across and into their receivers. Cato forced himself on to his feet, drew some deep breaths and indicated Petronius. 'Get him to the hospital immediately.'

As the optio carried out the order Cato made his way up on to the rampart and squeezed past the archers until he found Macro. The prefect smiled a greeting.

'Cato! You made it. The rest of the men?'

'I lost six from my party, and there's been no sign of Sycorax.'

'I know,' Macro replied flatly. 'But we'll keep looking out for him and his men. Meanwhile, see there.' He pointed out across the wall at the onagers. One was roaring with flames, the crackle clearly audible from where they stood. The other was still alight, but even as they watched the enemy was successfully smothering the flames. Shortly afterwards they had put that fire out.

'Never mind,' Macro said with a note of satisfaction. 'It'll be out of action for a while and the other one's destroyed. That's improved our chances no end. Good job, Cato.'

Cato tried to feel some satisfaction at his achievement, but he felt hollow and empty and bone weary. If Sycorax and his men had been lost, then the raid had been costly indeed, whatever it may have achieved. He felt guilty to have been the cause of the men's death and for an instant he stared out over the wall, past the burning faggot and the bodies spread around it, out over the desert, trying to penetrate the darkness to the place where he had been forced to leave Glabarus, as if half expecting to see the man stagger out of the darkness. But Glabarus must be dead. And Sycorax and the others too. It would be better if they were dead, Cato realised. The enemy would show little mercy to any Roman soldiers they took alive.

He spread out his arms slightly and lowered his head as he leaned on the wall. Macro looked at him.

'You're done in, lad. Best go and get some rest.'

'I'll wait a while, sir. In case Sycorax makes it back.'

'I'll look out for him,' Macro said gently. 'You get some rest, Centurion. That's an order.'

Cato looked up and met his friend's eyes. He thought about protesting, then knew that Macro was right. There was nothing to be gained by tiring them both out.

'Very well, sir. Thank you.'

Cato took one last look at the burning onager and hoped that he had bought his comrades enough time to justify the sacrifice of Glabarus, Sycorax and the others. He'd know soon enough, when the next day dawned.

CHAPTER TWENTY-SIX

As soon as the flames on the surviving onager had been extinguished the Parthian engineers started making repairs, and the sounds of their labours could be heard through the rest of the night. At first light Macro and Cato climbed the corner tower to survey the results of the previous night's raid. The first onager was little more than a black, charred skeleton. A short distance away the other onager almost looked undamaged as the enemy swarmed round it. Fresh torsion cords had been fitted and they were busy tightening them with long levers, several men to each, straining every muscle to wring the very last measure of power from the weapon's throwing arm.

'Won't be long before that's back in action,' Cato muttered. 'They've been busy.'

'You don't know the half of it,' Macro replied, and gestured towards the ground in front of the fort. 'Shortly after you returned, they began removing the traps. We tried throwing torches out for the archers to see their targets, but the enemy had screens, and just ducked behind them the moment the first arrows began to fly. They only stopped at daybreak.'

Cato looked down and saw that a large swath of the defences had been cleared, the pits filled in and the caltrops removed. Bannus and his men could now approach almost as far as the ditch on the side of the fort where the ruined gatehouse stood. When the time came for the enemy to make their attack, little would stand in the way between them and the men of the cohort. Cato glanced at the gatehouse. Some attempt had been made to prepare a breastwork out of the rubble. It continued the line of the wall and Macro had posted enough men behind it to convince the enemy that the Romans would not easily surrender the gatehouse. A shallow bluff, Cato realised. The moment the repaired onager was ready to recommence the bombardment, it would batter down the breastwork and send the Romans scurrying for the shelter of the inner wall.

'No sign of Sycorax and the others?'

'Not yet,' Macro replied quietly. 'I don't expect we'll be seeing them again.'

Cato shook his head wearily. 'All those men lost, and we only managed to destroy one weapon.'

'One destroyed. One damaged. That's a good result by any measure, Cato. You've halved the weight of their bombardment and set them back a while until the repairs are complete. You and the others did as much as could reasonably be expected. So don't go and put yourself down, and don't rubbish the effort of those men who didn't make it back last night,' Macro said frostily. 'In the circumstances we had to try something, or just sit here and wait for them to come to us. We did the right thing.'

'Maybe, but if it just postpones the inevitable, then that's small comfort. I wonder if the men who . . .' Cato's voice faded as his gaze was drawn to a group of men working close to the burned onager. They had been busy cutting away the salvageable timber and constructing something on the ground next to the remains of the siege weapon. Now several small parties of the enemy were distributing lengths of jointed wood, fashioned in some kind of crosspiece. He pointed them out to Macro.

'What are they up to?'

The older officer strained his eyes for a moment and shook his head. 'Beats me. Framework for a ram housing, maybe.'

As they watched there was a brief commotion in the enemy camp and then a crowd of men marched towards the siege engines. As they got closer Cato could see that they were jostling a small party of captives with dark tunics and smeared skin. He felt a sinking feeling in his guts as he recognised one of the prisoners.

'I think that's Sycorax . . .'

Even as he watched them approach the hastily arranged constructions lying on the ground Cato could guess what was coming next, and he felt his stomach clench and feared he was going to be sick. The prisoners were split up, one man being dragged to each crosspiece. The tunics were torn from their bodies and then they were held down against the wood while heavy iron nails were driven through their wrists and ankles. The sound of the hammer blows rang out over the open ground, accompanied by terrified screams of agony from the Roman prisoners.

Neither Macro nor Cato spoke as they watched the first of the makeshift crosses raised into position, and lowered heavily into the post hole that had been dug for the base. There was an audible thud and the forceful impact caused one of the prisoner's wrists to tear loose so that his mangled arm dropped and he gave a piercing shriek. The enemy were not fazed by the incident. One of them calmly set a siege ladder up against the rear of the cross, climbed up, reached over the beam to grasp the torn arm and nailed it back into place. Fortunately the torment of the prisoner was such that he passed out after the first few blows, to the relief of his comrades watching in horror from the walls of the fort. The respite was short-lived, however, as one by one the other prisoners were raised up until a line of crosses extended some distance in front of the surviving onager.

Cato felt a bitter acid taste in his mouth as he swallowed. 'That's what'll be in store for any of us they take alive, I imagine.'

'Yes,' Macro replied softly. 'Bannus is trying to get the wind up our boys.'

'Then I think he's succeeded.' Cato glanced along the wall and saw one of the auxiliaries bent over, vomiting on to the catwalk.

'Of course,' Macro continued flatly, 'there's a nice ironic touch there for his own side. After all the rebels we've crucified over recent years, now we're on the receiving end. Listen to 'em! They just love it.'

As the last cross rose up the enemy cheered loudly, and then their tone quickly changed to cruel laughter and derisive taunts and jeering as their victims writhed in agony and blood ran down beneath their arms and stained their bare chests bright red.

'They've had their fun,' Macro growled. 'Now it's our turn. Archers!' He turned to the men on the wall. In amongst them were sections of men armed with compound bows. 'Archers! Shoot on that crowd! Shoot, damn you!'

His obvious rage spurred the men into action. After hastily stringing their bows, the fastest of them notched their arrows, drew back the strings and angled the shafts high before releasing them. The first, ragged volley fell into the crowd, taking down a handful of the enemy before they could scatter and run for cover. More were struck down as the arrows fell with increased intensity. Then a shaft struck one of the Romans on the crosses, burying itself in his throat, so that he jerked, struggled a moment and then hung limp and quite still.

'They're hitting our men!' Cato said in a horrified tone. 'Stop them!'

'No.' Macro shook his head. 'That's what I'd hoped for.'

Cato turned and stared. 'What?'

Macro ignored him and turned to shout to the archers. 'That's it, boys! Keep it up! Stick it to 'em!'

The archers kept shooting as fast as they could, and had no time to follow the passage of their arrows, and so were unaware that they were hitting their comrades at first. Macro waited until the enemy had dispersed and the prisoners had been silenced before he gave the order for the archers to cease shooting. Only then were they fully aware of the result of their handiwork, and they gazed towards the enemy lines in numbed silence, until Macro's bellowed order echoed across the fort.

'First century will remain on watch! All other centuries to breakfast!'

When the men moved away from the wall slowly Macro thumped his fist down on the parapet. 'Officers! Get your men moving! They're not paid by the bloody hour!'

He glared at the officers as they hurried to carry out his command and soon only a thin screen of auxiliaries remained, spread along the wall. Then Macro nodded with satisfaction. 'I don't want our men exposed to that display any more than necessary. I want their minds on the fight, not on what might happen after it.'

'If they know what Bannus has in store for them, then they'll fight to the death.'

'Maybe,' Macro replied. 'But they'll not fight as well, if I give 'em the chance to dwell on the fate of those poor buggers.'

Cato could see the sense of that. Macro had demonstrated a fine understanding of how soldiers' minds worked, and even if the men at Fort Bushir were doomed Macro would see to it that their minds were concentrated on killing as many of their enemies as possible before they were cut down in turn. His friend was professional to the very last, Cato realised. And, at some point in the next few days, there was every chance that that last moment would indeed come. Cato looked back towards the bodies hanging from the crosses.

'Was it really necessary to kill them?'

Macro sniffed. 'What would you have done? Left them there to die a slow, agonising death? It was an act of mercy, Cato.'

Cato frowned as an unpleasant thought entered his mind. He turned to his friend. 'What if I had been captured along with Sycorax and the others last night? Would you have given the order for the archers to shoot me?'

A bemused look flitted across Macro's face. 'Of course I would, Cato. Without an instant's hesitation, and believe me, if you had been nailed up alongside those men, you'd have thanked me.'

'I'm not sure about that.'

'In any case, I wouldn't have given you the choice.' Macro smiled grimly, before he continued in an earnest tone, 'And if it had been me out there, I'd have expected you to do the same. The thing is, I'm not sure you'd have the balls to go through with it . . . Well?'

Cato looked at him for a moment and then shook his head. 'I don't know. I just don't know if I could do that.'

Macro pursed his lips sadly. 'You're a good man. A good soldier, and a good officer most of the time. If we get out of his, then one day you'll have a command of your own, and I won't be there. That's when you'll have to make the really tough decisions, Cato. You can count on it. The question is, are you ready for that?' He looked hard at his young friend for an instant and then punched him lightly on the shoulder. 'Think it over. Meanwhile, I want you to make sure that the gatehouse is as ready as it can be before Bannus gets that onager back into action.'

'I don't think there's any point to that, sir. He'll batter our repairs down quickly enough.'

'The point is that it keeps our men busy, and stops them thinking too much. That includes you. It also shows Bannus and his friends that the Second Illyrian's not going to give up, roll over and wait for our enemies to stick the boot in. We're better than that. Understand what I'm saying?'

'Of course,' Cato replied testily. 'I'm not a fool.'

'Far from it. But even the most brilliant minds can still learn something from those of us with experience, eh?' Macro smiled. 'Now see to it that you do a decent job of that breastwork.'

'Yes sir.' Cato nodded. 'I'll do my best.'

'Of course you will. I'd expect nothing less. Don't just stand there, Centurion. Get moving!'

All morning the men toiled at raising the breastwork over the remains of the gatehouse, and strengthening the inner wall. Mindful of Macro's words, Cato drove them hard and permitted them few rest breaks as they thickened the makeshift defences and added to the height of the inner wall. If the enemy managed to force their way through this last obstacle then the Second Illyrian Cohort would be wiped out. As the men toiled within the fort, the enemy continued to clear away more of the traps laid outside, their workers screened by a thin line of archers ready to take a shot at any target that revealed itself up on the wall. Behind them the engineers sweated under the bright sun to make the surviving onager serviceable once again. Shortly after noon the enemy at last drew away from the siege engine as the throwing arm was carefully ratcheted back, engineers checking the weapon for any further sign of damage as it prepared to bombard the fort again. At length they were satisfied that it was safe to proceed. A curt order was shouted, the locking lever snapped back and the throwing arm swept up and hit the cross beam with a loud thwack as the missile was released, soaring up into the air and then arcing down towards the gatehouse. At once Cato and the work party dropped their tools and scrambled down behind the wall into cover.

The Parthian siege engineers were first rate, or at least very lucky, thought Cato, as the first shot smashed into the breastwork and knocked a gaping hole in the top of the rebuilt defences. The bombardment continued with an endless cycle of clanks, a crack and the crash and rumble of masonry. After the first missile had landed, Cato pulled his men back behind the inner wall and climbed a corner tower to watch proceedings as the hot afternoon wore on. The gradual destruction of the remains of the gatehouse was carried out in a methodical and complete manner, beginning with the wall and then simply pounding the rest into a pile of loose rubble that would make a practical breach for Bannus and his army to assault. As the light began to fade and the desert sand shimmered hot and bright red in the wash of the setting sun, the onager at last fell still and the men inside the fort no longer had to press themselves into the shelter of a wall and cringe as the rocks crashed down. When he was sure that the bombardment had ceased, Cato sent for Macro. The prefect joined him behind the destroyed gatehouse and took a few tentative steps on the rubble.

'They'll be able to climb over this easily enough.'

'When do you think they'll come?' asked Cato.

'Hard to say.' Macro looked up at the sky, already darkening to a velvet blue pierced by the first of the evening's stars. 'I reckon they'll wait until first light when they'll be able to see how the attack is progressing.' Macro shrugged. 'At least that's what I would do in their boots.'

Then they heard the sounds of drums being beaten and the harsh blare of a trumpet.

'What's that?' Cato asked. 'What are they up to now?'

'How should I know?' Macro grumbled. 'Come on, let's have a look.'

He beckoned to Cato to follow him and started to climb over the piles of stone, slabs of rock and splintered wooden beams. As they reached the top of the mound of rubble Cato stared towards the enemy camp. A large number of men were forming up opposite the gatehouse, comfortably outside arrow range. The sun, low in the sky, bathed them in an orange hue that glinted off their weapons like molten bronze.

'Nice!' Macro nodded towards the wash of colour along the distant skyline. 'Although I think the view is wasted on our friends out there. They've got other things on their minds.' He turned to Cato with an apologetic expression. 'Seems I was wrong. They're not prepared to wait until tomorrow morning. They're going to attack the fort at once.'

CHAPTER TWENTY-SEVEN

While the enemy massed their forces outside, Macro hurriedly gave orders for the defence of the fort. The cornicen sounded the alarm and the men came running from their barracks blocks, equipment in hand, and went to their stations on the parade square in the lengthening shadows of the headquarters building. In addition to the duty century still on the walls, there were nine other centuries of infantry and four cavalry squadrons who would fight dismounted. There was no time for the customary pre-battle speech to whip up the unit's fighting spirit. Instead, Macro quickly commanded that the cavalrymen stand firm as a reserve. One century was sent to each of the other walls while the six remaining centuries were sent to the wall facing the enemy.

Macro turned to Cato. 'I want you in charge of the inner wall. I'm going to need to stand back from this fight and take overall command. So I want my best officer in the most critical position.'

'Thank you, sir. I swear I won't let you down.'

'If you do, then neither of us is going to live to regret it.' Macro forced himself to laugh. 'So don't let those bastards get past you.'

'I won't,' Cato replied. 'We'll hold them back until Symeon and his friends arrive.'

'Oh, he'll be here,' Macro said confidently. 'If I'm any judge of character, he's the kind of man who'd never miss a fight. So let's make sure we leave him a few of those Parthians to take care of.'

Cato smiled. 'I'll see what I can arrange.'

Macro stuck his hand out. 'Good luck, lad. We're going to need it tonight.'

Cato grasped his friend's hand firmly. 'Good luck to you too, sir.'

Macro nodded and there was awkward stillness between the two of them and Macro wondered if they would still be alive to greet each other in the morning. Cato seemed to guess what he was thinking and said quietly, 'We've faced tougher enemies in our time, sir.'

'Ah, but that was in the Second Legion.' Macro glanced round at the men filing off the parade ground to take up their positions. 'These auxiliaries aren't even close to being a match for legionaries. But they look competent,' he conceded grudgingly. 'We'll know their quality soon enough. Now, off you go.'

As Cato caught up with his men and led the main force to its position on the wall facing the enemy, he thought once more of Symeon and hoped that Macro's assessment of the man was right. But even if it was, would the men that Symeon knew at Petra be prepared to honour their pledge to the Romans? Cato was not sure. He had too little knowledge of the peoples of the eastern frontier to judge their character. All he, and every other man in the cohort, could do was hope. They would be saved by Symeon and the Nabataeans or die. The Roman forces in Syria would not come to their aid. That was almost certain. Longinus was counting on Bannus to destroy Bushir, and with it the men who knew of his disloyalty to the Emperor. Cato smiled to himself. It would be good to live through this just to see the appalled expression on the Governor's face.

When he reached the inner wall, Cato placed two centuries on the fighting platform behind the breastwork. Those who were armed with bows were sent on to the walls on either side of the ruined gatehouse, and on to the roofs of the buildings behind the inner wall. Every arrow and javelin that could be spared by the other centuries in the fort was piled up in front of the remaining four centuries, which had been placed under the command of Centurion Parmenion to act as an immediate reserve. The first wave of Judaean rebels to enter the breach was going to be met by a hail of missiles from three sides. Cato could well imagine the devastating effect and hoped that it would be enough to break their spirit. If they could only be persuaded to give up the siege and return to their villages, now, before enough blood was spilt to give Rome and Judaea an insatiable taste for it. If Bushir fell, then the whole province was doomed to years of fire, sword and death on a terrible scale. Therefore, hard as it seemed, Cato must make sure that he and his men slaughtered the first wave of attackers with as much savage, ruthless brutality as they could manage.

As the last of the men quietly took up their positions the sun began to set, burnishing their faces and armour in a warm red glow. It was a small mercy that the rapidly fading glare of the sun made it impossible to see the enemy bearing down on them, but the Romans could clearly hear the cheers and triumphant cries as the rebels moved towards the breach. As they closed on the fort there came a rhythmic rapping of spears and blades against the rims of shields and the air was filled with the harsh din that swelled and magnified the sense of threat that lay beyond the mound of rubble where the gatehouse once stood.

Cato pulled himself up on to the fighting platform and shuffled past his men until he stood at the centre of the inner wall. He shifted his shield round to the front and drew his sword as the sound of the enemy's approach rose to a deafening pitch. On the main wall, the first of the archers began to loose their arrows at the target still hidden from those manning the inner line of defence. Slingshot whipped back at them, almost at once finding the first Roman casualty of the night's assault; a lead shot smashed the hand of one of the archers. Cato watched as the man dropped his bow, clutching his hand to his chest as he straightened up behind the rampart. At once a second missile struck him in the face and he pitched backwards off the wall.

Glancing at the men on either side of him Cato was reassured to see that most of them stood ready, staring steadily at the rubble in front of them. Some looked as nervous as Cato felt and he knew he must say something to encourage them.

'Steady, lads! They're just lambs to the slaughter. So don't disappoint them!'

Cato was relieved to see that remark raise some smiles and even a little laughter. But the shallow mirth was short-lived as the exchange of missiles suddenly grew more fierce and three more Romans toppled from the main walls. Then Cato saw the tips of the first spears appear over the crest of the rubble and blocks of stone, pitch black against the red horizon. He tightened his grip on his sword and turned to shout an order to the men standing ready behind the inner wall.

'Make sure you feed those javelins to the front as quick as you can!'

He turned back just as the first of the enemy appeared over the crest, kicking up a cloud of dust as they scrambled into the breach. Arrows shot down on them from either side and several fell out of sight, but more took their place and charged up the uneven and shifting slope into the fort with a shrill war cry. A black wave of silhouettes surged forward, over the crest, and then stumbled down into the gloomy killing zone in front of the inner wall.

'Prepare javelins!' Cato called out. The men on the wall raised their javelins and swung their arms back. Cato waited a moment, allowing more men to struggle over the rubble to give his men a densely packed target. Then he raised his sword.

'Ready! . . . Loose javelins!'

With a collective grunt of effort the auxiliaries threw their arms forward, releasing the iron-tipped shafts into the raging mob pressing into the small area in front of the inner wall. Scores of the Judaean rebels were struck down, pierced through by the Roman javelins. The cries of triumph that had been on their lips a moment earlier died with them and there was a brief hush inside the fort as the attackers stalled for a moment in shock at the effect of the first volley. On the Roman side, the auxiliaries were already taking up the replacement javelins handed to them from behind and readying them for the next volley.

Cato filled his lungs and shouted out, 'Release at will!'

A steady shower of javelins rained down on the enemy packed in front of the inner wall and more and more bodies littered the ground as the shafts of javelins spiked up like thickets of reeds. And still the Judaeans came on, emerging from the thick dust as they scrambled into the fort, and added to the tightly packed target making it impossible for the Romans to miss. Cato felt sick as he watched the slaughter. Already the ground was almost covered with dead and injured, drenched in blood, and he had to fight the impulse to order his men to stop. The dreadful killing must continue if they were to shatter the enemy's will to fight on.

For what seemed an age the Judaeans kept coming, and those caught in the trap began to cry out in panic, and shout in frustration and rage as they could neither press forward to engage the Romans nor move back, away from the terrible rain of javelins. The constant pressure from behind, from those as yet unaware of the massacre taking place inside the fort, continued to press on those at the front, forcing them to their deaths.

Then, at last, somehow, word spread back beyond the breach and the order was given to call off the attack. Still showered with javelins and shot at with arrows the Judaeans began to retreat, pressing back as they scrambled over rubble and the bodies of their comrades until they had gone, retreating into the fading purple light of dusk. Cato sheathed his sword and gazed upon a nightmare scene of tangled bodies, javelin shafts at every angle and dark blood splashed over it all. Yet there was still life amid the tide of human destruction. Here and there bodies writhed in agony or shifted feebly as the injured moaned and cried for help, or a merciful end. Cato turned away and jumped down from the fighting platform, striding round the base of the inner wall until he reached the ladder that led up to the main wall and climbed the rungs. From the height of the wall he could see across the ground towards the enemy camp. The Judaeans were streaming away from the fort, encouraged on their way by the arrows still flying after them from the walls. A few of the enemy, more resolute than their companions, were standing their ground and whirring slings overhead as they loosed slingshot back at the Romans.

Cato leaned over the breach and stared at the bodies piled before the inner wall. There had to be more than a hundred of them, and maybe twenty or thirty more shot down outside the gatehouse. The losses of this first assault had been terrible and Bannus would have a hard time trying to persuade his men back into the breach, Cato reflected. He raised his head and glanced towards the enemy camp, wondering what Bannus would be thinking as he beheld the failure of the first attempt to overrun the fort.

'Sir!' One of the archers beside him anxiously gestured to Cato to get down. 'Once those bloody slingers see the crest on your helmet you'll draw their fire like bees to honey.'

As if on cue, the air was filled with the zip of slingshot and Cato ducked down. He nodded to the archer gratefully. 'Thanks for the warning.'

'Warning?' The man's eyebrows rose in surprise. 'Wasn't warning you, sir. Just didn't want them all aiming my way.'

'Oh.' Cato laughed. 'Thanks anyway.'

The archer shrugged and then notched another arrow and looked cautiously over the rampart for a suitable target. Suddenly he bobbed up, loosed his arrow, and ducked down. An instant later a lead shot cracked into the other side of the rampart. With the walls still bathed in the fading light, and the desert before them swallowed up by shadows Cato realised that the advantage would be with the slingers until the last rays of the sun had died away.

He turned to the archers. 'Keep it up until they're out of range. Pick your targets! I don't want anyone to waste arrows. We're going to need them.'

They exchanged a quick salute and then Cato climbed back down into the fort to rejoin the men on the inner wall. So many of the enemy had died right up against the base of the wall that they were already providing the basis of a ramp and Cato decided to deal with that straight away. He looked for Centurion Parmenion in the gloom and beckoned him over.

'We need to get those bodies away from the inner wall. Take two of the reserve centuries and get the enemy dead out of the fort. Put them in view of the attackers. Make a pile of the bodies, something they can see. Once that's done pick up the serviceable javelins out there and bring them back inside the wall. Got that?'

'Yes sir,' Parmenion replied. 'After what they did to Sycorax we'll show them that two can play games with morale.'

Cato clapped him on the shoulder. 'That's the idea. Get our men to work.'

While Parmenion bellowed his orders Cato returned to the main wall to keep watch on the enemy. The Judaeans had fallen back some distance and their leaders were doing their best to rally them for another attempt. Already, some fires were being lit in the Judaean camp and torches were held high, illuminating men at work rolling bundles of sticks towards the fort. At the same time, soldiers with the conical helmets of Parthians were straining to wheel the surviving onager closer to the target. Cato glanced down and saw that Parmenion and his men had lowered ladders over the inner wall and were already busy lifting the bodies under their shoulders and dragging them up the mound of rubble, down the far side and on to a growing pile just in front of the breach. Some of the enemy were still living, and the auxiliaries despatched them with quick thrusts to the heart, or cut their throats, before dragging them away.

As darkness closed in over the desert, and the first stars twinkled coldly in the ink-black sky, the enemy came on again. There was a warning shout and a moment later the men who had been tasked with clearing the bodies away began to scramble back over the inner wall, pulling the ladders up behind them.

This time there was no arrogant roar of triumph, no rousing rattle of sword and spear against shield rim, just a silent approach of a dark mass of men, stealing towards the fort. They stopped just outside arrow range and waited as the onager was brought forward. A flickering torch filtered through the mass and then a fire flared up in a brazier, close by the onager, revealing the mass of men huddled round the huge weapon.

It did not take long to see what they were waiting for. A faggot was placed in the cup of the onager and quickly set on fire before the throwing arm was released with a metallic clank and an instant later the thud of the restraining bar. The faggot blazed up into the night sky, trailing flickering tongues of flame, sailing towards the fort until it struck the top of the rampart in a brilliant shower of sparks and bounced over the wall and crashed down into the street beside a stable block. A moment later the first fire arrow followed, then more, until a regular bombardment of fire arrows fell on the fort, interspersed with large flammable bundles of kindling wood, doused with oil, bursting on to the buildings inside the walls. The lack of rain had made the timbers of the fort dry and combustible and soon several fires had broken out beyond the breach.

Cato looked back from the inner wall as flames engulfed the end of one of the nearby barrack blocks. He climbed down and strode over to Centurion Parmenion at the head of the troops held in reserve. Most of the soldiers were crouching nervously, waiting for the next incendiary missile to come over the wall, as Cato approached.

'We have to deal with those fires before they get out

of control. Take two centuries from the reserve, form them into fire parties and set them to it.'

'Yes sir.'

As Parmenion sent his men off to fight the fires, Macro came up to check on Cato's situation. He nodded towards the flames with a grim expression. 'Reminds me of that fight we had with the Germans in that village close to the Rhine.'

'I remember it well, sir. That was the first time I faced an enemy. I was an optio then.'

'So you were.' Macro reflected. 'That was over three years ago. Seems longer. Much longer. Although it was you who set fire to the defences last time.'

'And here we are, about to be burned out of our shelter once again.'

'We'll have to see about that.' Macro nodded towards the inner wall. 'How has it been? I saw the start of their attack from one of the towers.'

Cato recalled the earlier slaughter with a strained expression. 'They got caught in front of the wall, as we'd hoped.'

'Gave them a good hiding, then?'

'Yes.'

'And our side? Many casualties?'

'Only a few.'

'Good,' Macro said with satisfaction. 'I'm sure they'll be back. Not quite so cocky next time, so you'll have a fight on your hands.'

'I imagine so. Have they tried any attacks on other walls?'

They were interrupted as a highly angled fire arrow clattered off the ground close by and shattered in a spray of brilliant sparks. Both officers instinctively flinched away, and then continued their conversation. Macro jerked his thumb over his shoulder.

'There was a feint towards the east wall. Nothing serious, just an attempt to draw off men from this position.'

'Here they come!' a voice cried from the main wall.

Cato swung round, cupping a hand to his mouth. 'To arms! Get on the wall! Fire parties, carry on!'

The auxiliaries on the fighting platform raised their shields, and held their javelins ready as they stared out at the dark mass of the gatehouse ruins.

'I'll join you,' Macro muttered to Cato. 'This is where the fight will be decided.'

'We could certainly use you here, sir.'

Macro clapped him on the shoulder, and then bellowed to the auxiliaries around him. 'Right! Let's make 'em regret that they ever decided to mix it with the Second Illyrian!'

CHAPTER TWENTY-EIGHT

The two centurions picked up spare shields that had been stacked near the javelins and made their way up on to the fighting platform. Behind the inner wall the fires in the fort still blazed despite Centurion Parmenion's attempts to bring them under control. Cato knew that they would be clearly silhouetted for the enemy slingers and archers, but at least the flames provided some illumination of the pile of rubble stretching up before the inner wall. The archers on the wall were already loosing arrows on to the approaching enemy as swiftly as possible. Slingshot whipped back at them from the darkness, and the steady barrage of fire arrows and incendiary missiles hurled by the onager continued arcing over the wall and flaring down on to the buildings behind.

The Judaeans came up the rubble slope as before, but this time they stopped just beyond the crest, beyond the range of the javelins, and began whirring slings over their heads.

'Slingshot!' Cato cried out in warning to his men. 'Keep those shields up!'

Then the air was filled with the whip-whup of shots, moments before they struck the face of the wall and the auxiliaries' shields in a cacophony of sharp raps. The Judaeans made no attempt to advance any further, but continued to keep up a heavy bombardment of those manning the wall, while others concentrated their shots on the archers on the walls to either side of the ruined gatehouse. It did not take long to clear the archers away as they were cut down by the lethal slingshot, or were forced back to take cover further along the wall. Once they had been dealt with the slingers turned their attention to the inner wall. Every so often a shot found its way past one of the shields and struck home with bone-shattering force.

Macro risked a quick glance over the rim of his shield. Satisfied that the enemy were still halted on the other side of the rubble, he ducked back down and drew a deep breath so that he could be heard above the din of the slingshot strikes.

'Second Illyrian! Take cover behind the wall!'

The men needed no encouragement to duck down out of sight of the slingers and they squatted behind the breastwork, lowering their shields to rest beside them. Macro turned and met Cato's eyes.

'Seems that they've learned their lesson well. No more frontal assaults until we've been softened up.'

Cato was taking a last glance at the enemy from beneath the shelter of his shield. A stone glanced off the central boss with a shattering ring. He felt the impact through his shield arm and winced as he dropped down. 'Softened up? More like tenderised.'

Macro laughed. 'Let 'em try. As long as this wall's between us there's not much they can do to cut down our numbers.'

'Maybe,' Cato replied quietly. 'But they must know that too.'

'Meaning?'

'Meaning that there must be a reason for them to want us to keep our heads down.'

Macro lowered his shield on to the fighting platform. 'They're up to something. I'll be back in a moment.'

He slid off the fighting platform and ran along behind it until he reached the ladder leading up to the main wall. There would be a nasty instant when he emerged in full view of the slingers in the breach, and, bracing himself, he launched himself up the rungs. There was a shout and two slingshots whipped close by, then Macro threw his body up on to the rampart and rolled out of sight. One of the men immediately scurried over and protected him with his shield. Catching his breath Macro nodded his gratitude and then went over to the wall. Making sure that he was sheltered behind one of the crenellations, he peered over the top.

Behind the screen of slingers in the breach there was

the pile of bodies from the first assault and beyond that the silent mass of Judaean rebels waiting to attack. As Macro watched them by the wavering orange glow of the torches that ringed the onager, he noticed them pull aside as something passed through the crowd. As yet he could not make out what it was. Then one of the enemy, sharper-eyed than his comrades, spied the prefect's head and loosed a shot at the ramparts. It struck the masonry above Macro's head and chips of stone burst from the wall, several striking Macro in the face, one laying open the flesh at the corner of his left eye.

'Shit!' He recoiled backwards, clutching at his face. 'Shit. Bastard.'

His fingers came away coated in blood and Macro hurriedly undid his neckcloth and mopped the wound. His left eye still had vision, but it was badly blurred and the pain in the socket was searing.

'Sir?' The auxiliary who had protected him with his shield loomed in front of Macro. 'Shall I send for the surgeon?'

'No!' Macro winced. 'I've had worse. I'll be fine.'

The auxiliary looked at him doubtfully and then shuffled away. Macro tried to staunch the flow of blood before he tried again to see what the enemy was bringing forward. The front ranks split open and gave way to a score of men carrying an iron-tipped beam of wood. So that was it, Macro realised. A battering ram. He slithered back to the edge of the rampart and this time he decided not to risk the ladder but lowered himself over the side of the wall a bit further along, and dropped heavily to the ground below. He hurried back to Cato. His friend winced as he saw the wound on Macro's face.

'Sir, you'd better get that seen to.'

Macro shook his head. 'No time for that. We're for it now. They're bringing up a ram. It'll be here any moment.'

They took a quick glance over the breastwork and saw that the slingers were already moving aside as the men carrying the ram struggled up the rubble slope and heaved their burden over the crest and down into the fort. Behind them massed the Judaeans, clutching an assortment of shields and weapons, as well as several ladders, all washed in a pale yellow glow from the fires burning inside the fort. On either side the slingers continued to rain their missiles down on the breastwork. Once the men carrying the ram had cleared the rubble they made straight for the middle of the inner wall where Cato and Macro had taken their position.

'All right!' Macro shouted at the men on either side. 'When I give the command, on your feet. Save your javelins for the men carrying the ram.'

He held his hand out for a javelin, and turned back to Cato as his friend hefted the shaft of his own weapon. 'Ready?'

'Yes, sir.'

'Second Illyrian! Up and at 'em!' Macro rose behind his shield, Cato at his side, and then the rest of the men.

Below them, the men at the ram glanced up, but did not hesitate as they lumbered on. Macro raised his arm, balanced the javelin and took aim with the iron head, before he hurled it with all his strength. The weapon flew towards the man at the head of the party carrying the ram, but he saw it and ducked to one side so that the javelin missed him and tore through the forearm of the man behind. Macro swore and reached back for another javelin. Even as he had missed, many of his men had not, and several of the attackers went down, pierced by the lethal iron heads of the weapons. As soon as they fell, replacements rushed up from the dense mass behind and took their place at the ropes that had been fastened round the timber shaft. The reappearance of the Romans above the breastwork provoked the slingers to renew their furious bombardment and there was a sharp cry from the auxiliary standing next to Cato as he was struck in the face with a dull crack. The auxiliary dropped his javelin and let his shield drop for a moment and was immediately hit in the shoulder, the impact driving him round as his knees buckled. Cato could not spare him any help as he hurled his second javelin and turned back to the men behind the wall for another without waiting to see if his throw had been true.

'Get that man to the medics!'

Hands grasped the injured auxiliary and hauled him off the fighting platform. An instant later another man had taken his place, javelin raised and ready to throw. On the other side of the wall, the ground was strewn with wounded and dead, but the survivors had reached the wall and, as someone shouted the time, they swung the ram back and then forward with all their might. Cato felt the platform quake beneath his feet and a section of the breastwork in front of him fell away.

'Get them!' he shouted to his men desperately. 'Get them!'

The auxiliaries responded to the order with a frenzy of hurled javelins that struck down so many men that the enemy could no longer hold the ram and it sank to the ground, until more Judaeans rushed forward, snatched up the rope holds and swung the ram back, and forwards into the wall. This time the impact nearly knocked Cato and Macro off their feet and another large chunk of the makeshift wall collapsed. Macro grabbed Cato's arm and pulled him down behind the breastwork.

'The wall's going to give way soon. Get down and get some men ready to hold the breach. You have to keep them out. Go!'

Cato jumped down from the fighting platform. Glancing back as he felt another blow from the ram he saw loose chunks of stone leap from the wall. He turned back to the reserve force, and became aware that a line of casualties was being treated by medical orderlies by the side of the nearest barracks block. He turned to the closest optio. 'What are the wounded doing here? Get them to the hospital.'

The optio shook his head. 'Can't, sir. The fires have cut us off from the centre of the fort. They have to be treated here.'

Cato looked beyond the optio, down the street between the barracks blocks. At the end of the buildings flames and smoke barred his view. Just then a couple of men from Centurion Parmenion's fire-fighting party emerged from the smoke and bent over coughing. They carried smouldering mats in their hands and a moment later they went back to try to beat the flames out. Cato turned back to the optio.

'Find Centurion Parmenion. Tell him he has to clear a way through. I don't care how he does it, but it must be done, or we're going to be caught between the fire and the enemy.' Cato thrust the optio on his way and turned to the other auxiliaries standing to behind the wall.

'Reserve units! On me!'

The men hurried over and formed up in a solid column, shields to the front and javelins now grounded and angled forward, ready to serve as spears. In front of them the wall shook and showered chunks of rock on to the ground under another blow from the ram. On the fighting platform Macro was desperately ushering the men away from the collapsed breastwork so that they would not be caught in the falling masonry when the ram breached the wall. The next blow came, and another, and then after a slight delay the wall fell outwards in a rush of debris and a swirling cloud of dust. Cato clenched his hand tightly round the shaft of his javelin and raised it towards the gap in the inner wall that was wide enough for two men to get through at a time.

'Forward!' he shouted, and the reserve tramped towards the gap, keeping pace as their shields rose and the tips of their javelins were lowered towards the enemy. The first of the Judaeans burst through the red-tinted cloud of dust, his battle cry dying on his lips as he fell straight on to the points of two of the auxiliaries to the side of Cato. They ripped their weapons from the man's guts and closed on the gap in the wall, just as more men scrambled through it, screaming and waving their swords in the glow of the flames licking up into the night sky above the fort. For an instant there was a gap of a spear's length between the two sides and then the Judaeans were pressed up against the broad oval Roman shields, hammering away at them with the pommels of their swords, or slashing at any part of the defenders that came within reach of their blades. The first rank of auxiliaries could not wield their javelins in the crush and thrust them back to the men behind before drawing their swords and hacking and thrusting at the enemy before them. Those in the second and third ranks held their javelins overhead and stabbed at the faces in the front rank of the enemy horde trying to force its way through the breach.

Above the rasp and scrape of weapons and the grunts and shouts of the men packed around him, Cato heard

Macro's voice shout a warning to the men still on the wall.

'Ladders! They're bringing ladders up! Draw swords!'

Cato's awareness of the fight raging on either side of the breach suddenly faded as he felt the point of a blade slice into his calf. He groaned with pain and rage through gritted teeth and glanced down. A small, lithe boy had dropped low and squeezed under his shield, even though he risked being trampled to death. He had a short curved dagger in his hand and drew it back to strike again at Cato's leg. Without a thought, Cato slammed the bottom rim of his shield into the back of the boy's neck. The child spasmed, dropped the knife and slumped to the ground. Before Cato's mind could even register that he had felled a child, a horribly scarred face appeared at the top of his shield, and a point of a levelled sword flickered forwards. Cato just had time to turn his head aside and the sword struck his cheek guard and was deflected over his shoulder. For an instant Cato was dazed by the blow, but by the time the white splashes had faded from his vision one of his men had sliced almost through the man's arm and he fell away with a scream. Cato shook his head to try to clear the dizziness and pushed forward again, ramming his shield into the tightly packed press of bodies trying to force their way into the fort. There was no longer any room for any general exchange of blows as the men from both sides were crushed against each other by the pressure of the rear ranks and the struggle became simply a question of strength. Cato leaned his shoulder into the back of his shield and braced his legs and shoved against the enemy.

On the fighting platform Macro looked down into the breach and was relieved to see that the Judaeans were being held back for now. The wavering crest of a centurion in the heart of the struggle showed that Cato still lived and was leading his men from the front. Then Macro snatched his eyes away from the breach and glanced back into the heart of the fort. Fires were raging all around the fight for the inner wall and even as Centurion Parmenion and his men were busy trying to extinguish the flames fresh incendiary arrows and clay pots of inflammables continued to cross the wall in high flaring arcs before plunging down and adding to the blaze. The men around Macro were in danger of being caught between the flames and the force assaulting the breach. There was only one thing to be done, Macro decided grimly. They must hold the inner wall at all costs, and then drive the enemy off so that they could turn their efforts towards fighting the fires, before the Judaeans could summon up the courage to make another attempt to break in.

On either side of the breach the enemy were trying to throw their assault ladders up against the breastwork. Each time the arms of the ladders slapped against the walls the auxiliaries frantically tried to thrust them back, before the first of the attackers could swarm up the rungs and fight his way over the wall. Directly in front of Macro, two roughly hewn shafts of wood appeared and he sprang towards the wall, shield raised and sword held ready. An instant later a turbaned head appeared, the metal spike of a conical helmet protruding from the cloth. Dark eyes glared at Macro, and the man hissed through clenched teeth as he climbed another rung and paused to take a swing at the Roman officer with the heavy sword in his spare hand. Macro swept his blade across to block the blow and then punched the heavy brass pommel into the man's face, knocking him cold, and he fell back on to the men at the base of the ladder, dropping his weapon at Macro's feet. At once Macro thrust the ladder away from the wall, then glanced to his left and saw an enemy atop another ladder battling it out with a legionary. He turned, stepped towards the ladder and slammed the point of his sword into the man's chest. The impact thudded down Macro's arm and the man died with an explosive grunt as the blow drove the air from his lungs. Macro wrenched the sword free and the body tumbled down the rungs.

There was no immediate threat and Macro looked round again and saw that the auxiliaries were still holding the enemy back. They had not been able to gain a foothold anywhere on the wall and Cato had them stalled in the breach of the inner wall. Now was the time to break their will. Macro's toe stubbed against a loose rock on the fighting platform and he glanced down at it in anger, then smiled. He sheathed his bloody sword and snatched the rock up. Taking quick aim he hurled it into the mob pressing up against Cato and his men. The rock struck a man on the side of the head and his eyes rolled up and he slumped back as he lost consciousness, blood coursing from the tear in his scalp. Macro snatched up another rock, from the wall this time, and hurled it into the crowd. He looked across the gap to a handful of auxiliaries staring forward, waiting to be attacked, while the ladder parties were trying to assault the wall a little further away.

'You men!' Macro bellowed across the gap and they turned to him at once, conditioned to the imperative tone of the parade ground. 'Use rocks, javelins, whatever you can get your hands on and hit them. Like this!'

Macro looked down, saw the enemy's sword, grabbed it and hurled it into the mob, grinning with satisfaction as the blade struck another attacker in the shoulder. The auxiliaries began to pluck loose chunks of masonry from the wall and rained them down on to the heads of the enemy packed helplessly below them. It was impossible to miss, and the Judaeans could only watch as the Romans picked them off in a killing frenzy. A few of them tried to hurl stones back but were thwarted by the men crowding around them. At last those in the less compact part of the crowd outside the breach began to give way. At once the pressure of the back ranks eased and Cato and his men began to creep forward, heaving their shoulders against the insides of their shields. As the pressure in front of them eased they increased their pace, bearing the attackers back into and through the breach. As the crest of Cato's helmet appeared on the far side of the inner wall and then more Romans appeared, a low moan of despair rose up from the enemy ranks. They began to back away, even as the more resolute of their comrades screamed at them to keep fighting. But once the contagion of fear and uncertainty spread there was no stopping it, and the enemy fell back from the inner wall, clambering awkwardly up the rubble slope and out of the fort.

As they retreated, Cato seized the chance to press home the advantage, and waved his troops on.

'They're running for it! Get after them! Cut 'em down!'

The men poured out of the breach behind him and quickly spread out across the body-strewn area in front of the wall as they chased after the enemy. Moments ago the Judaeans had been pressing home their attack and now they were fleeing for their lives. Cato was shocked by the sudden reversal in the tide of the battle, and then he regained control of himself and ran forward with his men, chasing the enemy back up the rubble slope. He reached the crest and paused at the sight of the enemy streaming away from the fort like rats in the loom of the flames from the fort and the torches of the enemy lines. He could not risk this brief moment of victory rushing to his men's heads, or they would be annihilated. Quickly he sheathed his sword and cupped a hand to his mouth.

'Second Illyrian!' he bellowed as loud as he could. 'Second Illyrian, on me! Back inside the fort! Now!'

The nearest men heard and turned to respond, reluctantly giving up the chance to slaughter more of the enemy. A few others carried on a few paces before their blood rage faded and they retreated towards the fort. But a handful, maddened with battle rage, charged on and were lost amid the dark shadows of the Judaean ranks. Cato waited for the last of his men to clamber down the rubble slope, then turned to follow them, ducking as a slingshot zipped close overhead. Macro was waiting for him in front of the breach, grinning.

'I tell you, Cato, you're losing it. A few more wild charges like that and I'm sending you into the arena. You'd scare any gladiator out of his skin.'

Cato felt himself blush, instantly angry that he had made himself look so foolhardy.

'Oh, come now.' Macro clapped him on the shoulder. 'You and the lads did well. They won't be coming back again in a hurry.'

'Maybe not in a hurry,' Cato conceded. 'But they will be back.'

'Of course they will.' Macro nodded over his shoulder at the flames rising up from the buildings a short distance behind the inner wall. 'Meanwhile we've got other problems to worry about . . .'

CHAPTER TWENTY-NINE

They made their way back through the breach and went to find Centurion Parmenion. The veteran officer was working alongside his men pulling down the cohort's stables in an attempt to create a firebreak so that there was still a way through to the rest of the fort for the men defending the breach. A short distance away fire was consuming the granary and the roaring of the flames was punctuated by explosions of sparks from the building's timbers. Cato and Macro felt the heat hit them as they approached Parmenion and Macro had to squint as his eyes began to sting. Parmenion ordered his men to continue the work as he made his report to the prefect. His face was streaked with sweat and grime.

Macro pointed towards the stables. 'Where are the horses?'

'Scrofa took them to the far side of the fort, sir. He's tethering them along the east wall.'

'Fair enough,' Macro conceded. 'Good job. Better

move the hostages there as well, in case the fire spreads to their cells. Now then, what's the news on the fire?'

'We're not going to be able to stop it spreading, sir. This firebreak's only going to divide it, keep an avenue open for you and the boys on the inner wall, if you get pushed back.'

'If we lose the wall, we lose the fort,' Macro responded bitterly.

'Maybe not,' said Cato. 'Not immediately at least. If we lose the wall then we have to use the fire as the next line of defence. It won't burn itself out for some hours.'

'And then?' Macro tipped his head to one side. 'Well? What then?'

It was a good question, Cato realised. The answer was straightforward. 'Then they march over the ashes and massacre us. Or we try to make a break for it. Leave a few men behind to make it seem as if the wall is still being defended, while the rest of us head out of the eastern gate and try to get as far from the fort as possible before daybreak. After that, head north to the Decapolis.'

Parmenion shook his head. 'They'd cut us to pieces if they caught us in the open. Those Parthians would pepper us with arrows so that we'd have to stop and cover ourselves with shields. They'd pin us down until the rest of Bannus' force turned up and finished off what was left. Battle of Carrhae, all over again.'

'All right, then,' Cato responded. 'We try something

else. Something they can't possibly expect.' His eyes gleamed with excitement.

'Here we go again,' Macro muttered, turning to Parmenion. 'Brace yourself . . . All right, Cato, let's hear it.'

'If we stay on the wall, the flames will either get us or force us out of cover so that we'd have to face them on the ground outside the walls. If we retreat through the firebreak and close it off with burning debris, then we're just postponing being slaughtered a few hours.'

'Yes. So?'

'So we leave some men to man the walls, take the cohort out of the eastern gate, circle round and strike at their camp.' Cato looked from one man to the other. 'Well?'

Parmenion shook his head. 'That is the most hare-brained idea I've ever heard. No offence, or anything.'

'None taken. But what's the alternative? You're already agreed that we can't just wait and see what happens. Bannus won't be expecting us to take the initiative.'

'With good reason!' Parmenion snorted. 'He outnumbers us four or five to one.'

'Which is why he won't even think it is us.'

Parmenion frowned. 'What do you mean?'

'I think I know what the lad's thinking,' Macro interrupted. 'We hit them from the north, making as much noise about it as we can, and Bannus might just think that it's a relief force from Syria. Is that it, Cato?'

Cato nodded. 'They just might.'

Parmenion chuckled mirthlessly. 'And when morning comes and they see exactly how few we are, they just might take us for lunatics.'

Cato ignored him and kept his attention focused on his friend. 'We could carry it off, sir. If we strike from the darkness, the enemy will have no idea of the size of the force attacking them. They'll assume the worst and panic. It'll take a while before they even guess at the truth, and by then we could have scattered them, burned the surviving onager and sacked their camp. It'll take Bannus days to recover.'

Macro was not yet fully convinced. 'What if it goes wrong? If they don't run, but stand their ground, then we'll be given a good kicking.'

'No worse than if we just stayed put and waited for a good kicking here in the fort.'

'Good point,' Macro conceded. 'All right, we'll give it a try. After all, we've nothing to lose.'

'Except our sanity,' Parmenion muttered. 'And our lives.'

Macro glanced round at his officers, all those who could be spared for the operation. Parmenion and the others were manning the west wall and towers, doing their best to move around as much as possible to give the impression that there were far more men defending the breach than was the case. Macro was briefing the rest of the officers in the courtyard of the headquarters building. During the night Scrofa, Postumus and the men of the reserve squadron had been busy creating a firebreak along the route that bisected the fort, pulling down buildings on either side and carrying off the combustibles. The fire had raged across half of the fort and finally seemed to be shrinking in intensity now that it had exhausted its fuel. Unfortunately, not before it had gutted the prefect's quarters. All the fine murals and furniture that Scrofa had surrounded himself with had already been consumed by flames.

'The trick of it will be to get our men into position without alerting the pickets that Bannus has established round the fort. That's why we have had to wait for the fire to die down – can't risk them seeing us quit the gate. A party of scouts will go out ahead of the main force and clear the pickets on the north side so they can't give any warning to Bannus. We'll have to go carefully until we clear the belt of defences, but then I want the cavalry to run down the pickets closer to the enemy camp. Centurions Scrofa and Postumus will be in command of the cavalry squadrons. Once the pickets are dealt with they will move half a mile north of the enemy camp and form up on the flanks. Centurion Cato and I will follow with the infantry. When the line is complete we'll approach in silence for as long as possible and when I give the signal we sound every horn we have. Make sure the men give it full voice when they respond. I want

Bannus to think every Roman soldier between here and Armenia is charging down on him. Tell your men to go in hard. They're to charge on until they hear the recall. At that point everyone is to retire through the breach, covered by the cavalry.' Macro opened his hands. 'That's it. Any questions?'

Centurion Postumus raised his arm.

'Yes?' Macro growled.

'Who dreamed up this nightmare?'

Macro glared at him for a moment before he turned back to address the rest of the cohort's officers. 'That's it then. I know it's a tough job, but we're in a bitch of a situation, gentlemen, and there's not much else we can do. If this works, then we'll have bought ourselves a few more days, and perhaps frightened off many of the men Bannus managed to recruit from the local villages. All right then. Get your kit and join your units. Dismissed!'

The officers tramped out of the courtyard and Cato edged closer to Macro and muttered, 'I think we need to keep an eye on Postumus, sir.'

'Fair enough, but he's in the same boat as us. He fights or dies. We can trust him that far at least.'

Cato glanced at Macro wearily. 'If you say so.'

Macro frowned. 'How long since you had any rest, Cato?'

'Not for two days, at least. Same as you.'

'I can take it, but you look done in.'

'I am,' Cato admitted. 'But there's nothing I can do about it until after the attack on their camp.'

'No. You can sleep afterwards maybe.'

'Yes. Afterwards.' Cato forced a smile. 'One way or another.'

The Roman column slipped out of the eastern gate in the third hour before dawn. The men had blackened their faces and limbs with ash and charred wood. Since they would have to march quickly into position and then chase down the more lightly armed men in Bannus' army, they had been ordered to leave their body armour behind. Each man carried his shield and was armed with a javelin and short sword, and wore a strip of white linen on his sword arm for identification. As the four cavalry squadrons trotted ahead and then turned to the left and moved round the fort's defences, the infantry advanced as quickly as they could, out of step, so as not to give themselves away by the rhythmic tramp of Roman army boots. Macro and Cato marched at the head of the column. Cato was shivering in the cold night air and hoped that the march round the fort would warm him up so that he didn't have to clench his teeth to stop them chattering. The auxiliaries had been threatened with dreadful punishment if they dared to speak and the column moved forward in silence, only the noise of their boots breaking the hush, until they turned off the stony track and then the sand muffled the sound almost entirely.

Almost at once they came across two bodies, sprawled on the ground. Macro halted the column and paused to turn one over with his boot.

'Seems that the scouts have done a good job,' he said in an undertone. 'I just hope they get them all without any trouble. If not . . .'

'They'll do fine,' Cato reassured him. 'Every man in the cohort knows what's at stake.'

'It's down to the gods then,' Macro concluded as he raised his arm and waved the column forward. 'I just hope Fortuna doesn't think I've used up my allotment of luck.'

'Of course you haven't,' Cato replied softly. He had grown used to Macro's superstitious tendencies, and had long since given up any attempt to talk his friend round to a more rational view of the world. Cato even doubted that there were any such things as gods. But the belief in them certainly served a purpose, helping most men to bridge the gap between knowledge and experience, and Cato had resigned himself to having to humour the superstitions of others, and even be seen to go along with them.

'Don't you think I've run out of luck?' Macro whispered. 'I wonder, given all the shit that's flown in my direction since we arrived in Judaea.'

'No, sir,' Cato replied patiently. 'For the most part you have made your own luck. Fortuna has just topped it up from time to time. We really shouldn't talk.'

'No.' Macro quickened his pace slightly so that he

drew slightly ahead of Cato, and then advanced, his ears and eyes straining to detect any sign of movement ahead of them. To their left the walls of the fort were clearly visible in the glow of the dying embers and the silhouettes of Parmenion's men could be clearly seen manning the towers and patrolling the walkway. As they marched in a wide arc round the fort the enemy camp came into view: a sprinkling of fires, twinkling in the distance. Half a mile to the north of the camp was a slight fold in the landscape that had been chosen as the site where the force would form up. When Macro judged that they had skirted round far enough to avoid being detected he changed course and began to lead the column towards the enemy camp at a tangent. Now was the most dangerous moment. If they were spotted before they could deploy for attack Bannus could bring the full weight of his army to bear and the Romans would be overwhelmed in short order.

As they approached the fold in the ground, there was no shout of alarm, no call of a trumpet to indicate that the enemy had detected their presence. Then, at last, the ground began to slope down and there ahead of them lay two darker masses separated by a stretch of open ground: the small forces of cavalry sent ahead of the main column. Cato pointed them out to Macro who nodded, and led the column to a point midway between them. As the column deployed, a horseman trotted down the line and stopped when he saw the crests on Macro's and Cato's helmets.

'Sir?'

Macro at once recognised the quiet voice as Scrofa's.

'Is that the prefect?'

'Yes. Come here.' Macro beckoned to him. 'Anything to report?'

'We took care of their outlying pickets, sir. Their relief came out of camp a short while back. We took care of them too. Surprised them quickly enough to stop anyone raising the alarm.'

'Good. But the men coming off watch will be expected back. We'll have to attack at once.'

Cato had a sudden thought. 'Wait. Perhaps there's a way to maximise the surprise of the attack.'

'What?' The gloomy shape of Macro turned towards him. 'What do you mean?'

Cato looked up at Scrofa. 'The bodies of the relief. Where are they?'

'Just over there.' Scrofa pointed to the ground rising up in the direction of the enemy camp.

'Cato,' Macro cut in. 'What are you thinking of doing?'

'They're expecting a party of men to come off watch. What if I, and some of our men, took their place? We overpower the guard on the edge of the enemy camp, and I signal you to approach. Sir, we could be inside the camp before they even knew we were here.'

Macro considered the plan briefly. 'All right then, Cato. It's worth a try. What signal will you use?'

Cato thought quickly. As they had approached the camp earlier he had seen the braziers burning round the perimeter of Bannus' army. 'I'll wave a torch from side to side. That should do it.'

'A torch. Very well, but don't take unnecessary risks. If they see through you, just shout and we'll come.'

'Yes, sir. I'd better get going.'

Cato saluted the prefect and turned to the nearest men in the line stretching out on either side. 'This section! Follow me.'

He led the men up the slope in the direction that Scrofa had indicated, and just before the crest they found the bodies of the enemy relief pickets. Ten men, scattered in a loose heap, mostly dead from the injuries they had sustained in the brief skirmish, and a few with cut throats: the men who had been wounded, but could not be left alive to give any cry of warning.

'Get their robes on,' Cato ordered. He reached down to the nearest body and winced as his fingers closed on a wet and sticky patch of cloth. Forcing himself to continue, he pulled the heavy wool cloak off the body and draped it over his shoulders. He finished the disguise with the man's padded leather helmet and then turned to inspect the rest of his party. They stood in native cloaks and turbans and helmets. Cato was satisfied that they would pass for the enemy in the darkness. At least, no one would take them for Romans. He turned towards the enemy camp.

'Let's go.'

They set off across the stony sand, heading for the nearest corner of the camp, where the two onagers had originally been positioned. There had been little attempt to organise the camp in an ordered manner. Only a few large tents were clustered in the centre for Bannus and his lieutenants. Some of the army had constructed scratch-built shelters of skins stretched over flimsy wooden frames fashioned from slender, flexible lengths of wood that they had brought with them. The rest slept in the open, as close to a fire as they could get. By the surviving onager five men stood round a brazier on this side, clearly intent on keeping warm rather than doing an efficient job of keeping watch. Cato lowered his head a little as he marched towards them, as if they might somehow see from his face, at a distance in the dark, that he was not Judaean. As they marched into the light of the brazier one of the enemy turned to them and called out a greeting. The tone was friendly enough and good-humoured, so Cato raised a hand and waved as he made for them, shifting his shield round so that only the edge of the frame showed beyond his cloak. The man continued talking as they approached, and then paused, clearly inviting a response. Cato quickened his pace and nodded his head. The man frowned, and just as Cato and the others reached the brazier, his eyes widened in alarm and he snatched at the sword hanging at his side. Cato leaped forward, his sword rasping from its scabbard, swinging round and up so that the edge sliced into the man's head with a dull crunch that dropped him immediately. The other men round the brazier looked on in stunned surprise before they realised what was happening. By then it was too late. Cato's men sprang on them, and in a brief frenzy of savage thrusts and cuts from their short swords all the sentries were cut down and lay sprawled on the ground. Cato pointed to a cart parked behind the burned remains of the first catapult. 'Hide the bodies.'

While the others hurriedly dragged the dead away and then returned and stood around as their replacements, Cato fashioned a torch from some of the kindling lying to one side of the brazier. He plunged it into the fire, waited a moment until the slender twigs and brush were ablaze, then drew it out, stepped towards Macro and the others waiting out of sight in the darkness and held the torch high as he waved it steadily from side to side. Then he turned and thrust the torch into the brazier and stood with the others, waiting. It would take a while for Macro to march the cohort up to the edge of the camp. Until then Cato and his party would have to stand in for the men on watch. He gazed towards the eastern horizon, beyond the fort, and stared for a moment. There was definitely the faintest glimmer of light along the horizon that just demarcated the land from the sky. Cato turned to look for the first sign of the approaching cohort, but it was still too dark to pick them out. A little while after Cato had given the signal a man approached them from inside the camp. He gave a brief wave as he passed by and was singing softly to himself as he headed out into the darkness.

'Where the hell is he going?' one of Cato's men whispered.

Cato rounded on him angrily. 'Where do you think? He's having a shit.'

One of the other men chuckled. 'Then he's going to have the surprise of his fucking life.'

'Quiet!' Cato hissed.

The sound of the man's singing continued from the darkness a little longer, then abruptly stopped. An instant later, he came scurrying back towards the men gathered round the brazier, wrenching his robes back down over his legs. He jabbed an arm back towards the desert and began gabbling away in excitement. Cato said nothing, and when the man glanced at Cato's face his eyes widened in astonishment.

Cato had drawn his sword and now raised it quickly and punched the hilt into the man's nose. He reeled back, and Cato hit him again, a shattering blow to the temple, and he collapsed. 'Sorry about that,' Cato muttered.

Moments later the first of the Romans emerged from the darkness and closed on the perimeter of the enemy camp. Cato turned to the other men in his party. 'Time to drop the disguise.'

They stripped off the enemy's garments and turned towards the Judaean camp. Cato watched as the cohort approached. He could see the outline of Macro's helmet at the centre of the line as they came on at a measured pace to keep formation. Then they were visible in the pools of light cast by the nearest fires.

'Second Illyrian!' Macro's voice bellowed out of the night. 'Charge!'

At once the air was split with the sound of trumpets and a great roar tore out of the auxiliaries' throats as they rushed towards the camp. They raced through the nearest campfires thrusting their javelins at the men lying on the ground. Beyond them the rest of the camp began to stir to life, men struggling up from their sleep, blinking their eyes and then staring in surprise, and then terror, towards the Roman soldiers pouring out of the desert. Cato and his men ran in to join their comrades and stabbed their javelins at the Judaeans scrambling away from them. One of the auxiliaries paused to bend down and pull at a silver chain round the neck of a man he had just killed and Cato grabbed his arm and wrenched him up, thrusting him on towards the centre of the camp.

'Don't stop for anything! Keep going forward. Kill and move on!'

Away to his side, Cato heard the thrumming of hooves as Scrofa and his cavalry rode along the side of the camp for a short distance, and then turned in and charged the men who were arming themselves to meet the Roman infantry. On the other flank Postumus with the other two squadrons would be doing the same and Cato finally let go of the anxiety that had been coiled up in his breast. The plan had succeeded, the enemy had been taken by surprise. Now they must exploit the surprise as brutally as possible. He ran on, thrusting his javelin at any enemy still moving on the ground, or crossing his path as he angled towards the centre of the Roman line cutting its way across the enemy camp. True to Macro's orders the cornicens and bucinators continued to blow their instruments for all they were worth and the air was filled with the harsh blare of the signal to charge. The men too were adding to the din, shouting their war cries as they slaughtered the enemy without mercy. Already Cato was stepping over scores of bodies, dead and the injured, writhing and crying out, all illuminated by the glow of the campfires.

The Romans swept forward, a wave of death rushing across the camp, leaving bloodshed in their wake. Away to the east the faint light that Cato had discerned earlier was now a distinct pallid glow along the horizon and he felt an instant of panic grip his heart. As soon as the enemy realised how few men were attacking them they would surely turn on the Romans. Yet still the Judaeans and their Parthian allies fled before the enemy streaming across their camp. Cato caught up with Macro as the Roman line approached the cluster of tents at the heart of the site. The prefect was exultant and beamed with pleasure as he caught sight of Cato.

'We've beaten them! The bastards are buggering off in all directions.'

For a moment Cato shared in his friend's triumphant mood, and then he noticed that he could see almost across the entire extent of the camp. His heart sank as he faced Macro.

'It's getting light.'

'All the better to see them run!'

'It cuts both ways, sir. They'll soon see that they outnumber us. We'd better begin to withdraw.'

'Withdraw?' Macro shook his head, and gestured to the men who had run past them, still cutting their paths across the enemy camp, killing all in their way. 'We've beaten them, I tell you. We have to push on while their spirit's broken.'

'Of course, sir. As long as we're ready to give the order to retreat when the time comes.'

Macro nodded and turned to run on with his men, beckoning to Cato to follow him. By the time they had reached the far side of the camp, dawn was spreading across the sky, and even though the sun had not breached the horizon there was plenty of light to illuminate the land stretching out around the fort. The camp was littered with bodies, and Romans were hunting down those who had hidden at first but were now making a break for it, sprinting for the gaps in the Roman lines. Spread out across the desert were thousands of men and horses, some of which had been mounted by Bannus' Parthian allies. Already the enemy was slowing down, regrouping and starting to fight back against the scattered Romans. The cavalry squadrons of Scrofa and Postumus were also dispersed; many had ridden far too deeply amongst the enemy and were now in danger of being cut off.

Macro and Cato drew up at the edge of the camp, breathless as they surveyed the scene with growing anxiety.

'We've done all we can do, sir,' Cato panted. 'We've won our victory. Let's not lose it now. Give the order for the recall.'

Macro hesitated, torn between the desire to press the attack home, to keep killing the enemy and break their will, and the knowledge that his men were in danger now.

'All right then,' he conceded at last, and turned back towards the command party of standard bearers and trumpeters who had been following their prefect across the fort. He drew a breath and called out, 'Sound the recall!'

Moments later the signal blasted out and the auxiliaries began to draw up, abandoning their pursuit of the enemy. A few hotheads carried on heedlessly, but even they began to respond as the enemy stopped fleeing as soon as they saw the Romans begin to withdraw and form up by their standards. Already Cato noticed that their leaders were hurriedly rallying their men, and over by a group of horsemen the Parthians were banding together and would soon have a large enough force to take on their attackers. Cato could imagine the carnage they would wreak if they got the chance to bombard the Romans with arrows before they reached the safety of the walls of Fort Bushir.

'Come on!' Macro bellowed, waving angrily to the men straggling back from the pursuit. 'Hurry up!'

The tide of battle was changing before their eyes. Already the Judaeans were starting to turn on the Romans, chasing after those who had let their battle rage carry them too far. As Cato watched, a group of Judaeans caught up with one of the auxiliaries and knocked him to the ground. The man rolled on to his back and tried to cover himself with his shield, then Cato lost sight of him as the enemy crowded round and hacked at the victim at their feet, their sword blades rising and falling in a frenzy.

Cato turned to Macro. 'If we don't make a move for the fort now, we'll never reach it.'

Macro glanced round. It was over half a mile to the breach where the gatehouse had once stood. The enemy would run them down long before they got there if they delayed any longer. Macro faced his men. 'Second Illyrian! Back to the fort, double time! Scrofa! Postumus! On me!'

As the centurions and optios of the infantry relayed the orders and turned their men back towards Bushir, the two cavalry commanders trotted over to Macro. They had lost only a handful of men in the pursuit of the enemy and most had already returned to their standards, although several were still trying to fight their way back through the rallying Judaeans.

Macro addressed them hurriedly, one eye on the enemy streaming back towards the camp. 'I want the cavalry to screen our retreat. Pull your men back to the edge of the camp facing the fort. Form them in line and charge anyone that looks threatening, Once we make the breach you can fall back and the archers will cover you from the wall.'

Postumus exchanged a quick glance with Scrofa before he replied. 'That's madness. You'll get us killed.'

'That can happen to soldiers,' Macro said coldly. 'This isn't a bloody debating society, gentlemen. Those are your orders and you will carry them out. Go!'

Scrofa wheeled his mount round and spurred it back towards his command. Postumus glared at Macro for a moment and then followed his former commander.

'Come on.' Macro patted Cato's arm and started trotting after the column of infantry hastening back to the fort. Around them ran the last of the stragglers. There was a pounding of hooves and the cavalry galloped by in a cloud of dust to take up their allotted positions. Once past the camp they turned outwards and formed a line, Scrofa's men to the left of the breach, Postumus' to the right, leaving a gap for the infantry to pass through. Cato and Macro caught up with the rear century and joined the ranks. Glancing back over his shoulder Cato was shocked to see some Judaeans sprinting after him, no more than fifty paces behind. A handful of them stopped abruptly and began to whirl slings overhead.

'Look out!' Cato shouted. 'Slingshot!'

He turned and presented his shield, just in time to save himself from a stone that cracked off the top edge of his shield and rattled over the top of his helmet. One of the other men was not so lucky and was struck in the back at the base of his spine. His legs went dead and he flopped forward with a cry of pain and surprise. One of his comrades stopped and hurried back to his side.

'Leave him!' Macro ordered, thrusting him back towards the column. Cato turned back and ran to catch up, tensing his shoulders and ducking his head slightly as if that might make him significantly less of a target. More shot whipped by and this time fate spared the Romans any further casualties. They were closing up on the cavalry screen and Macro called out, 'Cavalry! Charge them! Now!'

Scrofa and Postumus waved their swords to the front and the grim-faced cavalrymen edged their mounts forward. They trotted past Macro and Cato and the Judaeans who were pursuing them slithered to a halt as they realised their danger, and began to fall back. However, beyond them Cato could see a line of horsemen trotting towards the Roman cavalry. The Parthians came on, bows held ready and sword scabbards slapping the flanks of their mounts. The men caught between the two lines of horsemen ran from the narrowing gap, desperate to escape the clash. Macro and Cato continued towards the fort, casting glances back over their shoulders. Suddenly Macro stopped and turned.

'What the hell is he doing?'

Cato fell back and joined him in time to see Postumus' squadrons veer to the right, cutting diagonally across the enemy front. Postumus swept his arm forward and shouted an order that Macro and Cato could not quite catch the sense of. His cavalry increased their speed and galloped away from the camp, towards the north. As they did so Scrofa reined in and his men halted, perhaps a hundred paces from the enemy. He turned to watch as Postumus and his men rode off.

'The bastard's running out on us!' Macro said in astonishment.

'The fool,' Cato muttered. 'Where does he think he can escape to?'

'Who cares?' Macro turned back to the men pursuing them. Scrofa and his men were all that now stood between the infantry heading for the fort and the enemy horde, desperate to chase after them and wipe them out. 'Only Scrofa can save us now.'

CHAPTER THIRTY

Scrofa stared at the oncoming Parthians, then glanced back at Macro, as if looking for guidance. Macro swore softly and muttered, 'You have your orders, man. Bloody well carry them out.'

'He's going to run for it too,' Cato decided, grabbing his friend's arm. 'We have to go. Now!'

'Wait!' Macro raised his arm and thrust it out towards the enemy. Scrofa was still for a moment, then he nodded. With a formal, final salute to Macro he swept his sword towards the Parthians and shouted the order to charge. His men spurred their horses on, and holding their shields close and clutching their spears tightly they raced towards the Parthians. Macro shook his head in wonder, before Cato pulled his arm insistently. The two officers turned away and ran down the track to catch up with the rest of the column hurrying back to the safety of the fort. Behind them there was a pounding of hooves for an instant and then the clash and ring of sword blades, the thud of blows landing on shields, shrill whinnies from terrified horses and the savage war cries of fighting men, and the screams of the wounded.

Ahead of them the first of the infantry centuries had reached the breach and was scrambling up the blood-stained rubble. Parmenion leaned over the wall to the side, desperately waving the men on. As more of the infantry arrived, the units struggling up the rubble merged into a single mob of frantic men, while their comrades jostled forward at the base of the mound, anxiously looking over their shoulders. When Macro and Cato reached them they looked back and saw that Scrofa and his men were locked in a terribly unequal fight with the Parthians and would surely be cut to pieces as the price they paid for saving their comrades. Cato glanced away to the north and saw that Postumus and his friends were already little more than dark blots amid a haze of kicked-up dust. Already, a large number of Parthians were racing after them, determined not to let them escape, and Cato found himself hoping that Postumus was saved for as horrible a death as the Parthians could conceive.

He turned back and saw that the auxiliaries were still struggling to climb up the rubble slope. 'If this carries on much longer none of the cavalry will survive.'

'Come on you men!' Macro bellowed in frustration. 'Move yourselves!'

'Prefect!'

Macro turned towards the voice and saw Centurion

Parmenion waving at him from the wall, an excited expression on his face.

'What is it?'

'There, sir! Look over there!' Parmenion thrust his arm out and stabbed his finger to the south.

Macro thrust his way through the men and clambered a short distance up the slope so that he could see. An instant later Cato was at his side and both officers scanned the desert in the direction Parmenion had indicated. At first the swirling dust stirred up by Bannus' army made it hard to discern what was causing Parmenion to be so animated. Then a fluke of breeze shifted the dust and Cato saw beyond the enemy. There was another body of men, hundreds of them, mounted on horses and camels, riding out of the desert directly towards the Judaeans. Now Macro could see them and he punched his fist into the air. 'It's Symeon! Symeon!'

The men around him paused and turned to look and then took up Macro's cry. Cato, true to his cautious nature, looked hard at the approaching riders and did not join in the cheering. There was no possible way of telling who they were at this distance. But now the enemy had seen the men riding down on them and at once they turned away from the fort. The blind pursuit of the hated Romans dissolved in an instant and they were fleeing for their lives once again. There was light enough to see clearly, and their leaders began to rally some of their men, forming them up to face the oncoming threat. But most just ran, across the camp, instinctively heading in the direction of the villages they had left to join Bannus in his struggle against the Romans. Only when he saw them break and run did Cato allow himself to believe that it was Symeon, or at least allies of some kind. The men around him were cheering wildly and now the auxiliaries began to flow in the other direction, out of the fort and back towards the enemy camp. Macro and Cato slithered down the rubble after them.

Ahead, the survivors of Scrofa's cavalry slumped wearily in their saddles and stared in confusion as the Parthians suddenly turned and fled from the scene, galloping away as fast as their mounts would carry them, heedless of their former allies as they rode through and over them. When Macro reached the scene he looked round.

'Where's Scrofa?' He turned. 'Scrofa!'

'There, sir.' Cato pointed. A short distance away, beneath a riderless horse, lay a crumpled body in a rich red cape, the helmet bearing the crescent of an officer. Near him lay the bodies of two Parthians. Macro and Cato hurried over and knelt down beside Scrofa, shifting him gently on to his back. Scrofa's eyes flickered open. He stared round with a dazed expression when he saw the two officers looming over him.

'Macro . . .' he said quietly. 'I'd hoped they'd got you too.'

Macro smiled. 'No such luck.'

Cato caught his eye and nodded towards Scrofa's side.

The broken stump of an arrow shaft protruded from the former prefect's chest, just below his heart. Frothy blood oozed out of the wound. Macro turned his gaze back to Scrofa's face. 'That was quite a charge you led there. You saved us.'

'So it seems.' He smiled weakly and then his face screwed up in agony for a moment, before the pain receded. 'Who would have thought I'd ever save your lives? There's no justice.'

'Enough of the hard man act, Scrofa. It doesn't suit you.'

Scrofa's lips flickered into a smile. 'But I was a good soldier in the end, wasn't I?'

'You were. I'll make sure that everyone knows it.'

'You do that . . . One other thing.'

'What is it?'

'Postumus . . .' Scrofa raised his head with a struggle and suddenly gripped Macro's hand tightly. 'Swear to me you'll make that bastard pay. For running out on us. For his treachery . . .'

'Don't worry about Postumus. Last I saw of him he was being run down by scores of Parthians. He'll not get away. And if he does, and we take him alive, I'll make sure he knows what you thought of him before you—' Macro broke off in embarrassment. 'Well, you can tell him yourself. Once you've recovered.'

Scrofa slumped back and whispered, 'No such luck . . .'

'Wait!' Cato leaned over him. 'Scrofa! You said treachery. What treachery?'

Scrofa's eyes fluttered and he spasmed, his body arching as the muscles tensed. Then abruptly he relaxed and sank back on to the sand, head lolling to one side. Cato snatched his wrist and felt for a pulse, but there was nothing and he let the arm drop down to Scrofa's side. 'He's gone.'

Macro stared at him for a moment and shook his head. 'You know, I never thought he had it in him to go out like a hero. It took guts to do what he did. I was wrong about him.'

'No, you were right about him, up until the end.' Cato rose to his feet. 'This was his redemption. He knew that. I saw it when he saluted you. He was lucky to get his chance to do some good before he died.'

'Lucky?' Macro stood up. 'You have a funny idea of luck, Cato.'

'Maybe.' Cato looked round. The auxiliaries were spread out across the camp, chasing after the Judaeans. This time it was no ploy to gain time. The enemy was routed and the Romans' wild triumph and bloodlust was unrestrained. Ahead of them rode the new arrivals, mercilessly running down the Judaean rebels and those Parthian allies who had been unhorsed.

Macro noticed a small group of horsemen riding across towards them. At their head was Symeon, and as they approached and reined in Macro recognized Murad amongst his companions and they exchanged a smile. Symeon slid down from his mount and grasped Macro's arms and planted a kiss on each of his cheeks.

'Prefect. Thanks be to Yahweh that you are safe! You too, Centurion Cato.' Symeon gestured towards the riders sweeping across the desert after the enemy. 'Apologies for not arriving sooner, but we made the best time we could.'

'Who are all these men?' Macro asked. 'I was expecting some help, not a bloody army.'

'Those men work for the caravan cartels. Caravan escorts. Mostly mercenaries, but good men.'

'They certainly seem to be taking satisfaction in their work. How did you get hold of so many of them?'

'My friends gave their word to repay you for saving that caravan.'

'Well, they've certainly returned the favour,' Macro responded. 'Now we have to find Bannus, make sure that he's taken alive if he isn't dead already. He needs to be made an example of.'

'Bannus?' Symeon turned and pointed down the road towards Heshaba. 'I saw a party of horsemen ride that way as we attacked. Perhaps twenty or thirty. Most were Parthians. He could have been with them.'

'More than likely,' Macro replied. 'I'll have to go after him.'

'Ride with us,' Symeon offered. 'We know the lie of the land. You'll not get far on your own. No Roman would. Besides, I have my own business to settle with Bannus.'

Macro thought for a moment. 'All right then. But first tell your men they can quarter in the fort if they wish. We can feed and water them. I'll leave Centurion Parmenion in command, and give him orders to look after your men. He can also have our hostages released. We've no further need of them now. Wait here. Cato!'

'Yes, sir?'

'Find us two good mounts, and suitable kit and provisions for hunting down Bannus.'

'Yes, sir.' Cato looked at him with an anxious expression.

'What's the matter?'

'It's that village that worries me, sir. The one that sheltered me and Symeon.'

'What about it?'

'Symeon said Bannus was heading in that direction, and he'll need to water his horses, and find provisions himself, before he goes any further. Bannus is a desperate man. In his current frame of mind who knows what he'll do when he gets there?'

'Well, we'll find out soon enough,' Macro responded soberly. 'Now, let's not waste any more time.'

He turned and strode back towards the fort.

Cato had a sick feeling in his stomach the moment they turned the last corner in the track leading down the wadi towards the village of Heshaba early in the afternoon. They had seen a trail of smoke from some distance away and now the village was in view below them, beneath a dark billowing cloud. Several of the houses in the centre of the village were burning fiercely and some of the inhabitants were trying to beat the flames out, while others formed a chain from the water trough in the village square, throwing buckets of water on to the flames. Symeon looked aghast and spurred his mount into a gallop at the sight, and the rest of the small column hastened after him. They tethered the horses to a clump of olive trees outside the village and ran through to the square. Several villagers lay dead to one side amidst great puddles of blood, all of them with cut throats. Symeon snapped a series of orders at his men and they went to help fight the fires as best they could. Cato looked round in alarm.

'Where's Miriam? I can't see her.'

Symeon looked round anxiously, then pointed up the street to where a woman sat slumped against the side of a building, in the shade. 'I think that's her. Come on.'

They ran over to the woman, who was sitting cross-legged and nursing her head in both hands as she wept.

Symeon crouched down beside her. 'Miriam?'

She wiped her eyes and looked up, revealing a cut and bruised cheek. She seemed dazed and confused for an instant before some clarity of thought returned to her. She swallowed and cleared her throat. 'What have we done to deserve this?'

'What happened?' Symeon asked gently. He took her hand and stroked it. 'Miriam, what happened?'

She looked up at him, lips quivering. 'Bannus. He came here with some men. They demanded food and the little gold and silver that we have. When my people protested Bannus seized the nearest family, and killed them, one by one, until we gave him what he wanted.' She looked round at Cato and Macro. 'He took my son's casket . . . and . . . and he took my . . . my Yusef.' Her face crumpled and she began to weep again, great sobs of despair and sorrow racking her thin frame. Symeon tenderly placed his arm round her shoulder and stroked her hair with his spare hand.

'Yusef?' Cato frowned. 'Why would he take Yusef? It doesn't make sense. If he's trying to escape us why burden himself with a prisoner?'

'Not a prisoner,' Miriam mumbled. 'A hostage. He recognised you, Symeon, when you attacked him this morning. He knows you are coming after him, and he knows you would not allow Yusef to come to any harm. So he took him with them.'

'All right,' said Macro. 'I can understand the boy, but this casket? What's that about?'

Miriam replied quietly. 'Bannus claims to be the one who is continuing the work of Jehoshua. He had a large following amongst our people. They would place great value on the contents of the casket.'

'Treasure?'

Miriam shrugged. 'A kind of treasure. Now it's in the hands of Bannus and he will want to use it to claim that he is the rightful successor to my son.'

'What's in the casket?' Macro asked Symeon.

'I don't know,' Symeon replied. 'Only Miriam knows.'

Macro turned back to her. 'Well?'

She shook her head and Macro sighed impatiently. 'So don't tell me . . . Anyway, Bannus has the casket, he has a hostage and he has a head start on us. Do you know which way he went?'

'Yes.' Miriam looked up and cuffed her tears away. 'He said to tell Symeon to find him in Petra.'

'Petra?' Cato was confused. 'Why Petra? And why tell us where he is going?'

'He wants to speak to Symeon. Somewhere he can talk in safety.'

'Makes some sense,' Symeon conceded. 'Petra's neutral even if these friends of mine are not. They've been an enemy of Judaea in the past, but now they're concerned that Rome has her eye on Nabataea. Bannus is counting on their king's mistrust of Rome. Bannus thinks he'll be safe there.'

'How long ago did they leave?' Macro interrupted. 'Miriam?'

'Just before noon.'

'It's what, two days' ride to Petra?'

Symeon nodded. 'Two days, or quicker if you force the pace.'

'Could we catch up with him?'

Symeon shrugged. 'We could try.'

'Then let's get moving — we've wasted enough time here.' Macro saw the hurt in Symeon's expression as he comforted Miriam and was aware of Cato's disapproving frown. He turned to Miriam and tried to sound reasonable and reassuring. 'Listen, Miriam, the sooner we set off after them, the better chance we have of getting your grandson back for you, and that casket.'

Miriam suddenly grabbed his hand and looked into Macro's eyes with an intense expression. 'Swear to me that you will bring Yusef back to me! Swear it!'

'What?' Macro looked angry and tried to pull his hand back, but the woman gripped him with surprising strength. 'Look, I can't swear it. But I'll do my best.'

'Swear it!' she insisted. 'As Yahweh is your witness.'

'I don't know about any Yahweh,' Macro replied uneasily. 'But if you want me to swear by Jupiter and Fortuna, I will, if it helps you.'

'By your gods then,' she assented. 'Swear to return Yusef to me.'

'I swear I will do my best,' Macro compromised, then turned to Cato and Symeon. 'Now let's get going.'

He strode back towards the horses. Symeon squeezed Miriam's shoulder gently one last time, then set off after Macro, calling out to his men to leave the fires and come with him. Cato hesitated a moment. He was sick of the suffering that he had witnessed in this province. Sick of his part in its perpetuation. The image of the boy he had slammed his shield down on to flashed through Cato's mind. A boy the same age as Yusef. He felt a great sadness settle on him like a heavy burden. Something had to be done about the situation. Cato needed to bring some good out of it all. Just to feel clean again. 'Miriam?'

She looked up.

'We will find him, and bring him back,' said Cato. 'I promise I won't rest until we do.'

CHAPTER THIRTY-ONE

'So where's this city of yours?' Macro asked as they rode down the worn track between the steep-sided hills.

Symeon gestured to his right. 'In there.'

Macro and Cato turned towards the sheer rock faces towering up on the other side of the valley. There seemed to be no break in the cliffs, and rising up in the distance beyond were the rocky peaks and crags of yet higher hills.

'Rocks, rocks and more rocks,' Macro grumbled. 'Petra – the name says it all.'

Cato nodded wearily. He was at the end of his endurance. There had been no rest in the days of Bannus' assault on Fort Bushir, and afterwards they had ridden relentlessly down the line of the mountains that ran along the Jordan valley, pursuing Bannus and the small band of his followers who had survived their defeat at Bushir. Symeon, at the head of a select party of the Nabataeans, had driven them on, grim-faced, forever scanning the way ahead for the least sign of Bannus. They had sighted him once, from the peak above the village of Dana. Before them stretched a vista of smaller mountains and hills that gave out on to the wide barren basin of the lower Jordan valley. The air was so dry and clear that little of the detail was lost in the distance and from where they stood they could see the foothills on the far side of the valley, thirty or forty miles away. Even Macro was impressed by the spectacular vista. Then Murad gave a shout and pointed towards the hills further to the south. A thin column of tiny black specks was climbing a distant ridge, and a faint puff of dust marked their progress. Symeon shouted a command and they set off again, riding hard to catch up, but soon the distant horsemen had crested the ridge and disappeared from sight.

They rode until dusk made further progress danger-ous and then camped in the open, rising at the first hint of light to continue the chase. So it was that two days after leaving Heshaba they approached Petra in the blistering heat of noon. As they descended into the valley that led to the entrance of the city they passed a caravan heading north: hundreds of camels piled high with goods bound for the luxury-loving Hellenic cities of the Decapolis. Symeon, Murad and the others exchanged greetings with the men in charge of the caravan and stopped a moment for a brief conversation before they made their farewells and the caravan continued climbing the track at a slow steady pace.

Symeon reined his horse in alongside Macro and Cato. 'I asked them if there had been any new arrivals in Petra earlier today, or yesterday.'

'And?' Macro responded.

'It seemed that Bannus arrived at first light. They saw a party of horsemen enter the siq as the camels were being loaded. They had a boy with them, and a number of Parthians. It has to be Bannus.'

'Siq?' Cato asked. 'What is the siq?'

Symeon smiled at him. 'The siq is Petra's secret weapon. You'll see what I mean the moment we pass into it.'

They rode on, into the base of the valley, and became aware of a growing sound of voices, the braying of donkeys and the deeper grunt of camels, and then the track turned round a spur of rock and ahead of them lay a vast open area filled with men and beasts. Porters struggled with great bundles of goods: rolls of cloth, tightly bound packages of spices and fine glassware carefully packed in straw and placed in wicker baskets. Caravans were being loaded for the cities of the north, while others, unladen, were preparing to return to the great trading ports of Arabia for their next consignment of luxuries. Cato looked round eagerly. He had never seen the like of some of the people who thronged the great natural marshalling arena of Petra – brown-skinned, silk-robed men with narrow eyes, and dark hair in plaits. He pointed them out to Symeon and asked who they were.

'They're from the east. The furthest east a man can go,

so I'm told. I don't know much about them, except that they are as rich as men can be, thanks to Roman and Greek gold and silver. The amount of treasure passing through Petra is almost beyond imagination, Cato. I am surprised you Romans aren't being bled white by such an outpouring of your wealth.'

'You've never been to Rome, have you?'

'Not yet. But I will, one day.'

'Then you'll see why Rome can afford these luxuries. There is nothing the richest men cannot buy. Their coffers are that deep.'

'For the moment perhaps,' Symeon mused. 'But no empire, however rich, can continue indulging itself at such a rate, surely?

'I don't know,' Cato admitted. 'I've never thought about it.'

Symeon shrugged. 'Then maybe you should.'

After Symeon had dismissed his Nabataeans they rode on, threading through the marshalling arena until they reached a broad road that led towards the rock cliffs. The road was paved and gently cambered with a drainage ditch on either side. There was plenty of traffic along the route, more porters, merchants and mercenaries like the men who rode with Symeon and Murad. On either side of the road were tombs, carved into the rock with great skill so that the facades looked like freestanding columns. Then the road curved round a large rock formation and Cato and Macro saw a small but solid-looking gateway built across the road. Behind it soared sheer cliffs of red rock marked with darker and lighter bands of stratification. There was a narrow fissure between the cliffs that led back into the mountains. Symeon turned to his Roman companions.

'That, my friends, is the siq.'

The gateway was guarded by a score of men in fine robes and polished scale armour that gleamed brilliantly when they stood directly in the sunlight, out of the shade of the cliffs. Before the gate stood a crowd waiting to pay their toll to go through, while a steady stream of people passed by in the opposite direction. Symeon indicated that they should dismount, and led them over to join the crowd entering the siq. The crowd slowly shuffled forward until Symeon approached the table set up by the entrance. A smiling, over-indulged official greeted him in Aramaic.

Symeon responded, indicating the size of his party, and the official quickly rattled some beads across an abacus to work out the toll. Symeon took out his purse and handed over some silver coins, and the official slipped them into the slot atop a big chest to one side of the table. He was about to wave them through when he spotted Macro and Cato and his eyes narrowed suspiciously. He raised his hand to halt Symeon and shot some questions to him in a hostile tone. Symeon responded as reasonably as he could, but the official became increasingly ill tempered and finally shouted an order to the guards by the gate.

Macro stepped towards the table. 'What's going on?'

'Our friend seems to have taken exception to you. There were some Parthians amongst a party seeking entry to Petra early this morning. Now there are two Romans. He wants to know why representatives of the great powers are suddenly so interested in visiting Petra.'

'But we're not representatives. We're just hunting down Bannus. Tell him.'

'I did. I said I have a house here and that you are my guests. He didn't believe me. He says he must detain you and is going to inform the palace that you are being held.'

'Detain? You mean arrest?' Macro frowned. 'Not likely.'

A squad of six guards approached from the gatehouse and Macro's hand slid down to the handle of his sword. He drew it a short distance from the scabbard, before Cato pressed the pommel back down.

'Macro, that's not going to help. Please don't. We can't afford to cause any trouble.'

'Bollocks.'

'This won't help us to take Bannus prisoner, and return Yusef to his mother.'

Macro turned from Cato to the approaching guards, and then back to Cato again with a deep sigh of resentment and frustration. 'All right then.'

The guards halted in front of the table and their leader approached the two Romans warily. He gestured towards their swords and Cato and Macro reluctantly drew them and handed them over. Then he indicated the entrance to the siq.

Cato turned to Symeon. 'Where are they taking us?'

'To the cells under the royal palace. Don't worry, I'll do what I can to get you out of there as soon as possible.'

'That would be nice,' Macro said coldly. 'If it's not too much trouble.'

The leader of the guards spoke to them, more insistently this time, and thrust his finger towards the siq. Cato stepped into the middle of the group of guards, and after a moment's hesitation Macro followed him and they marched away. Once they had passed through the gate the rock faces closed in on both sides so that in places only a few men could stand abreast. Overhead the cliffs blocked out all but a thin sliver of open sky, and in places an overhang threw the passage into dim shadow. The route was paved and a small water channel ran alongside to prevent flooding. Those ahead of the small party had to squeeze to one side to permit them to pass as the guards and their prisoners made their way along the winding path into the city.

'You can see why Pompey was never able to bring the Nabataeans to heel,' Cato said quietly. 'If this is the only way into Petra then a small force could hold an army at bay for ever.'

'There has to be another way in,' Macro replied. 'A path through the mountains, or at least something scaleable. Surely?'

'Maybe not. How else could Nabataea have resisted every conqueror passing through the region?' Cato looked up at the cliffs in wonder. 'It's a miracle that anyone ever found this entrance in the first place.'

They turned a corner and ahead of them a narrow fissure of light split the cliffs from top to bottom. A short distance beyond the opening was an enormous structure, a temple, built from massive columns. Only when they got closer did Cato realise this was no construction, but had been carved from solid rock.

'Will you just look at that,' Macro marvelled as they emerged from the siq and could see the entire edifice, fiery red in the sunlight angling down across it. They had emerged into a narrow canyon, stone-paved and filled with market stalls and the stands of bankers, just as in any large city of the empire. Except that there were no temples surrounding the market, just red cliffs. The guards steered them across the market area and round another corner and there, at last, the city of Petra revealed itself to them. Great tombs, carved into the rock, lined the broad thoroughfare leading into the heart of the mountain-bound city. More stalls lined the route and ahead, rising above a low spur of a hill, was a sprawl of magnificent palaces and temples. As they emerged from the tomb-lined street the cliffs opened out and the rest of the city came into sight, a mass of houses and streets covering the small rises in the ground that surrounded the basin at the heart of Petra. The guards and prisoners marched down a wide straight street, colonnaded on both sides, until they reached a broad flight of steps rising up the hill to the right upon which rested the great palace of the kings of Nabataea. They climbed the steps, but headed away from the large brass-covered doors of the main entrance towards a small, discreet door at the side. Beyond, a staircase descended beneath the palace and then a torchlit tunnel doubled back towards the street they had walked down. At the end of the tunnel was a line of cells with small barred openings that looked down into the street. The leader led them past the first cells, some of which contained a handful of wretched individuals living in their own filth as they awaited judgement or served out their punishment.

Cato nudged Macro. 'Look there.'

Macro glanced to the side as they passed the bars of the last cell but one. Inside, sitting against the stone walls, were several Parthians, still wearing the scaled armour that they had fought in outside Fort Bushir. The eyes of the Parthians followed the new arrivals as they passed by and were ushered into the next cell. The leader of the guards closed the barred door and slid the bolts into place, and then marched off with his men, leaving the two Romans to themselves.

Macro went over to the window and stepped up on to the bench below it so that he could see through the bars. Outside, people passed by, not bothering to cast a glance at the face of the prisoner staring at them from the dim recess at the base of the palace.

'Not the best of results,' he said grimly.

'Symeon will sort the situation out. He'll have us released as soon as possible.'

'You seem to place great confidence in that man.'

Cato had slumped down against the wall and felt the urge to sleep closing in on him like a shroud. His eyes felt heavy and he closed them for a moment. Yet he was piqued by Macro's comment. 'Confidence? Yes, I suppose so. He seems to know what he's doing. And it's thanks to him that Bannus was defeated at Bushir, remember?'

'Fair point,' Macro replied flatly, continuing to stare out between the bars. 'I just hope he can get us out of this shithole.'

'Colourful,' Cato muttered, and then finally succumbed to his exhaustion as his chin dropped on to his breast and he fell asleep.

A hand grasped his shoulder and shook him roughly. Cato stirred. 'Leave me alone,' he mumbled. 'Go away, Macro.'

The hand shook him again, more forcefully this time, and Cato raised his head, opened his eyes and made to protest again. Only it wasn't Macro. Murad grinned at him and said something in his own tongue while he waved a finger mockingly at the young Roman officer. Macro was standing behind him.

'What's going on?' Cato asked.

'Seems that Symeon has sent us a few necessaries.' Macro gestured to the floor of the cell and Cato saw a bundle of clothes and a small basket of bread and meat. Murad smiled, pointed to the food and then to his mouth.

'Good! Eat. Eat.'

Cato nodded. 'I get the point, thanks.'

He rose up stiffly and rubbed his lower back and buttocks, still aching from two days in the saddle. Outside in the street it was dark and the cell was illuminated by three flames of an oil lamp on the ground beside the door. Macro squatted down and tore off a hunk of bread and popped it into his mouth. As he chewed he gestured towards a wax tablet resting on top of the bundle of clothes. 'He sent us a message as well.'

'What does it say?'

Macro started to explain, but he had too much bread in his mouth to talk properly and he began to chew furiously for a moment before he gave up and tossed the tablet over to Cato. 'See for yourself,' he managed to say.

Cato picked it up and began to read. Symeon had been to see the royal chamberlain to explain the situation and request that the Romans be released. The trouble was that Bannus had beaten him to it, and had already informed the chamberlain that these were Roman spies sent to investigate Petra's defences. Symeon had protested their innocence on this charge. Accordingly, the chamberlain had decided to see all parties first thing in the morning. Symeon had sent them a change of clothes and some of the local scented oil, and had paid the palace guards to bring them some water for washing so that they might present themselves in a decent state to the chamberlain. He concluded by saying that he was still trying to discover where Bannus was staying, that Yusef was safe and the casket was still in Bannus' possession.

Cato lowered the tablet and glanced down at himself. His skin was still streaked with dark smudges of the ash he had blackened himself with for the attack on the enemy camp. The sweat he had shed over the course of two days' riding under the glare of the sun had caused dust to stick to his skin and work its way into every pore and crease. Glancing up at Macro he could see that his friend looked equally dishevelled. Murad pointed towards a tub in the corner of the cell and mimed washing his face.

Cato nodded and bent down to untie his bootlaces. 'What hour is it?'

'No idea,' Macro admitted. 'I fell asleep a short time after you. Only woke up when they let Murad into the cell.'

Once his boots were off, Cato reached for the hem of his tunic. Murad muttered something and quickly backed away and knocked on the door. A moment later the bolt slid back and a guard pulled it open. Murad turned and waved to them both and was gone. The guard shut and bolted the door behind him.

Macro chuckled. 'Seems that they're not too keen on

exposing bare flesh around here. I noticed that in the street. No idea how they can bear so much clothing in this heat.'

Cato continued to strip. When he was naked he reached into the tub and discovered that there was a brush resting in the bottom. After he had scrubbed his skin down and dabbed himself dry he examined the clothes that Murad had brought them. There was a light linen tunic for each of them, as well as a flowing robe of some fine material he had never encountered before, and two pairs of lightweight sandals.

'Nice,' he muttered and began to dress.

Macro took his turn at the tub, and then looked at the clothes suspiciously. 'I'd rather wear my army tunic.'

'It's filthy, it's torn and it stinks of horse-sweat.'

'So?'

'So it's hardly going to impress this royal chamberlain that Symeon mentioned. Besides,' Cato raised his arms so that the folds of the fine material hung from his thin frame, 'these clothes feel very comfortable. Very comfortable indeed. You'll see.'

'Huh!' Macro snorted. 'You look like a high class whore.'

'Really?' Cato smiled mischievously. 'Then just wait until I try on that scented oil.'

Shortly after the sun had appeared above the hills that surrounded the city, the guards came for Macro and Cato.

Macro had made a poor show of wearing the clean garments provided for him and the robe hung untidily from his broad shoulders, folds of it overflowing the army belt that he wore loosely about his waist. Earlier, he had refused point blank to wear one drop of the scented oil from the ornate vial that Murad had placed carefully beside the clothes.

'I will not stink like some two-sestertian tart!' he fumed.

Cato tried to reason with him. 'When in Rome—'

'That's precisely the fucking point! We're not in Rome. If we were then I wouldn't have to take part in this fancy dress nonsense.'

'Macro, there's a lot riding on this. Not least the question of our getting out of this cell. We can't do anything from here. We have to make a good impression on the local powers. So please, arrange those clothes properly at least. And, if you're not going to wear the oil, you'd better make sure you stand downwind of the chamberlain.'

'Ha bloody ha,' Macro grumbled, but he began to pluck the folds of the unfamiliar garb into place. When it came to the sandals, Macro was surprised to discover how comfortable they felt after the sturdy army boots he had grown so accustomed to. Not, of course, that he would admit as much to Cato.

'All right then. I'm ready. Let's go.'

They were taken up the tunnel from the cells. As they

passed the Parthians, still held in the next cell, Macro winked at them. 'Enjoy the hospitality, lads.'

'What's the point?' asked Cato. 'They can't understand you.'

'I'm out here in clean clothes, while they're stuck in a nasty dark cell. What's not to understand?' Macro grinned.

The chamberlain saw them in the court he held adjacent to that of the King. It was a grand hall, lined with columns that soared up to a ceiling covered with geometric patterns picked out in gold. A low dais with an ornate chair and side table stood at the end of the room and light flooded in through shuttered windows high up on the walls. In one corner a caged bird was singing a beautiful but mournful song over and over again. A guard indicated that they were to stand in front of the dais and then turned away and left them, closing the doors behind him.

'What now, I wonder?' Cato said softly.

They stood in silence for a while, expecting the imminent arrival of the chamberlain and his retinue, but no one came, and the repetitive song of the bird continued to echo off the walls until Macro felt a compulsion to wring its neck and jam the carcass on a roasting spit. Fortunately for the songbird, the doors suddenly opened again and Symeon was shown into the room. He smiled at the sight of the two Romans.

'There! You look a lot more civilised.' He gave Macro a quick appraisal. 'Well, less like barbarians at least.'

'What's happening?' Macro asked. 'We've been waiting here for ages. Where's this bloody chamberlain?'

'He's been conferring with his advisers. The arrival of Bannus, and then you two, has created something of a difficult situation for the Nabataeans.'

'How so?'

Symeon glanced round before he lowered his voice and continued. 'One of the Parthians who entered the city with Bannus claims to be a prince of their royal household. If the Nabataeans continue to hold him prisoner, they risk offending Parthia. They've heard that the Parthians are massing forces close to Rome's Syrian frontier. If there's a war between Rome and Parthia, and Parthia wins, then Nabataea cannot afford for there to be any bad will between them. On the other hand, Bannus and his Parthian friend are responsible for attempting to launch a rebellion in Judaea. If the Nabataeans release this Parthian prince and his friend Bannus, they risk offending Rome.' Symeon paused to let it sink in. 'You can see the problem. At the moment they are trying to verify the Parthian's claim.'

'But that could take weeks.'

'Apparently not. Parthia sent an ambassador to the Nabataean king recently. They're at his palace on the Red Sea. The chamberlain has sent word to the King about the situation and asked that he return, with the ambassador, to Petra.'

'How long will that take?' asked Macro.

'Several days.'

Macro pressed his lips together to contain his frustration. 'I am not going to be stuck in that bloody cell for that long. You can tell that to your bloody chamberlain.'

At the sound of footsteps approaching Symeon glanced towards the door. 'I think you'll be able to tell him yourself.'

The doors opened again, and a small crowd entered the hall, in the wake of a tall thin man, richly dressed. The chamberlain's retinue of clerks and advisers took their positions on and around the dais. The chamberlain ignored Symeon and the two Romans until he had settled in his seat. Then he looked towards them and smiled an insincere politician's smile.

'I apologise for the inhospitable manner of your entry to our city.'

His Greek was cultured and flawless. He sounded more Greek than most Greeks, Cato decided as the chamberlain continued addressing them.

'Symeon has made representations to me that you be released into his custody for the duration of your stay in Petra. I will grant this, on the following conditions: first, that you swear an oath not to attempt to quit the city; second, that you confine your movements to the centre of Petra, and make no effort to reconnoitre our defences; third, that you avoid all contact with Bannus and his Parthian allies. If you encounter them in the street you will ignore them. Any breach of

these conditions will result in your immediate reincar-
ceration.'

'Reincar-what?' Macro muttered to Cato.

'They'll chuck us back in the cell.'

'Oh.'

The chamberlain looked at them. 'Are you willing to
accept these conditions?'

Macro nodded. 'We are, sir.'

'Very well. Do I have your oath to abide by these
conditions?'

'I swear it.'

'And your friend?'

'I swear it also,' Cato responded.

'Good! That is settled then. Bannus and the Parthian
prince have sworn the same oath, so there will be no
trouble between you while you are under our jurisdiction.' There was no doubting the imperative undertone of
his statement and the Roman officers nodded their assent.

'So, then,' the chamberlain continued. 'What is it that
Rome would ask of the Nabataean kingdom, in respect
of the present situation?'

Macro frowned as he tried to follow the gist of the
chamberlain's words. Fortunately Cato had a firm grasp
of Greek and was able to reply on their behalf. 'We want
the safe return of the boy taken hostage by Bannus. We
want the return of a casket that belongs to the boy's
family, and we want Bannus.'

'And what of the Parthian prince?'

Cato looked to Macro for a decision. Macro opened his mouth, paused and then raised a finger. 'Just a moment please, sir.' He turned to Cato and whispered, 'What do you think? Should we let that Parthian bastard off the hook?'

'I don't see what else we can do,' Cato replied, with a quick glance at the chamberlain who was clearly less than amused by Macro's informal request for an intermission. 'You heard what Symeon said. Nabataea dare not risk offending Parthia. For that matter, I doubt that the Emperor would want to present Parthia with any grievance against Rome. I'd say we drop any claim we have on him and concentrate our efforts on Bannus.'

Macro thought it over. It made sense in the circumstances, even though he was reluctant to lose his moral claim for revenge against the Parthian who shared the responsibility for the deaths of so many men of the Second Illyrian. He swallowed his anger and turned back to the chamberlain. 'We lay no claim on the Parthian.'

A visible ripple of relief swept through the Nabataean officials. The chamberlain gestured to one of the guards and spoke in their tongue. The guard bowed and turned to a side door. He opened it and beckoned to someone waiting outside. A moment later, Bannus entered the hall. He glanced round and for a moment there was no expression on his face as he caught sight of Symeon and the two Romans. Then his eyes narrowed slightly, betraying his bitter hatred. The chamberlain called out to him and indicated that he should stand to one side of the dais, some distance from his enemies.

'Bannus,' he began, 'these representatives of Rome demand that you are handed over to them.'

'No!' Bannus cried out. 'You must not betray me. I came here to ask for asylum. Is this how Nabataea treats its guests?'

'I do not recall extending an invitation to you,' the chamberlain replied with another of his smiles. 'Therefore you are not our guest.'

'Nevertheless, I would ask you for shelter, for protection against a common enemy.'

'Enemy?'

'I speak of Rome.'

'We are not at war with Rome. They are not our enemy.'

'Yet they will be. Rome is not simply another kingdom. It is a contagion. They will never cease to covet the lands of others. If they would have my land, poor as it is, as a province of their empire, then how do you imagine they would look upon the wealth of Nabataea?'

The chamberlain did not reply. He spared Cato and Macro a quick glance before returning his attention to Bannus. 'What evidence do you have that Rome has any designs on Nabataea?'

'Evidence?' Bannus smiled. 'Why, all the evidence of history. There is not a land that they have conquered wherein they did not look across its frontier with a view to the next conquest. Their appetite for expansion is insatiable. Only when those peoples who are not yet under the Roman yoke realise their common danger will we be free of their tyranny. If you hand me over to them, then you betray all those who would defy Rome, and all those, in the fullness of time, who *should* defy Rome.'

'You refer, of course, to the kingdom of Nabataea.'

'I do.'

The chamberlain's staff looked at each other uneasily. But their master simply stared at the Judaean as he reflected on their exchange. At length, he turned to Macro and Cato. He frowned. 'Who speaks for you?'

Macro turned to Cato and spoke in an undertone. 'I can't keep up with this in Greek. You'll have to speak for us. But be careful, mind. Play it straight and don't try anything too clever. All we want is Bannus, the boy and that woman's casket.' He turned back to face the chamberlain. 'My companion Centurion Cato will speak for us.'

Cato hissed, 'Are you sure about this, Macro?'

'Quite sure. Now get on with it.'

The chamberlain fixed his stare on Cato. 'Is it true? Does Rome intend to annex our kingdom?'

Cato felt his heart beating wildly inside his chest. For a moment he was too terrified to respond. How could he? He was a junior officer, albeit one with a mission assigned to him by the Emperor's chief of staff, Narcissus. But he could not deny Bannus' accusation, because he simply did not know the extent of imperial policy.

'Sir,' he began hesistantly, 'I am a soldier. I have no idea what my masters in Rome intend for this region. All that I do know is that Judaea is a Roman province, under the rule of Roman law, and that this man, Bannus, is a brigand and an outlaw who tried to provoke a rebellion against us. Therefore he is a common criminal, and all that my prefect and I seek is the chance to bring him to justice.'

'Justice!' Bannus laughed bitterly. 'What justice will I receive at the hands of Rome? You'll nail me up on a cross at the first opportunity, just as you did to Jehoshua, and all the others who led the resistance against Rome.'

Cato did not reply to this charge, since it was true. Instead he tried a different tack. 'As I said, I have no knowledge of the Emperor's plans for his empire, but this I do know. If a kingdom offers shelter or any other form of succour to an enemy of Rome, such as Bannus, then I am certain that the Emperor would not be well disposed towards that kingdom. Particularly since someone like Bannus would pose an ongoing threat to the stability of the Roman province of Judaea, as long as he is permitted to live . . . on the very border of the province.'

The chamberlain understood the thrust of Cato's last words and nodded, folding his hands together as he contemplated the situation. Bannus looked to him, trying hard to conceal his desperation.

'Before you decide to hand me over to these Roman

scum, I have to tell you that I am no simple brigand. No outlaw. I made a treaty with Parthia. That is why their prince is serving under my command.'

'Bollocks!' Macro snapped, the word echoing round the hall. Cato winced as his friend jabbed his finger out towards Bannus and continued angrily, 'How can you make a treaty with Parthia? You're nothing but a criminal.'

'I am no criminal,' Bannus replied, his voice suddenly dropping into a more calm, almost serene, tone. 'I am the rightfully anointed king of my people. I am the *mashiah*.'

'Blasphemer!' Symeon spat. 'How dare you?'

He took several steps towards Bannus before the chamberlain quickly gestured to his guards and they drew their swords, hurriedly interposing themselves between the two men. Symeon was forced to stop in his tracks, breathing hard and glaring at Bannus. He forced himself to calm down and raised his hands to indicate that his rage was under control. 'Forgive me, sir. But this man, who crawls lower than the belly of a snake, outrages the religion of my people with such a claim.'

'Really?' Bannus smiled. 'Didn't our friend Jehoshua once claim to be the *mashiah* ? Or did someone claim that on his behalf ?'

Symeon coloured and Cato saw him clench his fists so tight that they blanched, hard and cold as rock.

'Now I lay claim to that title,' Bannus continued. 'And as the leader of my people I am perfectly entitled to enter into treaties with Parthia. For their part, they recognise me as an allied ruler. That being the case, I do not think that Parthia would look too kindly on my being surrendered to these petty officials from a small outpost on the frontier of their empire.'

'Petty official?' Macro started. 'Me? Why, the little bastard! I'll have him!'

'Enough!' shouted the chamberlain. 'Silence!'

His voice echoed round the hall, and only the songbird continued with its unending and unchanging sequence of notes. The chamberlain glanced towards the bird cage and muttered to one of his advisers, and the man slipped discreetly across to the corner of the hall, picked up the cage and hurriedly carried it from the room. Macro gave vent to a small sigh of relief.

The chamberlain drew himself up in his chair. 'I cannot make a ruling on this matter today. It is beyond the range of my responsibilities. I hereby defer the question to his majesty who will hear the details on his return to Petra. Both parties are bound by their oaths, and I hereby authorise the release of the two Roman officers into the charge of Symeon. The Parthian prisoners will also be released, once they have sworn their oaths. The royal court will reconvene to rule on this matter when his majesty returns. That concludes this hearing. Gentlemen, you may leave.'

CHAPTER THIRTY-TWO

Symeon took them to his home on the side of the hill opposite the palace. It was a modest house by the standard of many Nabataeans who lived off the caravan trade. The plain door gave on to an atrium with a small courtyard beyond. Rooms led off from the courtyard and a narrow staircase led upstairs to the sleeping quarters. Symeon had one slave, an elderly man by the name of Bazim who maintained the house and cooked for his master when Symeon returned to Petra from his travels.

'It's not very grand,' Symeon said as he showed them inside, 'but it's all I need and it's the closest thing I've ever had to a home. Come, Bazim's prepared a room for you. I imagine you're both still tired from the journey here, and a night in the cells hasn't helped much.'

'Thank you,' said Cato. 'I'd like that.'

'Then rest. We'll talk again tonight, over a meal. Meanwhile, if there's anything you need just ask Bazim. I have to go out now.'

'Oh?'

'Yes, there's some business that needs attending to. I have to meet Murad and some of the caravan cartels. It'll take most of the day.'

'We'll see you later then,' said Macro.

Symeon smiled, and turned to leave the house. When the door had closed behind him Macro let out a jaw-cracking yawn and arched his back. 'I'm all in. Bazim!'

The slave shuffled out of his small room at the end of the hall. 'Master?'

'You speak Greek?'

'Of course, master.'

'Good for you. Now show me to this room you've made ready.'

'Yes, master. Over here.' He led them to the rear of the courtyard and through a small passage, and they emerged in a walled garden. Bright plants climbed a trellis that stretched over the nearest half of the garden giving a cool shaded area. In one corner was a large room with a plain bed on either side. The sound of running water caught Macro's ear and he looked round in surprise.

'There's a fountain over there.' Macro crossed the garden and stood in front of the small basin into which a thin jet of water tumbled from the mouth of a brass lion on the wall. He reached his hands into the water and relished the cooling flow over his skin. In the time since he and Cato had first landed in Caesarea water had been such a precious commodity that to see a fountain here in Symeon's house seemed like something of a miracle.

Bazim approached from behind. 'My master thought you might like to rest where you could hear the sound of running water.'

Macro smiled. 'He was right. Bless him.'

He leaned forward and doused his head in the spray, shaking it off as he stood back up, sending glittering droplets across the paving slabs of the sunlit courtyard. For a moment, he was transported back to his childhood, to the long summer days when he swam with his friends in a small stream that fed into the Tiber. Then the moment was gone, and he was aware once again of how tired he felt. He trod wearily across to the room that Bazim had prepared.

'Hey, Cato! Where have you got to?'

Inside the room, his friend was already asleep, still in his borrowed robes, head resting on a bolster and mouth agape as he breathed heavily. Macro smiled. Cato had beat him to it, keen to fall asleep before Macro's snoring could keep him awake. As Macro kicked off his sandals he noticed that Cato still wore his. He hesitated a moment, then padded over to his friend and pulled the sandals off gently and placed them on the floor. Then he lay down on his own bed, smiling at the comfort afforded by the thick bedroll. In the background the water gurgled pleasantly and dappled sunlight filtered through the foliage on the trellis. Macro closed his eyes. He could do with a few days of this, and he found himself hoping that the King of Nabataea did not return to his capital too soon.

As his thoughts returned to the reason for their presence in Petra, Macro's mood soured. Somewhere out there in the streets and houses of the city lurked Bannus and his Parthian friends. Whatever the King decided to do on his return, there would be a reckoning, Macro vowed. Bannus must not be allowed to survive and breed yet more rebellion in the troubled, long-suffering province of Judaea.

The days passed slowly and Cato and Macro quickly grew frustrated by the restrictions placed on their movements in the city. Especially Cato, who was fascinated by the sheer peculiarity of the vast tombs and temples that had been carved from the rock with such skill. By day they explored the market, and marvelled at the range of luxury items that rivalled all but the most prestigious establishments in Rome. There was a library where Cato discovered a collection of maps, many of which detailed lands that no Roman had heard of, let alone seen. For his part, Macro was content to sample the food and the wine and catch up on his sleep in the cool garden of Symeon's house. Soon after their arrival Symeon informed them that he had discovered where Bannus and the Parthians were staying. A rich merchant on the other side of the city had offered them his home. He had no love of Rome, like many Nabataeans who viewed any expansion of the Empire with anxiety.

Then, one afternoon, when Cato was walking

through the precinct of the great temple in front of Petra's wide forum, Bannus emerged from a colonnade right in front of him. Both men automatically stopped and started to apologise before their eyes met and the words died on their lips. There was a tense silence and then Bannus made to move away.

'Wait!' said Cato. 'I want to talk. We have to talk.'

Bannus continued for a few paces before he stopped and turned. 'Aren't you forgetting the terms of the oath we took for the chamberlain?'

'No. But that was to stop us fighting. I just want to talk.'

'Talk?' Bannus smiled. 'What about? The weather? The price of corn? The withdrawal of Rome from Judaea?'

Cato ignored the sarcasm and pointed to a small wine shop on the far side of the forum. 'In there, in case we are seen together by any of the chamberlain's men.'

They made their way over to the wine shop in silence and sat on stools on opposite sides of a small table.

'Allow me,' said Bannus and ordered a jar of wine, before he turned back to Cato. 'So, talk.'

'Your revolt is over. Your army has been crushed and the survivors have returned to their villages.'

'I failed this time,' Bannus admitted. 'But there will be another rebellion. As long as the presence of Rome corrupts our land there will always be rebellion.'

Cato's heart sank. 'But you cannot prevail against

Rome. Your men are no match for the legions, you must know that.'

'That is why I made a treaty with Parthia.' Bannus smiled. 'I think even a Roman must have heard what happened to the army of Crassus at Carrhae. Or don't they mention that in your histories?'

'They mention it.'

'Then you must know that Parthia is more than a match for Rome on the battlefields of the east.'

'Perhaps. But if Parthia prevails, do you imagine for a moment that they would let Judaea exist as an independent state, despite what they may have promised you?'

Bannus shrugged. 'If they try to impose their rule on us we will rebel against them as we have against Rome.'

'And be defeated again.' Cato shook his head. 'Can't you see? Judaea is fated to be a vassal of one empire or another. Like many other states. Most of them have found their place in our world and are prosperous and peaceful enough. Why should that not be true of Judaea?'

'You've spent too long in the company of that traitor, Symeon.' Bannus sneered. 'Just because it is true of other provinces does not justify imposing your rule on us. We are different, and we want our sovereignty back. Until that happens, there can be no peace.'

Cato stared back at him in silence for a while. Inside he felt the ache of despair. Bannus was a fanatic. There was no reasoning with such men. He decided to change the subject. 'Very well. I understand your position. But it will take time to build another army. So what is the point of keeping the boy, Yusef ? He has served his purpose. You no longer need a hostage.'

'Yusef stays with me.'

'Why?'

'He is the son of the founder of our movement. He needs to be made aware of his heritage. In time he can serve as my lieutenant. With him at my side, and with the relics of his father in my hands, we will be able to win back those who have forgotten the true way.'

'You mean Miriam and her people?'

'Them, and communities like them, in every city across the eastern world. At the moment they are confused. Miriam, and traitors like Symeon, have been corrupting the message of Jehoshua, telling his supporters that armed resistance is futile and that we must use peaceful means to win over our enemies. That we must have faith in the long term.' He stared at Cato. 'Tell me, Roman, what can faith achieve that force can't? Liberty grows from the point of a sword. That is my creed. That was the creed of Jehoshua, before he weakened at the moment of crisis. That is the creed which Miriam and Symeon and their followers have betrayed. It is the creed I will teach Yusef, and one day he will ride at my side at the head of our army when we liberate Jerusalem. Only then will we have fulfilled the dream of Jehoshua.'

'With you as the *mashiah*, naturally.'

'Of course. I have inherited the role from Jehoshua.'

Cato was aware of something that had been said a moment earlier, and frowned. 'What did you mean, "before he weakened"?'

'Ah.' Bannus leaned forward and smiled. 'Why don't you ask your friend Symeon about that? About how it all ended? Now, please excuse me, but I really don't think that there is much purpose in continuing this discussion. If we ever meet again, Roman, then I will kill you.'

He stood up and strode out of the wine shop and across the forum. Cato watched him until he disappeared up a side street. A feeling of tired despair filled his heart like a lead weight. He had hoped to reason with the man and try, at least, to persuade him to release Yusef. All now depended on the will of the King of Nabataea.

That night, as they dined in Symeon's garden, Cato was nervous. For the rest of the day, he had dwelt on Bannus' remarks about Symeon and was determined to find out what lay behind the intense hatred between the two men. As Bazim cleared away the platters of *mensaf*, and brought them a jug of spiced, heated wine, the three men sat quietly for a moment staring at the stars that shone so brilliantly in the clear sky. A full moon hung over the dark outline of the cliff that towered over the royal palace.

Then there was a dull rap at the door and they heard Bazim's slow footsteps as he went to answer it. After a moment he emerged from the house and handed his master a small, hinged wax slate. Symeon flipped it open and scanned the message inside.

'It's from the chamberlain. The King returned to Petra at dusk. He is in session with the chamberlain and his advisers. Their decision will be communicated to us in the morning.'

'Good!' Macro thumped the cushion of his seat. 'We'll have that bastard Bannus in our hands and we can settle the matter once and for all.'

Symeon looked at him. 'You seem very confident that the King will decide in your favour.'

'Why shouldn't I be confident? He's got more to fear from Rome than Parthia.'

'That may be true, Prefect, but for pity's sake don't say such things in front of anyone else here in Petra. The last thing we need now is anyone stirring up anti-Roman hysteria.'

Macro was chastened and took a sip of wine. 'Just telling it the way it is.'

Symeon chuckled. 'Which is why you're an accomplished soldier, and not a diplomat.'

'And thank fuck for that.' Macro raised his glass. 'Sooner an honest fighter than a man who fights honesty any day.'

Symeon clapped his hands. 'An aphorism is born!'

'I spoke to Bannus today,' Cato blurted out.

The others stopped smiling and turned to stare at him. Macro recovered first. 'What the hell did you do that for? You want to get us thrown back in that bloody cell?'

'No.'

'Well then.' Macro shook his head in exasperation. 'Why did you do it?'

'I tried to persuade him to hand over Yusef.'

'He said no, I take it.'

'He said that, and more.' Cato's eyes turned to Symeon. 'Bannus told me I should ask you what happened to Jehoshua, at the end.'

Symeon breathed in deeply and looked down into the dark red liquid in his glass. There was a long silence, in which Macro attracted Cato's attention and raised his eyebrows. Cato gestured to him to be patient. At length Symeon spoke.

'I'll tell you what happened, then you'll understand why there is now only a deep hatred between Bannus and myself. You already know that we were both followers of Jehoshua, but in those days we were also friends. The best of friends, like brothers really. There was a third friend, but I'll tell you about him in a minute. We joined the movement because Jehoshua held out the promise of freeing Judaea. As he drew more and more people to follow him some began to say he was the *mashiah*. He ignored them at first, but after a while he seemed to become attracted to the idea. I confess, I encouraged him in this. I am ashamed of it now, given what happened. Anyway, the prophecy of the *mashiah* is quite specific. He must liberate Jerusalem, assume the throne of David and lead Judaea to victory over the rest of the world.'

'That's a tall order,' Macro said quietly.

'Quite.' Symeon smiled faintly, and continued. 'So, with several thousand of our followers behind us, we set out for Jerusalem. It began well enough. The streets were lined with people who greeted us hysterically and showered blessings on Jehoshua. We managed to take over the precincts of the Great Temple. Jehoshua ordered that the moneylenders and the tax collectors be kicked out of the temple and their records destroyed. You can imagine how well that went down with the poor amongst his followers. Then we took over the armoury of the temple guards. At first we were carried away with the elation of it all. All that remained was to confront the Sanhedrin, persuade them to come over to our side and rise up against the Roman garrison.'

'What were they doing about it?' Macro interrupted. 'The garrison? Surely they would have intervened the moment you took over the temple?'

'They shut themselves up in Herod's palace. At the time the tensions between my people and the Roman officials were at breaking point. There had been riots a few years earlier, and the procurator did not want to risk inflaming the situation again. So they did nothing.'

Macro sat back with a look of disgust. 'I'd have sorted you lot out in short order.'

'I imagine you would. But you are not Pilate. Anyway,

the Sanhedrin refused to come over to us. You have to understand that the high priests were drawn from the richest, most powerful families, and Jehoshua believed that Judaeans had to be freed from poverty and exploitation as much as from Roman tyranny. He had assumed that the Sanhedrin would place their nation before their purses, and was thrown aback by their refusal to cooperate. That's when he lost it. Suddenly, he said that we could not win by force of arms. We must win the argument. We must win the battle for the hearts and minds of our enemies.'

'Hearts and minds.' Macro laughed. 'Where have I heard that one before? Shit, when will people ever learn . . . Sorry, please go on.'

'Thank you.' Symeon frowned before he continued. 'When we heard him utter this new line, we were horrified. Bannus and I met in secret, and decided he had to go. The movement needed a more resolute leader or there would be no revolt. No new kingdom of Judaea. So we decided to betray Jehoshua. Hand him over to the authorities. They would surely execute him and we would have a martyr, as well as a new leader.'

'Who?' Cato asked. 'You or Bannus?'

'Me. Bannus would be my lieutenant.'

'Some friends you turned out to be,' said Macro. 'With friends like you and Bannus what need had Jehoshua of enemies?'

'You don't understand, Prefect,' Symeon replied

intensely. 'We loved Jehoshua. We all did. But we loved Judaea more. We had to save our people. What is the life of one man, however much he is loved, when weighed against the fate of an entire nation?' He paused and sipped from his glass. 'So we prepared a message, telling the authorities where they could find Jehoshua. There was only one man close to us whom we could trust to deliver the message, the third friend in our circle that I told you of earlier. His name was Judas. Even so, we did not dare to tell him what was in the message. So Judas took the message to the Sanhedrin. Jehoshua was arrested, tried, tortured and executed. His followers were stunned. Too stunned to react to events. Before the day was out the Roman troops were on the streets arresting the ringleaders and disarming and dispersing their followers. I managed to escape, with Bannus, through the sewers. Once we got out of Jerusalem we split up. He went north to continue the struggle. I went south, to Petra. For a while I was desolated, too ashamed of what we did, to care about anything. But slowly, I built a new life for myself and began to travel, to rebuild my connections with the surviving members of the movement, like Miriam. I did not realise at first that I had changed. I had been young and inexperienced and had never seen a battle in those days. To think that I ever believed we could beat the legions!' He shook his head. 'The romance of great causes and the folly of youth just leads to death. Eventually I came to realise that Jehoshua had been right in the end; we could not defeat Rome with swords, only with words, with ideas. Bannus never accepted that.'

'And Judas?' Cato asked. 'What became of him?'

Symeon bowed his head in shame. 'As soon as he realised what had been contained in the message, he hanged himself.' Symeon's voice trembled. 'I've never been able to forgive myself for that . . . So now you know my story.' Abruptly, he rose from his couch, bowed his head and quickly walked back into his house.

Macro watched him go, then turned to Cato with a pitying expression. 'This place is one endless bloody tragedy. The sooner we finish the job and get out of here the better. I've had enough of it. I'm sick of them. All of them.'

Cato did not reply. He was thinking of Yusef. Now he was more determined than ever that the boy must be rescued from Bannus and returned to Miriam. Only then could that small fragment of the cycle of destruction and despair be broken.

The messenger came early in the morning. Macro and Cato were eating a breakfast of figs and goats' milk when Symeon emerged from the house with a smile. 'The King has agreed to hand Bannus over to us. The Parthian prince will be returned to his kingdom. Soldiers are already on the way to the house where Bannus and his friends are staying, with orders to arrest them.'

Cato felt a lightness in his chest. 'Then it's over.'

'Yes.' Symeon smiled. 'It's over, and there will be some peace in Judaea, for now. The King has asked that we come to the palace to formally conclude matters, as soon as we receive the message.'

Macro jumped up, rubbing the sticky remains of his meal on the folds of his tunic. He beamed. 'Well? What are we waiting for?'

They were shown into the chamberlain's hall once again, and this time provided with chairs. A few clerks and officials sat with them, waiting for the chamberlain and the King to appear. For a while Macro sat contentedly, then he became slowly irritated by the growing delay and started tapping his foot, the sound echoing faintly off the walls, until Symeon reached over and held his knee still.

'Where's the bloody King, then?' Macro grumbled. 'We've been waiting ages.'

A side door opened and a clerk scuttled in and whispered something to one of the chamberlain's advisers. The adviser glanced towards the Roman officers before he nodded to the clerk and crossed the hall towards Cato and Macro.

'Something's wrong,' said Cato. 'Something's happened.'

'What do you mean?' Macro whispered irritably. 'What could be wrong?'

'Shhh.'

The adviser bowed his head to them and addressed Symeon in the local tongue. Cato watched Symeon's response and saw the look of shock.

'What is it?'

Symeon held up his hand to silence Cato and let the adviser finish his message. Then he turned to Macro and Cato.

'Bannus has gone. When the soldiers arrived at the house to arrest him this morning the Parthians were still there, but Bannus was not in his room. Two horses are missing from the stables of the owner of the house. The soldiers immediately sent word to the guards on the entrance to the siq to stop anyone leaving the city. They were too late. The siq guards reported that a man left Petra at first light. He claimed to be a merchant, and he had a boy with him.'

CHAPTER THIRTY-THREE

Macro and Cato waited while Symeon rode into the wide mouth of the wadi and scanned the ground before him, looking for tracks. As the patch of stony ground gave way to the bright red sand he found what he was looking for and beckoned to the others. Macro and Cato urged their mounts forward, picking a route through the rocks until they reached their companion. Symeon had dismounted and pointed out the hoof imprints.

'Definitely horses.' He stood up and followed the line of the tracks stretching out into the sand until they faded in the distance, in line with the edge of a large dune and one of the vast towers of rock beyond.

'It has to be Bannus,' Cato commented. 'Who else would ride into a wilderness like this?'

Macro grunted. He had finally consented to wear a headdress like the local people and was now grateful that it was keeping the sun off his head. Even so, it was three days since they had galloped out of the siq, desperately

478

trying to catch up with Bannus. Initially there had been no indication which direction he had taken, but then the pursuers had chanced on a shepherd boy in the hills half a day's ride to the south of Petra who had seen a man and a boy ride past, heading south. Symeon and the two Romans had followed, moving from sighting to sighting and once finding the smouldering remains of a small fire. They were already far off the established caravan routes and heading towards the deep desert of Arabia. A chance sighting of a puff of dust in the distance had drawn them to this vast expanse of red sand that formed the bed of a giant maze of sheer rock formations, known to the nearest tribes as Rhum. No horseman had any reason to be in a place like this, unless he was on the run.

'Bannus,' Symeon agreed, and remounted. He drew in his reins and they continued riding into the vast mouth of the wadi, which stretched out for miles ahead of them. The tracks were easy enough to follow, and Cato wondered why Bannus had chosen to cross terrain that would leave proof of his passing in such an obvious manner. But then, Bannus would be desperate, especially if he knew that he was being followed. The Nabataeans had immediately sent messengers south with a description of the man and so there would be little chance of hiding in that direction. All that was left to Bannus now was Arabia, and the hope that he could cross it and then ride north to his friends in Parthia. He no longer cared about hiding his tracks, only about putting as much distance as possible between him and his pursuers.

They rode on, the soft impact of the horses' hooves providing the only sound amid the desolate landscape surrounding them. At the end of the wadi the tracks bent to the left and headed across a wide open stretch of sand, broken up by a handful of dunes, towards another rock formation two or three miles away. It was late in the afternoon and already long dark shadows stretched across sections of the desert. Halfway across this expanse Symeon halted them at the base of a dune and dismounted.

'I'm going to have a look from the top. See if I can see any sign of him.'

'I'm coming too,' Cato decided and jumped down.

'There's no need.'

'I'm worried about Yusef. I have to see for myself.'

Symeon shrugged and started to climb the side of the dune.

Cato turned to Macro. 'Won't be long.'

Macro reached for his canteen and took a small swig. 'If you see any sign of water, let me know.'

Cato smiled, then moved off, following Symeon's tracks up the dune. As soon as the slope made itself apparent the going became difficult as the sand shifted downhill under his feet, to such an extent that it felt as if he was making no progress at all. But eventually, exhausted, he flopped down beside Symeon and scanned the way ahead. On the far side of the dune the sand continued for another mile before it reached the rock formation. Now Cato could see that there was a cleft in the rocks that ran from top to bottom. At the base of the cliffs was a small clump of shrubs and a handful of stunted trees.

'There's water there.'

'That's not all.' Symeon strained his eyes. 'Look again.'

This time Cato saw it, the tiny shapes of two horses, almost lost against the shrubs, and the figure of a man, or a boy, sitting in the shade of one of the trees.

'I can only see one of them.'

'Calm yourself, Cato. We've seen no sign of a body since we've been following him. No body, no blood. I'm sure Yusef is over there with him.'

Cato wanted to believe it. 'All right then, what shall we do?'

'We have to wait. If we approach him now he'll be sure to see our dust the moment we emerge from behind this dune. So we wait until dark, and then ride in. We can stop some distance before the rocks and continue on foot. If we can surprise Bannus then we might be able to grab Yusef before he can do anything.'

'Right.' Cato nodded. 'That's the plan then.'

The sun had sunk far below the rims of the peaks of Rhum and cast the whole area into dark shadow as the three horsemen reined in a quarter of a mile from the cleft in the rocks ahead. A small dune, little more than a fold in the land, concealed them from Bannus and they left their horses hobbled to prevent them from wandering into sight before the trap could be sprung. Then, stripping down to their tunics and taking only their swords with them, the three men crept forward.

Bannus had succeeded in lighting a fire and the glow of the flames cast an orange bloom on to the lowest reaches of the cliffs. As they crept forward Cato saw Bannus take a chunk of bread out of the saddlebag resting on the ground by his side. He bent over a bundle of rags on the ground and dropped the bread beside it. The rags moved and Cato realised it was Yusef. Tied up, but alive. As they drew close to the fire Cato saw that there was no cover between them and Bannus. If he looked into the desert he would surely be able to see them before long.

They continued, with painstaking caution, until they were within fifty paces of the fire and could hear the crackle of the flames and the hiss of the burning wood. Bannus was sitting with his side to them. Opposite him Yusef had managed to wriggle up into a sitting position and was eating the bread, held between his bound hands.

Macro tapped Cato's arm and indicated that he was going to circle round behind Bannus, and Cato nodded that he understood. Both he and Symeon silently drew their swords and lay still, pressing themselves into the fine sand as Macro slid slowly to the right in a wide arc round behind Bannus until he was in line with his back, the fire, and Yusef beyond. Then Macro began to creep forward, in slow, gradual movements, until he was within twenty feet of his target. With pounding heart, and hardly daring to breathe, he eased himself up from the sand, drawing his feet under him then rising up, sword in hand, bracing himself to spring towards Bannus' back.

Over Bannus' shoulder Macro saw the boy suddenly gasp and start up, wide-eyed.

'What is it?' Bannus snapped, then a sixth sense made him spin round and he saw Macro launch himself forward. At once Bannus leaped up and sprinted round the fire, snatching out his curved dagger as he went. Cato and Symeon ran in towards the fire. Before any of them could stop him, Bannus had hauled the boy from the ground and now had his forearm locked across Yusef's throat, pinning him to his chest. The other hand was extended, fist clenching a dagger whose blade gleamed in the firelight.

'Stand back!' Bannus screamed. 'Stand back! One step closer and I swear I'll gut the boy!'

Macro stood only a spear's length away, crouching low, sword point raised. The others were slightly further off, and spread out, so that Bannus had to keep twisting his neck to keep them all in sight.

'Don't move!'

Yusef raised his bound hands and started to claw at the hairy forearm across his throat.

'He can't breathe,' Cato said calmly. 'Bannus, you're killing him.'

Bannus stared back suspiciously for an instant, and then relented, loosening his grip just enough to let Yusef gasp some air into his lungs.

'That's better,' said Cato. 'Now, we have to talk . . . again.'

'We said all we had to say last time.'

'There's no escape now, Bannus. You must surrender. But you can do one good thing before it's over. Spare the boy and return him to Miriam.'

'No!'

'What choice have you got?' Cato pleaded. 'We cannot let you escape again. Let him go.'

'No. Symeon! Saddle my horse. You, Roman – the short one. Your mounts have to be nearby. Bring them here!'

'Fetch them yourself, fuckwit,' Macro growled.

Bannus raised his blade to Yusef's face and, with a deft flick, nicked his cheek. The boy yelped with pain as a thin trickle of blood coursed down his cheek and across Bannus' forearm.

'Next time, I'll take one of his eyes out. Now get the horses, Roman.'

Symeon looked on in horror before he turned to Macro. 'For pity's sake do as he says.'

'I am not going to let him escape,' Macro said firmly. 'Whatever he threatens to do to the boy. It ends here.'

'Macro, I beg you.' Symeon's voice was broken with anxiety. 'Not the boy. He's all that Miriam has.'

Macro did not reply, and did not take his eyes off Bannus as he stood poised to strike. So it was Cato who first noticed the figures emerging from the darkness of the desert. A dozen camel riders in dark robes, quickly fanning out so that the five figures by the fire were surrounded.

'Macro,' Cato said softly. 'Sheathe your sword, slowly.'

Symeon and Cato did the same and turned towards the new arrivals. There was a moment of stillness in which Cato felt himself and his companions scrutinised by the silent riders. Bannus lowered his knife, but kept his arm firmly round Yusef.

Cato whispered, 'Symeon, who are they?'

'Bedu.' Symeon raised a hand in greeting and spoke to the newcomers. A voice replied in kind and one of the riders edged his camel closer. At a series of tongue clicks and taps from his crop the camel's front legs folded, then the back legs, and the rider eased himself from the saddle. He lowered his veil and stared at them all with dark eyes before he started speaking to Symeon again. Then he turned and snapped out some orders to his men and they also began to dismount. One of the men who had been in the shadows held the reins of the three horses that had been left in the desert.

'What do they want?' Cato asked.

'Water. There's a spring in that fissure. He says it belongs to his tribe and that we are trespassing.'

Macro edged closer to the others. 'Fine, so what does he intend to do about it?'

The Bedu leader ordered some of his men to collect waterskins and they disappeared into the fissure. Then he turned back to Symeon and spoke again.

'He wants to know what we are doing here.'

Cato glanced at Macro. 'We've nothing to hide. Tell him the truth.'

There was another exchange before Symeon relayed the details. 'I told him Bannus is our enemy. I asked him if he would let us take Bannus and the boy and leave. He said no.'

'No?' Cato felt a chill in the back of his neck. 'Why not? What does he want from us?'

'He demands that we pay a price for trespassing on their land.'

'What price? We have nothing of value.'

Symeon smiled faintly. 'Except our lives.'

'They mean to kill us?'

Macro's hand tightened on his sword handle. 'Let them bloody try.'

'Not quite,' Symeon replied. 'He said that since we were enemies, we should finish our fight here, in the light of this fire. One of us will fight Bannus. If our man wins we can leave with the boy. If Bannus wins, he leaves with the boy and you two will be killed.'

'I don't understand.' Macro frowned, then he glanced at Symeon. 'You're going to fight him?'

'Yes.'

'No. Let me. I'm trained for this. I'll have a better chance.'

'Prefect, I know how to fight, and this has been a long time coming. Besides, I told the Bedu leader that I would fight.'

Bannus had overheard all this, and smiled. 'Nothing I'd like better.'

'Release the boy,' Cato said.

'Why not?' Bannus brought out his knife again and cut Yusef's bonds. As the ties fell away Yusef hobbled a few steps away from Bannus and collapsed on the sand. Symeon rushed over to him and held the boy's shoulders.

'Yusef, are you all right?'

The boy nodded.

'I'll have you back with your people in a few days, I swear it.'

Bannus laughed. 'Only if you kill me first, old friend.'

Symeon looked up at him. 'I will kill you Bannus. It's the only way to cure your sickness.'

'Sickness?'

'What else can it be when a man is so determined to continue a pointless fight that he no longer cares how many die as a result?'

'I do it for my people!' Bannus protested. 'You abandoned them long ago. What would you understand of our struggle?'

'That it's doomed. You cannot fight Rome and win.'

487

'I can and I will,' Bannus said with deliberation. 'It's just a question of time.'

Symeon shook his head sadly and held Yusef closer. The leader of the Bedu approached them and spoke to Bannus, pointing to a clear space of ground beside the fire. The Bedu had tethered their camels for the night and now sat in a loose circle about the makeshift arena.

'It's time,' Symeon said.

The Bedu leader pushed them gently towards the clearing, guiding Macro, Cato and Yusef to one side. Then he calmly pressed the two Romans down on to their knees and barked an order to his men. Four came over to stand behind them, and they felt hands on their shoulders and then the cold steel of daggers at their throats. The Bedu shouted to Symeon and the latter nodded, drawing his curved sword. A short distance from him Bannus sheathed his dagger and pulled out his own blade, dropping into a crouch as he eyed Symeon warily.

For a moment the two men stood staring at each other, blades held out, ready to strike or parry. Then Bannus took a few steps to the side, edging round so that the fire was behind him, throwing him into silhouette. At once Symeon circled to cancel the advantage. As he took his last step, Bannus leaped forward, slashing down with his fine curved blade. Symeon expertly parried the blow and swept his sword round to the side, where it rang sharply off the hilt that Bannus had snatched across to block the cut. It had been the work of an instant, the sound of the last clash biting through the air even before the first clatter had faded. Both men drew back and stood, carefully balanced, weighing each other up.

Symeon stepped forward and feinted, and feinted again, but Bannus' blade did not move.

'You're going to have to try harder than that . . .'

'You talk too much,' Symeon replied quietly, then thrust at his opponent's head, flicking his wrist at the last moment so the blade cut over Bannus' blocking move and sliced towards his temple. Bannus had no choice but to duck and stagger back to avoid the blow and Symeon launched a series of attacks, which Bannus just managed to ward off in a rapid chorus of ringing blades. At the last moment, as Bannus was pressed towards the Bedu at the edge of the clearing, he powered forward, inside the arc of Symeon's blade, and crashed into his chest, sending Symeon spinning backwards. As they broke contact, Bannus sliced his blade past the other man's side and its finely sharpened edge cut through the folds of Symeon's tunic and laid open a long cut on his chest.

Symeon grunted with pain and clapped his spare hand to the wound, raising it up red and dripping a moment later.

Macro winced and turned his head carefully towards Cato. 'Not good.'

Keeping his eyes fixed on Symeon, Bannus called out mockingly, 'Romans! Your friend is too old, too slow. It will be over soon. Better take your leave of each other now.'

Symeon appeared to sway a little and Cato swallowed nervously. Then with what seemed an effort, Symeon lowered himself into a fighting crouch again and gestured to Bannus to come at him. 'If you think you can beat me.'

'Only too happy to oblige.' Now Bannus moved in to attack in a neatly worked sequence that Symeon met with an equally accomplished series of parries and blocks, but at the end of the attack, as Bannus drew off, Symeon was breathing heavily and blinking his eyes. Cato felt a sick sense of resignation as he saw the blood flowing freely from Symeon's wound and dropping to the ground to soak into the red sand.

'How much longer can you last, old friend?' Bannus moved his blade from side to side, keeping his distance from Symeon as he continued his taunts. 'You're bleeding to death, steadily weakening. I just have to bide my time, make a few more cuts, and then it is over. You're dead, and Yusef is mine. Just as I defeat you, so I will defeat Rome one day.'

'No!' Symeon roared, and lumbered forward, his blade flashing yellow and red in the firelight as he slashed at his enemy's head. There was little finesse in his attack, just sheer brute force as he beat away at Bannus' sword. Bannus, grim-faced, nimbly warded off the blows and stepped lightly aside, scrambling back as Symeon paused for breath, panting hoarsely.

'You've had your chance,' Bannus said coldly. 'And I'm tired of playing with you. Now it's time to end this. Goodbye, Symeon.' The last words were snarled through gritted teeth as he charged at Symeon. There was a flurry of blows and each was parried with a scrape of steel as Symeon found it more and more difficult to defend himself. Then Bannus suddenly jumped to one side and cut down viciously. The edge of his blade cut deep into Symeon's sword arm and his fingers went limp. The sword dangled a moment then hit the sand with a dull thump.

Symeon did not cry out but bit his teeth together and moaned deep inside his chest. Bannus stood over him, sword raised and a triumphant sneer on his lips. 'It's ended just as I knew it would. Now it's time for you to join Jehoshua.' He stepped forward and raised his sword. Cato leaned his head back and shut his eyes. Macro stared ahead with steely contempt for his imminent death.

As the sword blade poised over Symeon's head there was a sudden explosion of movement. Symeon's good hand snatched the dagger from Bannus' belt, and the blade turned up as it rose, in one fluid movement. It was over so quickly that the first Macro was aware of it was when he saw the hilt of the dagger under Bannus' chin and the red spike of its point where it had burst through the top of his skull. Bannus stood for a moment with a stunned expression on his face, mouth slightly agape. Then his arms slumped down and the sword dropped from his lifeless hands and he collapsed by the fire, his legs kicking once in a wild spasm.

For a moment all was still, then Symeon rose unsteadily to his feet and looked down at Bannus. 'As I said. You talk too much.'

Cato opened his eyes, surprised that he was still alive. Then he saw Bannus sprawled at the feet of Symeon. 'What happened?'

Macro glanced at him. 'You missed that? Sometimes I despair at you, lad.' Then he looked round at the Bedu warriors behind him, put his finger gently against the blade still at his throat, and eased it to one side, with a smile. 'If you don't bloody mind, that is?'

The Bedu warriors moved away from them and Macro and Cato hurried across to Symeon, who was swaying now. They eased him down on to the sand and Cato tore strips from Bannus' tunic. The wounds looked clean by the light of the fire and the Romans bound Symeon's wounds. Yusef watched from his original position, still shaken by what he had just witnessed, and all that he had endured over the days since he had been taken from his people. As soon as he had finished bandaging Symeon, Cato took the bedroll from Bannus' saddle and wrapped it round the boy's shoulders.

Now that their entertainment was done, the Bedu largely ignored them and set about preparing their camp for the night. They cooked a meal over the fire and the leader beckoned the others to join them and share their food. Symeon was given pride of place and the Bedu warriors talked animatedly to him about the fight until he was too weak to continue, and begged them to let him sleep. Cato made up his bedroll and helped Symeon down and then covered him with a cloak to keep him warm once the fire died down. He did the same for the boy and then sat with Macro staring across the flames at the Bedu warriors.

For a long time Macro said nothing, and then he finally muttered, 'That was close. Closest I've ever come to thinking I'd actually die.' He turned to his friend. 'Don't mind telling you, it scared the shit out of me.'

'You scared?' Cato chuckled. 'I don't believe it.'

'It's no joke, Cato. Seriously, no joke.' He turned to look at Symeon. Yusef had shuffled his bedroll closer to the wounded man and was resting his head against Symeon's uninjured side. 'That Symeon's a bloody marvel. Must have taken nerves of steel to wait for his chance like that. The problem of course is that he saved our lives.'

Cato could not hide his astonishment. 'That's a problem?'

'Oh yes. It means that now I owe him a favour.'

The Bedu had gone when Cato woke first the next morning. Only the faint impressions in the sand and the half buried mounds of camel dung remained to show they had camped there for the night. They had pilfered

Bannus' belongings and the casket that he had taken from Miriam lay open on the sand. A length of white cloth, with dark stains that might have been blood, spilled over the lid of the casket and a plain glazed cup lay a short distance away. Cato folded the shroud carefully and put it back in the casket, placing the cup safely in between layers of the material before he shut the casket and fastened the latch. The fire was dead and the ashes were no longer even warm. Bannus' body lay where it had fallen, and Cato dragged it away behind the bushes and buried it before the others were awake. Macro stirred next, sat up abruptly and looked round for the Bedu.

'Gone! How the hell did they do that?'

'You're not exactly a light sleeper.'

'Very funny. Where's Bannus?'

Cato jerked his thumb towards the bushes. 'Out of sight and out of mind. Where he belongs.'

Symeon's wounds felt stiff and he had to be helped into the saddle as they prepared to ride out of Rhum. Yusef insisted on riding the same horse that had carried him to this place. He took the reins and looked round at Cato. 'Where are we going?'

'Home.' Cato smiled. 'We're taking you home.'

CHAPTER THIRTY-FOUR

They rode into Heshaba several days later. The centre of the settlement was surrounded by the blackened shells of the houses that had been set on fire by Bannus and his men. A few curious faces turned out to see the four riders as they rode past, and once Yusef had been recognised people hurried to find Miriam and tell her that a miracle had happened.

Macro and Cato tethered their horses in the village square and helped Symeon down from his mount. The wound to his side was healing slowly, but the blow to his arm had severed too many muscles and tendons ever to recover fully and Symeon was coming to terms with the probability that he would never be able to wield a sword again. His fighting days were over. He sat heavily in the shade of a blackened wall and Cato went over to the trough to douse his head. Yusef made sure that Symeon was made comfortable when there was a sharp cry from the end of a street and the four new arrivals turned to the sound. Miriam was leaning one hand against a wall for support while she clasped the other to her mouth. As soon as he saw her Yusef sprang to his feet and sprinted across and threw himself into her arms. For a while they just held each other close, and then they continued into the square, walking arm in arm over to Symeon and the two Roman officers. Miriam bit her lip, struggling to hold back her tears as she spoke.

'I–I don't know how to thank you. I—' She looked down and shook her head slightly. 'I don't know the words to say how happy I am. How grateful I am. May God bless you all and keep you safe for the hereafter.'

'Well, thank you,' Macro responded awkwardly. 'I'm sure he will keep an eye on us, especially after all we've been through. We've earned it.'

'There's one more thing,' Cato said. He walked over to his horse, unbuckled a large saddle pouch and carefully took out Miriam's casket. 'Here you are.'

Miriam took the casket and stroked a hand softly across the lid. 'Again, thank you and bless you.' She looked up at Cato. 'I take it you have dealt with Bannus.'

'Yes.'

'Poor soul. Poor tormented soul.'

Macro looked at Cato in surprise and was about to open his mouth when Cato shook his head with a pleading expression. Then Cato looked round the village. 'What happens now? Are you going to rebuild the destroyed houses? We could help you.'

'No,' Miriam replied. 'I've been thinking things over

since Yusef was taken from me. There's no point. Heshaba will not survive in isolation. We cannot escape the world as I had hoped we could. There is no future for the vision of my son if we stay here. If we cannot escape the world, then we must re-join it.' She smiled. 'I suppose you might say that we cannot let the world escape us. Anyway, I've decided that we must go to the cities, and spread word of his teaching where there are ears to hear it.'

'Then I wish you well,' Cato replied. 'Though I'll be honest. Any movement that seeks to change the world by peaceful persuasion has got its work cut out. Chances are you will fail.'

'Maybe,' Miriam said. 'But we have to try. Or my son will have died for nothing.' She turned to Symeon. 'What about you? Are you still playing the great adventurer?'

Symeon indicated his bandaged arm. 'Those days are over, Miriam. There'll be no more fighting for me now.'

She nodded. 'No fighting perhaps. But you could always join us. We could use a man like you. One with your connections.'

'I'll think about it.'

'My son believed in you, Symeon.'

Symeon glanced quickly at Macro and Cato, but they remained expressionless. His guilty secret had died with Bannus and neither Cato nor Macro saw any reason to reawaken old wounds now. Not least on this day when Yusef had been restored to Miriam.

Symeon took her hand. 'We can talk about it later.'

'Very well.' Miriam turned to Macro and Cato. 'You've had a long ride. Can I offer you something to eat and drink? Some shelter?'

Macro shook his head. 'No. Thank you for the offer, but I have to return to Bushir. It's been too long since Cato and I were with our men. We have to return to duty, now that Bannus has gone. Maybe we'll see you later, before you and your people quit Heshaba.'

'Yes, Prefect. We'd be honoured.'

Macro smiled briefly and turned to Cato. 'Come on, we have to go.'

They clasped arms with Symeon for the last time and Cato laughed. 'You'll have to show me that trick with the knife some day. Next time I'll keep my eyes open.'

Symeon shook his head. 'I've had enough of weapons. Enough of death. That's all behind me now.'

'Really?' Macro looked disappointed. 'A pity.'

The two officers untethered their mounts and swung themselves up into the saddles. As they rode out of the village Miriam, Symeon and Yusef stood in the middle of the square for a while and watched them trot up the track that led out of the wadi. Miriam had the casket clutched tightly beneath her arm. Then Symeon placed his good arm about her shoulder and Yusef put his arm round her from the other side and they turned to walk towards the shelter that had been erected to serve as Miriam's temporary home.

* * *

Centurion Parmenion had not wasted any time since they had left in pursuit of Bannus. The enemy camp had been completely razed and only two mounds were left, marking the mass graves of the peasants that Bannus had led to their deaths. The gatehouse was almost rebuilt and the sentry in the tower challenged them correctly as they approached, even though he could hardly contain his surprise that the two officers had returned from their quest alive. Beyond the gate some of the barrack blocks had been rebuilt, and the prefect's house had been made habitable, if no longer luxurious. The other fire-damaged buildings had been demolished and swaths of the fort stood bare and blackened.

In the headquarters building they found Centurion Parmenion in the commander's office, surrounded by clerks and dictating orders. As soon as he had got over the surprise of seeing his commanding officer and Cato, Parmenion offered to give up his office with a rueful smile.

'Can't say I'd be sorry to be shot of all this paperwork, sir.'

'You seem to be doing a fine job. You can carry on with it until tomorrow.'

'Yes, sir.'

'Is there anything I should know before I get some sleep?'

Parmenion nodded. 'The hostages have been returned to the villages, as you ordered, and there's a dispatch from

Governor Longinus. It arrived yesterday, addressed to the prefect, in confidence. I didn't think I should open it.'

'You're the acting commanding officer, Parmenion.'

'I know that, sir. I just thought that I should wait. Until we heard something.'

'Where is it?'

'Just a moment, sir.' Parmenion crossed to the desk and opened a cabinet under the table. He took out a sealed package and handed it to Macro.

'I'll read this in my quarters. You'd better come with me, Cato.'

As they were leaving the office a thought struck Cato and he turned back to Parmenion. 'Centurion Postumus – what happened to him?'

'No one knows. After the battle I sent a patrol to look for him. We found his men, all dead, shot down with arrows. But no sign of him. Strange that.'

'Yes,' Cato said uneasily. 'Very strange.'

'I'm sure he'll turn up.'

'I imagine he will,' Cato replied as he left the office and strode off to catch up with Macro.

Macro opened the package as soon as they reached his quarters. The message was brief enough and he handed the document to Cato. It was an order from the staff of the Governor. The Second Illyrian Cohort was ordered to prepare to quit the fort at Bushir. They were instructed to proceed to Syria to join the army concentrating to counter the latest threat from Parthia.

Cato smiled. 'Seems that Longinus wants to keep a close eye on us.'

'I bet. Now that he knows that we're on to his game you can be sure he won't miss a chance to get rid of us. We're going to have to be careful out there, Cato.'

'Very careful. In the meantime there's work to be done. The cohort fought well enough, but they're not ready for a campaign season just yet.'

'No rest for us, then,' Macro grumbled as he poured two cups of wine and passed one to Cato. 'And we've got to write a report for Narcissus at some point.'

'I can handle that, if you like.'

'What should we tell him? That threat to the Empire. Was it Longinus, or Bannus? Either way, we've put a stop to it. Now we've just got Parthia to deal with. Shit, I could do with a nice long rest.'

'Look on the bright side, sir.'

'Bright side? What bright side?'

'At last you're going to see Syria. That's what you've always wanted, as long as I've known you.'

'Syria . . .' Macro mused contentedly and drained his cup. 'There is that.'

AUTHOR'S NOTE

It has been a great pleasure to research and write *The Eagle in the Sand*. From the beginning of the series I have wanted to take Macro and Cato east. It is long overdue for poor Centurion Macro, who has been fantasising about the lure of the east. On this occasion the reality has been rather grittier than he had hoped. Maybe next time.

Some readers might feel that I have taken a few liberties with the story of the most famous of the Judaean rabble-rousers executed by Rome – Jehoshua, or Jesus as he has come to be known. To them I would recommend Neil Faulkner's *Apocalypse*, a quite superb account of the background and history of the great revolt of AD 66. The various crosscurrents of political, religious and social class divisions are clearly analysed in great detail, and Faulkner is adept at making telling comparisons with the more recent history of the region. I cannot recommend this book highly enough to anyone keen to discover more about Judaea in the first century.

Most of the landscape depicted in this novel remains unchanged and I have tried to convey the starkness and the spectacle of the eastern frontier as tangibly as possible. Bathing in the Dead Sea was as much a novelty for me as it was for Macro, and it is hard to describe the awesome experience of Petra. Even though I had read extensively about the city (and watched Indiana Jones gallop through the siq!) nothing can prepare a visitor for the moment when they emerge from the narrow chasm to be confronted by the towering edifice of the 'Treasury'. And that was only the start of an unforgettable day's exploration of the site. Petra's man-made magnificence is matched by the natural spectacle of Wadi Rum (as it is known these days), a sprawling area of blood-red sand divided up by great walls of rock. The epic scale of the place is made yet more impressive by the silence, and it provides a fitting arena for the final conflict of the novel.

Jordan has some of the most impressive classical ruins in the world. The theatre at Amman is virtually intact, and the remains of some of the other cities of the Decapolis have been extensively excavated. Of particular note are Jerash, and Umm Qais where the visitor can sit high up in a theatre made of black stone and gaze out across Jawlan to Lake Tiberias, and then turn to see Nazareth. And yet the site that impressed me more than anything else was the most desolate and hard to reach, namely the desert fort of Q'sar Bashir. Even the Jordanian Ministry of Tourism was not quite sure where it was. Fortunately

King Abdullah put me in touch with a friend of his, Samer Mouasher, who was able to guide us to the site. The walls and towers of Bashir still rise up from the rock and sand, and the masonry dislodged by an earthquake over two centuries ago still lies where it fell. A visitor can scale some of the towers, and from the top the vista of sand stretches out to the horizon on all sides. I was struck by the hubris of an empire that could build a formidable fort in such an isolated position. 'Look on my works, ye Mighty, and despair!' Shelley had nailed the sensation precisely.

As we drove on to Petra, every detail of the fort stayed in my mind, and I knew that I had found the perfect inspiration for the setting of Macro and Cato's latest adventure.

Simon Scarrow
March 2006